PENGUIN CLASSICS

THE STEPPE AND OTHER STORIES

ANTON PAVLOVICH CHEKHOV, the son of a former serf, was born in 1860 in Taganrog, a port on the Sea of Azov. He received a classical education at the Taganrog Gymnasium, then in 1879 he went to Moscow, where he entered the medical faculty of the university, graduating in 1884. During his university years he supported his family by contributing humorous stories and sketches to magazines. He published his first volume of stories, *Motley Tales*, in 1886 and a year later his second volume, *In the Twilight*, for which he was awarded the Pushkin Prize. His most famous stories were written after his return from the convict island of Sakhalin, which he visited in 1890. For five years he lived on his small country estate near Moscow, but when his health began to fail he moved to the Crimea. After 1900, the rest of his life was spent at Yalta, where he met Tolstoy and Gorky. He wrote very few stories during the last years of his life, devoting most of his time to a thorough revision of his stories, of which the first comprehensive edition was published in 1899–1901, and to the writing of his great plays. In 1901 Chekhov married Olga Knipper, an actress of the Moscow Art Theatre. He died of consumption in 1904.

RONALD WILKS studied Russian language and literature at Trinity College, Cambridge, after training as a Naval interpreter, and later Russian literature at London University, where he received his Ph.D. in 1972. Among his translations for Penguin Classics are *My Childhood*, *My Apprenticeship* and *My Universities* by Gorky, *Diary of a Madman* by Gogol, filmed for Irish Television, *The Golovlyov Family* by Saltykov-Shchedrin, *How Much Land Does a Man Need?* by Tolstoy, *Tales of Belkin and Other Prose Writings* by Pushkin, and five other volumes of stories by Chekhov: *The Party and Other Stories*, *The Kiss and Other Stories*, *The Fiancée and Other Stories*, *The Duel and Other Stories* and *Ward No. 6 and Other Stories*. He has also translated *The Little Demon* by Sologub for Penguin.

DONALD RAYFIELD was born in 1942 and educated at Dulwich College, London, and Magdalene College, Cambridge. He is Professor of Russian and Georgian at Queen Mary College, University of London. He has written a number of monographs, notably *Anton Chekhov: A Life* and *Understanding Chekhov*, and is currently working on *Stalin and the Hangmen* and on a Georgian–English dictionary.

ANTON CHEKHOV

The Steppe and Other Stories

Translated with Notes by RONALD WILKS
With an introduction by DONALD RAYFIELD

PENGUIN BOOKS

PENGUIN BOOKS

Published by the Penguin Group
Penguin Books Ltd, 80 Strand, London WC2R 0RL, England
Penguin Putnam Inc., 375 Hudson Street, New York, New York 10014, USA
Penguin Books Australia Ltd, 250 Camberwell Road, Camberwell, Victoria 3124, Australia
Penguin Books Canada Ltd, 10 Alcorn Avenue, Toronto, Ontario, Canada M4V 3B2
Penguin Books India (P) Ltd, 11 Community Centre, Panchsheel Park, New Delhi – 110 017, India
Penguin Books (NZ) Ltd, Cnr Rosedale and Airborne Roads, Albany, Auckland, New Zealand
Penguin Books (South Africa) (Pty) Ltd, 24 Sturdee Avenue, Rosebank 2196, South Africa

Penguin Books Ltd, Registered Offices: 80 Strand, London WC2R 0RL, England

www.penguin.com

First published 2001

025

Set in 11/12.5 pt PostScript Monotype Fournier
Typeset by Rowland Phototypesetting Ltd, Bury St Edmunds, Suffolk
Printed and bound in Great Britain by Clays Ltd, Elcograf S.p.A.

CONTENTS

INTRODUCTION

An interesting game (invented by the drama specialist Harai Golomb) can be played with Chekhov's plays: leave one minute, two minutes, three minutes, and so on, before the curtain falls on the last act and see how completely you change your understanding of the play with each exit. We can play the game with Chekhov's work. Imagine that tuberculosis had killed him not in 1904, but in 1897, 1891 or 1884, and how differently we would view him. A Chekhov who had died in the Moscow clinic in April 1897, leaving no *Three Sisters* or *Cherry Orchard*, would not be seen as a dramatist (despite the existence of *The Seagull* and *Uncle Vanya*), but almost solely as the progenitor of the modern short story, a prose poet who relegates plot, characterization and moral argument to equal or even lesser status than atmospheric mood. A Chekhov who had stopped with this volume (after all, his journey across Siberia to Sakhalin might very well have killed him in 1890 or 1891), leaving no *Ward No. 6*, *Black Monk* or *Ariadna*, might appear as a gifted disciple of Russia's elder generation of great novelists, Turgenev, Tolstoy and Leskov, refining, miniaturizing their techniques, but as yet unable to match their cosmic vision or moral authority, or to devise a narrative language of his own.

Had Chekhov died at the age of twenty-four, of the haemorrhage that he suffered in 1884, only a very perceptive critic would have been able to discern the embryonic genius in a dozen or so of the two hundred five-page stories he had published ever since he had started medical school in 1879. (And, three years later, if Chekhov had not taken down his doctor's brass plate, his desertion of literature for medicine might still have passed unlamented.)

There are no sharp breaks or blinding lights in Chekhov's development; nevertheless, it was a development. The works of this volume are in no way juvenilia – we have excluded from this collection, however interesting, anything written before the end of 1886, when Chekhov had qualified, both as a doctor and as a writer. But the stories in this volume represent a Chekhov who is more self-conscious and more conventional – more dependent on the opinions of editors, critics and readers – than in his later work. The level of genius in 'A Dreary Story' or 'The Steppe' is not demonstrably lower than in the late work, but we can hear the author thinking, we can see the ties to the texts of the masters – to Tolstoy or Gogol – and the view of the world that emerges is not yet as hauntingly ambiguous as it is to become. Good and evil, heroes and villains still loom large in Chekhov's fiction; the author can still justify the ways of art, science, morality and logic to his reader.

In his twenties, and in the supposedly stagnant eighties of Russia's nineteenth century, Chekhov the writer was still an unusual phenomenon. Forty years ago the cliché of the nineteenth-century Russian writer was evoked by Russia's wittiest dissident writer Andrei Sinyavsky (1925–97), in a satirical monologue, a short story called 'The Graphomaniacs': 'They lived on country estates, they knew a foreign language from birth and, in between balls and duels, wrote their novels which were immediately published in all languages of the globe.' Chekhov had no country estate (until 1892), he was not a member of the gentry, he was nearly forty before he had learnt enough French to read a newspaper, he attended neither balls nor duels and in his lifetime was virtually unknown in most of Western Europe. His life was more like that of the Soviet writer as Sinyavsky portrayed it: 'the problem of three meals a day, paying for the gas, your shoes have worn out and you owe the typist for two hundred pages at a rouble a page . . . was this mind of genius really brought up on rotten hamburgers?'

Anton Chekhov and his elder brothers, looking back at how far sheer talent had brought them, used to exclaim: 'Did such genius really come out of an earth closet?' True, their origins were humble: but Chekhov's father had the qualifications to produce genius; like Dickens' and Ibsen's fathers, he was a bankrupt shopkeeper.

Taganrog, down south, on the Sea of Azov, may have had no sewerage or piped water, but it did have an opera house and an enterprising theatre, not to mention a good grammar school. Some of Chekhov's teachers were alcoholics, sadists (among them the father of the 'iron' Felix Dzerzhinsky who was to lead Lenin's secret police) and police informers. Others, however, were original minds, even published writers. Taganrog gave Chekhov and his brothers a disrespectful, anti-metropolitan and multi-ethnic ethos which no amount of Moscow and St Petersburg sophistication could efface. It also provided the scheme of a southern provincial town to infuse much of Chekhov's work: its cherry orchards and cemetery statuary are to recur right until Chekhov's valedictory work, *The Cherry Orchard*. Its heterogeneous population of merchants, officials, vagabonds, its unhappy provincial heroines were also to populate – sometimes recognizably for themselves – much of Chekhov's early prose.

Taganrog's churches played an important, even oppressive, part in Chekhov's formative years. His father's tyrannical reign as a cantor gave Chekhov a knowledge and love of the Russian liturgy and its music unparalleled in any other major writer, except Nikolay Leskov. The rhythms of his prose are infused with the psalmodic periods of the Russian *akathistos* (a psalm improvised by the priest) and the Byzantine hymns for each event in the church calendar, the *troparia*. At the same time, as he was soon to admit, kneeling on frozen church floors in the early hours of the morning, a torture that alternated with parental thrashings, gave Chekhov an insuperable aversion to religion – in fact to any ideological system. This forced him as a writer to embrace doubt and uncertainty, and prevented him from adopting any of the mantles, Christian or secular, that so many Russian prose-writers felt compelled to don.

The education Chekhov received was like an English public school, minus sport, homosexuality and corporal punishment, strongly oriented towards the classics and to Orthodox Christianity. True, he read most of Tolstoy, Dostoyevsky and modern European literature when he had already become a writer himself, but lacking the culture of Russia's gentry literati was not altogether a disadvantage, since it led him to seek his own literary paths.

Chekhov's first writing was controlled by the strict formulas of the editors of the comic, satirical and didactic weekly magazines who first bought his work when he became an indigent medical student in Moscow. Their demands for simplicity, precision, topicality, exactness and conformity to a sometimes paranoiac censorship were not entirely inhibiting factors for a writer's development. Like many writers, Chekhov also learnt economy, dispassionate observation and irony from his medical training. Writing a *historia morbi* for each new case in hospital gave him a new technique for story-writing: 'A Dreary Story', 'Ward No. 6', 'The Black Monk', 'The Bishop' are all stories built on the progress of a disease – angina, paranoia, tuberculosis, typhoid – and the parallel disintegration of a persona. As a doctor, Chekhov may not have been particularly distinguished, but what survives of his medical essays are terse models of autopsies that served as kernels for fictional stories. Perhaps it is significant that, though mediocre in surgery, Chekhov had high marks for gynaecology and psychiatry; he had an almost numinous gift for diagnosing fatal illness in colleagues, literary or medical, and he had the patient listening ear which marks off the best psychiatrists and best novelists. Though he deserted medicine as a career (treating first only friends and relatives, then afterwards only peasants), medicine did not desert Chekhov. The doctor as saint in countless stories and the doctor as observer, god, villain or clown in all the plays but the last testify to the parallels that Chekhov, wittingly or not, drew between his 'mistress', literature, and his 'legitimate wife', medicine.

Medicine had other values for the writer: the medical profession was the stratum in society that the Russian state feared. Its publications were uncensored, its political defiance respected. To be a doctor gave Chekhov a pride that none of the privations and humiliations of Grub Street could break.

A stubborn independence distinguishes Anton Chekhov from his elder brothers. One, Alexander, was a polyglot and polymath, whose letters show a Boswellian talent for self-parody; but dependence on alcohol and sex reduced him from leader of the family to clown. Nikolay, an artist with the talent of a Daumier, was destroyed spiritually, even before he collapsed physically, by similar factors –

plus tuberculosis. Chekhov's defining feature is a refusal to be dependent, on other human beings, their money or their opinions, on drugs, on sex. His brothers' disastrous lives furnish material for many of his stories: they also served as a horrible warning.

If Anton Chekhov had a need, it was for a replacement father-figure. This is what saved him from remaining a gifted, productive – even prolific – hack. He admired, first of all, that most under-estimated of the major Russian novelists, Nikolay Leskov: in Chekhov's prose the elusiveness of the narrator, the tendency to infuse a narrative with lyricism, the indifference to the preoccupations of Western European writers stems from Leskov's influence. (Leskov was the only prose fiction writer whom Chekhov's father read.) Leskov was a cantankerous, isolated figure. Their initial encounter, when Leskov poured salad oil over the young Chekhov's head to anoint him, was followed by mutual estrangement. By the mid 1880s, a deep but qualified admiration for Tolstoy's morality, lapidary prose technique and sceptical analysis of all abstractions and received ideas had aroused in Chekhov a deeper admiration: some years were to pass before a personal encounter with Tolstoy (and a doctor's refusal to accept Tolstoy's more extreme pontifications on sex, science and the cosmos) led Chekhov to distinguish between Tolstoy the heroic man, the writer of genius and the preacher of absurdities – but the influence, however moderated, remains in Chekhov's work.

The third of these senior influences was decisive: it was Aleksey Sergeyevich Suvorin, the St Petersburg newspaper magnate, publisher, political *éminence grise*, who had marked out Anton Chekhov's potential. The Russian intelligentsia preferred, if they could afford to do so, to stay clear of Suvorin: they were horrified by Suvorin's tragic aura (his family was beset by suicide and sudden death), Mephistophelean personality and apparent lack of political or moral principle (he was a consistent nationalist conservative anti-semitic radical, with pronounced private anarchic tendencies). Suvorin was twenty-six years older than Chekhov, but they had much in common: Suvorin too came from the provincial peasantry, was exploited by indigent relatives, and had, like Anton Chekhov, a fondness for the company of actresses and for wandering round cemeteries.

Suvorin paid three times as much and gave twice as much space as the Moscow editors to the writers who filled his paper's Wednesday and Saturday supplements. His readers were more sophisticated, too: they, like their editor, had a salacious streak, they wanted dangerous women and wicked Jews in their stories; but they were prepared to have ambiguity and lyricism and to do without mockery and flippancy. Suvorin's newspaper was once compared to a zoo whose animals were fed and watered by a kindly keeper: Chekhov was the elephant in this zoo, and the only animal encouraged to take walks abroad.

Many Russian writers, especially the radical left, regarded with distaste Chekhov's alliance with the Suvorin family – the alliance weakened only at the end of the 1890s, when Suvorin and his heir's anti-semitism became embarrassing. Quips flew through St Petersburg: 'Suvorin the father, Suvorin the son and Chekhov the Holy Ghost.' But from Suvorin's paper it was possible for Chekhov to graduate, belatedly, to the conventional avenue for a novice Russian writer: the thick monthly journals to which the intelligentsia and gentry subscribed. Only then, from 1888 with the publication of 'The Steppe' could Chekhov have the freedom to write at as much length as he chose, for a fee which allowed him to write at his own pace. To survive as a writer for the Moscow weeklies, Chekhov would have had to go on writing two or three stories a week under various pseudonyms. Under Suvorin he could live like a bourgeois on a story a week; on the monthly journals, two or three longer tales a year were sufficient to raise the writer's income to that of a gentleman.

Suvorin was not only a *deus ex machina* who found work and pensions for Chekhov as well as his parents and siblings; he was a friend who for several years tried to persuade Chekhov to marry his daughter (at first as a child of eleven) and share the family fortune. Here Chekhov began to show his mettle, what Suvorin called his flint, against what Chekhov called Suvorin's 'weak character'. Never was a Dr Faust better defended against a Mephistopheles: one of Chekhov's mistresses had happened to be a certain Lily Markova, who had been the Suvorin family governess: Chekhov knew all Suvorin's terrible secrets. Because he understood – and shared –

Suvorin's depression, this was a basis for a friendship almost unique between publisher and writer. Suvorin was also an influence – if only by reaction, for his salacious stories and anti-semitic plays evoked in Chekhov a powerful retort. Furthermore, Suvorin and his family served as material to Chekhov, to the amusement of Suvorin's second wife, to the indignation of his sons and hangers-on. The lonely professor of 'A Dreary Story', like Professor Serebryakov of *Uncle Vanya* tormenting his young wife, is only one example of the use to which Chekhov could put his friends: the most extreme, perhaps, was the suicide of Suvorin's young son, Volodya, in 1887, which Chekhov reworked in a story of that name and again in *The Seagull*.

Suvorin and his cronies had recognized in Chekhov's Moscow stories an extraordinary evocation of nature, a gift for a single brush-stroke to convey a picture. Under Suvorin, Chekhov now developed a psychology for his heroes, and particularly his heroines. The fourth story in this volume, 'Verochka', is not Chekhov's best-known story, but it is a landmark in its sensitive use of the non-encounter for a story. Russian dramatists had always distinguished themselves by their ability to remove from classical comedy its key element: the wedding bells for the young couple in the final act. In Alexander Griboyedov's *Woe from Wit* (1827), a variation of Molière's *The Misanthropist* and the most remarkable verse comedy ever written inside or outside Russia, the heroine is publicly humiliated while her admirer calls for a carriage to take him far away. The hero of Gogol's *Marriage* leaps through a second-floor window rather than go through with the betrothal which his friend has worked so hard to arrange for him. Turgenev's *Home of the Gentry* (*A Nest of Gentlefolk*), where the heroine goes to a nunnery instead of marrying the hero, is another precedent. Never, however, had Russian literature achieved such a touching tragi-comedy of non-communication, of the failure of the male to fulfil his role of hunter and decision-maker, as in Chekhov's 'Verochka': the strength of the story is in its complete absence of moralizing or even morality, in the way that nature seems to predetermine the failure of the encounter, even to symbolize the mystery of non-motivation in the mist that pervades the air.

Chekhov had found his scene. Although he was to become a

landowner and gardener only six years later, the garden is in his work, as in medieval romance or in Turgenev's novels, the setting for the crucial events and non-events in human life. In Chekhov's case one can go further: his stories take their indirect lines and fuzzy boundaries not from literary, but from horticultural technique. In gardens, paths should lead you circuitously back to an exit which was your entrance; the boundaries between the artificial garden and the natural landscape should be invisible. Thus the protagonists of 'Verochka', as of many Chekhov stories and plays, end up in the same predicament with which they began, only now with a knowledge of the circularity in their existence. Chekhov has found a pattern for a story, a couple thrown together – a feckless but well-meaning male visitor to a provincial girl, literally leading her up the garden path and then failing to utter the expected words that will bring the story to an end. We will encounter this pattern again and again, but with ever subtler variations: it is there in the sub-plot of 'A Dreary Story'; it is the primary theme, much more cruel, in 'A Visit to Friends'; it is to be found in the plays – Dr Astrov and Sonya in *Uncle Vanya*, Lopakhin and Varya in *The Cherry Orchard*.

At the end of 1887, the same year and in the same newspaper – Suvorin's *New Times*, in which 'Verochka' was printed – Chekhov published 'The Kiss'. Here, too, at the end the hero deliberately refuses to take the opportunity to make sense of a brief encounter, when he decides to sleep alone in a peasant hut rather than accept the invitation to the general's house where, on his last visit, he was kissed by a mysterious young woman in the dark, by mistake. The mood of 'Verochka' is pathetic – we feel for the heroine who is given no explanation. In 'The Kiss' the erotic encounter was a mistake, no forsaken woman is suffering, and the situation is touchingly comic. The lonely hero's name Ryabovich, 'pock-marked', mutes our sympathy for his obsessive reaction; moreover we see him as one of a group of unmarried, unhappy and dull officers. Yet Ryabovich is the victim of the same forces as the hero of 'Verochka'. If the autumnal mists cool the ardour of Verochka's admirer, Ryabovich is compelled by the smell of spring in the poplar trees, the lilacs and the roses, to a frenzy of erotic introversion (Chekhov's acute sense of smell, which reminds one of the decadent sympathies of a Huysmans, shows itself in the importance of scents in determining the reactions of his characters.)

'The Kiss' met with a very positive response – partly because of Chekhov's extraordinary ease in conveying a military milieu, something he was not to attempt again until the play *Three Sisters*. Mainly, perhaps, such stories evoked a positive reaction because they reminded the Russian reader of Maupassant. Chekhov's work of the mid 1880s has much in common with Maupassant: extraordinary economy of language, an ability to penetrate the inner life of another social element (Maupassant too could write about officers), a fondness for highly sexed heroines, a love of rivers, seascapes and fishing. 'The Kiss' has the symmetry of a Maupassant story and, if it lacks the melodrama or violent action so characteristic of Maupassant, that lack was yet to be appreciated by Chekhov's readers as a positive advance. We will find Maupassant often mentioned, even loudly praised, in Chekhov's fiction; Maupassant's fine tale, *A Life*, where a patrician estate falls into ruin and is sold to the heroine's exploiters, was to provide much material for *The Cherry Orchard*. For a while, too, Chekhov shared Maupassant's modest view of the modern writer as an honest artisan providing workmanlike prose for an era in which the great writers (whether Flaubert and Stendhal, or Turgenev and Dostoyevsky) had become canonized and new genius was still to be born.

Yet Chekhov's modesty could not have been entirely sincere. Unlike Maupassant, he intuits forces in the universe which are not mere chance, and he is not content to limit himself to portrayal and condemnation of human folly. Chekhov's medical training had given him a deeper, more tragic philosophy than Maupassant's; his passion for Russia's harsh nature, too, has a less hedonistic side than Maupassant's enjoyment of the Côte d'Azur.

Nature, whether in the garden or the wild, dominating and directing the behaviour of the human beings who mistakenly believe they control nature, was what drew the envious attention of older writers to Chekhov's early work. In 1887 Chekhov revisited nature. Taking a substantial advance from Suvorin, for the first time in several years, he crossed Russia from north to south to revisit not just the town where he had grown up but the steppe and forest landscapes he remembered as a child. (There were, it now transpires, other reasons for the journey: an infatuated woman desperately waiting for him in Taganrog.) If any external experience that transformed Chekhov can be identified, it is this revisiting of childhood landscapes: they had vanished. A Welshman called Hughes had established coal mining in what had been the Switzerland of the Don and built a coal-mining town, Khiuzovka: the forests were put to the axe to make pit-props, slag heaps despoiled the steppes. Lyricism about landscapes is central to Gogol's and Turgenev's work. Chekhov is different, for he is the first 'green' writer in the modern sense: he mourns the irreversible destruction of nature by man and implies that nature might be better off without man. Of the stories that resulted from this journey south, 'Panpipes' is perhaps the most poignant in lamenting the dried-up rivers, the disappearing birds and mammals, the deforestation.

Something of a dream of Eden underlies this sense of an irreversible fall. In Chekhov's only novel, a half-spoof, half-serious detective story of 1884 known as *The Shooting Party*, the most striking element is the evocation of an estate run wild in which exotic trees (ignoring the realities of the Russian climate) create a *Douanier* Rousseau jungle, while human beings degenerate into liars and murderers. The peasants of 'Panpipes', dismayed and upset by the disappearance of their environment, are to find their dismay echoed for a long time in Chekhov's work. He gives their phrases to the forest-loving doctor in his plays *The Wood Demon* and *Uncle Vanya*. The chopping down of trees is to be a typical token of the villain: right until the victorious Natasha in *Three Sisters*, celebrating her victory in driving (by breeding) the sisters out of their house by announcing that she will destroy a maple tree and an avenue of firs. From now on in Chekhov's work characters are assigned the roles of dendrophiles or dendrophobes: they are to be judged by their effect on the environment. Not to have planted a tree becomes nearly as great a sin as having chopped one down.

For Chekhov's critics, however, to give a moral and political lead was the prime duty of a conscientious writer. As Chekhov escaped from Suvorin's zoo to become a self-sufficient writer, nobody reproached him directly for his lowly provincial origins, but it was clear that the public had expectations of an extended prose piece that would have to be structured along a plot and thus express a philosophy and take a stand: Chekhov's claim to metropolitan nobility (at least of spirit) would be decided by the idealistic nature of the stand he adopted.

The extended piece, for which stories such as 'Panpipes' appear to be studies, was 'The Steppe'. It is not actually Chekhov's longest work: *The Shooting Party* is twice as long but, as it appeared in Chekhov's lifetime only in daily newspaper instalments, it passed unnoticed. 'The Steppe' was commissioned for a very different readership from Suvorin's *New Times* – the prestigious liberal monthly the *Northern Herald*. The story was successfully nominated for a prestigious prize; it was literally a masterpiece in that it proved that Chekhov had finished his apprenticeship to other writers and to professional editors. But 'The Steppe', for all the wonderment at its evocation of southern landscapes, left critics puzzled.

Where is the plot? A boy leaves his home town (presumably Taganrog), to be taken by strangers to begin his schooling in Kiev, on the other side of the Ukraine. A journey, centred on a carriage, is a conventional enough European and Russian device, from Laurence Sterne and Gogol to Chekhov. But the boy-protagonist is handed over to a convoy of drovers, the purpose of the priest who had taken him is forgotten and then turns out to be unimportant. The boy finally arrives in Kiev and we have no hint of what will happen, just as we have only odd hints of why it has happened in the first place. Delight at the story in Suvorin's circle turned to frustration: a sequel was suggested – one in which little Yegorushka would become a suicidal adolescent, like Suvorin's third son. Critics could not see in 'The Steppe' the thread holding together a succession of literary pearls – the Jewish innkeeper scene, fishing for crayfish, the thunderstorm – and felt betrayed.

Perhaps it is in response to the strong prejudice in the Russian reader that literature should make him not just happier, but elevated and enlightened, that after 'The Steppe' we find the influence of Tolstoy as a writer becoming very marked in Chekhov's work. Undoubtedly, the success of 'The Steppe' made Chekhov secure from poverty or pressure: in the sixteen years left to him he wrote far less than in the previous seven, and he wrote very little comic work, and almost nothing that he did not want to write. But there was a catch in this freedom: public expectations brought his prose closer to the structures and themes that Tolstoy, who was after all the only novelist of genius to have survived into the mid 1880s, had made a norm.

Public recognition also led Chekhov into the theatre – the history of the Russian theatre is made by writers, with the exception only of Griboyedov and Alexander Ostrovsky (1823–86), the almost single-handed creator of the Russian tragic repertoire, who were not professional playwrights but poets or novelists who, after proving themselves masters, then ventured, like fools rushing in where angels fear to tread, into the theatre. Had Chekhov perished in 1890, it is unlikely that there would have been many performances of *Ivanov* let alone of *The Wood Demon*. If *Ivanov* has merit, it is in the way that Chekhov reworks many characters, for example the dispossessed Jew, the morally bankrupt intellectual landowner, from prose fiction into drama, and in the way the play parodies and thus attacks Suvorin's successful but anti-semitic play *Tatyana Repina*. *The Wood Demon* of 1889 is all the more disastrous as a play for taking the material of 'A Dreary Story' and of 'Panpipes' and failing to make it work as theatre. Two ignoble factors explain Chekhov's first venture into drama: firstly, a virulent love–hate of the theatre, its repertoire and denizens – he was drawn to actresses yet felt them to be 'Machiavellis in skirts'; secondly, because through the theatre a Russian writer established an audience and readership in circles, aristocratic and provincial, that did not read the 'thick monthlies'; thirdly, because of the highly efficient Russian Society of Playwrights and Composers, even a moderately successful play in Russia was a pension – authors collected up to ten per cent of the gross box office for every performance in any town. Over the next two decades, *Ivanov* thus earned Chekhov more than all the stories he was to write.

Great Chekhovian theatre was only to arise out of more and more mischievous attempts to upset the conventions of the Russian stage – and out of the painful symbiosis that Chekhovian drama would establish with Stanislavsky's and Nemirovich-Danchenko's revolutionary Moscow Art Theatre. In this early period, *Ivanov*, *The Wood Demon* and the vaudevilles brought Chekhov only an income: literary esteem could come only as his prose took on more novel-like forms.

Tolstoy weighs somewhat heavily on a number of stories of the mid eighties. Not that Tolstoy's use of language affected Chekhov – his own copy of *War and Peace* is scored with red underlinings marking disapproval of Tolstoy's repeated metaphors and sermonizing syntax: one character in Chekhov is to remark that Tolstoy writes with a plasterer's trowel, not a painter's brush. Sometimes, however, Chekhov makes an interesting experiment out of Tolstoyanism: he preaches neither 'simplification' nor 'non-resistance to evil', but explores the morass into which honest people stray when they try to put these precepts into practice. Tolstoyanism shows its mark in the technique of seeking the concrete reality behind an abstraction or a pretended virtue, to look for hypocrisy and lies in the words of the characters and to show the reader what is really happening by monitoring the protagonists' unconscious body language and internal stream of consciousness. Tolstoyan influence can also be seen in Chekhov's temporary adoption of a secure judgemental authorial stance.

The best of these Tolstoyan works is probably 'The Name-day Party' – it is one of the half-dozen Chekhov works which Katherine Mansfield used as models to evolve her own prose (her *The Garden Party* is likewise a party spoiled by a catastrophe which the celebrants do everything to suppress). 'The Name-day Party' punishes hero and heroine, hosts who have hidden their own misapprehensions and neglected their moral duty in order to impress their guests, with a dramatically disastrous ending; it is full of allusions to *Anna Karenina* in the hero's hay making, the worried pregnant heroine's seeking solace from a peasant, in the parallel of a gathering thunderstorm and miscarriage.

Undergoing Tolstoy's influence was as much a process of inoculation as were Chekhov's early years spent singing in church: the essential aesthetic element remained, the ideology evaporated. In a year or two the initial influence is assimilated and even to a certain extent rejected. 'A Dreary Story' has Tolstoyan allusions, Tolstoyan parallels, but is not Tolstoyan. Common sense, an aesthetic sensing of the limits between art and philosophy, a doctor's confidence in science and the unknowability of absolute right and wrong have overcome the temptation to pontificate. Perhaps the key element in Chekhov's medical training was a conviction that only those qualified in a profession were competent to practise it. Chekhov abjures moralizing because he is not a bishop and philosophizing because he is not a philosopher. Unlike Tolstoy, he is convinced that it is not for the writer to 'show the paths to paradise'.

In the course of 1888 and 1889 Chekhov's mood was clouded by serious tragedy: the moral collapse of his brother Nikolay was followed by a physical one, and in summer 1889 Nikolay had to be nursed (mainly by Chekhov's eldest brother Alexander) as he lay dying of tuberculosis, typhoid and drug addiction. Chekhov had seen two grandparents, several uncles and an aunt die of 'the white plague'; he, too, had haemorrhages, fevers and coughs and could estimate with fair exactitude his own shortened lifespan. The death of Nikolay brings a despair and depression into his work. Helplessness in the face of death was to expel from Chekhov the last assumptions of certainty or immortality. If 'The Steppe', which celebrates a lost primeval natural world, is a masterpiece, then 'A Dreary Story', which mourns the loss of all meaning in life, transcends anything that was written by Chekhov's contemporaries in Russia or Western Europe. It is not just a response to the great classics, it is a riposte to them.

One key element in the first-person narrative is that the hero, who has no surname, is a generally recognized hero: a professor of medicine. If there was one idol generally accepted by all ranks and ideological groups in Russia, it was the new generation of Russian medical scientists. Nikolay Stepanovich, who narrates his own last months, in many ways resembles the renowned surgeon, Professor Botkin, who was known to be dying of a liver cancer he himself refused to diagnose. The Tolstoy work which 'A Dreary Story' seeks to supersede is *The Death of Ivan Ilich*. Tolstoy's hero is a prominent civil servant, and no reader is particularly surprised that he is to find, as he dies in agony, that his life is meaningless. Chekhov's hero represents the summit of what is attainable to a human being. If Nikolay Stepanovich, the world authority on medicine, is in thrall to existential despair, what hope is there for anyone? Tolstoy consoles his dying man with a peasant lad to nurse him compassionately and a vision of light at the end of a black sack into which he is being sucked. There are no compassionate peasants or lights at the end of the tunnel in 'A Dreary Story'.

In technique, too, introspection and melancholy have moved Chekhov to a new plane: the interaction of thunderstorm and characters' moods and behaviour in 'A Dreary Story' has none of the obvious Romantic pathetic fallacy – it is an ironic, moving interaction of natural forces and human mood, with nothing of the moral metaphorical import of 'The Name-day Party'. For the first time, too, Chekhov has hit on a method of first-person narrative that reveals to the reader more than it appears to reveal to the narrator. The all-knowing Nikolay Stepanovich, noting every foible of the family and friends he is alienated from, is not aware that he is in love with his ward, the unhappy actress Katya, from and to whom he refuses all consolation. Here, too, for the first time in Chekhov, we have the hallmark of the mature work – the blurring of the boundary between protagonist and author. There is a distance between the hero–narrator, through whom we see all the rest of the action, and the silent, ubiquitous authorial presence, which has the empathy of an actor for his role. Nikolay Stepanovich expresses hundreds of opinions, usually contemptuous, on his postgraduate students, the city of Kharkov, Brahms, the theatre, fame, the family, Russian literature. Many are to recur in Chekhov's later work, to acquire an authorial stamp, but for the first time in Chekhov's work we can no longer mark the frontier between the author and the protagonist: yet another major conventional orienteering aid for the reader has been abolished, and we are deprived of our ability to pass judgement.

The depression of 1889 that found expression in this morbidly ironic if heroic work was only deepened by the increasing boldness of Russia's critical rabble, who disapproved of Chekhov's distancing himself from Tolstoyan certainties while adopting a Tolstoyan type of plot. Some critics talked of plagiarism, others of 'unprincipledness'. The more understandable failure of *The Wood Demon* added humiliation: Chekhov was told by the distinguished actor Lensky to abandon the theatre since he did not even know the alphabet of drama composition.

The old conflict between the doctor and the writer was renewed, and Chekhov decided on a response which might have been suicidal, both literally and artistically: in spring 1890 he set off on a journey across the freezing damp of Siberia to the penal colony of the island of Sakhalin, Russia's Devil's Island and Botany Bay all in one, to investigate the conditions of the prisoners there. The primary motive was certainly to demonstrate that he had more compassion for suffering humanity than any of the critics who accused him of indifference, of refusing solutions to the problems raised; the journey was also a flight from the inordinate demands of relatives, friends and mistresses; lastly, it was an emulation of heroism, notably of the conquistador–explorer, discoverer of the wild horse, Nikolay Przhevalsky, who had died in Central Asia and whose obituary Chekhov had just written, in the form of an anonymous panegyric.

The dividing line between Chekhov's early and mature work is not a neat fracture point: 'A Dreary Story' has features of the mature work, just as the very last pieces take up themes, scenery and mood of the early work. If there is a temporal and spatial cut-off point, then the journey to Sakhalin marks it. Some elements disappear for ever from Chekhov's works. First, there are now very few saints, heroes, villains, monsters. Evil resides not in single human beings, or even in families, but in a system. It was the prison colony, prisoners and guards, who made a collective evil: the most horrific psychopath, murderer or hangman was as an individual the usual mix of the sympathetic and horrible. The reluctance to judge and categorize becomes absolute in Chekhov's work after Sakhalin. Secondly, a poetic element that reminded Russian readers of the elegies of Pushkin and the metaphysical lyrics of Fyodor Tyutchev (1803–73), Russia's most powerful if least prolific lyrical poet, enters Chekhov's works. The absolute certainty of death forces characters to look at life with disbelief and even with renewed capacity for enjoyment.

A year spent abroad also gave Chekhov the benefits of a sabbatical. Very little of his work refers to, let alone is set in, Siberia or Sakhalin. (Likewise, for all his frequent and prolonged visits to St Petersburg, Chekhov only once set a story there.) On his return to Russia Chekhov did not settle down; the following spring he set off with the Suvorins on his first visit to Western Europe (another setting which he uses very rarely, despite four further visits, including almost an entire year spent in Nice). Not until summer 1891 did he suddenly revert to frenzied work, simultaneously writing *The Island of Sakhalin*, his largely unrecognized *magnum opus*, one of his longest, most ambitious stories, 'The Duel', and a number of explosive shorter stories.

The obsession with death in Chekhov's work reaches its apogee in a story which appears at first sight to be just a fictionalized account of observations on his long sea journey, as he returned with a pet mongoose from Sakhalin to Odessa. The ship was carrying largely soldiers and guards returning from duty in the prison colony. One of them dies and the body is thrown to the sharks in the Indian Ocean. The tubercular man's last moments and the extraordinary green light that suffuses the sky as his body goes overboard, however, makes 'Gusev' a work that, once read, cannot be forgotten. The green light (in fact, the colour green) is to permeate all Chekhov's work, right until Natasha's dress in *Three Sisters*, as a horrible omen of death.

The frantic summer spent in a magnificent country house at Bogimovo is perpetuated in many later Chekhov stories (for example, 'The House with the Mezzanine'). The mansion still stands but is now a mental hospital for survivors of shellshock in World War II – as though Ward No. 6 had come back into reality – and its gardens are now a pig farm. It is as though Chekhov had determined to recover all critical reputation that he had lost during his absence over the previous year and a half. The result, 'The Duel', was the last major work he published in Suvorin's *New Times*; over the autumn and winter of 1891 the story took up all the space that Suvorin had reserved for fiction, thus earning the resentment of those writers who now had no outlet.

'The Duel' is Chekhov's most conventional work: it has two heroes who represent opposing sets of opinions, one precise, scientific and western, the other vague, intuitive and Slavonic; their ideological and moral enmity is crystallized in a duel which ends farcically. What clearer reminiscence of Turgenev could there be? It is hard to think of a major Russian writer of the nineteenth century who did not write a story that could have been entitled 'The Duel'. Likewise, Chekhov has placed his characters in the claustrophobic setting of a Black Sea garrison town (suspiciously like Sukhumi), a Wild West setting (one might sometimes think) that lends itself to the taut plotting. The build-up to the duel (and even its apparently salutary consequences for both parties) also follows classical lines. The differences, however, are more important than the similarities to conventional duelling novels. For one thing, neither party's views command much respect: they are rationalizations on the one hand of the aesthete (Layevsky) and his incurable idleness and on the other hand of the scientist (von Koren) and his involuntary hyperactivity. What distinguishes this ideological battle from those in Dostoyevsky, Tolstoy or Turgenev is Chekhov's subtle authorial preference for a third way, the way of the inarticulate or uncomprehending non-combatants. The absurd mediator Dr Samoylenko declares that if he stopped loving a woman he would make it his life's work to hide the fact, unlike the 'honest' cad Layevsky or the 'honest' bluff Przhevalsky-like conquistador von Koren. The Tatar innkeeper does not care whether people worship Allah or Jehovah, as long as they respect God. The naïve deacon interrupts the duel (over which an ominous green light is falling) and prevents a clear resolution of conflict. And not least, a group of indigenous Caucasians sit in a circle on the other side of a river by which the querulous Russians are picnicking and tell each other stories in a language which none of the colonists can understand. Doctor, deacon, Tatar and Abkhaz natives have an instinctive talent for peace and harmony which no proponent of any ideology can achieve – in this lies the novel and powerful import of 'The Duel' and it is thus that Layevsky's absurd self-justification seems to accuse Tolstoy of hypocrisy and misogyny and scientific rationalism of brutal destructiveness. Above all, like Maupassant's best prose, so the narrative of 'The Duel' is dominated by the sea: it drowns out soliloquies, it drives back the travellers. As in Chekhov's mature work – 'The Lady with the Little Dog', for example – the sea represents a natural force not just more powerful but more significant than us, and those that recognize natural forces (the Tatar, the deacon, the doctor, the Abkhaz) have the advantage over the articulate intellectuals who occupy the foreground of the narrative.

If Sakhalin was the greatest trauma in Chekhov's life, its consequences took time to make their mark. 'Ward No. 6', perhaps the most pessimistic work that Russian literature has ever produced, was not written until Chekhov himself had prepared what he hoped would be his own idyllic interlude, a refuge in the country. 'The Duel' with its reconciliation, even partial redemption, with its cast all alive at the end of the story, is a deceptively happy conclusion to the first period of Chekhov's development.

FURTHER READING

Gordon McVay (tr.), *Anton Chekhov: A Life in Letters* (London: Folio Society, 1994), the best selection and translation of letters.

Brian Reeves (tr.), *The Island of Sakhalin* (Cambridge: Ian Faulkner, 1993).

SECONDARY LITERATURE: GENERAL BOOKS

Toby W. Clyman, *A Chekhov Companion* (Westport/London: Greenwood Press, 1985), a very valuable if expensive collection of essays, with extensive bibliography.

P. Debreczeny and T. Eekman (eds), *Chekhov's Art of Writing: A Collection of Critical Essays* (Columbus: Slavica, 1977).

Thomas Eekman (ed.), *Critical Essays on Anton Chekhov* (Boston: G. K. Hall, 1989), 208 pp.

W. Gerhardie, *Anton Chekhov: A Critical Study* (London: Macdonald, 1974), 'Bloomsbury' Chekhov, but well-informed.

R. L. Jackson, *Chekhov: A Collection of Essays: 20th-Century Views* (Englewood Cliffs, New Jersey: Prentice-Hall, 1967).

R. L. Jackson (ed.), *Reading Chekhov's Text* (Evanston, Ill.: Northwestern University Press, 1993).

S. Koteliansky (tr., ed.), *Anton Chekhov: Literary and Theatrical Reminiscences* (New York: Blom, 1968).

Virginia Llewellyn-Smith, *Chekhov and the Lady with the Little Dog* (London: Oxford University Press, 1973).

V. S. Pritchett, *Chekhov. A Spirit Set Free* (London: Hodder & Stoughton, 1988).

Donald Rayfield, *Anton Chekhov: A Life* (London: HarperCollins, 1997).

T. Winner, *Chekhov and his Prose* (New York: Holt, 1966).

WORKS ON INDIVIDUAL STORIES IN ALPHABETICAL ORDER

'A Dreary Story'

Shoshana Knapp, 'Herbert Spencer in Čexov's "Skucnaja istorija" and "Duel": The Love of Science and the Science of Love', *Slavic and East European Journal* 29:3 (Fall 1985), pp. 279–96.

'The Duel'

Andrew Durkin, 'Allusion and Dialogue in "The Duel"' in Robert Louis Jackson (ed.), *Reading Chekhov's Text* (Evanston, Ill.: Northwestern University Press, 1993), pp. 169–78.

'Gusev'

Milton Ehre, 'The Symbolic Structure of Chekhov's "Gusev"', *Ulbandus Review*, New York, 2:1 (Fall 1979), pp. 76–85.

'The Kiss'

Nathan Rosen, 'The Life Force in Chekhov's "The Kiss"', *Ulbandus Review*, New York, 2:1 (Fall 1979), pp. 175–85.

'The Steppe'

Martina Bjorklund, *Narrative Strategies in Čechov's 'The Steppe': Cohesion, Grounding and Point of View*, Turku, 1993.

Jerome H. Katsell, 'Čexov's "The Steppe" Revisited', *Slavic and East European Journal* 22 (1978), pp. 313–23.

'Verochka'

Joseph Conrad, 'Čexov's "Verocka": A Polemical Parody', *Slavic and East European Journal* 14 (1970), pp. 465–74.

CHRONOLOGY

1836 Gogol's *The Government Inspector*
1852 Turgenev's *Sketches from a Hunter's Album*
1860 Dostoyevsky's *Notes From the House of the Dead* (1860–61)
Anton Pavlovich Chekhov born on 17 January at Taganrog, a port on the Sea of Azov, the third son of Pavel Yegorovich Chekhov, a grocer, and Yevgeniya Yakovlevna, née Morozova
1861 Emancipation of the serfs by Alexander II. Formation of revolutionary Land and Liberty Movement
1862 Turgenev's *Fathers and Sons*
1863–4 Polish revolt. Commencement of intensive industrialization; spread of the railways; banks established; factories built. Elective District Councils (*zemstvos*) set up; judicial reform
Tolstoy's *The Cossacks* (1863)
1865 *Lady Macbeth of Mtsensk* (1864) by Leskov, a writer much admired by Chekhov
1866 Attempted assassination of Alexander II by Karakozov
Dostoyevsky's *Crime and Punishment*
1867 Emile Zola's *Thérèse Raquin*
1868 Dostoyevsky's *The Idiot*
1868 Chekhov begins to attend Taganrog Gymnasium after wasted year at a Greek school
1869 Tolstoy's *War and Peace*
1870 Municipal government reform
1870–71 Franco-Prussian War
1873 Tolstoy's *Anna Karenina* (1873–7)
Chekhov sees local productions of *Hamlet* and Gogol's *The Government Inspector*

1875 Chekhov writes and produces humorous magazine for his brothers in Moscow, *The Stammerer*, containing sketches of life in Taganrog

1876 Chekhov's father declared bankrupt and flees to Moscow, followed by family except Chekhov, who is left in Taganrog to complete schooling. Reads Buckle, Hugo and Schopenhauer

1877–8 War with Turkey

1877 Chekhov's first visit to Moscow; his family living in great hardship

1878 Chekhov writes dramatic juvenilia: full-length drama *Fatherlessness* (MS destroyed), comedy *Diamond Cut Diamond* and vaudeville *Why Hens Cluck* (none published)

1879 Dostoyevsky's *The Brothers Karamazov* (1879–80). Tolstoy's *Confession* (1879–82)

Chekhov matriculates from Gymnasium with good grades. Wins scholarship to Moscow University to study medicine

Makes regular contributions to humorous magazine *Alarm Clock*

1880 General Loris-Melikov organizes struggle against terrorism

Guy de Maupassant's *Boule de Suif*

Chekhov introduced by artist brother Nikolay to landscape painter Levitan with whom has lifelong friendship

First short story, 'A Letter from the Don Landowner Vladimirovich N to His Learned Neighbour', published in humorous magazine *Dragonfly*. More stories published in *Dragonfly* under pseudonyms, chiefly Antosha Chekhonte

1881 Assassination of Alexander II; reactionary, stifling regime of Alexander III begins

Sarah Bernhardt visits Moscow (Chekhov calls her acting 'superficial')

Chekhov continues to write very large numbers of humorous sketches for weekly magazines (until 1883). Becomes regular contributor to Nikolay Leykin's *Fragments*, a St Petersburg weekly humorous magazine. Writes (1881–2) play now usually known as *Platonov* (discovered 1923), rejected by Maly Theatre; tries to destroy manuscript

1882 Student riots at St Petersburg and Kazan universities. More discrimination against Jews
Chekhov is able to support the family with scholarship money and earnings from contributions to humorous weeklies

1883 Tolstoy's *What I Believe*
Chekhov gains practical experience at Chikino Rural Hospital

1884 Henrik Ibsen's *The Wild Duck*. J.-K. Huysmans' *À Rebours*
Chekhov graduates and becomes practising physician at Chikino. First signs of his tuberculosis in December
Six stories about the theatre published as *Fairy-Tales of Melpomene*. His crime novel, *The Shooting Party*, serialized in *Daily News*

1885–6 Tolstoy's *The Death of Ivan Ilich* (1886)
On first visit to St Petersburg, Chekhov begins friendship with very influential Aleksey Suvorin (1834–1912), editor of the highly regarded daily newspaper *New Times*. Chekhov has love affairs with Dunya Efros and Natalya Golden (later his sister-in-law). His TB is now unmistakable
Publishes more than 100 short stories. 'The Requiem' is the first story to appear under own name and his first in *New Times* (February 1886). First collection, *Motley Tales*

1887 Five students hanged for attempted assassination of Tsar; one is Lenin's brother
Tolstoy's drama *Power of Darkness* (first performed in Paris), for which he was called nihilist and blasphemer by Alexander III
Chekhov elected member of Literary Fund. Makes trip to Taganrog and Don steppes
Second book of collected short stories *In the Twilight*. *Ivanov* produced – a disaster

1888 Chekhov meets Stanislavsky. Attends many performances at Maly and Korsh theatres and becomes widely acquainted with actors, stage managers, etc. Meets Tchaikovsky
Completes 'The Steppe', which marks his 'entry' into serious literature. Wins Pushkin Prize for 'the best literary production distinguished by high artistic value' for *In the Twilight*,

presented by literary division of Academy of Sciences. His one-act farces *The Bear* (highly praised by Tolstoy) and *The Proposal* extremely successful. Begins work on *The Wood Demon* (later *Uncle Vanya*). Radically revises *Ivanov* for St Petersburg performance

1889 Tolstoy's *The Kreutzer Sonata* (at first highly praised by Chekhov)

Chekhov meets Lidiya Avilova, who later claims love affair with him. Tolstoy begins to take an interest in Chekhov, who is elected to Society of Lovers of Russian Literature

'A Dreary Story'. *The Wood Demon* a resounding failure

1890 World weary, Chekhov travels across Siberia by carriage and river boat to Sakhalin to investigate conditions at the penal colony (recorded in *The Island of Sakhalin*). After seven months returns to Moscow (via Hong Kong, Singapore and Ceylon (Sri Lanka))

Collection *Gloomy People* (dedicated to Tchaikovsky). Only two stories published – 'Gusev' and 'Thieves'. Immense amount of preparatory reading for *The Island of Sakhalin*

1891 Severe famine in Volga basin (Chekhov organizes relief)

Chekhov undertakes six-week tour of Western Europe with Suvorin. Intense affair with Lika Mizinova

Works on *The Island of Sakhalin*. 'The Duel' published serially. Works on 'The Grasshopper'

1892 Chekhov buys small estate at Melikhovo, near Moscow; parents and sister live there with him. Gives free medical aid to peasants. Re-reads Turgenev; regards him as inferior to Tolstoy and very critical of his heroines

'Ward No. 6' and 'An Anonymous Story'

1893 *The Island of Sakhalin* completed and published serially

1894 Death of Alexander III; accession of Nicholas II; 1,000 trampled to death at Khodynka Field during coronation celebrations. Strikes in St Petersburg

Chekhov makes another trip to Western Europe

'The Student', 'Teacher of Literature', 'At a Country House' and 'The Black Monk'

1895 'Three Years'. Writes 'Ariadna', 'Murder' and 'Anna Round the Neck'. First draft of *The Seagull*

1896 Chekhov agitates personally for projects in rural education and transport; helps in building of village school at Talezh; makes large donation of books to Taganrog Public Library

'My Life' published in instalments. *The Seagull* meets with hostile reception at Aleksandrinsky Theatre

1897 Chekhov works for national census; builds second rural school. Crisis in health with lung haemorrhage; convalesces in Nice

'Peasants' is strongly attacked by reactionary critics and mutilated by censors. Publishes *Uncle Vanya*, but refuses to allow performance (until 1899)

1898 Formation of Social Democrat Party. Dreyfus affair

Stanislavsky founds Moscow Art Theatre with Nemirovich-Danchenko

Chekhov very indignant over Dreyfus affair and supports Zola; conflict with anti-Semitic Suvorin over this. His father dies. Moves to Yalta, where he buys land. Friendly with Gorky and Bunin (both of whom left interesting memoirs of Chekhov). Attracted to Olga Knipper at Moscow Art Theatre rehearsal of *The Seagull*, but leaves almost immediately for Yalta. Correspondence with Gorky

Trilogy 'Man in a Case', 'Gooseberries' and 'About Love'. 'Ionych'. *The Seagull* has first performance at Moscow Art Theatre and Chekhov is established as a playwright

1899 Widespread student riots

Tolstoy's *Resurrection* serialized

Chekhov has rift with Suvorin over student riots. Olga Knipper visits Melikhovo. He sells Melikhovo in June and moves with mother and sister to Yalta. Awarded Order of St Stanislav for educational work

'Darling', 'New Country Villa' and 'On Official Duty'. Signs highly unfavourable contract with A. F. Marks for complete edition of his works. Taxing and time-consuming work of compiling first two volumes. Moderate success of *Uncle Vanya* at Moscow Art Theatre. Publishes one of finest stories, 'The Lady with the Little Dog'. Completes 'In the Ravine'. Begins serious work on *Three Sisters*; goes to Nice to revise last two acts

1900 Chekhov settles in the house built by him in Yalta. Actors from the Moscow Art Theatre visit Sevastopol and Yalta at his request. Low opinion of Ibsen
Sees *Uncle Vanya* for first time

1901 Formation of Socialist Revolutionary Party. Tolstoy excommunicated by Russian Orthodox Church
Chekhov marries Olga Knipper
Première of *Three Sisters* at Moscow Art Theatre, with Olga Knipper as Masha. Works on 'The Bishop'

1902 Sipyagin, Minister of Interior, assassinated. Gorky excluded from Academy of Sciences by Nicholas II
Gorky's *The Lower Depths* produced at Moscow Art Theatre
Chekhov resigns from Academy of Sciences together with Korolenko in protest at exclusion of Gorky. Awarded Griboyedov Prize by Society of Dramatic Writers and Opera Composers for *Three Sisters*
Completes 'The Bishop'. Begins 'The Bride', his last story. Begins *The Cherry Orchard*

1903 Completion of Trans-Siberian Railway. Massacre of Jews at Kishinev pogrom
Chekhov elected provisional president of Society of Lovers of Russian Literature
Completes 'The Bride' and the first draft of *The Cherry Orchard.* Arrives in Moscow for Art Theatre rehearsal of *The Cherry Orchard*; strong disagreement with Stanislavsky over its interpretation

1904 Assassination of Pleve, Minister of Interior, by Socialist revolutionaries. War with Japan
Chekhov dies of TB on 15 July at Badenweiler in the Black Forest (Germany)
Première of *The Cherry Orchard* at Moscow Art Theatre

NOTE ON TEXT

Chekhov's stories (like most of the literature of the time) were not first published as separate books, but appeared in magazines or newspapers such as *New Times*, or in the thick journals, chiefly *Russian Thought*. Some of the stories were subsequently published in separate selections, such as *Tales and Stories* (1894).

In 1899 Chekhov made over the copyright of all his work (with the exception of the plays) to the publisher A. F. Marks in return for 75,000 roubles. Although the terms seemed favourable at the time, many of Chekhov's friends felt he had been highly imprudent in signing the contract (Gorky unsuccessfully tried to get him to break the contract) as they considered the terms grossly inadequate. In addition the need to collate all the stories that had so far appeared in magazines and newspapers, together with meticulous editing and improving the material, taxed Chekhov sorely and was very time-consuming. The Marks edition was published in 1899–1901, in ten volumes, and reprinted in 1903. However, the main drawback of this edition was that the stories were not printed chronologically. The first scholarly edition, with full notes and commentary, was published in Moscow, 1944–51.

Between 1973 and 1983, the definitive thirty-volume edition, *Polnoye Sobraniye Sochineniy i Pisem* (*Complete Collected Works and Letters*) was published in Moscow, with extensive commentaries by leading Soviet Chekhov scholars. It is on this edition that these translations are based.

PATRONYMICS

Russian names consist of first name, patronymic and surname, the patronymic or middle name being derived from the father's first name. For example, Chekhov's middle name, Pavlovich, derives from his father's first name, Pavel. In formal speech first name and patronymic are usual: a servant addressing his master would use both first name and patronymic. But a master would use only a first name when talking to a servant.

However, Chekhov does now and then use the direct equivalent of the English 'Mr' and 'Mrs'. This is used to convey extreme formality; also, sarcasm on the part of the person using it – for example, when von Koren scoffs at Layevsky in 'The Duel'. In both cases I have retained this form of address.

The Steppe and Other Stories

The Steppe

(THE STORY OF A JOURNEY)

I

Early one July morning a dilapidated springless brichka – one of those antediluvian carriages in which only merchants' clerks, cattle dealers and impecunious priests travel in Russia these days – drove out of N—, the main town in Z— province and thundered along the post road. It rattled and squeaked at the slightest jolt – to the mournful accompaniment of a pail tied to the backboard. From these sounds alone and the pathetic leather strips dangling from its peeling chassis one could determine its great antiquity and fitness for the scrapheap.

Two residents of N— were seated in the brichka: a clean-shaven, bespectacled merchant in a straw hat by the name of Ivan Ivanych Kuzmichov who looked more like a civil servant than a merchant, and Father Khristofor Siriysky, senior priest of St Nicholas's Church at N—, a small, long-haired old man wearing a grey canvas caftan, a broad-brimmed top hat and a colourful embroidered belt. The first was deep in thought and kept shaking his head to ward off sleep. His customary, cold, businesslike expression was at odds with the good humour of one who had just bid his family farewell and had drunk a glass or two. The second was gazing at God's world in wonderment with his small moist eyes and with a smile so broad that it seemed even to take in the brim of his hat; his face was red and had a chilled look. Both Kuzmichov and Father Khristofor were on their way to sell wool. Just a few moments before, as they said farewell to their households, the two of them had heartily indulged themselves in cream doughnuts and despite the early hour had enjoyed a good drink . . . Both were in the best of moods.

Besides the above-mentioned gentlemen and Deniska, the coachman, who was tirelessly whipping the pair of sprightly bays, there was one other passenger in the carriage – a nine-year-old boy with a face that was brown from the sun and wet with tears. This was Yegorushka, Kuzmichov's nephew. With his uncle's permission and Father Khristofor's blessing, he was on his way to grammar school. His mother, Olga Ivanovna – Kuzmichov's sister and a minor civil servant's widow, who doted on educated people and refined company – had prevailed upon her brother to take Yegorushka on his wool-selling trip and deliver him to the school. And now this boy, with no idea where or why he was travelling, was sitting on the box next to Deniska, clinging to his elbow to stop falling off and bobbing up and down like a kettle on the hob. The rapid motion made his red shirt billow out from his back like a balloon and his new, coachman-style hat with its peacock's feather was constantly slipping onto the nape of his neck. He felt the most abject of mortals and just wanted to cry.

When the carriage passed the prison, Yegorushka looked at the guards slowly pacing up and down by the high white wall, at the small barred windows, at the glittering cross on the roof and he remembered how a week earlier, on the Day of Our Holy Lady of Kazan,[1] he had gone with his mother to the prison chapel to celebrate the festival. And before that, at Easter, he had visited the prison with Lyudmila, the cook, and Deniska, and taken Easter cakes, eggs, pies and roast beef. The convicts had thanked them and crossed themselves – and one of them had given Yegorushka a pair of hand-made tin studs.

The boy gazed at these familiar places as that hateful carriage flashed past them, leaving everything in its wake. After the prison, black, sooty smithies flew by, and then the snug green cemetery enclosed by a cobblestone wall. From behind this wall white crosses and tombstones nestling in the foliage of the cherry trees gaily peeped out and from the distance they resembled white patches. Yegorushka remembered that when the cherry trees were in bloom those white patches would merge with the blossoms in a sea of white. And when the cherries ripened the white tombstones and crosses would be flecked with crimson spots, like bloodstains. Under the cherry trees, behind the wall, Yegorushka's father and his grandmother, Zinaida Danilovna, slept day and night. When Grandmother had died they put her in a long narrow coffin and placed two five-copeck pieces over her eyes that would not close. Before she died she had been very much alive and used to bring him poppy-seed rolls from the market, but now she just slept and slept . . .

Beyond the cemetery were the smoking brickyards. Dense black smoke rose in great clouds from the squat reed-thatched roofs and drifted lazily upwards. The sky above the yards was murky and the big shadows cast by the clouds of smoke crept over the fields and across the road. Men and horses, covered in red dust, were moving about in the smoke by the roofs.

The town came to an end with the brickyards and the open country began. For the last time Yegorushka looked back at the town, pressed his face to Deniska's elbow and wept bitterly.

'Still blubbering, eh? Little cry-baby!' said Kuzmichov. 'Mama's darling's snivelling again! If you don't want to come you'd better stay behind. No one's forcing you.'

'Never mind, Yegor my boy, never mind,' Father Khristofor said in a rapid patter. 'Never mind, boy . . . Call on God. It's for a good purpose you're travelling, not an evil one. As they say, knowledge is light and ignorance is darkness. Verily it is so!'

'Do you want to go back?' asked Kuzmichov.

'Ye-es I do!' sobbed Yegorushka.

'Then you should go back. No point in travelling all this way for nothing.'

'Never mind, my boy, never mind,' Father Khristofor continued. 'You must call on God. Now, Lomonosov[2] travelled like this with the fishermen, but then he became famous all over Europe. Intellect conjoined with faith brings forth fruit that is pleasing to God. What does the prayer say? "For the glory of our Creator, for the solace of our parents and for the benefit of church and country . . ." Yes, that's so.'

'But there's different kinds of benefit,' Kuzmichov said as he lit a cheap cigar. 'There's some who study for twenty years but still get no benefit from it.'

'That does happen.'

'Some folk benefit from learning, but there's others that get their brains all in a muddle. My sister's got no sense at all, she's always trying to be *so* refined and she wants Yegorushka to be a scholar. But she doesn't understand that with me in my line of business I could set him up for life. I'm telling you all this because if everyone became scholars or gentlemen there'd be no one left to do the trading or sowing. Everyone would starve to death.'

'But if everyone started trading or sowing there'd be no one left to acquire learning.'

Thinking that they had both said something weighty and compelling, Kuzmichov and Father Khristofor assumed solemn expressions and cleared their throats simultaneously. Having listened to their conversation and made nothing of it, Deniska shook his head, sat up and lashed both horses. There was silence.

And meanwhile a wide, endless plain encircled by a chain of hills was stretching out before the travellers. Huddling together and peeping out from behind each other, these hills melted away into the rising ground which extended from the right of the road to the very horizon and vanished in the lilac distance: here you can travel on and on without ever being able to make out where the plain begins or ends . . . Behind, the sun was already looking out over the town and quietly, without any fuss, it was beginning its work. At first, a long way ahead, where sky met earth, close to small barrows and a windmill which from the distance resembled a tiny man waving his arms, a broad, bright yellow band stole over the ground. A moment later a similar bright band lit up a little closer, crept off to the right and enfolded the hills. Something warm touched Yegorushka's back, a band of light that had crept up from behind darted between the carriage and horses and rushed away to meet other bands – and suddenly the whole wide plain cast off its early morning penumbra, smiled and sparkled with dew.

Newly-mown rye, coarse steppe grass, spurge and wild hemp – everything that had been half-dead, reddish-brown and darkened by the intense heat, washed by the dew now and caressed by the sun – came to life, to blossom anew. Arctic petrels cheerfully cried as they skimmed over the road, gophers called to each other in the grass, from somewhere far to the left came the lapwings' plaintive song. Frightened by the carriage, a covey of partridges took wing and flew towards the hills, softly trilling. Grasshoppers, cicadas, field-crickets and mole-crickets struck up their monotonous chirring in the grass.

But after a short while the dew evaporated, the air became stagnant and once more the disappointed steppe took on its cheerless July aspect. The grass drooped and life stood still. The brownish-green, sun-baked hills, appearing lilac from afar with their soft muted tints, the plain and the hazy distance, and that overarching sky – so breathtakingly deep and transparent in the steppes where there are no forests or high mountains – now seemed endless and numb with anguish . . .

How sultry, how forlorn! The carriage races along and all Yegorushka can see is that same sky, plain, hills . . . The music in the grass grows hushed. The petrels fly off, the partridges vanish. Rooks idly hover over the withered grass: all of them are alike and they make the steppe look even more monotonous.

A kite skims the earth with an even sweep of its wings, suddenly stops in mid-air as if brooding over the tedium of existence and then flaps its wings and shoots off like an arrow over the steppe. Why did it fly and what did it need? That was a mystery. Far away the windmill waved its sails.

Now and then brief glimpses of white skulls or boulders break the monotony; an ancient grey monumental stone or a parched willow with a dark-blue crow on its topmost branch looms up for a fleeting moment, a gopher darts across the road – and once again tall weeds, hills, rooks flash before the eye.

But now, thank heavens, a cart laden with sheaves of corn approaches. On the very top lies a young peasant girl. Sleepy and exhausted by the heat she raises her head to look at the people coming towards her. Deniska gapes at her, the bays stretch their muzzles towards the sheaves, the carriage screeches as it grazes the cart and prickly ears of corn brush Father Khristofor's hat like a besom.

'Can't you see where you're going, you fat lump!' shouts Deniska. 'Gawping like you bin stung by a bee!'

The girl smiles sleepily, moves her lips and lies down again . . . And then a solitary poplar appears on a hill. God alone knows who planted it and why it was there. It was hard to take one's eyes from its graceful trunk and green attire. Was that beautiful tree happy? Scorching heat in summer, biting frosts and blizzards in winter, terrifying nights in autumn when you see only pitch darkness and hear nothing but the wayward, angrily howling wind. But worst of all, you are alone, alone all your life . . .

Beyond the poplar a bright yellow carpet of wheat stretched from the crest of the hill down to the road. Up on the hill the wheat had already been cut and gathered into sheaves, but at the bottom reaping was still in progress. Six reapers were standing side by side swishing their cheerfully gleaming scythes in unison. The movements of the women who were binding the sheaves and the gleaming scythes told of blistering, stifling heat. A black dog with its tongue hanging out ran from the reapers towards the carriage, probably meaning to bark, but stopped halfway and casually looked at Deniska as he threatened it with his whip: it was too hot for barking! One woman stood erect, clutched her tormented back with both hands and followed Yegorushka's red calico shirt with her eyes. Whether it was the colour that pleased her or whether she was thinking of her children, she stood motionless for a long time watching him pass.

But now the wheat too had flashed by and once again there stretched that scorched plain, those sun-baked hills, the sultry sky; again a kite hovered over the earth. And in the distance that windmill was waving its arms again, still resembling a tiny man swinging his arms. One grew weary of looking at it and it seemed to be running away from the carriage, never to be reached.

Father Khristofor and Kuzmichov sat in silence. Deniska shouted as he whipped the bays. Yegorushka was no longer crying, but looked around apathetically. The burning heat and the tedium of the steppes had exhausted him. He felt that he had been travelling and bobbing up and down for ages, that the sun had been baking his back for an eternity. They had not even travelled seven miles, but already he was thinking: 'It's time we stopped for a rest!' The good-humoured look had gradually faded from Uncle's face, leaving only that matter-of-fact detachment which lends an implacable, inquisitorial expression to a lean, clean-shaven face, especially when it is bespectacled and when nose and temples are covered in dust. But Father Khristofor never stopped looking at God's world in wonderment and smiling. Not saying a word, he was thinking about something agreeable and cheerful, and a kindly, genial smile was fixed on his face. The intense heat, it seemed, had made that agreeable, cheerful thought congeal in his brain . . .

'Tell me, Deniska, do you think we'll catch up with the carts today?' asked Kuzmichov.

Deniska glanced at the sky, sat up, whipped the horses and replied, 'We'll catch 'em up by nightfall, God willing . . .'

There was a sound of barking. Six huge steppe sheepdogs suddenly leapt out as if they had been lying in ambush and rushed to meet the carriage with ferocious howls. All of them, exceptionally vicious, with shaggy spiderish muzzles and red-eyed with malice, surrounded the carriage, jealously hustled each other and set up a hoarse baying. They were filled with passionate loathing and seemed ready to tear horses, carriage and men to shreds. Deniska, who loved to tease and wield his whip, rejoiced at the opportunity, assumed an expression of malicious glee, leant over and lashed out at one of the dogs. This made them howl even more and the horses raced off. Yegorushka, who could barely hold on to the box, realized as he looked at the dogs' eyes and teeth that he would be torn to pieces in a trice should he fall off. But he felt no fear, looked at them with the same malicious glee as Deniska and only regretted that he had no whip in his hands.

The carriage drew level with a flock of sheep.

'Stop!' cried Kuzmichov. 'Whoa!'

Deniska flung his whole body backwards and reined in the horses. The carriage came to a halt.

'Come here!' Kuzmichov shouted at the drover. 'Get those blasted dogs off will you!'

The old drover, ragged and barefoot, with a warm fur cap, a filthy bag on his thigh and a long crook in his hands – a regular Old Testament figure – called off the dogs, doffed his cap and went over to the carriage. An identical patriarchal figure was standing stock-still on the other side of the flock, impassively surveying the travellers.

'Whose flock is this?' asked Kuzmichov.

'Why, it's Varlamov's!' the old man replied in a loud voice.

'It's Varlamov's!' repeated the drover on the other side of the flock.

'Tell me, did Varlamov pass this way yesterday or didn't he?'

'No, he didn't. But his bailiff did . . . that's a fact . . .'

'Let's go!'

The carriage rolled on, leaving the drovers and their vicious dogs behind. Yegorushka reluctantly peered at the lilac distance ahead and now he had the feeling that the turning windmill was getting nearer. It grew larger and larger until it loomed up in all its bulk and he could see its two sails quite clearly. One was old and patched, the other had been made from new wood only recently and was gleaming in the sun.

Although the carriage was travelling in a straight line, for some reason the windmill began to recede to the left. On and on they drove, but still it kept moving to the left, never disappearing from view.

'That's a fine windmill Boltva's built for his son!' remarked Deniska.

'But I can't see his farm.'

'It's over there, on the other side of the gully.'

Boltva's farmstead soon appeared, but the windmill still did not recede and kept up with them, looking at Yegorushka and waving its shiny sail at him. What a sorcerer that windmill was!

II

Towards noon the carriage turned off the road to the right, continued for a short distance at walking pace and came to a stop. Yegorushka heard a most delicious, soft gurgling, and he felt as though some totally different kind of air had brushed his face like cool velvet.

From a hill stuck together by nature from colossal unsightly rocks a thin stream of water was running through a pipe of hemlock wood put there by some unidentified philanthropist. Limpid, gaily sparkling in the sunlight and softly murmuring, as if it imagined itself a powerful raging torrent, it swiftly ran away somewhere to the left. Not far from the hill the little stream broadened out into a small pool. The sun's scorching rays and the burning soil drained its strength as they thirstily drank from it, but a little further on it had most probably joined up with another similar small stream, since about a hundred steps from the hill there grew along its course lush green sedge, from which three snipe flew up crying when the carriage approached.

The travellers settled down by the stream for a rest and to feed the horses. Kuzmichov, Father Khristofor and Yegorushka sat down on a felt mat they had spread out in the sparse shade produced by the carriage and the unharnessed horses and started eating. That agreeable, cheerful thought which had congealed in Father Khristofor's brain from the heat simply craved expression after he had slaked his thirst with water and eaten a hard-boiled egg. He glanced at Yegorushka affectionately, chewed for a while and began:

'I was student too, my boy. From my earliest years God endowed me with intelligence and understanding, so that I wasn't like the others when I was your age and I gladdened my parents' and tutors' hearts with my powers of comprehension. Before I was fifteen I already spoke Latin and composed verses in Latin as well as in Russian. As I remember, I was crosier-bearer to Bishop Khristofor. One day after Mass – as I recall it was the name-day of the most pious Tsar Alexander Pavlovich of Blessed Memory – as the bishop was unrobing in the chancel he looked kindly at me and asked, "*Puer bone, quam appellaris?*" And I replied, "*Christophorus sum.*"[3] And he replied, "*Ergo connominati sumus*" – that is, we were namesakes, so to speak. Then he asked in Latin whose son I was and I replied – in Latin too – that I was the son of Deacon Siryisky, of Lebedinskoye village. Seeing how quick and lucid my replies were the bishop blessed me and said, "Write and tell your father that I shan't forget him and that I'll keep you in mind." When the priests and holy fathers who were in the chancel heard this exchange in Latin they were not a little surprised either and each one showed his pleasure by praising me. I hadn't grown whiskers yet, but I could read Latin, French and Greek, I knew philosophy, mathematics, secular history and all the sciences. The Lord gave me the most wondrous memory. I only had to read something once or twice and I knew it by heart. My tutors and patrons were astonished and assumed that I would become an outstanding scholar, a luminary of the church. I did contemplate going to Kiev to continue my studies, but my parents wouldn't agree to this. "You'll be studying all your life," my father said, "so when can we expect to see you again?" Hearing this, I gave up my studies and took up a church appointment. Of course, I never became a scholar – but then, I didn't disobey my parents. I was a comfort to them in their old age and gave them a decent funeral. Obedience means more than fasting and prayers!'

'I reckon you must have forgotten every single thing you learnt!' observed Kuzmichov.

'And is it surprising? Praise be to God, I'm in my seventies now. I still remember a little bit of philosophy and rhetoric, but I've completely forgotten languages and mathematics.'

Father Khristofor screwed up his eyes, reflected for a moment and softly said:

'What is substance? Substance is an independent entity needing no other for its effectuation!'

He twisted his head round and laughed from emotion.

'Nourishment for the spirit!' he said. 'Verily, matter nourishes the flesh, but spiritual sustenance feeds the soul!'

'Learning's all very well,' sighed Kuzmichov, 'but we'll have learned our lessons all right if we don't catch up with Varlamov!'

'That man's not a needle in a haystack, we'll find him. He's wandering around somewhere in these parts.'

The familiar three snipe flew over the sedge and in their shrill cries there was a note of alarm and annoyance at having been driven off the stream. The horses steadily champed and whinnied; Deniska bustled around. Trying to demonstrate how completely indifferent he was to the cucumbers, pies and eggs that his masters were eating he embarked upon the slaughter of the horseflies and common flies that were clinging to the horses' bellies and backs. Uttering peculiar, viciously exultant cries of triumph from deep in his throat, he swatted his victims with gusto and when he missed he grunted with frustration, following with his eyes every single one that was fortunate enough to escape death.

'Deniska! What are you up to? Come and eat!' Kuzmichov said with a deep sigh to show he had eaten his fill.

Deniska meekly went over to the felt mat and selected five large yellow gherkins known as 'yellties' (he did not dare take any of the smaller, fresher ones), picked out two hard-boiled eggs that were black and cracked, after which he timidly, as if afraid of being struck on his outstretched arm, touched a small pie with his finger.

'Help yourself! Go on!' urged Kuzmichov.

Deniska took the pie with determination, walked some distance away and sat down on the ground with his back to the carriage, whereupon such a loud chewing was heard that even the horses turned round and eyed Deniska suspiciously.

When he had eaten, Kuzmichov took a sack containing something out of the carriage.

'I'm going to sleep now,' he told Yegorushka. 'Now, mind no one takes this sack from under my head.'

Father Khristofor removed his cassock, belt and caftan. Yegorushka took one look and was absolutely amazed. Not for one moment had he supposed that priests wore trousers, but Father Khristofor was wearing real canvas trousers tucked into his high boots and a short, coarse cotton jacket. Seeing him in a costume that was totally unbecoming to someone in holy orders and with that long hair and beard, Yegorushka thought he bore a striking resemblance to Robinson Crusoe. When he had unrobed, Father Khristofor lay down face to face with Kuzmichov in the shade under the carriage and they closed their eyes. After he had finished chewing Deniska stretched himself out belly upwards in the full glare of the sun and closed his eyes too.

'Mind no one steals the horses!' he told Yegorushka and immediately fell asleep.

Silence fell. All that could be heard was the snorting and champing of the horses and the snores of the sleepers. Some way off a solitary lapwing wailed and there was an occasional squeak from the three snipe that had flown up to see if the uninvited guests had left. The stream softly lisped and gurgled, but none of these sounds broke the silence or stirred the lifeless air – on the contrary, they made nature still drowsier.

Gasping from the heat which he found particularly oppressive after his meal, Yegorushka ran to the sedge and from there he surveyed the locality. He saw exactly what he had seen that morning: the plain, hills, sky, the lilac distance. Only, the hills were nearer and there was no sign of the windmill which had been left far behind by now. From behind the rocky hill where the stream was flowing rose another, smoother and wider, with a tiny hamlet of five or six farmsteads clinging to it. Around the huts there were no people, trees or shade to be seen and it was as if the hamlet had choked in the burning air and withered away. For want of something to do Yegorushka caught a fiddler-cricket in the grass, raised it to his ear in his fist and for a long time he listened to it playing its fiddle. Tiring of this music, he chased a swarm of yellow butterflies that had flown to the sedge to drink and he did not notice that he had come back to the carriage again. Uncle and Father Khristofor were fast asleep; now they would be sleeping for another two or three hours until the horses had rested. How could he pass the long hours and where could he escape the heat? No easy task . . . Without thinking, Yegorushka put his lips under the stream that was flowing from the pipe. His mouth became cold and there was a smell of hemlock. At first he drank eagerly, then he forced himself until the sharp coldness had spread from his mouth all over his body and the water had streamed over his shirt. Then he went to the carriage and watched the sleeping men. Uncle's face still expressed that same cool detachment. A fanatical businessman – even in his sleep or at church prayers when they sang 'And the Cherubim'[4] – Kuzmichov was constantly thinking about deals and he could not put them out of his mind for one minute. And now he was probably dreaming of bales of wool, wagons, prices, Varlamov . . . But Father Khristofor, a gentle, easy-going, easily-amused man, had never in his whole life been involved in a single deal that might have coiled itself around his soul like a boa constrictor. In all the numerous business deals he had undertaken in his time he was attracted less by the business itself than by the bustle and social contact – part and parcel of every undertaking. Therefore, in the present expedition, he was not so much interested in the wool, Varlamov, prices, as in the long journey, the wayside conversations, sleeping under a carriage and eating at odd hours . . . And now, judging from his expression, he was most probably dreaming of Bishop Khristofor, Latin disputations, his wife, cream doughnuts and everything that Kuzmichov could not have been dreaming of.

While Yegorushka was watching those sleepy faces, suddenly there came the unexpected sound of quiet singing. A woman was singing, some way off, but where the song was coming from and from which direction was difficult to determine. That soft, lingering, dirge-like song could be heard first to the right, then to the left, then up above, then from under the ground, as if some invisible spirit were hovering over the steppe and singing. As he looked around, Yegorushka could not make out where that strange singing was coming from. But then, when he had grown used to it, he fancied that the grass might be singing. Through its song, the half-dead, already doomed grass, plaintively and earnestly – and without any words – was trying to convince someone that it was guilty of no crime, that the sun had scorched it without reason. It insisted that it passionately wanted to live, that it was still young and would have been beautiful but for the burning heat and drought. Although guilty of no crime, it still begged someone for forgiveness and swore that it was suffering intolerable pain, melancholy, self-pity . . .

Yegorushka listened for a while and now it seemed that the doleful, lingering song had made the air even more sultry, hot and motionless. To drown the sound he ran to the sedge, humming and trying to stamp his feet. From there he looked in every direction – and then he saw the singer. Near the last hut in the hamlet stood a peasant woman in a short petticoat, as long-legged as a heron; she was sowing. White dust lazily floated down the hill from her sieve. Now it was obvious that she was the singer. A few yards from her a small boy, wearing only a smock and with no cap on his head, was standing quite still. As though bewitched by her song he did not move and kept looking downwards at something – most likely Yegorushka's red shirt.

The singing stopped. Yegorushka wearily made his way to the carriage and to while away the time played with the stream of water again.

Again he heard that droning song. That same long-legged woman was still singing in the hamlet, beyond the hill. But then he suddenly grew bored again. He left the pipe and looked up. What he saw was so unexpected that it rather scared him. On one of the large, cumbersome boulders above his head stood a small chubby boy wearing only a smock, with a large protruding stomach and thin little legs – the same boy who had been standing near the peasant woman. In blank amazement, open-mouthed, unblinking and not without some apprehension, as though he was seeing an apparition, he was inspecting Yegorushka's red shirt and the carriage. The colour of the shirt attracted and delighted him, whilst the carriage and the sleepers underneath made him curious. Perhaps he himself did not realize that the pleasant red colour and his curiosity had lured him down from the hamlet and now he was probably surprised at his own daring. For a long time Yegorushka looked him up and down – and he in turn Yegorushka. Neither said a word and both felt rather awkward. After a long silence Yegorushka asked, 'What's your name?'

The stranger's cheeks puffed out even more. He flattened his back against a rock, opened his eyes wide, moved his lips and replied huskily, 'Titus.'

The boys said nothing more to each other. After another silence and without taking his eyes off Yegorushka, the mysterious Titus hauled one leg up, felt around with his heel for a point of support and scrambled up the rock. From there, staring at Yegorushka as he retreated and apparently afraid he might be struck from behind, he clambered up onto the next rock and carried on climbing until he disappeared altogether over the crest of the hill.

As he followed him with his eyes Yegorushka clasped his knees and lowered his head. The sun's burning rays were scorching the nape of his neck and his back. Now that doleful song would die away and then waft towards him in the stagnant, sultry air; the stream gurgled monotonously, the horses champed and time seemed to be dragging on endlessly, as if it too had congealed and come to a stop. A hundred years seemed to have passed since morning . . . Was it not God's wish that Yegorushka, the carriage and the horses should become transfixed in that air, turn to stone like the hills and remain in that same place for eternity?

Yegorushka raised his head and looked ahead with glazed eyes. The lilac distance which until then had been motionless suddenly gave a wild lurch and together with the sky raced somewhere even further off. It dragged the brown grass and sedge after it and Yegorushka was whisked away with extraordinary speed in the wake of the fast-receding distance. Some mysterious force was silently bearing him somewhere and the stifling heat and that wearisome song were following in hot pursuit. Yegorushka bowed his head and closed his eyes.

Deniska was first to awake. Something had bitten him, because he jumped up, quickly scratched his shoulder and muttered, 'You rotten brute, damn and blast you!'

Then he went to the stream, slaked his thirst and took a long time to wash himself. His snorting and splashing roused Yegorushka from his drowsiness. The boy looked at Deniska's wet face covered with drops of water and large freckles, which created a marbled effect, and asked, 'Are we leaving soon?'

Deniska looked up to see how high the sun was.

'Shouldn't be long,' he replied.

He dried himself on his shirt-tail, assumed a very solemn expression and started hopping about on one foot.

'Come on, I'll race you to the sedge!' he said.

Although Yegorushka was utterly exhausted by the heat and drowsiness he still hopped after him. Deniska was about twenty and employed as a coachman. He was intending to get married – but he behaved like a little boy. He adored flying kites, racing pigeons, playing knucklebones and tag, and was always getting involved in children's games and quarrels. His masters had only to go out or fall asleep for him to start amusing himself with some sport such as hopping on one foot or throwing stones. Every adult, on seeing the genuine enthusiasm with which he romped about in children's company, found it hard to refrain from commenting 'What an oaf!' But children found nothing strange in this invasion of their domain by the big coachman: 'He can play with us as long as he doesn't start fighting!' they would say. Similarly, small dogs don't find it at all strange when large, well-meaning dogs intrude on them and start playing with them.

Deniska outstripped Yegorushka and this evidently gave him great satisfaction. He winked and to prove that he could hop on one foot over any distance suggested that Yegorushka hop with him along the road and back to the carriage without stopping.

Yegorushka declined this proposal, since he was already feeling terribly weak and breathless.

Suddenly Deniska pulled an extremely grave face – something he didn't do even when Kuzmichov gave him a severe telling-off or brandished his stick at him. Listening hard, he slowly went down on one knee and his face took on that fearful, stern expression that people display when they hear heretical talk. He fixed his eyes on one spot, slowly raised his hands above his wrists in the form of a scoop and then suddenly dropped on his stomach and clapped his hands together.

'Got him!' he cried in a husky, exultant voice, stood up and placed a large grasshopper before Yegorushka's eyes. Convinced that this must be enjoyable for the grasshopper, Yegorushka and Deniska stroked its broad green back with their fingers and touched its whiskers. Then Deniska caught a fat fly that had gorged itself on blood and offered it to the grasshopper. With the utmost nonchalance, as if it had been friends with Deniska for a very long time, the grasshopper moved its large visor-like jaws and bit off the fly's belly. Then they released the grasshopper and the pink lining of its wings glittered as it settled in the grass and immediately began trilling its song. They released the fly too; it preened its wings and flew off towards the horses minus its belly.

A deep sigh came from under the carriage. Kuzmichov had woken up. He quickly raised his head, anxiously peered into the distance and one could tell from his glance, which indifferently by-passed both Yegorushka and Deniska, that his first thoughts on waking were about wool and Varlamov.

'Get up, Father Khristofor! It's time to go!' he said in alarm. 'You've slept enough – we've probably missed out on the deal now anyway. Deniska! Harness the horses!'

Father Khristofor awoke with the same smile as when he had fallen asleep. His face was crumpled and wrinkled from sleep and seemed half its normal size. After washing and dressing he unhurriedly took a small soiled psalter from his pocket, turned his face to the east and started reading in a whisper and crossing himself.

'Father Khristofor!' Kuzmichov said reproachfully. 'It's time to go, the horses are ready, but you . . . for heaven's sake!'

'Won't be long,' Father Khristofor muttered. 'I must read today's portion of the Psalms first – I didn't get round to it earlier.'

'Your psalms can wait!'

'Ivan Ivanych, I have to read a portion every day. I mustn't neglect it.'

'God won't call you to account for it.'

For a full quarter of an hour Father Khristofor stood still, facing the east and moving his lips, while Kuzmichov looked at him almost with loathing and kept impatiently twitching his shoulders. He was particularly incensed when after each 'Glory' Father Khristofor took a deep breath, quickly crossed himself and repeated three times in a deliberately loud voice so that the others had to cross themselves as well:

'Hallelujah, hallelujah, hallelujah, Glory to Thee, Oh Lord!'

Finally he smiled, glanced up at the sky, put the psalter back in his pocket and said, '*Fini!*'

A minute later the carriage moved off. It was just as if it were travelling backwards, not forwards, for the passengers saw the same scenes as in the morning. The hills were still sinking in the lilac distance and there seemed no end to them. There were fleeting glimpses of tall grass and small stones, strips of stubble flashed by and those same rooks, together with a kite which was steadily flapping its wings, flew over the steppe. The air became even more immobile from the heat and the silence, and submissive nature was numbed in that deathly hush. No wind, not one bright fresh sound, not even one small cloud.

But now at last, when the sun was sinking in the west, the steppe, the hills and the air could bear the oppressiveness no more: exhausted, all patience gone, they endeavoured to cast off the yoke. From beyond the hills there suddenly appeared an ash-grey, fleecy cloud. It exchanged glances with the steppe, said 'I'm ready', and frowned. All of a sudden something seemed to snap in the stagnant air, there was a violent gust and the wind whirled over the steppe, whistling and roaring. At once the grass and last year's weeds began to murmur, while along the road dust eddied and spiralled, raced over the steppe and, drawing after it straw, dragonflies and feathers, soared towards the heavens in a black rotating column and darkened the sun. Far and wide over the steppe dashed tumbleweeds, stumbling and leaping; one of them, caught up in the whirlwind, span round and round like a bird and flew into the sky, where it turned into a black speck and vanished from sight. A second, then a third sailed after it and Yegorushka could see two of them colliding in the azure heights and grappling like wrestlers.

A bustard took flight just by the roadside. Bathed in sunlight, its wings and tail flashing, it resembled an angler's bait or a pond moth whose wings appear to blend with its antennae when it darts over the water, so that it seems to have antennae growing at the front, at the back and along its sides . . . Quivering in the air like an insect and displaying all its many colours, the bustard soared to a great height in a straight line and then, probably taking fright at the cloud of dust, flew off to one side – and its flashing could be seen for a long time afterwards . . .

And then a corncrake, alarmed by the whirlwind and unable to understand what was happening, rose from the grass. It flew after the wind and not into it – unlike all other birds. As a result its feathers grew ruffled, it swelled to the size of a hen and took on a very angry, intimidating look. Only the rooks, which had grown old on the steppe and were used to all its commotions, calmly hovered over the grass or, ignoring all else, casually pecked away at the hard earth with their thick beaks.

From beyond the hills came the dull roar of thunder; there was a sudden breath of freshness in the air. Deniska cheerfully whistled and whipped the horses. Father Khristofor and Kuzmichov held on to their hats and strained their eyes towards the hills. How welcome a light shower would be!

Just one small effort, it seemed, just one more exertion and the steppe would have prevailed. But an invisible, oppressive force gradually fettered both wind and air and settled the dust; and once again silence fell, as if nothing had happened. The cloud went into hiding, the sun-baked hills frowned, the air humbly grew still and somewhere only frightened lapwings wailed and bemoaned their fate . . .

Evening quickly set in.

III

A large single-storey building with a rusty iron roof and dark windows appeared in the twilight gloom. It was called an inn although it had no stable-yard and stood completely exposed in the middle of the steppe. A little to one side was the dark patch of a miserable little cherry orchard with a hurdle fence, while beneath the windows stood drowsy sunflowers, their heads heavy with sleep. A miniature windmill set up to frighten the hares off was rattling away in the orchard. Around the inn there was nothing to be seen or heard but the steppe.

No sooner had the carriage stopped by the canopied porch than joyful voices came from the inn – one a man's, the other a woman's. The door creaked on its block and in the twinkling of an eye a tall skinny figure loomed up by the carriage, swinging its arms and coat-skirts. It was Moses Moisevich the innkeeper, a middle-aged, extremely pale-faced man with a handsome jet-black beard. He was wearing a black, threadbare frock-coat which dangled loosely from his narrow shoulders as if suspended from a clothespeg and every time he threw up his hands, whether in joy or horror, its skirts flapped like wings. Besides this frock-coat, the innkeeper was wearing broad white trousers that were not tucked into his boots and a velvet waistcoat with a pattern of reddish-brown flowers resembling gigantic bed-bugs.

When he recognized his visitors, Moses at first stood rooted to the spot from a rush of emotion, then he threw up his hands and groaned. The skirts of his frock-coat flapped, his back bent double and his pale face twisted into a smile that seemed to be saying that the sight of the carriage was not only agreeable but excruciatingly sweet.

'Ah, goodness me, goodness me!' he gasped in a thin singsong voice, fussing so much that his wild contortions prevented the passengers from leaving the carriage. 'Such happy day this for me! Ah, what ever shall I do first! Ivan Kuzmichov! Father Khristofor! What pretty young gentleman is sitting on the box – or may God punish me! Ah, goodness me, why am I standing here like this and not inviting guests into parlour? Come in, I most humbly beg you! Welcome! Let me take your luggage . . . Ah, goodness me!'

As Moses was rummaging around in the carriage and helping the guests out, he suddenly turned around and cried, 'Solomon! Solomon!' in such a frenzied, strangled voice that he sounded like a drowning man calling for help.

'Solomon! Solomon!' a woman's voice repeated from inside the inn.

The door creaked on its block and in the doorway appeared a shortish, young red-headed Jew with a large beaked nose and a bald patch surrounded by wiry, curly hair. He was wearing a short, exceedingly shabby jacket with cutaway flaps and short sleeves, and short woollen trousers – all of which made him look as short and skimpy as a plucked fowl. This was Solomon, Moses' brother. Without a word of greeting and with a rather strange smile he approached the carriage.

'Ivan Kuzmichov and Father Khristofor are here!' Moses told him in a tone that intimated he was afraid Solomon might not believe him. 'Ay vay, what surprise to have such lovely people suddenly dropping in on us like this! Come on, Solomon, take their things. This way, my honoured guests!'

Shortly afterwards Kuzmichov, Father Khristofor and Yegorushka were sitting at an ancient oak table in a large, gloomy, empty room. This table was almost totally isolated, since, apart from the wide sofa upholstered in oil-cloth that was full of holes and three chairs there was no other furniture in that large room. As for the chairs, not everyone would have dignified them by that name. They were a pathetic semblance of furniture, covered with oil-cloth that had seen better days and with backs that had been bevelled with such unnatural severity they closely resembled children's toboggans. It was hard to imagine what comforts that mysterious carpenter who had so mercilessly bent those chairs' backs had in mind and one was inclined to think that it was not the carpenter who was to blame, but some vagrant Hercules who, intent on vaunting his strength, had first bent the chairs' backs, tried to straighten them but had only bent them even more. The room had a sombre look. The walls were grey, the ceiling and cornices grimy and the floor was full of cracks and gaping holes of unfathomable provenance (one was inclined to think they had been produced by the heel of that same Hercules), and you felt that even if a dozen lamps were to be hung in that room it would still be as dark as ever. Neither walls nor windows displayed anything remotely resembling decoration. However, on one wall, in a grey wooden frame, hung a list of regulations under a two-headed eagle[5] and on another, in a similar frame, there was some kind of engraving with the inscription 'Man's Indifference'. To what men were indifferent was impossible to ascertain, since the engraving had faded appreciably with time and was considerably fly-blown. There was a musty, sour smell in the room.

After leading his guests into the room, Moses renewed his contortions, throwing his arms up, bending up and down and uttering joyful exclamations – all this he considered essential in order to give an exceptionally courteous, friendly impression.

'When did our wagons pass by?' Kuzmichov asked him.

'One wagon train came past this morning, Ivan Kuzmichov, and another stopped for rest and meal and left in early evening.'

'Oh . . . did Varlamov come by or didn't he?'

'No, he didn't, Ivan Kuzmichov. But yesterday morning his bailiff Grigory passed by and he told me that Varlamov had most likely gone over to the Molokan's[6] farm.'

'Excellent. That means we'll catch the wagons up in no time at all – then we'll go on to the Molokan's.'

'But what you thinking of, Ivan Kuzmichov?' Moses said in horror, throwing up his hands. 'Where are you going to spend night? Now, you can enjoy nice little supper and stay here for night and tomorrow, God willing, you can drive off and catch up with anyone you have to!'

'I'm sorry, Moses, but we just haven't the time. Some other occasion, perhaps. We'll stay another quarter of an hour, but then we must be off. We can stay at the Molokan's overnight.'

'Quarter of hour!' shrieked Moses. 'Do you have no fear of God! Now, don't force me to hide your caps and lock door! At least have a bite to eat and some tea!'

'We've no time for tea and sugar and all that stuff,' said Kuzmichov.

Moses leaned his head to one side, crooked his knees and spread his hands out as if warding off blows; with that same painfully cloying smile he started begging them:

'Ivan Kuzmichov! Father Khristofor! Please do me favour and have tea with me! Am I really such wicked man that you refuse to drink tea with me? Ivan Kuzmichov!'

'All right then, we'll have some tea,' Father Khristofor sighed sympathetically. 'That won't hold us up.'

'Oh, all right,' agreed Kuzmichov.

Moses sprang into action, gasped joyfully, cringed – just as if he had leapt from cold water into the warm – and ran to the door.

'Rosa! Rosa!' he cried in that frenzied, strangled voice in which he had summoned Solomon.

A minute later the door opened and in came Solomon with a large tray. After putting it on the table he looked sarcastically to one side and then smiled as strangely as before. Now, by the light of the small lamp, one could see every detail of his smile. It was extremely complex and expressed a variety of feelings – but predominant was one of blatant contempt. It seemed that he was thinking about something both funny and stupid, that there was someone whom he despised and just could not bear, and that he was pleased about something and was waiting for the right moment to produce a hurtful sneer and then laugh his head off. His long nose, fat lips and cunning, protruding eyes seemed tense from this urge to roar with laughter.

'Solomon, why didn't you come over to the fair at N— this summer to do your Jewish impersonations?' asked Kuzmichov, peering at his face and smiling sarcastically.

Two years before, as Yegorushka also remembered very well, Solomon had performed scenes from Jewish life in one of the booths and enjoyed great success. The mention of this made no impression whatsoever on Solomon. Without a word of reply he went out and soon returned with the samovar.

When he had completed his duties at the table he stepped to one side, folded his arms on his chest, stuck one leg out and fixed his sarcastic eyes on Father Khristofor. In his posture there was something provocative, overbearing and contemptuous and at the same time extremely pathetic and comic, because the more threatening it became the more sharply it accentuated his short trousers, docked jacket, grotesque nose and his whole wretched plucked, bird-like figure.

Moses brought a stool from another room and sat down a little way from the table.

'Good appetites! Here's the tea and sugar!' he said, attending to his guests. 'Drink your fills! Such rare visitors, so rare! Really, it must be five years since I saw Father Khristofor! And is no one going to tell me who that handsome little gentleman is?' he asked, tenderly looking at Yegorushka.

'He's my sister Olga's son,' Kuzmichov replied.

'And where's he off to?'

'To school. We're taking him to the grammar school.'

Out of politeness Moses showed surprise and meaningfully twisted his head.

'That's very good!' he said, wagging his finger at the samovar. 'That's good! And you'll be such fine gentleman when you leave school that we'll all have to take hat off to you! You'll be clever, rich – and so grand! And Mama will be so pleased! Oh, that's very good!'

He was silent for a while, stroked his knees and then continued in a politely jocular tone, 'You'll have to forgive me, Father Khristofor, but I must report you to the Bishop for robbing merchants of their livelihood! I'll get myself an official form and write and tell him that Father Khristofor doesn't have much money, so he's gone into business and started selling wool!'

'Well, it's something I thought up in my twilight years,' laughed Father Khristofor. 'I've changed profession from priest to merchant, my friend. Actually I should be at home now saying my prayers, but here I am galloping around like a Pharaoh in his chariot . . . Ah, vanity . . . !'

'But you'll make plenty money!'

'Do you think so? I'll get more kicks than copecks! The wool isn't mine, it's my son-in-law's, Mikhail's!'

'But why didn't he go himself?'

'Why? . . . because he's still wet behind the ears. It's all very well buying wool, but when it comes to selling it he has no idea – he's still very young. He spent all his money, wanted to make a bundle and then go and cut a dash, but he's been running around all over the place and no one will even give him what he paid for it. For a whole year the lad knocks around and then he comes to me and asks, "Papa, do me a favour, please sell the wool for me. I haven't a clue about these things!" So true! Yes, the moment things go wrong he comes running to Papa, but before that he managed very nicely without him! He didn't come to me for advice when he was buying it, but now it's Papa he wants! But what can Papa do? If it weren't for Kuzmichov, Papa wouldn't have done a thing. Children are nothing but trouble!'

'Yes, big trouble, I can tell you!' sighed Moses. 'I've got six of my own. This one to school, another to the doctor's, a third needs coddling – and when they grow up they give you even more trouble. But it's nothing new – it was the same in the Holy Scriptures. When

Jacob had little childrens he wept, but when they grew up he wept even more!'

'Hm . . . yes,' agreed Father Khristofor, pensively glancing into his glass. 'Personally speaking, I've done nothing to anger God. I've lived my allotted span as happy as anything . . . I've fixed my daughters up with good husbands, set my sons up in life. And now I'm free. I've done my duty and I can go wherever I like. I live nice and quietly with my wife, eat, drink and sleep, enjoy my grandchildren, say my prayers and I ask for nothing more. I live off the fat of the land and I don't need anything from anybody. Never in my life have I known sorrow and if the Tsar for example were to ask me now, "Is there anything you need? What would you like?" I'd tell him *nothing*! I want for nothing – and I can thank God for that. There's no happier man than me in the whole town. Only, I've sinned a lot – but after all, only God is sinless. Isn't that true?'

'Of course it's true.'

'Well then, I've lost my teeth of course, my poor back aches from old age, I get short of breath and all that . . . I do have illnesses – the flesh is weak! But as you can see for yourself I've lived my life to the full. I'm in my seventies! You can't go on for ever – you mustn't outstay your welcome!'

Father Khristofor suddenly remembered something, snorted into his glass and laughed so much he had a coughing fit. Moses laughed as well – and he too had a coughing fit, out of politeness.

'It's an absolute scream!' Father Khristofor said with a helpless wave of the arm. 'My eldest son Gabriel comes to stay with me. His line is medicine – he's a district doctor down in Chernigov[7] . . . Right, so I tell him, "I'm a bit short-winded . . . and there's one thing and another . . . Well, you're a doctor, so cure your father!" He immediately makes me undress, does some tapping and listening, kneads my stomach, performs different tricks and then he tells me, "Papa, you need compressed air treatment".'

Father Khristofor laughed convulsively until the tears came, and then he got up.

'"Confound your compressed air!" I said. "Confound your compressed air!"' As he said this he laughed and waved his arms. Moses stood up, too, hands on stomach, and burst into peals of shrill laughter, just like a yapping lapdog.

'Confound your compressed air!' repeated Father Khristofor, guffawing.

Laughing two notes higher, Moses had such a paroxysm of mirth he could barely keep his footing.

'Oh, my goodness!' he groaned in mid guffaw. 'Let me get my breath . . . You're real comedian you are. Oh, you'll be death of me!'

He laughed and talked, but at the same time he kept giving Solomon timorous, suspicious looks. The latter was standing in the same posture as before and smiling. Judging from his eyes and his grin he genuinely despised and hated people, but this was so at odds with his plucked-hen appearance that Yegorushka construed his defiant attitude and sarcastic, supercilious expression as deliberate clowning, calculated to amuse the honoured guests.

After drinking about six glasses of tea in silence, Kuzmichov cleared a place in front of him on the table, picked up his bag – that same bag he had kept under his head when he slept under the carriage – untied the string and shook it. Bundles of banknotes tumbled out onto the table.

'Let's count them while we have the time, Father Khristofor,' said Kuzmichov.

Moses was embarrassed at the sight of the money, stood up and, since he was a sensitive man reluctant to pry into others' secrets, he tiptoed from the room, balancing himself with his arms. Solomon stayed where he was.

'How many in the one-rouble packets?' Father Khristofor began.

'They're in fifties. The three-rouble notes are in nineties, the twenty-fives and hundreds are in thousands. You can count seven thousand eight hundred out for Varlamov and I'll count Gusevich's. Now, mind you don't make any mistakes!'

Never in his life had Yegorushka seen such a huge pile of money as was now lying on the table. There must have been a really vast amount, since the pile of seven thousand eight hundred roubles that Father Khristofor had put aside for Varlamov seemed exceedingly small in proportion to the rest of the bundle. At any other time so much money might have stunned Yegorushka and led him to consider how many buns, dough-rolls and poppy-cakes he could have bought with that pile. But now he looked at it indifferently, conscious only of the revolting smell of rotten apples and kerosene it gave off. Exhausted by the bumpy carriage ride, he felt terribly drained and all he wanted was to sleep. His head dropped, his eyes kept closing and his thoughts were tangled like threads. Had it been possible he would gladly have leant his head on the table, closed his eyes to avoid seeing the lamp and those fingers moving over the pile of banknotes and allowed his sluggish, sleepy thoughts to become even more muddled. As he struggled to stay awake he saw the lamp, the cups and the fingers double, the samovar swayed and the smell of rotten apples seemed even sharper and more revolting.

'Ah, money, money, money!' sighed Father Khristofor, smiling. 'You bring nothing but trouble. I dare say my Mikhailo's asleep, dreaming that I'll be bringing him a pile like this.'

'Your Mikhailo hasn't a clue,' Kuzmichov said in a low voice, 'he's like a fish out of water, but *you* understand and can see things straight. As I said, you'd do better if you let me have your wool and went back home. Oh yes, I'd give you fifty copecks over and above my own price – and that's only out of respect for you.'

'No, thank you very much,' sighed Father Khristofor. 'I appreciate your concern . . . Of course, if I had the choice I wouldn't hesitate, but as you know very well, the wool isn't mine . . .'

In tiptoed Moses. Trying not to look at the heap of money out of delicacy, he crept up to Yegorushka and tugged the back of his shirt.

'Come with me, young sir,' he said in an undertone. 'I'll show you such lovely little bear! Such fierce, grumpy bear! Oooh!'

Sleepy Yegorushka stood up and lazily plodded after Moses to have a look at the bear. He entered a small room where, before he saw anything, his breath was taken away by that sour, musty smell which was much stronger here than in the large room and was probably spreading all over the inn. Half of the room was taken up by a large double bed covered with a greasy quilt and the other by a chest of drawers and piles of every conceivable kind of clothing, ranging from stiffly starched skirts to children's trousers and braces. On the chest of drawers a tallow candle was burning.

Instead of the promised bear Yegorushka saw a big, very fat Jewess with her hair hanging loose, wearing a red flannel dress with black dots. She had great difficulty in manoeuvring the narrow space between bed and chest of drawers, emitting protracted, groaning sighs as if she had toothache. At the sight of Yegorushka she assumed a sorrowful look, sighed long and deep and before he had time to look round put a slice of bread and honey to his lips.

'Eat it, dear,' she said. 'Your mama's not here and there's no one to feed you. Eat up.'

Yegorushka began to eat, although after the fruit drops and poppy-seed cakes which he had at home every day he didn't care much for the honey, half of which was a mixture of wax and bees' wings. While he was eating, Moses and the Jewess looked on and sighed.

'Where are you going, dear?' asked the Jewess.

'To school,' Yegorushka replied.

'How many children does your mama have?'

'There's only me, no one else.'

'Oh dear!' sighed the Jewess, looking up. 'Your poor, poor mama! How she'll cry! How she'll miss you! In a year's time we're taking our Nahum to school, too. Oh dear!'

'Oh, Nahum, Nahum!' sighed Moses, the skin twitching on his pale face. 'He's such sickly child.'

The greasy quilt moved and there emerged a child's curly head on a very thin neck. Two black eyes gleamed and stared inquisitively at Yegorushka. Still sighing, Moses and the Jewess went to the chest and started discussing something in Yiddish. Moses spoke in a deep undertone and for the most part his Yiddish sounded like a non-stop 'gal-gal-gal', whilst his wife answered him in a shrill 'too-too-too', like a turkey-hen. As they were conferring another curly little head on a thin neck peeped out from under the greasy quilt, then a third, then a fourth. If Yegorushka had possessed a vivid imagination he might have fancied a hundred-headed hydra lay under that quilt.

'Gal-gal-gal,' boomed Moses.

'Too-too-too,' twittered the Jewess.

The conference finished when the Jewess plunged her hands deep into the chest of drawers, unfolded some kind of green rag and took out a large heart-shaped rye cake.

'Take it, dear,' she said, handing it to Yegorushka. 'You've no mama now, no one to give you nice presents.'

Yegorushka put the cake in his pocket and retreated to the door as he could no longer bear to breathe that acrid, musty air in which the innkeeper and his wife lived. When he returned to the main room he settled comfortably on the sofa and let his thoughts wander.

Kuzmichov had just finished counting the banknotes and was putting them back in the bag. He paid them little respect and unceremoniously bundled them into the dirty bag – indifferently, as though they were so much waste paper.

Father Khristofor was chatting to Solomon.

'Well, Solomon the Wise,' he asked, yawning and making the sign of the cross over his mouth. 'How are things with you?'

'What things do you mean?' asked Solomon, giving him a venomous look, as if some crime were being hinted at.

'Well . . . I mean, things in general. How are you getting on?'

'Getting on?' Solomon repeated, shrugging his shoulders. 'The same as everyone. As you see, I'm a servant. I'm my brother's servant, my brother's the visitors' servant and his visitors are Varlamov's servants – and if I had ten million roubles Varlamov would be my servant.'

'And why should he be your servant?'

'Why? Because there's no gent or millionaire who wouldn't lick a dirty Jew's boots to make an extra copeck. Now, I'm a dirty Jew and a beggar, everyone looks at me like I was a dog, but if I had money Varlamov would be making as much a fool of himself in front of me as Moses is in front of you.'

Father Khristofor and Kuzmichov exchanged glances. Neither of them understood Solomon. Kuzmichov gave him a stern, severe look and said, 'How can you compare yourself with Varlamov, you idiot!'

'I'm not such a fool as to compare myself with Varlamov,' replied

Solomon, giving the two of them a sarcastic look. 'Although Varlamov's Russian, at heart he's a dirty Jew. All he lives for is money and profit, but I burnt my money in the stove. I don't need money or land or sheep, and people don't have to be frightened of me and take their hats off when I go past. That means I'm cleverer than your Varlamov and more like a human being!'

A little later, in his deep drowsiness, Yegorushka could hear Solomon speaking about the Jews in a hurried, lisping voice that was hoarse from the loathing that was choking him. At first he spoke in correct Russian, but then he lapsed into the tone of those fairground tellers of tales from Jewish life, breaking into that same exaggerated Yiddish accent he once used at the fair.

'Hold on!' Father Khristofor interrupted. 'Just a moment! If you don't like your faith you'd better change it. Anyone who scoffs at his own faith is the lowest of the low.'

'You just don't understand!' Solomon rudely cut him short. 'We're talking at cross purposes.'

'That only goes to show how stupid you are!' sighed Father Khristofor. 'I instruct you to the best of my ability and you go and lose your temper. I talk to you calmly, like a father, and you start gobbling away like a turkey! You're a queer fish, no mistake!'

In came Moses. He looked in alarm at Solomon and his visitors and once more the skin on his face twitched nervously. Yegorushka shook his head and looked around, catching a fleeting glimpse of Solomon's face just as it was three-quarters turned towards him and when the shadow of his long nose bisected the whole of his left cheek. That contemptuous smile, deep in shadow, those sarcastic, gleaming eyes, that arrogant expression and that whole plucked-hen's figure doubling and dancing before Yegorushka's eyes made him look less like a clown than something out of a nightmare – an evil spirit most likely.

'That brother of yours is a real madman Moses, God help him!' Father Khristofor said, smiling. 'You should fix him up with a job somewhere or find him a wife. He's not human . . .'

Kuzmichov angrily frowned. Once again Moses looked at his brother anxiously and quizzically.

'Solomon, get out of here,' he said sternly. 'Get out!'

And he added something in Yiddish. Solomon laughed abruptly and left.

'What's going on?' Moses asked Father Khristofor in alarm.

'He keeps forgetting himself,' replied Kuzmichov. 'He's a boor and he thinks too much of himself.'

'I thought as much!' Moses exclaimed, clasping his hands in horror. 'Oh, goodness me, goodness me!' he quietly muttered. 'Now, please be so kind as to forgive him and don't be cross. That's the kind of person he is. Goodness me! He's my own brother and I've had nothing but trouble with him. Why, did you know he . . .'

Moses curled his finger against his forehead.

'He's out of his mind,' he continued, 'a hopeless case. I just don't know what to do with him. He cares for no one, respects no one and fears no one. You know, he laughs at everyone, says stupid things and rubs everyone up wrong way. You won't believe it, but once when Varlamov was here Solomon said such things to him that he gave both of us taste of whip. Why did he have to whip me? Was it my fault? If God robbed him of brains it was God's will. But how was I to blame?'

About ten minutes passed and Moses still carried on muttering in an undertone and sighing.

'He doesn't sleep at night – he just keeps thinking, thinking and thinking. What he thinks about God only knows. And if you go near him at night he gets angry and laughs. He doesn't like me either . . . And there's nothing he wants. When Papa died he left us six thousand roubles each. I bought an inn, married, and now I have children. But he went and burnt all his money in stove. Such shame, such shame! Why did he burn it? If he didn't need it then why not give to me? Why burn it?'

Suddenly the door squeaked on its block and the floor shook with footsteps. There was a draught of air and Yegorushka felt as if a great black bird had swept past and flapped its wings right in his face. He opened his eyes and there was Uncle, standing by the sofa, bag in hand and ready to leave. Holding his broad-brimmed top hat, Father Khristofor was bowing to someone and smiling – not his customary soft, kindly smile, but a deferential, artificial smile which did not suit him at all. Meanwhile, Moses was trying to balance himself as though his body had broken into three and he was doing his best not to disintegrate altogether. Only Solomon seemed unconcerned and stood in one corner, arms folded, smiling as contemptuously as ever.

'Your Ladyship, please forgive us, it's not very clean in here,' groaned Moses with that painfully sugary smile, paying no more attention to Kuzmichov and Father Khristofor and trying only to stop himself falling apart by balancing his whole body. 'We're only simple folk, your Ladyship!'

Yegorushka rubbed his eyes. In the middle of the room there really was a 'ladyship' in the shape of a young, very beautiful, buxom woman in a black dress and straw hat. Before Yegorushka could make out her features, for some reason he recalled that solitary, graceful poplar he had seen on the hill that day.

'Was Varlamov here today?' a woman's voice asked.

'No, your Ladyship,' replied Moses.

'If you happen to see him tomorrow please tell him to drop in and see me for a few moments.'

Suddenly, quite unexpectedly, about half an inch from his eyes, Yegorushka saw velvety black eyebrows, large brown eyes and well-groomed, dimpled female cheeks, from which her smile radiated like sunbeams all over her face. There was the smell of some wonderful perfume.

'What a pretty little boy!' the lady said. 'Whose is he? Casimir, just take a look. How lovely! Heavens, he's asleep! Oh, my darling little pet!'

And the lady firmly kissed Yegorushka on both cheeks. He smiled and closed his eyes, thinking he was dreaming. The door squeaked and the hurried footsteps of someone coming in and out could be heard.

Two deep voices whispered:

'Yegorushka! Yegorushka! Get up now, we're leaving!'

Someone, apparently Deniska, set Yegorushka on his feet and took him by the arm. On the way Yegorushka half opened his eyes and once again he saw that beautiful woman in the black dress who had kissed him. She was standing in the middle of the room and gave him a friendly smile and nod as she watched him go. As he went to the door he saw a handsome, thick-set, dark-haired gentleman in bowler hat and leggings. He must have been the lady's escort.

'Whoa there!' someone shouted outside.

At the front of the inn Yegorushka saw a splendid new carriage and a pair of black horses. On the box sat a liveried footman with a long whip. Solomon was the only one to come out and see off the departing guests. His face was tense with the urge to start roaring with laughter and he seemed to be awaiting the guests' departure with great impatience so that he could laugh at them to his heart's content.

'Countess Dranitsky,' Father Khristofor whispered as he climbed into the carriage.

'Yes, Countess Dranitsky,' Kuzmichov repeated, also in a whisper.

The countess's arrival must have made a very strong impression, since even Deniska spoke in a whisper and only ventured to lash the bays and shout when the carriage had travelled several hundred yards and when, far behind, all that could be seen of the inn was a small dim light.

IV

Who then was this elusive, mysterious Varlamov of whom people talked so much, whom Solomon despised and whom even the beautiful countess needed? As he sat on the box next to Deniska drowsy Yegorushka was thinking about precisely that man. He had never set eyes on him, but he had very often heard people talk about him and frequently tried to visualize him. He knew that Varlamov owned tens of thousands of acres, about one hundred thousand head of sheep and had piles of money. Of his way of life and activities, all Yegorushka knew was that he was always 'hanging around these parts' and that he was in constant demand.

At home Yegorushka had heard a great deal about Countess Dranitsky as well. She too owned some tens of thousands of acres, a great many sheep, a stud farm and had a lot of money. However, she did not 'hang around' but lived on a magnificent estate, of which Kuzmichov – who was often there on business – and some people he knew told many wondrous tales. For example, they said that the countess's drawing-room was hung with the portraits of all the kings of Poland, that there was a large rock-shaped table-clock crowned by a prancing diamond-eyed golden horse with a golden rider who swung his sabre right and left whenever the clock struck. They said that the countess gave a ball twice a year to which she invited gentry and officials from all over the province and which even Varlamov attended. All the guests drank tea from water boiled in silver samovars and they ate the most exotic dishes – at Christmas, for example, they were served raspberries and strawberries – and they danced to a band that played day and night.

'How beautiful she is!' thought Yegorushka, recalling her face and smile.

Kuzmichov must have been thinking about the countess, too, as after the carriage had driven about a mile and a half he said, 'And that Casimir Mikhaylych swindles her right and left. Remember when I bought some wool from her two years ago? He netted three thousand from that deal alone.'

'What do you expect from a lousy Pole?' Father Khristofor said.

'But it doesn't worry her in the slightest. As they say – young and foolish and nothing upstairs!'

For some reason Yegorushka wanted to think only about Varlamov and the countess – particularly the countess. His drowsy brain utterly rejected prosaic thoughts, became muddled and retained only those fantastic, magical images that have the advantage that somehow of their own accord and with no effort from the thinker they spring to mind and then vanish without trace after a good shake of the head. And in fact there was nothing in his surroundings that might encourage pedestrian thoughts. To the right were dark hills which seemed to be concealing something mysterious and terrifying; to the left the whole sky above the horizon was suffused with a crimson glow and it was hard to tell if there was a fire somewhere or if the moon was about to rise. The far distance was as visible as by day, but now its soft lilac hue had faded, veiled by the twilight gloom in which the whole steppe was hiding – just like Moses' children under their quilt.

On July evenings quails and corncrakes no longer call, nightingales do not sing in wooded river-beds, there is no scent of flowers, yet the steppe is still beautiful and full of life. No sooner has the sun set and darkness enfolded the earth than the day's sorrows are forgotten and the steppe heaves a faint sigh from its broad bosom. A cheerful, youthful trilling that cannot be heard by day rises from the grass, as if it cannot see in the darkness how it has aged; chirring, whistling, scratching – those bass, tenor and treble voices of the steppe – everything blends in one unbroken din and against the background of these sounds it is pleasant to reminisce and to be sad. The monotonous chirring is as soothing as a lullaby. On and on you drive and you feel that you are falling asleep. But suddenly the abrupt alarm call of a wakeful bird reaches your ears, some vague sound, like a human voice uttering a long 'Ah-ah!' of astonishment rings out – and slumber seals your eyelids. Or you may be driving past a gully where bushes grow and you hear the bird called the 'sleeper' by steppe-dwellers crying 'I'm sleeping, I'm sleeping, I'm sleeping!' – whilst another bird guffaws or breaks into hysterical weeping – it is an owl. For whom are they crying? Who can hear them on the steppes? God alone knows, but their cries are filled with sadness and complaining. There is a scent of hay, dry grass and late flowers – dense, richly-cloying and soft.

Everything is visible through the haze, but colours and outlines are difficult to make out. All things appear in a different light. As you travel on suddenly you see a monk-like silhouette by the roadside. It is standing motionless, waiting and holding something in its hands. Can it be a highwayman? The figure approaches, grows larger – now it is level with the carriage – and then you see that it is no human being but a lonely bush or boulder. These motionless figures stand on the hills and lie in wait, hide behind the barrows, peep out from the grass – all of them resembling human beings, all arousing suspicion.

But when the moon rises the night grows pale and languorous. It is as if the darkness never existed. The air is crystal clear, fresh and warm, everything is perfectly visible and even individual stalks of grass by the road can be made out. Far and wide over that immense expanse skulls and rocks are visible. The suspicious, monk-like figures seem darker and more sinister against the bright background of night. That surprised 'Ah-ah!' rings out more often amid the monotonous chattering and disturbs the still air, or the cry of some wakeful or delirious bird is heard. Broad shadows pass over the plain like clouds across the sky and if you peer for long into the inscrutable distance, hazy, weird shapes loom up, towering one behind the other. It is all rather eerie. And if you look up at the pale-green, star-spangled sky where there is not one small cloud or speck, you will understand why the warm air is so still, why nature is on her guard and is afraid to stir: she is terrified and unwilling to forfeit even one moment of life. Only at sea or on the steppe at night, when the moon is shining, can you judge the sky's unfathomable depth and boundlessness. It is awesome, beautiful and inviting, looking down languidly and beckoning you – and your head grows dizzy from its blandishments.

On you drive for an hour or two . . . By the roadside you pass a silent, ancient barrow or a stone image put up by God knows whom and when. A night bird flies silently over the earth and gradually you recall all those legends of the steppe, wayfarers' stories, folk-tales told by some old nurse from the steppe, together with all that you yourself have seen and grasped with the spirit. And then, in the buzzing of the insects, in the sinister figures and ancient barrows,[8] in the depths of the sky, in the moonlight and in the flight of the night bird – in all that you see or hear – there are glimpses of triumphant beauty, of youth in its prime and a passionate lust for life. Your spirit responds to its beautiful, austere homeland and you long to fly over the steppe with the night bird. And in this triumph of beauty, in this abundance of happiness, you are conscious of tension and sad yearning, as if the steppe realizes how lonely she is and that her wealth and inspiration are lost to the world – unsung and unneeded – and through all the joyful clamour you can hear her anguished, despairing call for a bard, a poet to call her own!

'Whoa! Hullo, Panteley! Everything all right!'

'Yes, Ivan Kuzmichov, thank God.'

'Seen Varlamov, lads?'

'No, that we 'aven't.'

Yegorushka woke up and opened his eyes. The carriage had stopped. A long way ahead, to the right of the road, stretched a wagon train, around which men were scurrying. Piled high as they were with large bales of wool, all the wagons seemed very tall and bulging, the horses small and short-legged.

'Well, we're off to the Molokan's,' Kuzmichov said in a loud voice. 'The Jew said Varlamov would be spending the night there, so it's goodbye, lads. And good luck!'

'Goodbye Ivan Kuzmichov,' several voices answered.

'Now listen, lads,' Kuzmichov said briskly. 'What about taking the boy with you? He doesn't have to hang around with us. You can put him on one of your bales, Panteley, and let him ride with you for a bit. We'll catch you up later. Come on, Yegor, there's nothing to worry about!'

Yegorushka climbed down from the box-seat. Several pairs of hands caught hold of him and lifted him high up, and he found himself on something big, soft and rather damp from the dew. Now the sky seemed close to him and the earth far away.

'Here's your coat, laddie!' Deniska shouted from somewhere far below.

Yegorushka's coat and little bundle were thrown up and landed next to him. Disinclined to think about anything, he quickly placed the bundle under his head, covered himself with his coat, stretched his legs right out and laughed with pleasure, shrinking slightly from the dew. 'Sleep, sleep, sleep!' he thought.

'And don't you devils do him any harm!' Deniska's voice came from below.

'Goodbye lads, and good luck,' shouted Kuzmichov. 'I'm relying on you!'

'You don't have to worry, Ivan Kuzmichov!'

Deniska struck the horses, the carriage creaked and moved off, no longer along the high road but somewhere to the side. For a minute or so all was quiet, as if the wagon had fallen asleep and all that could be heard was the clattering of the pail on the backboard gradually dying away in the distance. Then someone at the front of the train shouted, 'Off we go, Kiryukha!'

The first wagon creaked, then the one after it, then a third. Yegorushka felt that the wagon in which he was lying was swaying as well as creaking. The train was on the move. Yegorushka took a firmer grip on the rope securing the bale, laughed once more with pleasure, adjusted the cake in his pocket and began to fall asleep the way he usually did in his bed at home . . .

When he awoke the sun was already rising. Screened by an ancient burial mound it was striving to spread its light all over the world, eagerly casting its rays everywhere and flooding the horizon with gold. Yegorushka felt that it was in the wrong place, for yesterday it had risen behind him and now it was very much further to the left. And the entire landscape was different from yesterday's. The hills had vanished and wherever you looked a brown, cheerless plain stretched away endlessly. Here and there small barrows stood out and yesterday's rooks were in flight. Far ahead were the white belfries and cottages of some village. As it was a Sunday the peasants were at home, baking and boiling – you could tell from the smoke issuing from every chimney and hanging over the whole village in a blue-grey, transparent mantle. Between the cottages and beyond the church a blue river was visible and beyond it the hazy distance. But nothing bore so little resemblance to yesterday's sights as the high road. Instead of a road something exceptionally wide with a majestic sweep of heroic proportions stretched over the steppe. It was a grey strip, much-used and covered with dust, like all roads, but it was many metres wide. The sheer scale of it bewildered Yegorushka and conjured up thoughts of the world of legend. Who travelled along it? Who needed all that space? It was strange and puzzling. You might have thought that seven-league stepping giants like Ilya Muromets or Solovey the Robber[9] still flourished in Russia and that knightly steeds had not become extinct. As Yegorushka gazed at the high road he imagined six lofty chariots riding abreast, like those he had seen in drawings in Bible story-books. These chariots were harnessed to teams of six wild, frenzied horses and their high wheels sent clouds of dust soaring to the sky. The horses were driven by men you might see in your dreams or who might take shape in thoughts of the fantastic. And how well all these figures would have harmonized with the steppe – had they existed!

On the right of the road, along its whole length, were telegraph poles carrying two wires. Growing ever smaller, they vanished from sight near the village, behind the cottages and foliage, and then reappeared in the lilac distance as very small thin pencil-like sticks thrust into the ground. Hawks, merlins and crows sat on the wires, indifferently surveying the moving wagons.

Yegorushka was lying on the very last wagon and had the entire train in sight. There were about twenty wagons in all, with one driver to every three. Near the last wagon, in which Yegorushka was lying, walked an old, grey-bearded man, as thin and stunted as Father Khristofor, but with a stern, thoughtful, sun-tanned face. In all probability this old man was neither stern nor thoughtful, but his red eyelids and long sharp nose gave his face that stern, cold expression typical of people given constantly to thinking serious, solitary thoughts. Like Father Khristofor he was wearing a broad-brimmed top hat – not the kind worn by gentlemen, but of brown felt and more like a truncated cone than a genuine topper. His feet were bare. Probably from a habit acquired during cold winters, when more than once he had had to stand and freeze by the wagons, he would keep slapping his thighs as he walked and stamping his feet. Noticing that Yegorushka was awake he looked at him.

'Oh, so you're awake, young fellow!' he said, hunching his shoulders as if from frost. 'Ain't you Ivan Kuzmichov's little boy?'

'No, I'm his nephew.'

'Kuzmichov's? Well now, I've taken me boots off and here I be hopping along barefoot. They're bad, me poor ole feet – the frost got to them – and it's easier walking without any boots . . . Easier, me lad . . . Without boots, I mean . . . So, you're his nephew then?

He's a good man, he's all right. God grant him health. Yes, he's all right . . . I mean Kuzmichov, like . . . He's gone to see the Molokan. Oh, Lord have mercy on us!'

The old man talked as if it were bitterly cold, slowly and deliberately, without opening his mouth properly. And he mispronounced labial consonants, stuttering over them as if his lips were frozen. Not once did he smile when he looked at Yegorushka and he had a stern look.

Two wagons ahead walked a man in a long, reddish-brown coat, with a whip in one hand and wearing a cap and riding-boots with sagging tops. He was not old, probably about forty. When he turned around Yegorushka could see that he had a long red face with a thin goatee and a spongy swelling beneath his right eye. Besides that very ugly swelling there was one further sharply striking distinguishing feature about him. With his whip in his left hand he would wave his right as if he were conducting an invisible choir. Occasionally he would put the whip under his arm and then conduct with both arms as he hummed to himself.

The next carrier had a long, rectilinear figure, sharply sloping shoulders and a back as flat as a plank. He held himself erect as if he were marching or had swallowed a poker. His arms did not swing, but hung like straight sticks and he walked stiffly somehow, like a clockwork soldier, scarcely bending his knees and trying to take the longest possible strides. Whereas the old man or the owner of the swelling took two strides he managed to take only one and as a result seemed to be walking slower than everyone else and lagging behind. His face was bound with a piece of rag and on his head something resembling a monk's cap was sticking up. He was dressed in a short Ukrainian coat covered in patches and baggy blue trousers over bast shoes.[10]

Yegorushka could not make out the men who were further ahead. He lay on his stomach, picked a hole in the bale and for want of anything else to do started twining threads of wool. The old man who was walking below turned out to be less stern and serious than one might have supposed from his expression. Once he started a conversation he did not stop.

'Where are you going?' he asked as he stamped along.

'To school,' replied Yegorushka.

'To school? Aha . . . well . . . Our dear Blessed Lady succour us! Well now, one brain's good, but two's better. God gives one man one brain, another two and another gets three . . . yes, another gets three and that's a fact . . . One brain you're born with, the second comes from studying and the third from living a good life. So, lad, it's a good thing if a man has three brains. It not only makes living easier, but dying too. Oh yes, dying . . . We're all going to die!'

The old man scratched his forehead, looked up red-eyed at Yegorushka, and continued, 'Last year Maxim Nikolayevich, a gent from Slavyanoserbsk,[11] took his young lad off to school too. I don't know how good he is at learning, like, but he's a good honest boy. God grant both of them health – they're fine gentlefolk, that they are. Yes, he took his boy off to school, too . . . But there ain't no establishment in Slavyanoserbsk as can teach you proper book learning like . . . No, that there ain't. But it's a nice town, nothing wrong with it . . . It's only an ordernary school, for simple folk, but there just ain't none there that teach the higher sort of learning. No, there ain't . . . that's a fact. What's your name?'

'Yegorushka.'

'Yegory – so you're a Georgy! Your name-day must be 23 April, same as St George the Dragon-Killer. My Christian name's Panteley . . . I'm called Panteley Zakharov Kholodov . . . Yes, we're all of us Kholodovs . . . As you may've heard tell, I hail from Tim,[12] in Kursk province. My brothers got thesselves on the town register, working as craftsmen. But I'm a plain peasant. And peasant I've been ever since. Seven years ago I went there . . . home, I mean. I've lived in the village as well as the town . . . As I says, I was in Tim. Thank God we were all alive and well then, but I'm not so sure about now. Perhaps someone's died. And it's high time they did, 'cos they're old, all of them – there's some what's older than me. Death's nothing to worry about, it's a good thing, but only if you don't go dying without repenting of your sins. An impenitent death is the devil's delight. And if you want to die having repented of your sins, so that the mansions of the Lord are not forbidden you, you must pray to the Holy Martyr St Barbara,[13] who intercedes for all of us. Yes she does – and that's a fact . . .'cos God's given her a special place in heaven, so everyone has the full right to pray to her about penitence.'

Panteley rambled on and apparently wasn't bothered whether Yegorushka heard him or not. He spoke sluggishly, mumbling to himself and without lowering or raising his voice, yet he managed to say quite a lot in a short time. Everything he said consisted of fragments that had very little connection with each other and which were completely devoid of interest for Yegorushka. Perhaps – on the morning after a night spent in silence – he was only talking because he wanted to make a roll-call of his thoughts, out loud, so that he could check that they were all present and correct. When he had finished with repentance he carried on with Maxim Nikolayevich from Slavyanoserbsk:

'Yes, he took his lad to school . . . yes, he did – that's a fact . . .'

One of the wagon drivers who was walking a long way ahead suddenly darted to one side and started lashing the ground with his whip. He was a sturdy, broad-shouldered man of about thirty with fair curly hair and clearly very strong and robust. Judging from the movements of his shoulders and his whip, from the eager way he stood there, he was lashing some living creature. A second driver, a short, thick-set man with a bushy black beard, his waistcoat and shirt outside his trousers, ran over to him and broke into a deep spluttering laugh:

'Look, lads, Dymov's killed a viper. I swear it!'

There are some people whose brain-power can be accurately gauged from their voice and the way they laugh. The black-bearded wagon driver was just one of those fortunates: both his voice and laugh betrayed utter stupidity. When he had finished lashing, fair-headed Dymov raised the whip from the ground and laughingly hurled something resembling a length of rope towards the wagons.

'That's no viper, it's a grass-snake,' someone shouted.

The man with the bandaged face and clockwork walk quickly strode over to the dead snake, looked at it and threw up his stick-like arms.

'You rotten bastard!' he cried in a hollow, tearful voice. 'Why did you have to kill a grass-snake? What harm has it done you, blast you! Ugh, killing a little grass-snake! What if someone did that to you?'

'You oughtn't kill grass-snakes – that's a fact . . .' Panteley calmly remarked. 'It's wicked . . . And that ain't no viper. It may look like one, but it's a harmless, innocent creature. It's man's friend . . . that grass-snake, like . . .'

Dymov and the black-bearded driver must have felt ashamed, for they laughed out loud and lazily strolled back to their wagons without answering the grumbles. When the last wagon had come up to the spot where the dead snake was lying the driver with the bandaged face stood over it, turned to Panteley and tearfully inquired, 'Tell me, grandad, why did he have to go and kill that snake?'

As Yegorushka could now clearly see, his eyes were small and dull, his face grey and sickly and seemingly lustreless too, while his chin was red and looked badly swollen.

'Tell me, grandpa, why did he kill it?' he repeated, striding along with Panteley.

''Cos he's stupid and he's got itchy hands – that's why he killed it,' replied the old man. 'Yes, it's wrong to kill grass-snakes – that's a fact. You know, Dymov's a real trouble-maker, he'll kill anything he can get his hands on. But Kiryukha didn't do nothing to stop him, like he ought to 'ave done. All he did was cackle and snigger. Now, don't you get angry, Vasya. Why get angry? They killed it . . . so to hell with them. Dymov's a trouble-maker and Kiryukha's plain stupid . . . Now, don't worry . . . Folks is stupid, they don't understand, so to hell with them. Now, take Yemelyan – he wouldn't hurt a fly – never . . . that's a fact. 'Cos he's an educated man and they're stupid . . . That Yemelyan, like . . . wouldn't hurt a fly.'

Hearing his name, the driver in the reddish-brown coat and with the spongy swelling who had been conducting those invisible choirs stopped, waited for Panteley and Vasya to draw level, and walked along with them.

'What's all this about?' he asked in a hoarse, strangled voice.

'Vasya's real fuming,' Panteley said. 'I told him a few things so he wouldn't get angry, like . . . Oh, me poor ole feet, they're frozen stiff! Ah-ah! They're hurting like mad 'cos it's Sunday, the Lord's day!'

'It's from all that walking,' observed Vasya.

'No, lad, it's not the walking. It's easier when I walk, but it fair kills me when I lies in bed and gets warm. No, it's better when I walk.'

Yemelyan, in his reddish-brown coat, positioned himself between Panteley and Vasya and waved his arms as if those two were about to sing. After a few flourishes he dropped them and grunted despairingly.

'Me voice 'as gone!' he said. 'It's a real calamerty! All last night and all morning I seem to 'ave been hearing that triple "Lord have mercy" that we sang at the Marinovsky wedding. It's in me 'ead and in me gullet. I feel like I could sing it, but I'm just not up to it! I ain't got no voice!'

He silently pondered for a while and then continued, 'Fifteen years I was in the choir, I don't think no one 'ad a better voice than me in the whole Lugansk[14] factory. But I was darned stupid enough to go swimming two year ago in the Donets[15] and I ain't been able to sing one note proper ever since. Caught a chill in me gullet . . . And without me voice I'm as good as a workman with no 'ands.'

'Yes, that's a fact,' agreed Panteley.

'As I sees it, I'm done for – and that's that!'

Just then Vasya happened to catch sight of Yegorushka. His eyes glittered and seemed to grow even smaller.

'So, we've a young gent driving with us!' he said, hiding his nose in his sleeve as if overcome with shyness. 'Looks like a real tip-top driver! Now, you stay with us so's you can ride with the wagons and cart wool around!'

The thought of gentleman and wagon driver being combined in one and the same person must have struck him as most bizarre and witty, since he produced a loud titter and continued to develop the idea. Yemelyan also glanced up at Yegorushka, but cursorily and coldly. He was engrossed in his own thoughts and had it not been for Vasya he wouldn't even have noticed Yegorushka. Barely five minutes passed before he began waving his arms again. Then, as he described for his fellow travellers the beauty of the wedding anthem 'Lord have mercy' which he had remembered during the night, he placed his whip under his arm and began to conduct with both hands.

About a mile from the village the wagon train stopped by a well with a sweep. Lowering his pail into the well, black-bearded Kiryukha lay stomach-first on the framework and thrust his shaggy head, his shoulders and part of his chest into the dark hole so that Yegorushka could see only his short legs that barely touched the ground. When he saw the reflection of his head far below at the bottom of the well he was so overjoyed that he broke into peals of inane, cavernous laughter, echoed by the well. When he stood up, his face and neck were as red as a lobster. The first to run up for a drink was Dymov. He laughed as he drank, frequently turning away from the pail to tell Kiryukha something funny. Then he cleared his throat and produced five swear words loud enough for the whole steppe to hear. Yegorushka had no idea what they meant, but that they were bad he knew very well. He was aware of the silent revulsion his friends and relations felt for them. Without knowing why, he himself shared their feelings and had come to believe that only drunks and rowdies enjoyed the privilege of shouting such words out loud. He remembered the killing of the grass-snake, listened to Dymov's laughter and felt something akin to loathing for that man. As ill luck would have it, at that moment Dymov caught sight of Yegorushka, who had climbed down from his wagon and was walking towards the well.

'Looks like the old gaffer's given birth in the night!' he shouted, laughing out loud. 'It's a boy!'

Kiryukha choked with deep laughter. Someone else started laughing, too, but Yegorushka only blushed and finally concluded that Dymov was a very evil person.

With his bare head, light curly hair and unbuttoned shirt Dymov looked handsome and exceptionally strong. Every movement he made revealed a trouble-maker and a bully who knew his own worth. He flexed his shoulders, put hands on hips and laughed louder than the others, looking as if he were about to lift a colossal weight and thereby astonish the whole world. His wild, mocking look slid over the road, the wagons and the sky, settling nowhere, and he seemed to be looking for something else to kill – for want of anything better to do and just for a good laugh. Obviously he feared no one, would stop at nothing and probably couldn't have cared less what Yegorushka thought. But Yegorushka hated his fair head, his clean-cut face and his strength with all his heart, listened with fear and revulsion to his laughter and tried to think of some insult to fling at him by way of revenge.

Panteley also went over to the pail. He took a green lamp-glass from his pocket, wiped it with a cloth, dipped it into the pail and drank from it; then, after scooping some more water, he wrapped it in the cloth and put it back in his pocket.

'Why are you drinking from a lamp, grandpa?' Yegorushka asked in astonishment.

'There's some that drinks from buckets, others from lamps,' the old man replied evasively. 'Each to his own . . . if you likes to drink from a bucket then go ahead and drink your fill . . .'

'You little darling, you beauty!' Vasya suddenly said in a tender, plaintive voice. 'Oh, you little darling!'

His eyes glittered and smiled as he stared into the distance and his face took on the same expression as before, when he was looking at Yegorushka.

'Who are you talking to?' asked Kiryukha.

'It's a vixen . . . she's lying on her back, playing like a little dog.'

They all peered into the distance, searching for the vixen, but they could see nothing. Only Vasya, with those small, lacklustre grey eyes of his, was able to see anything and he was in raptures. As Yegorushka discovered later, his sight was amazingly keen – so keen that the desolate brown steppe was always full of life and content for him. He had only to look into the distance to see a fox, hare, great bustard or some other living creature that shunned human beings. To spot a fleeing hare or a bustard in flight is easy – anyone who has travelled the steppe has seen them – but it is not given to everyone to see wild creatures in their domestic habitat, when they are not running, hiding or looking around in alarm. But Vasya could see vixens at play, hares washing their paws, great bustards preening themselves, little bustards doing their courtship dance. Thanks to his keen vision, for Vasya there was another world – his own special world that was inaccessible to everyone else and which was no doubt absolutely delightful, for whenever he looked and went into raptures it was difficult not to envy him.

When the wagons moved on the church bells were ringing for morning service.

V

The wagon train drew up on a river bank at the side of the village. The sun was as fiery as yesterday and the air stagnant and cheerless. A few willows stood on the bank – their shadows did not fall on the ground but on the water, where they were wasted, while in the shade under the wagons it was stifling and oppressive. Azure from the reflected sky, the water eagerly beckoned.

The driver Styopka, an eighteen-year-old Ukrainian lad of whom Yegorushka was taking notice only now, in a long shirt without any belt and wearing over his boots wide trousers that fluttered like flags as he walked, quickly threw off his clothes, raced down the steep slope and plunged into the water. After diving about three times he floated on his back, his eyes blissfully closed. His face smiled and became wrinkled, as if he were being tickled, hurt and amused all at the same time.

On hot days when there is no escape from the sultry, stifling heat the splash of water and a swimmer's loud breathing are music to the ears. Dymov and Kiryukha took one look at Styopka, quickly undressed, laughed loud with anticipated pleasure and tumbled into the water one after the other. That quiet, humble stream resounded with snorting, splashing and shouting. Kiryukha coughed and laughed as if the others were trying to drown him. Dymov chased him and tried to grab his leg.

'Hey!' he shouted. 'Catch him! Hold him!'

Kiryukha was laughing and enjoying himself, but his expression was the same as on dry land: stupid and stunned, as if someone had sneaked up from behind and clubbed him with an axe butt. Yegorushka undressed, too, but instead of sliding down the bank he took a flying jump from a height of about ten feet. Having described an arc in the air he hit the water and sank deep – but he did not touch the bottom, since some strange power that was cool and pleasant to the touch caught hold of him and brought him back to the surface. Blowing bubbles and snorting, he came up and opened his eyes, but the sun was reflected in the river close to his face. First blinding sparks, then rainbows and dark patches darted before his eyes. Hurriedly he dived again, opened his eyes under the water and saw something dull green, like the sky on a moonlit night. Once again that power brought him up, stopping him reaching the bottom and staying in the cool. As he surfaced he breathed a sigh so deep that he had a sensation of great spaciousness and freshness not only in his chest but even in his stomach. And then, to make the most of the water, he indulged in every luxury: he lay on his back and basked, splashed, turned somersaults, swam on his stomach, his side, his back, and standing up, just as the mood took him, until he grew tired. The opposite bank, golden in the sunlight, was thickly overgrown with reeds and their beautiful clusters of flowers leaned towards the water. In one place the reeds shook and lowered their flowers with a dry crackling – Stepan and Kiryukha were 'tickling' crayfish.

'Look lads, a crayfish!' Kiryukha cried triumphantly, pointing out what was in fact a crayfish.

Yegorushka swam to the reeds, dived and started grubbing among the roots. As he delved in the slimy, liquid mud he felt something sharp and nasty – a crayfish, perhaps? – but just then someone grabbed his leg and hauled him to the surface. Gulping and coughing, Yegorushka opened his eyes and saw before him the wet, mocking face of Dymov the bully. That trouble-maker was breathing heavily and from the look in his eyes was evidently eager to carry on with his horseplay. He seized Yegorushka firmly by the leg and his other hand was already raised to grab his neck, but Yegorushka shrank from him with fear and repulsion, as if afraid the bully was going to drown him and managed to break free from his grasp.

'You fool! I'll smash your face in!' he muttered.

Feeling that this did not adequately express his loathing, he reflected for a moment and then added, 'You rotten swine! Son of a bitch!'

Just as if nothing had happened, Dymov paid no further attention to Yegorushka and swam off towards Kiryukha.

'Hey there!' he shouted. 'Let's catch some fish! Come on lads, let's fish!'

'Why not?' agreed Kiryukha. 'Must be loads of 'em here.'

'Styopka, run to the village and ask 'em for a net.'

'They won't give us one.'

'Oh, yes they will! Just ask. Tell 'em it's their duty as good Christians, seeing as we're all pilgrims – or as near as dammit!'

'You're right!'

Styopka emerged from the water, quickly dressed and without his cap, his wide trousers flapping, ran off to the village. After the clash with Dymov, the water lost all attraction for Yegorushka, so he climbed out and started to dress. Panteley and Vasya were sitting on the steep bank, dangling their legs and watching the bathers. Close to the bank stood Yemelyan, naked and up to his knees in water, clutching the grass with one hand to stop falling over and stroking his body with the other. With his bony shoulderblades and that swelling under the eye, stooping and clearly terrified of the water, he was a comical sight. His face was stern and solemn and he looked at the water angrily, as if about to curse it for having once given him a cold when bathing in the Donets and robbing him of his voice.

'Why don't you have a swim?' Yegorushka asked.

'Well . . . er . . . I don't fancy it,' replied Vasya.

'Why is your chin swollen?'

'It hurts . . . Once I worked in a match factory, young sir . . . The doctor said that was why me jaw got all swelled up. The air was bad in there. And besides me, three other lads got swollen jaws – with one of 'em it clean rotted away!'

Soon Styopka returned with a net. From their long stay in the water Dymov and Kiryukha were turning mauve and wheezing, but they set about fishing with great relish. At first they went along the reeds where it was deep. Here Dymov was up to his neck and the squat Kiryukha out of his depth. The latter was swallowing mouthfuls of water and blowing bubbles, while Dymov kept falling over and became entangled in the net as he stumbled on the prickly roots. They both noisily floundered and their fishing turned out nothing more than a pure frolic.

'Cor, it's deep!' croaked Kiryukha. 'We won't catch nothing 'ere!'

'Stop pulling, damn you!' cried Dymov as he tried to bring the net into position. 'Hold it there!'

'You won't catch nothing 'ere!' Panteley shouted from the bank. 'You're only scaring the fish, you silly fools! Try a bit more to the left, it's shallower there!'

Once a big fish gleamed above the net. Everyone gasped and Dymov hit out at the place where it had vanished, frustration written all over his face.

'Ugh, you lot!' cried Panteley, stamping his feet. 'You've let a perch get away! It's gone!'

Moving the net over to the left, Dymov and Kiryukha gradually managed to reach a shallow spot and there the fishing began in earnest. They were about three hundred yards away from the wagons now and they could be seen barely moving their legs, silently endeavouring to haul the net as deep and close as possible to the reeds. To frighten the fish and drive them into the net they thrashed the water with their fists, making the reeds crackle. From the reeds they went over to the far bank, trawled around with the net and then, with a disappointed look and knees held high, they returned to the reeds. They were in active discussion, but what they were discussing no one could hear. Meanwhile the sun was burning their backs, flies were biting them and their bodies had turned from mauve to crimson. They were followed by Styopka, bucket in hand, his shirt tucked right up under the armpits, holding the hem between his teeth. After each successful catch he held the fish high above his head so that it glittered in the sun.

'Look at that for a perch!' he cried. 'And we've caught five like that!'

Every time Dymov, Kiryukha and Styopka pulled in the net they could be seen rooting about for a long time in the mud, putting things in the bucket and throwing others out. Occasionally they passed something that was caught in the net from hand to hand, examined it with curiosity and then threw that away too . . .

'What've you caught?' came shouts from the bank.

Styopka gave some sort of answer but it was hard to make out what he was saying. Then he emerged from the water, grasped the bucket with both hands, forgot to let his shirt down and ran towards the wagons.

'This one's full!' he shouted, panting heavily. 'Give me another!'

Yegorushka peered into the bucket: it was full to the brim. A young pike poked its ugly snout out of the water, whilst around it teemed crayfish and minnows. Yegorushka touched the bottom and stirred the water with his hand. The pike disappeared under the crayfish and in its place a perch and a tench floated upwards.

Vasya too looked into the bucket. His eyes glinted and his face softened as it had done when he saw the fox. He picked something out, put it in his mouth and started chewing. There was a crunching sound.

'Lads!' Styopka cried out in astonishment. 'Vasya's eating a live gudgeon. Ugh!'

'It ain't no gudgeon, it's a chub,' Vasya calmly replied and carried on munching. He took the tail from his mouth, lovingly examined it and put it back. While he was chewing and crunching Yegorushka felt that it was no human being he was watching. Vasya's swollen chin, lacklustre eyes, his exceptionally keen eyesight, the fish tail in his mouth and the loving affection with which he chewed the gudgeon – all this gave him the appearance of an animal.

Yegorushka began to find his company tiresome. And besides, the fishing was over. He strolled by the wagons, reflected for a moment and plodded off to the village out of sheer boredom.

A few moments later he was standing in the church, leaning his forehead on someone's back that smelled of hemp and listening to the choir. The service was drawing to a close. Yegorushka understood nothing about church singing and felt indifferent towards it. He listened for a while, yawned and began examining people's backs and necks. One of these heads, reddish-brown and wet from the recent bathe, he recognized as Yemelyan's. At the back the hair had been cut evenly and higher than usual; the hair on his temples was also cut higher than fashion dictated; his red ears stuck out like burdock leaves and they seemed to sense they were out of place. As he studied the back of his head and his ears Yegorushka thought for some reason that Yemelyan was probably very unhappy. He remembered his conducting, his hoarse voice, those timid looks when he was bathing and he felt an intense pity for him. He had an urge to say a few kind words to him.

'I'm here!' he said, tugging his sleeve.

People who sing in choirs, whether tenor or bass, especially those who at least once in their lives have done some conducting, usually take a stern, hostile attitude to young boys. Nor do they lose this habit later in life when they no longer sing. Yemelyan turned to Yegorushka and scowled.

'No larking about in church!' he said.

Then Yegorushka made his way forward, to be nearer the icon-stand. There he saw some interesting people. At the front, to the right, a gentleman and lady were standing on a carpet. Behind each of them was a chair. Wearing a newly pressed tussore[16] suit, the gentleman was standing stock-still, like a soldier saluting, and he held his blue, clean-shaven chin high. There was an enormous amount of dignity in his stiff collar, his blue chin, small bald patch and cane. From this excess of dignity his neck seemed so tense and his chin strained upwards so forcefully that his head appeared ready to fly off and soar upwards at any minute. The lady, who was stout and elderly and wearing a white silk shawl, was holding her head to one side and she looked as if she had just done someone a favour and wanted to say, 'Ah, you don't need to thank me! I don't like that sort of thing . . .' All round the carpet was a dense throng of peasants.

Yegorushka went to the icon-stand and started kissing the local icons. Before each one he bowed to the ground and without rising looked back at the congregation; then he stood up and applied his lips again. The feel of the cold floor against his forehead was extremely pleasant. When the verger came from the chancel with a pair of long snuffers to put the candles out Yegorushka quickly leapt up from the floor and ran to him.

'Have they given out the communion bread yet?' he asked.

'There isn't any,' the verger replied crustily. 'And what would you be wanting it for?'

The service came to an end. Yegorushka left the church without hurrying and wandered around the village square. In his time he had seen many villages, squares, peasants and nothing that he saw now interested him in the least. For want of anything to do and to kill time one way or the other, he called at a shop over whose doorway hung a wide red calico strip. This shop consisted of two spacious, badly lit halves: in one half haberdashery and groceries were sold, whilst in the other there were barrels of tar, with horse-collars hanging from the ceiling. From this second half came the rich smell of leather and tar. The floor of the shop had been watered – and the water had probably been sprinkled by some great visionary or free-thinker, since the floor was completely covered with patterns and cabbalistic signs. Behind the counter, leaning his stomach on a desk, stood a fat, broad-faced, round-bearded shopkeeper. Evidently he came from the north. He was drinking tea through a lump of sugar and after every sip he heaved a deep sigh. His face was the picture of apathy, but every sigh seemed to be saying, 'You wait! I'll give you what-for!'

'A copeckworth of sunflower seeds please,' Yegorushka said.

The shopkeeper raised his eyebrows, came out from behind the counter and poured a copeckworth of sunflower seeds into Yegorushka's pocket, using an empty pomade jar as a measure. Yegorushka was reluctant to leave and he spent a long time inspecting the trays of cakes. Then he pondered for a moment and pointed to some fine Vyazma[17] gingerbreads that were mildewed with age.

'How much are these?' he asked.

'Two for a copeck.'

Yegorushka took out the cake given him by the Jewess the previous day.

'And how much are these?' he asked.

The shopkeeper took the cake in his hands, examined it from all angles and raised one eyebrow.

'This kind?'

He raised the other eyebrow and paused for thought.

'Two for three copecks.'

There was silence.

'Who are you?' asked the shopkeeper, pouring himself some tea from a copper teapot.

'I'm Ivan Ivanych's nephew.'

'But there's no end of Ivan Ivanyches!' sighed the shopkeeper. He glanced over Yegorushka's head at the door, was silent for a moment and then he asked, 'Would you like some tea?'

'Oh, yes please,' said Yegorushka, feigning reluctance, although he was longing for his usual morning tea.

The shopkeeper poured him a glass and gave it to him, together with a nibbled lump of sugar. Yegorushka sat on a folding-chair and drank. He wanted to ask another question – the price of a pound of sugared almonds – and had just begun when in came a customer. The shopkeeper put his glass to one side to attend to his business. He led the customer into the other half of the shop that smelt of tar and had a long conversation with him. This customer was obviously exceedingly stubborn and shrewd, kept shaking his head in disagreement and backing towards the door. The shopkeeper reassured him on some point and began pouring oats into a large sack.

'Call that stuff oats?' the customer said dolefully. 'They're not oats – they're just chaff. They'd make a cat laugh! I'm off to Bondarenko's, that I am!'

When Yegorushka returned to the river a small camp fire was smoking on the bank – the drivers were cooking their dinner. In the midst of the smoke stood Styopka, stirring the pot with a large, jagged spoon. A little to one side, their eyes reddened by the smoke, Kiryukha and Vasya were sitting down cleaning the fish. Before them lay the net, covered in slime and weeds – and in it were a gleaming fish and some crawling crayfish.

Having just got back from church, Yemelyan was sitting next to

Panteley, waving his arm and humming in a barely audible voice, 'To Thee we sing . . .' Dymov was wandering among the horses.

When they had finished cleaning the fish Kiryukha and Vasya dropped them all, together with the live crayfish, into the bucket, rinsed them and then emptied the whole lot into boiling water.

'Should I add some fat?' asked Styopka, skimming off the froth with a spoon.

'Whatever for? Fish provide their own sauce,' replied Kiryukha.

Before removing the pot from the fire Styopka added three handfuls of millet and a spoonful of salt. Finally he tasted it, smacked his lips, licked the spoon and grunted in self-satisfaction – this meant the stew was ready.

Everyone except Panteley sat round the pot and got to work with their spoons.

'Hey, you lot! Give the lad a spoon,' Panteley sternly remarked. 'I reckon he wants to eat too!'

'It's only plain peasant fare,' sighed Kiryukha.

'And there's nothing wrong with it – if that's what you fancy!'

They gave Yegorushka a spoon. He started eating, but he did not sit down and stood by the pot, looking into it as if into a deep pit. The stew smelled of fishy wetness and now and then a few scales popped up in the millet. It was impossible to scoop out the crayfish with a spoon and the diners picked them straight out of the pot with their fingers. In this respect Vasya displayed particular abandon, wetting not only his hands in the stew but his sleeves as well. But for all that Yegorushka found it very tasty and it reminded him of the crayfish his mother used to make at home on fast-days. Panteley sat to one side, chewing some bread.

'Why aren't you eating, grandpa?' Yegorushka asked.

'Don't eat crayfish . . . blow them!' the old man said, turning aside in disgust.

While they ate there was a general conversation from which Yegorushka gathered that, regardless of differences in age and temperament, all his new friends had one thing in common which made them alike: they were all people with a wonderful past and an appalling present. To a man they spoke ecstatically of their past, but almost contemptuously of the present. Russians like to reminisce, but they don't like living. Yegorushka was not yet aware of this and before the stew was finished he was firmly convinced that the men who were sitting eating around the pot had been humiliated and wronged by fate. Panteley said that in the old days – before the railways – he used to go with the wagon trains to Moscow and Nizhny-Novgorod, earning so much that he didn't know what to do with the money. And what merchants they were in those days, what fish they had, how cheap everything was! Nowadays the highways were shorter, the merchants stingier, the people poorer, the bread dearer. Everything had degenerated, dwindled to nothing. Yemelyan said that he had once sung in the choir at the Lugansk factory. He had possessed a remarkable voice and read music excellently, but now he was a mere peasant, living on the charity of his brother who sent him out with the horses and kept half of his earnings for himself. Vasya had once worked in the match factory; Kiryukha had been coachman to a very good family and used to be considered the best troika driver in the district. Dymov, son of a well-to-do peasant, had lived a life of pleasure, made merry and didn't have a care in the world. But the moment he was twenty his strict, harsh father, wanting him to learn a trade and afraid he might become spoilt at home, started sending him out to work as a wagon driver, like any poor peasant labourer. Styopka alone said nothing, but one could tell from his clean-shaven face that he had seen much better days.

Remembering his father, Dymov stopped eating and frowned. He scowled at his mates and let his eyes rest on Yegorushka.

'Heathen! Take your cap off!' he snapped. 'Do you think it's right eating with your cap on? Call yourself a gentleman!'

Without a word Yegorushka took off his cap. But by now the stew had lost all taste for him, nor did he hear Panteley and Vasya stand up for him. An intense feeling of anger towards that bully welled up inside him and he decided to do him some injury, come what may.

After dinner they all trudged off to the wagons and collapsed in the shade.

'Are we leaving soon, grandpa?' Yegorushka asked Panteley.

'We'll leave when God wills it . . . No good leaving now, it's too hot . . . Oh Lord, Thy will be done . . . Holy Mother of God! . . . Now, lie down, lad.'

The sound of snoring soon came from under the wagons. Yegorushka would have liked to go back to the village, but after a moment's thought he yawned and lay down next to the old man.

VI

All day the wagons stayed by the river and they left when the sun was setting.

Once again Yegorushka was lying on a bale of wool; the wagon gently creaked and swayed. Down below walked Panteley, slapping his thighs and muttering. As on the day before, the music of the steppes trilled in the air.

Yegorushka lay on his back, his hands under his head, gazing up at the sky. He watched the sunset take fire and then fade. Guardian angels covered the horizon with their golden wings and were preparing themselves for slumber: the day had passed calmly, serene and tranquil night had come and now they could rest peacefully in their heavenly home. Yegorushka saw the sky gradually darken and darkness descend on the earth; one after the other the stars began to shine.

If you look at the deep sky for long, without averting your gaze, your thoughts and your spirit somehow blend in a consciousness of solitude. You begin to feel desperately lonely and all that you had once considered near and dear becomes infinitely remote and trivial. The stars that have been looking down for thousands of years, the inscrutable sky itself and the darkness, so indifferent to man's short life – when you are confronted by them and try to fathom their meaning they oppress your spirit with their silence. Then you are reminded of the solitude that awaits all of us in the grave – and the reality of existence seems awful, terrible . . .

Yegorushka thought of Grandmother sleeping now in the

graveyard beneath the cherry trees. He remembered her lying in her coffin with bronze coins over her eyes; he remembered how they had then closed the lid and lowered her into the grave; he remembered the dull thud of clods of earth on the lid . . . He visualized Grandmother in her dark, narrow coffin, helpless and forsaken by all. He imagined her suddenly awakening, unable to understand where she was, knocking on the lid, calling for help and in the end growing faint with terror and dying a second death. He imagined that Mother, Father Khristofor, Countess Dranitsky, Solomon were dead. But try as he might to picture himself in the dark grave, far from home, abandoned, helpless and dead, he did not succeed. He could not admit the possibility of death for himself, personally, and he felt that he would never die . . .

Panteley, whose time was approaching, was walking down below, making a roll-call of his thoughts.

'Yes, they was fine gentlefolk,' he was muttering. 'They took their young lad off to school, but I 'aven't heard say how he's getting on . . . In Slavyanoserbsk there's no establishment as can make you all brainy, like . . . No . . . that's a fact . . . He's a good lad, that boy, no worries with him. When he grows up he'll be a help to his father. You're just a shaver now, Yegory, but when you're a grown man you'll keep your father and mother. That's what God's ordained – "Honour thy father and thy mother." I myself had little ones . . . but they was all burned to death in a fire. And me wife died too . . . and the children . . . that's a fact . . . The hut burned down on Twelfth Night eve. I wasn't at home, was on me way to Oryol[18] . . . to Oryol like. Marya jumped out into the street and she remembered the children was asleep in the hut so she ran back and was burned to death with the little ones . . . Yes . . . Next day all they found was bones . . .'

Around midnight Yegorushka and the drivers were once again seated around a small fire. While the dry brushwood was kindling Kiryukha and Vasya went to fetch some water from a gully. They vanished in the darkness, but the whole time one could hear them clanking their buckets and talking, which meant the gully wasn't very far away. The light from the fire lay on the ground in a large flickering patch; although the moon was bright, everything outside that red patch seemed impenetrably dark. The light shone into the drivers' eyes so that they could see only part of the road. In the darkness the wagons, bales and horses resembled vaguely shaped mountains and were barely visible. About twenty paces from the fire, where road and steppe converged, stood a wooden grave-cross, leaning to one side. Before they had lit the fire and he could still see a long way, Yegorushka noticed that there was an identical slanting cross on the other side of the road.

When Kiryukha and Vasya returned with the water they filled the pot and secured it over the fire. With the jagged spoon in his mouth, Styopka took up his post in the smoke near the pot and pensively gazed at the water as he waited for the first signs of scum. Panteley and Yemelyan sat side by side silently brooding. Dymov lay on his belly, his head propped on his fists, gazing at the fire. Styopka's shadow danced over him, so that his handsome face would be momentarily in darkness and then light up again. A short way off Kiryukha and Vasya wandered around gathering weeds and birch bark for the fire. Hands in pockets, Yegorushka stood by Panteley and watched the flames devouring the weeds.

Everyone was resting, musing, fitfully glancing at the cross over which the red patches were dancing. There is something melancholy, dreamlike and highly poetic about a lonely grave. You can hear its very silence and in that silence you sense the presence of the soul of the unknown being lying beneath the cross. Is that soul at peace on the steppe? Does it not grieve on moonlit nights? Around a grave the steppe seems sad, cheerless and pensive, the grass sadder and the grasshoppers' chatter more subdued. No passer-by would forget to mention that solitary soul in his prayers or stop looking back at the grave until it was far behind and veiled in darkness . . .

'Grandpa, why is that cross there?' asked Yegorushka.

Panteley looked at the cross, then at Dymov and asked, 'Mikola, isn't this where them reapers murdered the merchants?'

Reluctantly, Dymov raised himself on one elbow and looked at the road.

'That's the place all right,' he replied.

Silence followed. Kiryukha broke some dry stalks, bundled them together and thrust them under the pot. The fire flared up; Styopka was enveloped in black smoke and in the darkness the shadow of the cross darted down the road near the wagons.

'Yes, they was murdered,' Dymov said reluctantly. 'Some merchants, father and son, was travelling around selling icons. They put up at an inn not far from here – it's kept by Ignaty Fomin now. The old boy had a drop too much and took to boasting that he'd a pile of cash on him. As you know, merchants is a boastful lot, God save us, and he just couldn't help showing off to the people there. Well, at that time some reapers was staying the night at the inn. When they heard the merchant boasting like that they took note.'

'Oh Lord! Oh Mother of God!' sighed Panteley.

'So, next day, at first light,' continued Dymov, 'the merchants was about to go on their way when the reapers tagged along with them. "Let's all travel together, yer 'onner," they said. "It's more cheerful and it's safer, seeing as it's a bit off the beaten track around 'ere." So as not to break the icons the merchants had to go at walking-pace – and that suited the reapers down to the ground.'

Dymov rose to a kneeling position and stretched himself.

'Yes,' he continued. 'There weren't no trouble until the merchants reached this spot, when the reapers laid into 'em with their scythes. The son put up a good fight, grabbed a scythe from one of them and laid into 'em too. Well, as I don't have to tell you, the reapers came out on top, seeing as there was eight of them. They hacked at the merchants till there wasn't a piece of flesh left on 'em. After they'd finished their business they dragged 'em off the road, father on one side, the son on the other. Opposite this cross, on the other side, there's another one . . . Don't know if it's still in one piece . . . can't see it from here.'

'It's still in one piece,' said Kiryukha. 'Folks say they didn't find much money.'

'No, not much,' confirmed Panteley. 'A hundred roubles in all.'

'Yes – and three of them reapers died soon afterwards, seeing as the merchant gave 'em a right slashing with his scythe. They bled to death. The merchant chopped off one of the reaper's hands and they say he ran about three mile without it. They found 'im on a little hill near Kurikov. He was squatting with his head on his knees as if he was thinking hard. But when they looked closer they saw the spirit had departed – he was dead.'

'They found him from the trail of blood,' said Panteley.

Everyone looked at the cross and again there was a hush. From somewhere, probably the gully, came the mournful sound of a bird, 'Sleep! sleep! sleep!'

'There's many wicked folk in this world,' said Yemelyan.

'So many, so many!' affirmed Panteley, drawing closer to the fire – and from his expression he seemed scared. 'So many,' he continued in an undertone. 'I've seen so many of 'em in my time . . . wicked folk, like. I've seen many righteous folk, but sinners be beyond number. Save us and have mercy, Holy Mother! . . . I remember once – about thirty years ago, maybe more – I was driving a merchant from Morshansk.[19] He were a handsome fellow, very grand and he had pots of money . . . that merchant, like . . . He were a good man, right decent sort. So, we was driving along and we put up for the night at an inn. But in the north the inns ain't like they be in these 'ere parts. Up there the yards are roofed over, like cattle-sheds – rather like threshing-barns on the big farms – only them barns be a bit higher, like. So, we stopped at the inn and everything seemed all right. My merchant had a room to himself and I stayed with the horses – everything was as it should be. Well, lads, I says me prayers and before I goes to sleep I take a little stroll in the yard. It was pitch-black out there, couldn't see a darned thing. So I walk on a bit till I'm near the wagons and I see a twinkling light. What the heck could that be! The innkeeper and his wife must've long gone to bed and except me and my merchant there was no other guests. So what was that light? Well, I didn't like the look of it . . . I went a bit closer . . . to the light, like. Lord in heaven have mercy! Save us, Holy Mother! Level with the ground there's a little window with iron bars . . . in the house, like. So I lie down on the ground to have a look and as soon as I did the shivers ran up and down me spine.'

Trying not to make a noise, Kiryukha put another clump of weeds onto the fire. After waiting for the crackling and hissing to die down the old man continued, 'I look in and see a big cellar, all dark and gloomy . . . A small lamp's burning on a barrel and in the middle there's about a dozen men in red shirts with rolled-up sleeves – all sharpening long knives. "Oho!" I think, "this means we've fallen into a gang of robbers . . ." So what could we do? I run to the merchant, gently wake him up and say, "Now, Mister Merchant, don't you go panicking now, but we're in big trouble. We've landed in a robber's den." His face drops and he asks, "What are we going to do, Panteley? I've a pile of cash on me, it's for the orphans. As for my soul – that's in God's hands. I'm not afraid of dying, but it would be terrible to lose the orphans' money." Well, I was at my wits' end. The gates was locked, there was no escape, either by driving or running out of there. If there'd been a fence – well, you can climb over fences, but the yard was all roofed in . . . "Well," I says, "don't be afraid Mister Merchant, and say your prayers. Perhaps the Lord won't let any harm come to the orphans. Stay in your room and lie low. Meanwhile I'll try and think of something." Agreed. So I prays to God and he instructs me in me mind, like. I climb onto the carriage and ever so quiet, so no one could hear, I start stripping the thatch from the eaves. I make a hole and out I climb. Out, like . . . Then I run down the road as fast as I can. I run and I run – fair knackered myself, I did. Must've run about three mile in one breath – maybe more . . . Well, praise be to God, I see a village and run to one of the huts and bang on the window. "Good Christians!" I cries, "don't let a Christian soul perish." I wakes 'em all up. The villagers gather together and off we go. Some had ropes, others cudgels, some pitchforks. We go and break down the inn gate and head straight for the cellar . . . By then the robbers had sharpened their knives and were about to cut the merchant's throat. The villagers grabbed the lot of 'em, tied 'em up and hauled 'em off to the police. The merchant gave 'em three hundred roubles to show his thanks and he gave me five gold coins – *and* he made a note of my name, so's he could remember me in his prayers. It's said that later on they found piles of human bones in the cellar . . . Yes, bones, like. They used to rob folk and then bury 'em so there'd be no trace. Well, the executioners at Morshansk gave 'em a right old flogging.'

Having finished his story, Panteley surveyed his audience. They said nothing and simply looked at him. The water was boiling now and Styopka was skimming the froth.

'Is the fat ready?' Kiryukha whispered.

'Won't be long.'

Without taking his eyes off Panteley and apparently afraid he might start his next story without him, Styopka ran over to the wagons; soon he returned with a small wooden bowl and started rubbing the pork fat in it.

'Another time I was travelling – with a merchant, too,' Panteley continued in the same undertone and without blinking. 'As I remember now, his name was Pyotr Grigorych. A decent man, he was . . . that merchant, like. We put up at an inn, same as before, him in a room and me with the horses . . . The landlord and his wife seemed honest, kind folk all right – and the workers, too. But lads, I just couldn't get to sleep – I had a funny feeling and that was enough! The gates were open, lots of folk were around, but I fair had the creeps, didn't feel right at all. Now, everyone had long gone to bed . . . it was dead of night and soon it would be time to be getting up. There was I, lying all on me own in the carriage without closing me eyes – just like an owl. Then all of a sudden, lads, I hear a tapping – someone was creeping up to the carriage. I pokes me head out and sees a woman in just a shift, with nothing on her feet. "What do you want, me dear?" I asks. She was shaking all over – in a terrible state she was! "Get up, good man!" she says. "There's trouble . . . The master and his wife are up to no good. They want to do your merchant in. I heard the master and his wife whispering together – with my own ears I did." Well, my heart hadn't been aching for nothing! "And who might you be?" I ask. "I'm the cook." Fine. So I climb out of the carriage and go to the merchant's room. I wake him up and say, "Right, Pyotr Grigorych, there's something a bit fishy round here. You can catch up on your sleep later, sir, but get dressed now while there's time, so we can escape from evil while the going's good!" But the moment he started putting on his clothes the door opened and lo and behold! – Holy Mother of God! – into the room come the innkeeper and his wife, with three labourers. So the labourers was in it too! "That merchant's got pots of money, so let's share it out," says the innkeeper. All five had long knives . . . yes, a knife each. The innkeeper locks the door and says, "Say your prayers, travellers . . . But if you start yelling we won't let you finish them before you die." But how could we shout? Our throats were choking with fear, we weren't up to shouting then. The merchant bursts into tears and says, "Good Christians! You've decided to kill me because you've taken a fancy to my money. So be it. I'm not the first and I won't be the last. A lot of my fellow merchants have been murdered at inns like these. But why kill my coachman, good Christians? Why should he suffer because of my money?" And he says it all so pitiful, like! But the innkeeper replies, "If we spare his life he'll be the first to witness against us. It makes no difference whether we kill one or two – as well be hanged for a sheep as a lamb, I say. So, say your prayers, that's all – no point in talking any more!" Me and the merchant kneels down side by side, both of us weeping and we starts saying our prayers. The merchant was thinking of his children but I was still young then, I wanted to live . . . We look at the icon and we pray – oh, such a sorry sight it was – makes me weep even now! But the innkeeper's wife just looks at us and says, "You're nice people, so don't hold it against us in the next world and don't you go begging God to come down hard on us – we're only doing this because we need the money." We pray and pray, weep and weep – and God hears us. He took pity, like . . . So, just as the innkeeper grabs the merchant's beard to slit his throat there's suddenly one hell of a banging on the window from outside. We all quake in our boots and the innkeeper's arms dropped. Someone was banging and shouting, "Pyotry Grigorych! Are you there? Get ready, it's time to go!" When they saw someone had come for the merchant they all panicked and took to their heels. Well, we dashed into the yard, harnessed the horses and you couldn't see us for dust!'

'Who was that banging on the window?' asked Dymov.

'At the window? Must've been a saint or an angel, I reckons, as there was no one else about. When we drove out of the yard there wasn't a soul in the street. It was all God's doing!'

Panteley told a few more stories: all of them featured those same long knives and all were rich in flights of fancy. Had he heard these yarns from someone else? Or had he invented them himself in the remote past and then, when his memory grew weaker, began to confuse fact and fiction and could no longer tell one from the other? Anything was possible, but the strange thing was that now and throughout the journey whenever he happened to tell a story he showed a strong preference for fiction and never spoke about what he had actually experienced. Yegorushka took everything at face value and believed every word; but later he found it most odd that a man who in his time had travelled the length and breadth of Russia, who had seen and known so much, a man whose wife and children had been burnt to death, could think so little of his eventful life that whenever he was sitting by the camp fire he would either say nothing about it or talk about what had never even existed.

Over the stew everyone silently reflected on what they had just heard. Life really is frightening and full of marvels, so that however terrifying the stories you may tell in Russia, however much you may embroider them with bandits' dens, long knives and suchlike wonders, they will always strike your listeners as if they were true. Only someone highly skilled in interpretation will look on them sceptically and even he will not make any comment. The wayside cross, the dark bales, the wide expanse of steppe and the destinies of those gathered around the camp fire – all this was in itself so marvellous and terrifying that all that was fantastic about legends and folk-tales paled and could not be distinguished from real life.

Everyone ate from the pot, but Panteley sat on his own, away from the others, eating his stew from a wooden bowl. His spoon was different from the others and was made of cypress wood with a little cross at the end. As Yegorushka looked at him he remembered the lamp-glass.

'Why is grandpa sitting on his own?' he quietly asked Styopka.

'He's an Old Believer,'[20] Styopka and Vasya whispered in reply, looking as if they'd just mentioned some weakness or secret vice.

All of them sat in silence, engrossed in their own thoughts. After all those hair-raising stories no one felt inclined to talk about ordinary matters. Suddenly, in the silence, Vasya sat bolt upright, fixed his lacklustre eyes on some invisible point and pricked his ears up.

'What is it?' asked Dymov.

'Someone's coming,' Vasya replied.

'Where is he?'

'He's over there! I can just make out his dim white shape.'

Where Vasya was looking there was nothing but darkness. All of them listened hard, but they could hear no footsteps.

'Is he coming along the road?' asked Dymov.

'No, across the fields. He's coming towards us.'

A minute passed in silence.

'Perhaps it's the merchant what's buried here, haunting the steppe,' said Dymov.

Everyone cast a sidelong glance at the cross, looked at each other and suddenly burst out laughing – they were ashamed of being so scared.

'Why should he go haunting?' Panteley asked. 'Only them what the earth rejects wander around of nights. Now them merchants were a good lot . . . they received a martyr's crown . . . them merchants . . .'

But then footsteps were heard. Someone was hurrying towards them.

'He's carrying something,' Vasya said.

They could hear the dry grass rustle under the walker's feet and the tall weeds crackle, but in the glare of the fire nothing was visible. At last the footsteps sounded close by, someone coughed. The flickering light seemed to withdraw, a veil slipped from their eyes and the drivers suddenly saw a man standing before them.

Whether it was the flickering light or because everyone was anxious to see that man's face before anything else, oddly enough what struck them at first glance was not his face or his clothes, but his smile. It was unusually broad, good-natured, gentle – like that of a wakened child, one of those infectious smiles to which it is difficult not to respond in kind. After they had taken a closer look, the stranger turned out to be a man of about thirty, not at all good-looking – in fact, quite unremarkable. He was from the south, with a long nose, long arms and long legs. Everything about him was long, only his neck was so short it gave him a stooping look. He wore a clean white shirt with an embroidered collar, white baggy trousers and new high boots. In comparison with the drivers he looked the perfect dandy. He was carrying something large and white and at first glance rather strange, while over his shoulder peeped the barrel of a gun – which was also long.

When he emerged from the darkness and came into the bright circle he stopped dead in his tracks and for a full thirty seconds looked at the drivers as if he meant to say, 'Now, just admire that smile of mine!' Then he stepped over to the fire and beamed even more.

'How about some grub, lads?' he asked.

'Help yourself,' Panteley answered for everyone.

The stranger put what he had been carrying down by the fire – it was a dead bustard – and greeted them again.

Everyone went to have a look at the bustard.

'That's a fine big bird! What did you kill it with?' asked Dymov.

'Buckshot . . . wouldn't have got near it with grape . . . Come on, buy it, lads. I'll take twenty copecks.'

'And what shall we do with it? It'd be fine roasted, but boiled it'd be much too tough – we'd never get our teeth into it!'

'Oh, that's a nuisance! If I took it to the gents on the estate I'd get half a rouble for it. But it's a long walk – ten miles!'

The stranger sat down, unslung his gun and put it down by his side. He seemed listless and sleepy, and as he smiled and screwed up his eyes in the firelight he was evidently thinking the most agreeable thoughts. They gave him a spoon and he began to eat.

'And who might you be?' Dymov asked.

The stranger couldn't have heard the question, as he made no reply and did not even look at Dymov. Most likely that smiling man found the stew tasteless, for he chewed mechanically, lazily, first raising a full spoon to his mouth, then a completely empty one. He wasn't drunk, but he appeared to be a little touched in the head.

'I asked you a question – who are you?' Dymov repeated.

'Me?' replied the stranger with a start. 'I'm Konstantin Zvonyk, from Rovno, about three miles from 'ere.'

Anxious to make clear from the start that he was a cut above your ordinary peasant, Konstantin hastened to add:

'We keep bees and pigs.'

'Do you live with your father or have you got a place of your own?'

'I live in me own place now, set up on me own . . . Got married the month after St Peter's Day.[21] I'm a married man now, today's the eighteenth since I got spliced!'

'That's good!' Panteley exclaimed. 'A wife's a good thing – a blessing from on high!'

'So, his young wife's sleeping at home, all alone, while he's gadding around the steppe,' laughed Kiryukha. 'He's a queer fish all right!'

Just as if he had been nipped in the tenderest spot, Konstantin started, laughed and flushed.

'God, she's not at home!' he exclaimed, quickly taking the spoon from his mouth and surveying everyone in joyous amazement. 'She's not at home – she's gone to her ma's for two days. Yes, I swear it, off she went and now it's like I was a bachelor again!'

Konstantin waved his arm and shook his head. He wanted to go on thinking these thoughts, but the joy that lit up his face hindered him. As though he found it uncomfortable sitting there he changed position, laughed and waved his hand again. Despite his inhibitions about divulging his agreeable thoughts to strangers, he still had an overwhelming desire to share his joy with others.

'She gone to her ma's at Demidovo,' he said, blushing and shifting his gun. 'She's coming back tomorrow – she said she'd be back by dinner-time.'

'Do you miss her?' asked Dymov.

'Good God, how I miss her! What do you expect? Married only a few days and off she goes . . . Eh? Oh, she's a real bundle of mischief, God help me! She's wonderful, she's marvellous, always laughing and singing – real fireworks! When I'm with her me thoughts are all in a whirl, but without her I feel as if I've lost something and here I am wandering over the steppe like a fool! Been doing it since dinner and I'm all adrift!'

Konstantin rubbed his eyes, looked at the fire and laughed.

'So you must love her,' Panteley said.

'She's wonderful, absolutely marvellous,' Konstantin repeated, not listening. 'And what a housewife – so capable, so sensible! You won't find another like her in the whole province – not from common folk like us. And now she's gone away . . . But I know she misses me, I know! Yes, you little spitfire! She said she'd be back by dinner-time tomorrow . . . But what a business it was!' Konstantin was almost shouting now and he suddenly pitched his voice a tone higher and changed position. 'Now she loves me and misses me – but she didn't want to marry me, you know.'

'Now, you eat up,' said Kiryukha.

'No, she didn't want to marry me,' Konstantin continued. 'Three years I had a real ding-dong with her. I saw her at Kalachik Fair and fell madly in love – I was ready to hang myself for her, I was! I was in Rovno, but she was in Demidovo. We were best part of twenty miles from each other, so I couldn't do a thing. So I send matchmakers over, but she says, "Don't want to!" – the little minx! So I send her this and that, earrings, cakes, twenty pound of honey and still she says "Don't want to!" Would you believe it! Come to think of it, what sort of match was I? She was young, beautiful, full of pep, but I was old – nigh on thirty – and really *so* handsome! – me with me lovely beard thin as a nail and me nice smooth face a mass of pimples! If you think about it I didn't stand a chance. Only, I was well off, but them Vakramenkos are well off, too. They keep six oxen and two workmen. So, lads, I were in love, went right off me rocker I did! Couldn't sleep, couldn't eat. I were all befuddled, God save us! I was dying to see her, but she was at Demidovo . . . And what do you think – God strike me dead if I'm lying! I would walk over there three times a week to have a look at her. I stopped working. I was in such a stew that I even wanted to hire myself out as a labourer in Demidovo so as to be near her. I went through sheer hell! Me ma called in a wise old woman, me father was ready to give me ten good whackings. Well, I had to grin and bear it for three years, then I says to meself: to hell with it, I'll get a job as a cabbie in town. But it wasn't to be! At Easter I went to Demidovo to have one last look at her . . .'

Konstantin threw his head back and broke into such peals of light, cheerful laughter that it seemed he had just cleverly fooled someone.

'I see her near the stream with some lads,' he went on, 'and I get proper mad . . . I call her to one side and tell her all sorts of things – for a whole hour, maybe. And she falls in love with me! For three years she didn't love me but she falls for me 'cos of them words!'

'What words?' asked Dymov.

'The words? Can't remember. How could I? They flowed like water from a gutter – rat-tat-tat – non-stop. But now I couldn't say any of them words. So, she marries me. And now that little imp's gone to see her ma and here I am wandering around the steppe without her – I can't stay at home! Oh, I just can't stand it any more!'

Konstantin awkwardly freed his legs from under him, stretched out on the ground and propped his head on his fists. Then he stood up and sat down again. Everyone understood perfectly that here was a man happy in love, poignantly happy. His smile, his eyes, his every movement expressed overwhelming happiness. He kept fidgeting, not knowing what attitude to take and what he should do to avoid exhausting himself from an excess of delightful thoughts. Having unburdened himself to complete strangers he finally settled down and became lost in thought as he gazed at the fire.

At the sight of this happy man everyone felt dejected and wanted to be happy, too. Everyone became thoughtful. Dymov stood up, slowly walked around the fire and it was plain from his walk and the movements of his shoulderblades that he was feeling weary and depressed. He stood still for a moment, glanced at Kiryukha and sat down again.

The fire was dying down now. No longer did the light flicker and the red patch had grown narrow and dim . . . And the faster the fire died down the brighter the moonlight became. Now the whole width of the road, the bales, the wagon shafts, the champing horses could be seen. On the other side of the road was the dim outline of the other cross.

Dymov propped his cheek on one hand and softly sang some plaintive ditty. Konstantin smiled sleepily and joined in with his shrill little voice. They sang for about half a minute and stopped. Yemelyan gave a start, shifted his elbows and flicked his fingers.

'Lads,' he said imploringly, 'let's sing a sacred song!'

Tears sprang to his eyes as he repeated the request, pressing his hand to his heart.

'I don't know any,' said Konstantin.

All the others refused, so Yemelyan sang on his own. Conducting with both arms he tossed his head back and opened his mouth, but only a voiceless hoarse breathing burst from his throat. He sang with his arms, his head, his eyes and even with the swelling under his eye; he sang passionately, with anguish, and the more he strained his chest to extract but one note the hollower his breathing sounded.

Like all the others, Yegorushka was overcome with depression. He went to his wagon, climbed onto the bale and lay down. He looked at the sky and thought of that happy Konstantin and his wife. Why do people marry? Why are there women in the world? Yegorushka vaguely asked himself and thought: how pleasant it must be for a man to have a loving, cheerful and beautiful woman constantly by his side. For some reason thoughts of Countess Dranitsky came to mind. How pleasant to live with a woman like her, he thought. Most probably he would have been delighted to marry her himself had he not been so embarrassed at the thought. He recalled her eyebrows, the pupils of her eyes, her coach, the clock with the horseman. The quiet warm night descended upon him, whispering something in his ear and he felt as if that same beautiful woman were bending over him, smiling as she looked at him and wanting to kiss him.

Two small, ever-dwindling red eyes were all that remained of the fire. The drivers and Konstantin were sitting near them, dark and motionless, and there seemed to be far more of them than before. The two crosses were also visible and somewhere, far far away, a small red light gleamed – probably someone else was cooking his stew as well.

'"Dear old Mother Russia rules the wo-or-ld!"' Kiryukha suddenly sang in a wild voice, had a fit of coughing and fell silent. The echoing steppe caught up his voice and bore it away, so that the stupid nonsense itself seemed to roll over the plains on heavy wheels.

'It's time to go,' said Panteley. 'Get up, lads!'

While they were harnessing the horses, Konstantin strolled around the wagons, singing the praises of his wife.

'Goodbye, lads!' he shouted when the wagon train moved off. 'Thanks for the grub! I'm going on to that other fire. Oh, it's all too much!'

He soon disappeared into the gloom and for a long time they could hear him striding out towards the gleaming light, to tell the strangers there all about his happiness.

When Yegorushka awoke next day it was early morning and the sun had not risen. The wagons were standing still. Some man in a white forage cap and a cheap suit of grey cloth was sitting on a Cossack pony by the leading wagon, talking to Dymov and Kiryukha about something. About a mile ahead of the wagons were low white barns and cottages with tiled roofs; near the cottages neither yards nor trees were to be seen.

'What village is that, grandpa?' Yegorushka asked.

'Them's Armenian farms, lad,' replied Panteley. 'It's where the Armenians live . . . Decent folk – them Armenians . . .'

Having finished his conversation with Dymov and Kiryukha, the man in grey reined back his pony and looked towards the farms.

'It's real vexatious!' Panteley sighed, also looking at the farms and shrinking in the cool of the morning. 'He sent a man over to a farm for some bit of paper, but he ain't come back. He should've sent Styopka!'

'Who is he, grandpa?' asked Yegorushka.

'Varlamov.'

Heavens! Varlamov! Yegorushka quickly jumped up to his knees and looked at the white cap. In that short, grey-clad little man with his riding-boots, seated on an ugly little nag and talking to peasants when all respectable people were in bed it was hard to recognize the mysterious, elusive Varlamov, whom everyone needed, who was always 'hanging around' and was worth far more than Countess Dranitsky.

'He's not a bad man . . . real decent sort . . .' Panteley said, looking at the farms. 'God grant him health . . . he's a wonderful man – that Semyon Aleksandrych Varlamov . . . It's people like him lad, what keep the world going . . . that's a fact. The cocks ain't crowed yet but he's already up and about . . . Any other man would be asleep in bed or making tittle-tattle with visitors. But he's out on the steppe all day . . . running around . . . *He* don't miss out on a deal – oh no! A fine fellow!'

Varlamov didn't take his eyes off one of the farms and carried on talking, while his pony impatiently shifted from one foot to the other.

'Semyon Aleksandrych Varlamov!' cried Panteley, doffing his cap. 'Let me send Styopka. Yemelyan! Give 'em a shout! Tell 'em to send Styopka.'

But then at last someone on horseback rode away from the farm. Leaning heavily to one side, swinging his whip over his head as if performing some fancy tricks and wanting to astonish everyone with his daring horsemanship, he raced to the wagons with the speed of a bird.

'That must be one of his horse patrols,' said Panteley. 'He's got about a hundred of them patrols – maybe more.'

Drawing level with the first wagon the horseman reined in his horse, doffed his cap and handed Varlamov some kind of notebook. Varlamov removed a few sheets of paper from it and read them.

'And where's Ivanchuk's letter?' he shouted.

The horseman took the book back, examined the papers and shrugged his shoulders. He started speaking – most likely making excuses – and then he asked permission to return to the farm. Varlamov's pony gave a start as if his rider had suddenly grown heavier. Varlamov gave a start, too.

'Clear off!' he angrily shouted, shaking his whip at the horseman.

Then he turned his pony back and rode at walking pace past the wagons, still scrutinizing the papers. When he reached the last wagon, Yegorushka strained his eyes to get a better look. Varlamov was quite elderly. His simple, typically Russian face with its small grey beard was red, wet with dew and covered with little blue veins. It displayed that same matter-of-fact aloofness as Kuzmichov's, the same fanatical passion for business. But what a difference between him and Kuzmichov! Besides that habitual, businesslike detachment, Kuzmichov's face always betrayed anxiety and fear that he would not find Varlamov, that he would be late and thus miss out on a good price. Nothing remotely like this – so typical of your small, dependent businessman – was discernible in Varlamov's face or figure. This man fixed prices himself, ran after no one and depended on no one. However unremarkable his appearance, in everything else – even in the way he held his whip – you could see a man conscious of his own power and his established dominion over the steppe.

As he rode past Yegorushka he did not look at him; only his pony deigned to look at him with its large, foolish eyes – and most indifferently at that. Panteley bowed low to Varlamov who noticed this and, without taking his eyes off the papers and burring his consonants told him, 'Goot tay, grantpa!'

Varlamov's exchange with the horseman and that flourish of his whip evidently had a depressing effect on all the drivers: all of them looked serious. Demoralized by that powerful man's wrath, the horseman stood bareheaded by the front wagon, slackened the reins and said nothing, as if he could scarcely believe that the day had started so badly for him.

'He's a harsh old man,' muttered Panteley. 'Real harsh! But never mind . . . he's a good man . . . wouldn't harm no one without good reason . . . he's all right . . .'

After inspecting the papers, Varlamov put the book back in his pocket. As if reading his thoughts, the pony did not wait for orders, shuddered and tore off down the road.

VII

The following night the drivers made a halt and cooked their meal. This time everything was coloured by some indefinable melancholy from the very start. It was humid and everyone had drunk a great deal, without in the least managing to quench their thirst. The moon rose a deep crimson, sullen, as if she were ailing. The stars were sullen too, the mist thicker, the distance hazier. Nature seemed to be languishing in anticipation of some disaster.

Around the camp fire there was none of yesterday's animation and conversation. Everyone was depressed, everyone spoke listlessly and grudgingly. All Panteley could do was sigh and complain about his feet, every now and then raising the subject of 'dying impenitent'.

Dymov was lying on his stomach, silently chewing a straw. His expression was malevolent, weary, and showed revulsion, as if the straw had a bad smell. Vasya complained of jaw-ache and predicted bad weather; Yemelyan had stopped waving his arms and sat still, gloomily surveying the fire. And Yegorushka was wilting, too. The slow pace had exhausted him and the day's heat had given him a headache.

When the stew was cooked Dymov started picking on his mates – out of sheer boredom.

'Look, Old Lumpy's all sprawled out nice and easy over there – but he'll be first to the pot with 'is spoon!' he said, glowering at Yemelyan. 'Greedy-guts! Always tries to barge 'is way first to the pot. Just because he used to sing in a choir he thinks he's a gent. The roads are packed with singers like you begging for sweet charity!'

'What you picking on me for?' asked Yemelyan, angrily glaring back.

'To teach you not to be always first to the pot. Who d'ye think you are!'

'You're a fool, that's what,' Yemelyan said hoarsely.

Knowing from experience how such conversations usually ended, Panteley and Vasya intervened and urged Dymov not to pick quarrels for nothing.

'Fancy you in a choir!' the bully persisted with a contemptuous cough. 'Anyone can sing like that – you just sit in the church porch and sing, "Alms for Christ's sake!" Ugh, damn you!'

Yemelyan said nothing. His silence exasperated Dymov, who looked with even greater loathing at the ex-chorister.

'It's only because I don't want to dirty my hands on you, or I'd soon take you down a peg or two.'

'Why are you picking on me, scum of the earth! Have I ever done anything to you?' said Yemelyan, flaring up.

'What did you call me?' asked Dymov, drawing himself up; his eyes became bloodshot. '*What*? Scum am I? Yes? Well, take that! Now, go and look for it!'

Dymov snatched the spoon from Yemelyan's hands and flung it far to one side. Kiryukha, Vasya and Styopka jumped up and ran off to look for it, while Yemelyan stared imploringly and questioningly at Panteley. His face suddenly became small and wrinkled, started twitching – and the ex-chorister wept like a baby.

Yegorushka, who had long hated Dymov, suddenly felt that he was choking to death in that unbearably humid air and that the camp fire flames were scorching his face. He wanted to escape as quickly as possible to the darkness by the wagons, but that bully's evil, bored eyes drew Yegorushka to him. Longing to say something extremely insulting, he took a step towards Dymov.

'You're the worst of the lot!' he gasped. 'I can't stand you!'

After that he should have escaped to the wagons, but he felt rooted to the spot.

'You'll burn in hell in the next world!' he went on. 'I'm going to tell Uncle Ivan about you! Don't you dare insult Yemelyan!'

'Ooh, 'ark at 'im!' laughed Dymov. 'Little piggy's still wet behind the ears and thinks he can lay down the law! Fancy a clout on the ear-'ole?'

Yegorushka felt unable to breathe; suddenly he started shaking all over and stamped his feet – something that had never happened to him before.

'Hit him! Hit him!' he shrieked.

Tears spurted from his eyes. He felt ashamed and he ran staggering to the wagons. What impression his outburst had made he did not see. Lying on the bale weeping, he jerked his arms and legs and whispered, 'Mummy, Mummy!'

The men, the shadows around the camp fire, the dark bales, the lightning that was flashing in the far distance every minute – all this struck him as hostile and terrifying now. Yegorushka was horrified and he asked himself in despair how and why he had come to this unknown land, in the company of terrible peasants? Where were Uncle, Father Khristofor and Deniska? Why were they taking so long? Had they forgotten him? At the thought that he had been forgotten and left to the mercy of fate he felt chilled and so frightened that several times he felt like jumping off the bales and running headlong back along the road without looking behind him. But the memory of those dark, grim crosses which he was bound to pass on the way and the distant flashes of lightning stopped him. Only when he whispered 'Mummy!' did he feel a little better, it seemed.

The drivers must have been frightened, too. After Yegorushka had run away from the camp fire they first said nothing for a long time and then spoke in hollow undertones about something, saying that *it* was coming and they must hurry to escape from it. They quickly finished their supper, put out the fire and started harnessing the horses in silence. From their agitation and broken phrases they were clearly expecting some disaster.

Before they set off Dymov went over to Panteley.

'What's his name?' he quietly asked.

'Yegorushka,' replied Panteley.

Dymov put one foot on the wheel, gripped the cord that was tied around a bale and hauled himself up. Yegorushka saw his face and curly head. His face was pale, tired and serious – but no longer spiteful.

'Hullo, little boy!' he said softly. 'Come on, hit me!'

Yegorushka looked at him in amazement. At that moment there was a flash of lightning.

'It's all right – hit me!' Dymov repeated.

And without waiting for Yegorushka to hit him or speak, he leapt down and said, 'God, I'm bored!'

Then, swaying from one foot to the other and moving his shoulders, he idly sauntered along the string of wagons, repeating in a half-plaintive, half-irritated voice, 'God, I'm bored! Now, don't get the needle, Yemelyan,' he said as he passed him. 'What hopeless, wretched lives we lead . . . !'

Lightning flashed to the right and immediately flashed again in the distance, like a reflection in a mirror.

'Here, take this, Yegory,' Panteley shouted, handing up something large and dark.

'What is it?' asked Yegorushka.

'Matting. Cover yourself with it when it rains.'

Yegorushka sat up and looked around. The distance was noticeably darker and more than once every minute it winked at him with a pale light. The darkness was swerving to the right, as if pulled by its own weight.

'Grandpa, is there going to be a storm?' asked Yegorushka.

'Oh, me poor ole feet, they're frozen stiff!' chanted Panteley, not hearing him and stamping his feet.

To the left a pale phosphorescent streak flared and went out, as if someone had struck a match on the sky. From a long, long way off came a sound as if someone were walking up and down over an iron roof – probably barefoot, for the iron gave a hollow rumble.

'We're in for a real soaking!' cried Kiryukha.

Between the far distance and the horizon on the right there was such a vivid flash of lightning that it lit up part of the steppe and the point where the clear sky met the darkness. In one compact mass, with big black shreds hanging from its edge, a terrifying rain cloud was unhurriedly advancing. Similar shreds were piling up against each other and massing on the horizon to left and right. The tattered, ragged look of the cloud gave it a drunken, rakish air. There was a very distinct clap of thunder – no longer that hollow rumble. Yegorushka crossed himself and quickly put on his overcoat.

'I'm proper bored!' Dymov's cry carried from the leading wagons and his tone of voice showed that he was getting angry again. 'I'm bored stiff!'

Suddenly there was a squall so violent that it almost snatched Yegorushka's bundle and mat out of his hands. Wildly flapping and tearing in all directions, the mat slapped the bale and Yegorushka's face. The wind raced over the steppes, whistling, frantically whirling and raising such a din in the grass that neither the thunder nor the creak of wagon wheels could be heard above it. It was blowing from the black thundercloud, carrying with it dust clouds and the smell of rain and damp earth. The moonlight grew hazier, dirtier as it were, the stars frowned even more and the dust clouds and their shadows could be seen scurrying back somewhere along the edge of the road. By now, most likely, eddying and drawing dust, dry grass and feathers from the ground, the whirlwinds were soaring to the very height of the heavens. Close to that same black thundercloud clumps of tumbleweed were probably flying about – how terrified they must be feeling! But nothing was visible through the dust that clogged the eyes except flashes of lightning.

Thinking that it would start pouring that very minute, Yegorushka knelt and covered himself with his mat.

'Pantel-ey!' someone in front shouted. 'A . . a . . .' came in broken syllables.

'Ca-an't hear!' Panteley loudly chanted.

Once again those broken syllables.

The thunder roared angrily, rolled over the sky from right to left and then back again, dying out near the wagons at the front.

'Holy, holy, holy, Lord of Sabaoth,' whispered Yegorushka, crossing himself. 'Heaven and earth are filled with Thy glory.'

The black sky gaped wide, breathing white fire; immediately another thunderclap followed. Barely had it died away when there was such a broad flash of lightning that Yegorushka could suddenly see the whole wide road into the far distance, all the drivers and even Kiryukha's waistcoat. The black shreds on the left were already soaring upwards and one of them – rough and clumsy like a paw with fingers – was reaching towards the moon. Yegorushka decided to keep his eyes tightly closed, to pay no attention and to wait until it was all over.

For some reason the rain was a long time coming. Hoping that the thundercloud might pass over, Yegorushka peeped out from his mat. It was terribly dark and he could see neither Panteley, nor the bales, nor himself. He looked sideways where the moon had just been, but it was as pitch black there as on the wagon. The lightning flashes seemed even whiter and more blinding in the dark, so that they hurt his eyes.

'Panteley!' called Yegorushka: there was no answer. But now the wind gave a last tug on the mat and raced away somewhere. There was a steady, gentle sound and a large cold drop fell onto Yegorushka's knee; another trickled down his hand. Noticing that his knees were uncovered he wanted to rearrange the matting, but just then came the sound of pattering and tapping on the road, on the wagon shafts, on the bales: this was the rain. It appeared to have struck some kind of understanding with the matting and they started a conversation – rapid, cheerful but most irritating, like a pair of chattering magpies.

Yegorushka knelt – rather, squatted – on his shoes. When the rain started pattering on the mat he leant forward to shield his knees which were suddenly wet, but within a minute he felt a penetrating, unpleasant wetness from behind, on his back and his calves. He took up his former position, stretched out his knees under the rain and wondered how he could rearrange the matting that was invisible in the dark. But already his arms were wet, water ran down his sleeves and behind his collar, and his shoulderblades grew cold. So he decided to do nothing but sit still and wait until it was all over.

'Holy, holy, holy,' he whispered.

Suddenly, right over his head, with a fearful, deafening crash, the sky broke in two. He leant forwards and held his breath, expecting fragments to shower down on his neck and back. Inadvertently he opened his eyes and saw a blinding, intensely brilliant light flash five times – on his fingers, his wet sleeves, on the little streams flowing from the matting, on the bale and down on the ground. There was a fresh clap of thunder, just as loud and terrifying. The sky was no longer rumbling or crashing, but producing dry crackling sounds, like trees splintering.

'Crash! Bang! Crash!' the thunder distinctly articulated as it rolled over the sky, stumbled and collapsed somewhere over by the wagons or far behind with a spiteful, staccato crash.

Earlier, the lightning flashes had been merely frightening, but with thunder such as this they were truly menacing. Their eerie light penetrated his closed eyelids and sent a cold shiver all over his body. How could he avoid seeing them? Yegorushka decided to turn his face backwards. As if afraid someone was watching him, he cautiously went down on all fours, sliding his palms over the wet bale and turning round.

'Cra-ash!' went the thunder as it swept over his head, collapsed under the wagon and exploded.

Again his eyes happened to open and he saw a new danger: behind the wagon three enormous giants with long pikes were striding along. The lightning flashed on the points of their pikes, very clearly illumining their figures. These people were of vast dimensions, their faces covered, heads bowed and they were treading heavily. They seemed sad and despondent, and lost in thought. Perhaps they were not following the wagons with the intention of doing harm, but still there was something horrible in their being so close. Yegorushka quickly turned forwards. Trembling all over he shouted, 'Panteley! Grandpa!'

'Crash! Bang! Crash!' replied the sky.

As he opened his eyes to try and see if the drivers were still there, lightning flashed in two places and lit up the road into the far distance, the entire wagon train and all the drivers. Little streams of water were flowing along the road and bubbles were dancing. Panteley was walking near the wagons, his tall hat and shoulders covered with a small mat. His figure expressed neither fear nor anxiety, as if he had been deafened by the thunder and blinded by the lightning.

'Grandpa! Look at the giants!' Yegorushka shouted at him, sobbing.

But grandpa did not hear. Yemelyan was walking further ahead, covered in a large mat from head to foot which gave him a triangular shape. Vasya, who was completely uncovered, walked in his usual clockwork soldier fashion, lifting his legs high without bending his knees. In the brilliance of the lightning flashes the train did not appear to be moving, the drivers seemed transfixed and Vasya's upraised leg benumbed.

Again Yegorushka called out for grandpa. Receiving no reply, he sat quite still and no longer waited for the storm to end. He was convinced that the thunder would kill him, that his eyes would open inadvertently and that he would again see those fearsome giants. No longer did he cross himself or call out to the old man or think of his mother, but only grew numb from the cold and the certainty that the storm would never end.

But suddenly he heard voices.

'Yegorushka! Are you asleep?' Panteley shouted from below. 'Come on, get down! . . . The silly boy's gone deaf!'

'That was a storm and a half!' said some deep, unfamiliar voice, grunting as if the owner had just downed a goodly glass of vodka.

Yegorushka opened his eyes. Down below by the wagon stood Panteley, the triangular Yemelyan and the giants. The latter were now much shorter and on closer inspection Yegorushka could see that they were just ordinary peasants carrying iron pitchforks and not pikes on their shoulders. In the space between Panteley and the triangle was the lighted window of a small, low hut. So the wagons must have stopped in a village! Yegorushka threw off the mat, picked up his bundle and hurried down from the wagon. Now that there were people talking nearby and that there was a brightly lit window he no longer felt afraid, although the thunder still rumbled and crashed as before and lightning streaked the entire sky.

'That was a fine old storm, not bad at all, thank the Lord,' muttered Panteley. 'Me feet have gone a tiny bit soft from the rain, but it don't matter. Are you down yet, Yegorushka? Well, go into the hut . . . it's all right.'

'Holy, holy, holy . . .' Yemelyan said hoarsely. 'The lightning must've struck somewhere . . . Are you from these parts?' he asked the giants.

'No, from Glinovo . . . Yes, from Glinovo. We're working on the Plater estate.'

'Threshing, eh?'

'We does all sorts of jobs. Just now we're getting in the wheat. Cor, what lightning, what lightning! Ain't seen such a storm for many a long year!'

Yegorushka went into the hut and was greeted by a lean, hunchbacked old woman with a sharp chin. She was holding a tallow candle, screwing up her eyes and heaving lengthy sighs.

'What a storm the Lord's sent us!' she said. 'And our lads are out on the steppe at night. They'll be having a nasty time of it, poor dears! Now, take your clothes off, young sir.'

Trembling with cold and shrinking squeamishly, Yegorushka pulled off his drenched overcoat, planted his legs wide apart and stood there for a long time stock-still. The least movement brought a disagreeably damp and cold sensation. His sleeves and the back of his shirt were soaked, his trousers stuck to his legs and his head was dripping.

'Why are you standing like that – bandy-legs!' the old woman said. 'Come and sit down.'

Keeping his legs wide apart, Yegorushka went over to the table and sat on a bench near someone's head. The head moved, emitted a stream of air through its nostrils, chewed for a moment and subsided. From the head a mound covered with a sheepskin stretched along the bench: it was a peasant woman lying there asleep.

Sighing, the old woman went out and soon returned with a large water melon and a small sweet melon.

'Eat up, young sir . . . I've nothing else to give you,' she yawned, then rummaged around in a table drawer and produced a long sharp knife which was very similar to the type used by robbers to cut merchants' throats at inns. 'Please eat, young sir!'

Feverishly trembling, Yegorushka ate a slice of the sweet melon with some black bread, which made him feel even colder.

'Our lads are out on the steppe tonight,' sighed the old woman as he ate. 'Mercy on us! I ought to light a candle before the icon, but I don't know where Stepanida's put them. Come on, sir, eat up.'

The old woman yawned, reached backwards with her right hand and scratched her left shoulder.

'Must be nearly two o'clock,' she said. 'Soon it'll be time to be getting up. Our lads are out on the steppe tonight. Soaked to the skin they'll be, I dare say!'

'I'm sleepy, grannie,' Yegorushka said.

'Well, lie down young sir, lie down,' sighed the old woman, yawning. 'Lord Jesus Christ! There I was sleeping and suddenly I thought I could hear someone knocking . . . Then I woke up and saw it was a storm sent by God. I ought to have lit a candle, but I couldn't find one.'

Talking to herself she pulled some rags off the bench – probably her bedclothes – unhooked two sheepskin jackets from the nail by the stove and started making up a bed for Yegorushka.

'That storm's not letting up,' she muttered. 'Who knows, it could even start a fire somewhere . . . and our lads have to spend the night out on the steppe. Now, lie down young sir and go to sleep. Christ be with you, child. I'll leave the melon here – you might feel like a bite when you get up.'

The old woman's sighs and yawns, the regular breathing of the sleeping woman, the dim light in the hut and the patter of rain on the window all made Yegorushka feel sleepy. He was too shy to undress in front of the old woman, so he removed only his boots, lay down and covered himself with the sheepskin.

'Has the lad gone to bed?' came Panteley's whisper a minute later.

'Yes he has,' whispered the old woman in reply. 'Mercy on us! It just keeps thundering and thundering, no end to it.'

'It'll soon pass,' wheezed Panteley as he sat down. 'It's getting quieter now . . . The lads have gone off to the huts and two have stayed with the horses . . . the lads, like . . . they'll have to stay there . . . or them horses might get stolen . . . Yes, I'll sit down for a bit and then take me turn . . . I'll have to go or them horses'll be stolen . . .'

Panteley and the old woman sat side by side near Yegorushka's feet and spoke in sibilant whispers, punctuating their words with sighs and yawns. But Yegorushka just could not get warm. Although he was covered with a warm, heavy sheepskin, his whole body shook, his arms and legs were convulsed with cramps, his insides shuddered. He undressed himself under the sheepskin, but even this did not help. The shivers grew worse and worse.

Panteley went off to relieve the men and then came back, but Yegorushka still could not sleep and was shivering all over. Something was pressing down on his head and chest and crushing him. What it was he could not tell – was it the old people's whispering, or the strong smell of the sheepskin? The melons had left an unpleasant, metallic taste in his mouth. What was more, fleas were biting him.

'Grandpa, I'm cold!' he said, not recognizing his own voice.

'Sleep my child, sleep,' sighed the old woman.

Titus approached the bed on his thin legs and waved his arms; then he grew right up to the ceiling and turned into a windmill. Appearing different from when he had been sitting in the carriage, in full vestments and with a holy water sprinkler in his hands, Father Khristofor walked around the windmill, sprinkled it with holy water and it stopped turning. Yegorushka realized he was delirious and opened his eyes.

'Grandpa!' he called. 'Give me some water.'

No one replied. Lying there was unbearably stuffy and uncomfortable, so he got up, dressed and went outside. It was morning, the sky was overcast, but the rain had stopped. Shivering and wrapping himself in his wet coat, Yegorushka walked around the muddy yard, trying to hear something in the silence. He caught sight of a small shed with a half-open door made of thatch, peeped in, entered and sat down in a dark corner on a heap of dry dung.

His aching head was a jumble of thoughts and his mouth was dry and nasty from that metallic taste. He examined his hat, straightened the peacock's feather and remembered when he had gone with Mother to buy it. He put his hand in his pocket and took out a lump of brown, sticky paste. How had that mess got there? He thought for a moment and sniffed: it smelled of honey. Yes, it was that Jewess's cake. How terribly soaked it was, the poor thing!

Yegorushka inspected his coat. It was greyish, with large bone buttons and cut like a frock-coat. As it was something new and expensive, it had not hung in the hall at home but in the bedroom together with Mother's dresses and he was allowed to wear it only on holidays and church festivals. Looking at it, Yegorushka felt sorry for it and remembered that both he and the coat had been left to the mercy of fate, that neither of them would ever go back home and he sobbed so loud that he nearly fell off the heap.

A large white rain-drenched dog, with woolly wisps like curling-papers on its muzzle, came into the shed and eyed Yegorushka very inquisitively. Clearly it was wondering if it should bark or not. Deciding not to bark, it cautiously approached Yegorushka, ate the sticky paste and departed.

'They're Varlamov's men!' someone shouted in the street.

After a good cry Yegorushka left the shed, skirted a large puddle and made his way to the street. Right in front of the gates stood the wagons. As sluggish and drowsy as autumn flies, the wet drivers were wandering around nearby in their muddy boots or sitting on the wagons shafts. Yegorushka looked at them.

'How boring, how tiresome to be a peasant!' he thought. He went up to Panteley and sat next to him on a shaft.

'Grandpa, I'm cold!' he said, shivering, and he pulled his sleeves down over his hands.

'It's all right, we'll soon be there,' yawned Panteley. 'It's all right . . . you'll soon get warm.'

The wagons moved off early, when it was still cool. Yegorushka lay on his bale and trembled with cold, although the sun soon appeared and dried his clothes, the bale and the ground. Hardly had he closed his eyes when he saw Titus and the windmill again. With a feeling of nausea and heaviness all over his body he tried all he could to dispel those images, but hardly had they disappeared than that bully Dymov – red-eyed, fists upraised and bellowing – would throw himself on Yegorushka or would be heard complaining how bored he was. Varlamov would come riding past on his Cossack pony and that happy Konstantin would pass by with his smile and his bustard. How depressing, insufferable and tiresome all these people were!

Once, towards evening, Yegorushka raised his head to ask for a drink. The wagon train had come to a stop on a large bridge spanning a wide river. Down below dark smoke hung over the river and through it a steamer could be seen, with a barge in tow. Ahead, beyond the river, was an enormous, brightly coloured hill, dotted with houses and churches and at its foot a locomotive was shunting some goods wagons.

Never before had Yegorushka seen steamers or locomotives, or wide rivers, but now as he looked at them he was neither surprised nor afraid. His face did not show even the slightest trace of curiosity. All he felt was nauseous and he hurried to lie chest downwards on the edge of the bale. He was sick. Panteley cleared his throat and shook his head when he saw this.

'Our lad's real poorly!' he exclaimed. 'Must've caught a chill on his stomach . . . that lad . . . far from home. Oh, that's bad!'

VIII

The wagons had halted at a large commercial inn close to the quayside. As he climbed down from the wagon Yegorushka recognized a familiar voice. Someone helped him and said:

'We were already here yesterday evening . . . been waiting for you all day. We wanted to catch you up yesterday but we didn't manage it – we came a different way. Hey, you've made a right mess of your coat! You'll catch it from Uncle!'

Yegorushka peered into the mottled face of the speaker and remembered that this was Deniska.

'Your uncle and Father Khristofor are in their room at the inn,' continued Deniska. 'They're having tea. Come on!'

He led Yegorushka to a large, dark and dreary two-storey building similar to the almshouse at N—. After they had passed through a lobby, up some dark stairs and down a long corridor, Yegorushka and Deniska entered a small room where Kuzmichov and Father Khristofor were indeed sitting at a small tea-table. Both old men showed joy and surprise when they saw the boy.

'Aha, young sir!' intoned Father Khristofor. 'Mr Lomonosov in person!'

'Yes, it's His Lordship himself,' Kuzmichov said. 'Pray make yourself welcome!'

Yegorushka took off his coat, kissed Uncle's and Father Khristofor's hands and sat down at the table.

'Well, did you like the journey, *puer bone*?' asked Father Khristofor, showering him with questions, pouring him some tea and smiling his usual radiant smile. 'I bet it was boring, eh? And God save us all from travelling by wagon or ox-cart! On and on you go, you look ahead and the steppe's always the same ramblingly stretched-out affair as ever – you think it's never going to end! That's not travelling – it's a sheer abomination. Why don't you drink your tea? Come on, drink up. While you were trailing along with the wagons we pulled off a fantastic deal, praise be to God! We sold the wool to Cherepakhin at a price anyone would envy . . . Came out of it very well, we did.'

When he first saw his own people Yegorushka felt an irresistible urge to complain. He did not listen to Father Khristofor and wondered where to begin and what precisely he should complain about. But Father Khristofor's voice sounded so harsh and unpleasant that it prevented him from concentrating and only muddled his thoughts. After sitting for barely five minutes at the table he got up, went over to the sofa and lay down.

'Well now!' exclaimed Father Khristofor. 'And what about your tea?'

Still trying to think of something to complain about, Yegorushka pressed his forehead against the back of the sofa and suddenly burst out sobbing.

'Well now!' repeated Father Khristofor, getting up and going over to the sofa. 'What's the matter, Yegor? Why are you crying?'

'I-I'm ill!' murmured Yegorushka.

'Ill?' Father Khristofor said, disconcerted. 'That's no good, my boy. It's no good falling ill when you're travelling. Oh dear, no good at all . . . eh?'

He pressed his hand to Yegorushka's head and touched his cheek.

'Yes, your head's burning . . . you must have caught a chill . . . or it's something you've eaten . . . you must pray to God.'

'We could give him some quinine,' Kuzmichov said, rather taken aback.

'No, he should eat something warm. Yegorushka, would you like a nice little drop of soup? Eh?'

'No, I don't want any soup,' replied Yegorushka.

'Got the shivers?'

'I had them before, but now I feel hot. I'm aching all over.'

Kuzmichov went over to the sofa, touched Yegorushka's head, gave a troubled cough and returned to the table.

'Now, you'd better get undressed and go to bed,' said Father Khristofor. 'What you need is a good sleep.'

He helped Yegorushka undress, gave him a pillow, covered him with a quilt, laid Kuzmichov's coat over it, tiptoed away and sat at the table. Yegorushka closed his eyes and immediately had the feeling that he wasn't in the room at the inn at all, but on the high road, by the camp fire. Yemelyan was 'conducting', while red-eyed Dymov lay on his stomach eyeing Yegorushka mockingly.

'Hit him! Hit him!' Yegorushka shouted out loud.

'The boy's delirious,' Father Khristofor said in an undertone.

'It's a real nuisance,' sighed Kuzmichov.

'We must rub him down with oil and vinegar. With God's help he'll be better tomorrow.'

To free himself from these oppressive visions Yegorushka opened his eyes and looked at the light. Father Khristofor and Kuzmichov had finished their tea now and were whispering together. The former was happily smiling: obviously he was quite unable to forget about the handsome profit he had made on his wool. It wasn't the profit so much that cheered him as the thought of gathering his large family around him when he was back home, giving them sly winks and roaring with laughter. First he would string them along and tell them he had sold the wool at a loss – and then he would hand his brother-in-law Mikhailo a fat wallet. 'Here you are!' he would say, 'that's how to do business!' But Kuzmichov was not happy. His face expressed that same businesslike detachment and anxiety.

'If only I'd known Cherepakhin would pay that kind of price,' he said quietly, 'I wouldn't have sold Makarov those five tons back home. It's damned infuriating! But who would have guessed that prices here had gone up?'

A white-shirted waiter cleared the samovar away and lit the icon lamp in the corner. Father Khristofor whispered something in his ear. The waiter assumed a mysterious, conspiratorial expression, as if to say, 'I quite understand', and left, shortly to return and put a bowl under the sofa. Kuzmichov made up a bed for himself on the floor, yawned several times, lazily said his prayers and lay down.

'I'm thinking of going to the cathedral tomorrow,' Father

Khristofor said. 'I know one of the sacristans there. I really ought to go and see the Bishop after the service, but they say he's ill.'

He yawned and put out the lamp. Only the icon lamp was burning now.

'They say he's not receiving visitors,' Father Khristofor continued, disrobing. 'So I'll have to leave without seeing him.'

When he removed his caftan Yegorushka thought he was seeing Robinson Crusoe. 'Crusoe' mixed something in a saucer and went over to Yegorushka.

'Mr Lomonosov!' he whispered. 'Are you asleep? Sit up and I'll give you a rubdown with oil and vinegar. It'll do you good – only don't forget to say your prayers!'

Yegorushka quickly raised himself and sat up. Father Khristofor took his shirt off, winced and breathed jerkily, as though he himself were being tickled, and started rubbing his chest.

'In the name of the Father, the Son and the Holy Ghost . . . Lie with your face down . . . that's it. You'll be fine tomorrow . . . but don't let it happen again . . . heavens, you're on fire! I suppose you were out on the road in the storm, eh?'

'Yes, I was.'

'Then it's no wonder you're ill! In the name of the Father, the Son and the Holy Ghost . . . No wonder!'

When he had finished rubbing Yegorushka down, Father Khristofor put his shirt on, covered him up, made the sign of the cross over him and went out. Then Yegorushka saw him at prayer. Very likely the old man knew many different prayers, for he stood whispering for a long time in front of the icon. When he had completed his devotions he made the sign of the cross over the window, the door, Yegorushka and Kuzmichov, after which he lay down on a small sofa, without any pillow, and covered himself with his caftan. Out in the corridor the clock struck ten. Remembering how many hours were left until morning, Yegorushka wearily pressed his forehead against the back of the sofa and no longer made any attempt to rid himself of those vague, oppressive visions. But morning came much sooner than he expected.

He felt that he had not been lying there very long with his forehead against the back of the sofa, yet when he opened his eyes, slanting sunbeams were streaming towards the floor from both windows in the room. Father Khristofor and Kuzmichov had gone out. The room had been tidied and it was bright and cosy and smelt of Father Khristofor, who always had an odour of cypress and dried cornflowers about him (at home he made holy water sprinklers and decorated icon cases with cornflowers so that he was saturated with their scent). Yegorushka looked at the pillow, at the slanting sunbeams, at his boots which had now been cleaned and stood side by side by the sofa, and he burst out laughing. He felt it was odd not to be lying on that bale of wool, that everything around him was dry and that there was no thunder or lightning on the ceiling.

He leapt from the sofa and started dressing. He felt wonderful. Nothing remained of yesterday's illness, except a slight weakness in his legs and neck. Evidently the oil and vinegar had done their job. He remembered the steamer, the locomotive, the wide river he had glimpsed the day before and he hurried to get dressed so that he could run down to the quayside to look at them. When he had washed and was putting on his red shirt the lock in the door suddenly clicked and Father Khristofor appeared in the doorway in his top hat, carrying his staff and wearing a brown silk cassock over his canvas caftan. Smiling and beaming (old men who have just returned from church are always radiant), he placed a piece of communion bread and a packet of some kind on the table, and recited a short prayer.

'God has been gracious!' he exclaimed. 'Well, how are you?'

'I feel fine now,' replied Yegorushka, kissing his hand.

'Thank God for that . . . I'm just back from the service. I went to see an old sacristan friend of mine. He invited me for breakfast, but I didn't go. I don't like visiting people so early in the morning – blow it!'

He took off his cassock, stroked his chest and undid the packet without hurrying. Yegorushka saw a tin of unpressed caviare, a slice of smoked sturgeon and a French loaf.

'There, I happened to pass a fishmonger's, so I bought these,' Father Khristofor said. 'On weekdays one shouldn't indulge oneself, but I thought to myself that we have an invalid back at the inn, so I shall be forgiven! It's very good caviare . . . it's sturgeon . . .'

The white-shirted waiter brought in the samovar and a tray with crockery.

'Eat up now!' said Father Khristofor, spreading the caviare on a slice of bread and handing it to Yegorushka. 'Eat and enjoy yourself while you can, as the time is coming when you'll have to study. Now, mind you study attentively and diligently, so that you'll benefit from it. If you have to know something by heart you must learn it, but where you need to convey the inner meaning, ignoring the outer form, then do it in your own words, I say. And try and master every branch of knowledge. There are people who know mathematics backwards but are ignorant of Pyotr Mogila.[22] Others might know about Pyotr Mogila but can't tell you about the moon. Study, I say, so that you understand everything! You must study Latin, French, German, geography – history of course – divinity, philosophy, mathematics . . . And when you've mastered them all – taking your time over them and with prayer and application – you must take up a profession. Once you know everything, any career will be easy for you. Only, study and acquire grace. God will show you what you are destined to be – doctor, judge, engineer . . .'

Father Khristofor spread a little caviare on a small piece of bread, popped it into his mouth and continued, 'As Paul the Apostle says, "Be not carried about with divers and strange doctrines."[23] Of course, if it's black magic, or blasphemy, or summoning spirits like Saul,[24] or suchlike practices that are no good either to yourself or to others, then it's better not to study. You must absorb only what God has blessed. Just consider . . . the holy apostles spoke every tongue, so you must learn languages. Basil the Great[25] studied mathematics and philosophy, so you must study them as well. St Nestor[26] wrote history – so you must learn to write history too. Just do as the saints did . . .'

Father Khristofor sipped from his saucer, wiped his whiskers and turned his head.

'Good!' he said. 'I'm schooled in the old ways. I've forgotten a lot. What's more, I live differently from others. Really, there's no comparison. For example, it's very nice for people and for myself too if one can quote some Latin, or refer to something from history or philosophy in high society, over dinner or at a big gathering. It's the same thing when the assizes come round and everyone has to be sworn in – all the other priests go into their shells, but I'm on hail-fellow-well-met terms with the judges, prosecutors, barristers. I talk like a scholar to them, have tea with them, enjoy a good laugh and ask them questions about things I don't know. And they find it pleasant, too. So there you are, my boy . . . Learning is light, but ignorance is darkness. So study! Of course, it's not easy. Nowadays studying costs a lot of money . . . Your dear mother is a widow and lives on a pension. And besides . . .'

Father Khristofor looked anxiously at the door.

'Uncle Ivan will help you,' he continued in a whisper. 'He won't leave you in the lurch. He doesn't have children of his own and he'll help you. Don't worry!'

He looked grave and whispered even more softly, 'Only mind you don't forget your mother and Uncle Ivan – God forbid! Honour your mother, as the commandment bids us. Uncle Ivan is your benefactor, your guardian. If you become a scholar and you find other people a burden or despise them – God forbid – because they are stupider than you – then woe, woe unto you!'

Father Khristofor raised his hands and repeated in a thin voice, 'Woe, I say, woe unto you!'

Father Khristofor warmed to his theme, began to relish it as they say and would have continued until dinner-time, but the door opened and in came Uncle Ivan. He hastily greeted them, sat at the table and rapidly gulped his tea.

'Well,' he began, 'I've settled all the business. We should have gone home today, but there's still a problem with Yegorushka. We must find him a place to live. My sister told me she has a friend around here, Nastasya Petrovna. Perhaps she could take him in as a boarder.'

He rummaged in his pocketbook, took out a crumpled letter and read, '"Little Nizhny Street, to Nastasya Petrovna Toskunova, at her own house." We must go and see her right away. Oh, it's a real nuisance!'

Shortly after breakfast Uncle Ivan and Yegorushka left the inn.

'It's a real nuisance!' Uncle muttered. 'You just stick to me like a leech, damn you! All you and your mother want is book-learning and to be nice and refined, but you both give me no end of trouble!'

When they crossed the yard the wagons and drivers had disappeared – early that morning they had all gone down to the quayside. In a far corner stood that familiar dark shape – the carriage. The bays were standing nearby, eating their oats.

'Goodbye, brichka!' thought Yegorushka.

First they had a long walk uphill along a wide avenue, then across a large market square where Uncle Ivan asked a policeman the way to Little Nizhny Street.

'Well now,' grinned the policeman. 'That's *miles* from 'ere, over by the commons!'

On the way some cabs passed them, but Uncle allowed himself such extravagances as cabs only in exceptional circumstances and on major holidays. He and Yegorushka walked for a long time along paved streets, then along unpaved streets with footpaths and finally along streets that were neither paved nor with footpaths. When their legs and tongues had got them to Little Nizhny Street both were red in the face and, after removing their hats, they wiped away the sweat.

'Can you please tell me,' said Uncle Ivan, addressing a little old man sitting on a bench by a gate, 'where Nastasya Petrovna Toskunova's house is?'

'There ain't no Toskunova round 'ere,' replied the old man after a pause for thought. 'Perhaps it's Timoshenko you be wanting?'

'No, Toskunova.'

'Sorry, ain't no Toskunovas round 'ere . . .'

Uncle Ivan shrugged his shoulders and trudged on.

'You're wasting your time!' the old man shouted after him. 'If I says there ain't none, that means there ain't none!!'

'Tell me, dearie,' Uncle Ivan said, turning to an old woman on the corner selling seeds and pears from a tray, 'where's Nastasya Petrovna Toskunova's house?'

The old woman looked at him in surprise and laughed.

'Can she be living in a house of her own now?' she asked. 'Heavens, it's nearly eight years since she married her daughter off and left the house to her son-in-law. It's the son-in-law that lives there now.'

And her eyes seemed to be saying: 'How could those idiots not know a simple fact like that?'

'But where is she living now?' asked Uncle Ivan.

'Heavens!' repeated the old woman in amazement, clasping her hands. 'She's been in lodgings for ages. It's eight years since she made her house over to her son-in-law. Honestly!'

Most probably she was waiting for Uncle Ivan to be similarly surprised and exclaim: 'But that's not possible!' but he asked very calmly, 'So, where does she live?'

The fruit-seller rolled up her sleeves, pointed with her bare arm and shrilled, 'Now, go straight on and on till you come to a little red house. You'll see an alley to your left. Go down it and it's the third gate on the right.'

Uncle Ivan and Yegorushka reached the little red house, turned left into the alley and headed for the third gate on the right. On both sides of the very ancient gate stretched a grey fence with wide cracks in it. The right-hand section listed heavily forwards, threatening to collapse altogether, whilst the left sloped back towards the yard. The gate was still upright, but was apparently deliberating which would be more convenient – to fall backwards or forwards. Uncle Ivan opened the wicket-gate and both he and Yegorushka saw a large yard overgrown with tall weeds and burdock. About a hundred steps from the gate stood a red-roofed cottage with green shutters. A plump woman with her sleeves rolled up and her apron outspread was standing in the middle of the yard. She was scattering something on the ground and shouting in a shrill, piercing voice like the fruit-seller's, 'Chick, chick, chick!'

Behind her sat a ginger dog with pointed ears. On seeing the visitors it started barking tenor (all ginger dogs bark tenor).

'Who do you want?' shouted the woman, screening her eyes from the sun with one hand.

'Good morning!' Uncle Ivan shouted back, waving the ginger dog away with his stick. 'Tell me, does Nastasya Petrovna Toskunova live here?'

'She does. What do you want with her?'

Uncle Ivan and Yegorushka went over to her. She eyed them suspiciously and repeated, 'What do you want with her?'

'Perhaps *you* are Nastasya Petrovna?'

'Yes, I am!'

'Very pleased to meet you. Well now, your old friend Olga Ivanovna Knyazeva sends her regards. And perhaps you remember me – I'm her brother Ivan. We're all from the village of N—. You were born in our house and then you got married . . .'

There was silence. The plump woman stared vacantly at Uncle Ivan as if she neither believed nor understood. Then she flushed and threw up her hands. The oats spilled from her apron and tears spurted from her eyes.

'Olga Ivanovna!' she shrieked, breathless with excitement. 'My sweet darling! Oh, heaven save us, why am I standing here like an idiot? My dear little beautiful angel!'

She embraced Yegorushka, made his face wet with her tears and then broke down completely.

'Heavens above!' she said, wringing her hands. 'Olga's little boy! What joy! He's his mother all over, the spitting image! But why are you standing out in the yard? Please come inside.'

Crying, gasping for breath and talking as she went, she hurried into the house. The visitors wearily followed her.

'I'm afraid it's not very tidy in here,' she said, ushering the visitors into a small stuffy room filled with icons and flowerpots.

'Oh, goodness gracious! . . . Vasya! . . . At least open the shutters! My little angel! He's so adorable! And fancy me not knowing that Olga had such a dear little boy!'

When she had calmed down and grown used to her visitors, Uncle Ivan asked to speak to her in private. Yegorushka went into the next room where there was a sewing-machine, a cage with a starling in the window and as many icons and flowers as in the parlour. A little girl, sunburnt and as chubby-cheeked as Titus and wearing a clean cotton-print frock, was standing stock-still by the sewing-machine.

She stared at Yegorushka without blinking and evidently felt very awkward. Yegorushka looked at her in silence.

'What's your name?' he asked.

The girl moved her lips and seemed about to cry.

'Atka . . .'

(This meant Katka.)

'So, he'll live with you,' Uncle Ivan whispered in the parlour, 'if you'll be so kind, and we'll pay you ten roubles a month. He's not a spoilt boy, he's very well-behaved . . .'

'I don't know what to say, Ivan Ivanych!' whimpered Nastasya Petrovna. 'Ten roubles a month is good money, but taking in someone else's child really scares me! Supposing he falls ill or something? . . .'

When Yegorushka was called back to the parlour Uncle Ivan was already standing hat in hand and saying goodbye.

'What do you say then? So . . . he can stay with you now . . . Well, goodbye! You're going to stay here, Yegorushka,' he added, turning to his nephew. 'Behave yourself and do as Nastasya Petrovna says . . . Goodbye . . . I'll call back tomorrow.'

Uncle Ivan left and Nastasya Petrovna hugged Yegorushka again, calling him a little angel and tearfully began to lay the table. Within three minutes Yegorushka was sitting next to her, answering her endless questions and eating rich, hot cabbage soup.

That evening he was again sitting at the same table, propping his head on his hands as he listened to Nastasya Petrovna. Laughing and crying, she told him about his mother's younger days, about her marriage, her children . . . A cricket chirped in the stove and the lamp-burner faintly droned. The mistress of the house spoke in a low voice and every now and then dropped her thimble in her excitement. Every time she did so her granddaughter Katya would crawl after it under the table and stay there a long time, probably to look at Yegorushka's feet. Yegorushka listened and began to feel drowsy as he scrutinized the old woman's face, the wart with little hairs sticking out, the tear-stains. And he felt sad, so very sad. They made up a bed for him on a trunk and told him that if he felt hungry during the night he should go into the passage and help himself to some chicken under a plate on the windowsill.

Next morning Uncle Ivan and Father Khristofor came to say goodbye. Nastasya Petrovna was delighted and was about to prepare the samovar when Uncle Ivan, who was in a great hurry, waved his hand dismissively and said, 'We've no time for tea and sugar and all that! We're leaving right away.'

Before the farewells everyone sat in silence for a minute. Nastasya Petrovna sighed deeply and looked at the icons with tearful eyes.

'Well,' began Uncle Ivan, getting up, 'so you'll be staying here . . .'

That businesslike detachment suddenly vanished from his face, he flushed slightly, smiled sadly and said, 'Now, mind you study and don't forget your mother and do what Nastasya Petrovna Toskunova tells you. If you study hard, Yegorushka, I won't leave you in the lurch.'

He drew a purse from his pocket, turned his back to Yegorushka, fumbled for a while among his small change, found a ten-copeck piece and handed it to him. Father Khristofor sighed and without hurrying gave his blessing to Yegorushka:

'In the name of the Father, the Son and Holy Ghost . . . Study, my boy . . . work hard. If I die, remember me in your prayers. Here, take these ten copecks, it's a present from me as well.'

Yegorushka kissed his hand and burst into tears. Something deep down whispered that he would never see that old man again.

'Nastasya Petrovna, I've applied to the school already,' Uncle Ivan said, as if a corpse were laid out in the room. 'On 7 August you must take him for the examinations . . . Well, goodbye now. God be with you. Goodbye, Yegorushka.'

'You could at least have stayed for some tea,' groaned Nastasya Petrovna.

Through the tears that blinded his eyes Yegorushka could not see Uncle and Father Khristofor leave. He rushed to the window, but they were already out of the yard and the ginger dog that had just been barking ran back from the gate with an air of having fulfilled its duty. Not knowing why, Yegorushka leapt up and flew out of the house. When he was outside the gate Uncle Ivan and Father Khristofor were already rounding the corner, the first swinging his stick with the crook, the second his staff. Yegorushka felt that with these two men all he had lived through until then had vanished forever, like smoke. He sank exhausted onto the bench, shedding bitter tears as he greeted that new, unknown life that was just beginning for him.

What would that life be like?

Panpipes

Exhausted by the stifling air in the fir plantation and covered in cobwebs and fir-needles, Meliton Shishkin, the bailiff from Dementyev's farm, was wearily making his way, rifle in hand, to the edge of the wood. His dog, Lady, a cross between mongrel and setter, unusually thin and heavy with young, her wet tail between her legs, was plodding behind her master and trying her hardest not to get her nose pricked. The morning was dreary and overcast. A heavy spray fell from the trees that were thinly veiled in mist, and from the bracken, and the damp wood gave off a sharp odour of decay.

Ahead, where the plantation ended, stood silver birches and between their trunks and branches the misty horizon was visible. Beyond the birches someone was playing a rustic shepherd's pipe. The player produced no more than five or six notes, lazily dragging them out with no attempt at a tune – and yet in that shrill piping there was something utterly joyless and mournful.

When the plantation thinned out and small firs mingled with young birches, Meliton caught sight of the herd. Hobbled horses, cows and sheep wandered among the bushes, making the twigs crackle underfoot as they sniffed the grass in the wood. At the edge of the wood, leaning against a wet birch tree, stood an old shepherd, gaunt, bareheaded and wearing a coarse tattered smock. Deep in thought, he was gazing at the ground and to all appearances was playing his pipe quite mechanically.

'Good morning, gaffer! God be with you,' Meliton greeted him in a thin, hoarse voice which did not in the least match his enormous stature and large fleshy face. 'You're pretty good on those pipes, aren't you! Whose herd are you minding?'

'The Artamonovs,' the shepherd replied grudgingly and tucked the pipes away in the bosom of his smock.

'Then this wood belongs to the Artamonovs, too?' Meliton asked, looking around. 'Well, how about that – so it does! I almost got lost . . . Scratched my face all over on those brambles, I did.'

He sat down on the damp earth and started rolling a cigarette from a scrap of newspaper.

Like his thin reedy voice everything about this man was small – his smile, his tiny eyes, his little buttons and his cap perilously perched on his greasy, close-cropped head – and clashed with his height, his girth and his fleshy face. When he spoke and smiled there was something womanish, timid, submissive about his smooth-shaven podgy face and his whole appearance.

'Lord save us – what weather!' he said, rolling his head. 'They haven't got the oats in yet and this darned rain seems to have hired itself out for the autumn!'

The shepherd looked up at the drizzling sky, the wood and the bailiff's sodden clothes, thought for a moment and didn't reply.

'It's been like it all summer,' Meliton sighed. 'Bad for the peasants – and no joy for the masters either!'

Again the shepherd looked up at the sky, pondered and then said, slowly and deliberately, as if chewing every word, 'Everything's going one way . . . we must expect the worst.'

'And how are things here?' Meliton asked, lighting his cigarette. 'Seen any coveys of grouse on Artamonov Heath?'

The shepherd did not answer immediately. Again he glanced at the sky and to both sides, reflected for a moment and blinked. Evidently he attached no small importance to his words and to reinforce them tried to stretch them out with a certain degree of solemnity. His face displayed all the angularity and gravity of old age, and the saddle-shaped furrow running across it and his upwardly curling nostrils gave it a cunning, mocking look.

'No, can't say that I 'ave,' he replied. 'Yeryomka, our gamekeeper, said he sent up a covey on Elijah's Day[1] near Pustoshye, but I dare say he was lying. Ain't many birds about . . .'

'No, my friend, not many at all . . . it's the same everywhere! If you look at it practically the hunting's woeful, pitiful. There's just no game at all and what there is isn't worth soiling your hands for – it's not even fully-grown! So tiny it makes you feel real sorry.'

Meliton grinned and waved dismissively. 'What's happening in the world's enough to make you laugh – and that's all! Birds are so daft nowadays they sit on their eggs late and there's some that aren't off them come St Peter's Day. Oh yes!'

'Everything's heading the same way,' said the shepherd, raising his head. 'Last year there weren't much game and this year there's even less. You mark my words – in another five years there won't be any at all. As I see it, 'fore long there won't be birds of any kind left – let alone game-birds.'

'Yes,' agreed Meliton after pausing for thought. 'That's true.'

The shepherd laughed bitterly and shook his head.

'I'm just flabbergasted!' he exclaimed. 'What's become of 'em all? Twenty years ago, as I remember, there were geese here, cranes, ducks and black grouse – the place was swarming with 'em! The gents used to go out shooting and all you'd hear was bang-bang, bang-bang! There was no end of woodcock, snipe and curlews, and little teal and pipers was as common as starlings or sparrows, let's say – just swarms of 'em! And where have they all gone? Nowadays you don't even see birds of prey. Eagles, falcons, eagle-owls – all wiped out! There's not many beasts of any kind left. These days, my friend, you can count yourself lucky if you see a wolf or a fox, let alone a bear or a mink. Time was when there were even elk! For forty years I've been keeping an eye on God's works – year in year out – and as I see it everything's heading one way.'

'What way?'

'Towards what's *bad*, my lad. Towards ruination, it seems. The time's come for God's world to perish.'

The old man put on his cap and began to gaze at the sky.

'It's a real shame!' he sighed after a short silence. 'Lord, what a crying shame! Of course, it's all God's will – it wasn't us who made the world. All the same, my friend, it's a terrible shame. If a single tree withers away or, let's say, one of your cows dies, you feel sorry.

So what will it be like, my friend, if the whole world goes to wrack and ruin? There is so much that's good, Lord Jesus Christ! The sun, the sky, the woods, the rivers, living creatures – they've all been created and fashioned so they fit in with each other. Everything has its allotted task and knows its place. And all this must perish!'

A sad smile passed over the shepherd's face and his eyelids trembled.

'You say that the world's heading for ruin,' Meliton said thoughtfully. 'Maybe the world *will* end soon, but you can hardly take just birds as a sign.'

'It's not only birds,' said the shepherd. 'It's beasts as well – cattle, bees and fish . . . If you don't believe me ask any old man. Every one of them'll tell you that fish ain't anything like what they used to be. Every year there's less and less fish in the seas, lakes and rivers. Here in the Peschanka, as I remember, you could catch two-foot pike and there was burbot and ide and bream – all goodly-sized fish. But now you can thank your lucky stars if you catch a small pike or a six-inch perch. There's not even decent ruff. Every year it gets worse and worse and soon there won't be any fish at all! As for the rivers – they'll dry up, most likely!'

'You're right – that they will!'

'That's it! Every year they get shallower and shallower, there's no longer those nice deep pools there used to be, me friend. See those bushes over there?' asked the old man, pointing to one side. 'Behind them there's an old river-bed – "the backwater" it's called. In my father's day that's where the Peschanka flowed, but now look where the devil's taken it! It keeps changing course and you see, it'll keep changing course till it dries up altogether. Other side of Kurgasov there used to be marshes and ponds, but where are they now? And what became of all them little streams? In this very wood there used to be a stream with so much water in it the peasants only had to dip their creels in to catch pike, and wild duck used to winter there. But even at spring flood there's no decent water in it now. Yes, me friend, things are bad everywhere you look. Everywhere!'

There was silence. Lost in thought, Meliton stared before him. He wanted to think of a single part of nature as yet untouched by the all-embracing ruin. Bright patches of light glided over the mist and the slanting sheets of rain as if over frosted glass, only to vanish immediately – the rising sun was trying to break through the clouds and glimpse the earth.

'Yes – and the forests too,' Meliton muttered.

'And the forests too,' repeated the shepherd. 'They're being cut down, they catch fire or dry up and there's no new growth. What does grow is felled right away. One day it comes up and the next it's chopped down and so it goes on till there's nothing left. Ever since we got our freedom,[2] me friend, I've been minding the village herd and before that I was one of squire's shepherds too – grazed this very spot – and I can't remember one summer's day when I wasn't here. And all the time I keep watching God's works. I've been able to keep a close watch on things in me lifetime and as I sees it now all kinds of plants are dying out, whether it's rye, vegetables, flowers – everything's heading one way . . .'

'But people are better now,' observed the bailiff.

'How are they better?'

'They're cleverer.'

'Cleverer they may be, my lad, but what good is that? What use is being clever to those that's on the brink of ruin? You don't need any brains to perish! What use is brains to a huntsman if there's no game about? As I reckon, God's given folk brains, but he's taken their strength away. Folk have become feeble, mighty feeble. Take me, for example. I know I'm not worth a brass farthing, I'm the lowliest peasant in the whole village, but I still have me strength, lad. As you can see, I'm in me sixties, but I still mind the herd, come rain or shine. And at night I keep watch over the horses for a couple of copecks and I don't fall asleep or suffer from the cold. My son's cleverer than me, but just put him in my place and next day he'll be asking for a rise or he'll be off to the doctor's. Oh yes! I don't need nothing but bread – "give us our daily bread" as it is written. And me father ate nothing but bread – and me grandpa, too. But these days your peasant wants his tea and vodka and fancy white rolls. He needs to sleep from dusk to dawn, keeps going to the doctor's – pampers himself silly, he does. And why? Because he's grown feeble, he's got no backbone. He'd rather not sleep, but his eyes start to close – and there's nothing he can do about it.'

'That's true,' agreed Meliton. 'These days peasants are a useless bunch.'

'There's no escaping the fact, we get worse every year. Just consider the gentry, they're even feebler than the peasants now. These days gents might think they know everything, but they know things they don't need to know – and where's the sense in that? Fair breaks your heart to look at them . . . all skinny and weedy, like some Magyar or Frenchie. No class, no dignity – they're only gents by name. The poor devils've got no place in society, no work to do and you can never make out what they really want. Either they sit with their rod catching fish or they lie belly up reading a book. Or they're knocking around with the peasants and telling them all sorts of things. And there's those what's hungry and get jobs as clerks. And so they fritter their time away and it never enters their heads to try and get down to some real work. Time was when half the gentry were generals, but nowadays they're sheer trash!'

'They're very much poorer now,' said Meliton.

'They're poorer because God's taken their strength away. You can't go against God.'

Meliton stared fixedly at one point again. After a pause for thought he sighed the way steady, sober-minded people sigh and shook his head.

'And what's the reason for all this?' he said. 'It's because we sin so much, we've forgotten God and so the time is near when everything will come to an end. Honestly, you can't expect the world to last for ever. It mustn't outstay its welcome!'

The shepherd sighed and as if wishing to end that painful conversation he walked away from the birch and started counting the cattle in silence.

'Hey-hey-hey!' he shouted, 'where d'ye think you're all going, damn you! The devil himself's driven them into the firs! Halloo-loo-loo!'

He glared angrily and went over to the bushes to round up the herd. Meliton rose and strolled quietly along the edge of the wood.

He gazed at the ground beneath his feet and thought: he was still trying to remember at least one thing as yet untouched by death. Again, bright patches crept over the slanting belts of rain; they leapt into the tree tops and faded away in the wet foliage. Lady found a hedgehog under a bush and tried to attract her master's attention by howling and barking.

'You had an eclipse,[3] didn't you?' the shepherd cried out from behind the bushes.

'Yes, we did!' replied Meliton.

'I thought so. Everywhere folk are going on about it. It means, me friend, that there's disorder in heaven too. It didn't happen for nothing . . . Hey-hey-hey!'

After driving his herd out of the wood the shepherd leant against a birch, glanced at the sky and idly drew his pipe from his smock. As before he played mechanically, producing no more than five or six notes. The sounds that flew forth were hesitant, disjointed, wild and tuneless, as if he were holding the pipes for the very first time. But to Meliton, who was contemplating the world's impending ruin, there was something deeply mournful and heart-rending in his playing, something that he would have preferred not to hear. The highest, shrillest notes which trembled and broke off abruptly seemed to be weeping inconsolably, as though the pipe was sick and frightened, while the lowest notes somehow evoked the mist, the dejected trees and the grey skies. Such music harmonized with the weather, the old man and what he had been saying.

Meliton felt an urge to complain. He went up to the old man, looked at his sad, mocking face and muttered, 'And life's got worse, old man. It's more than flesh and blood can stand, what with bad harvests, poverty, cattle plagues the whole time, illness. We're racked by poverty, we are.'

The bailiff's podgy face turned crimson and took on a doleful, womanish expression. He twiddled his fingers as if looking for words to convey his vague feelings.

'I've eight children,' he continued, 'and a wife . . . my mother is still alive and all they pay me is ten roubles a month without lodging. The poverty's turned my wife into a real bitch and I'm on the bottle.

In actual fact, I'm a sober-minded, steady sort of chap, I've had some education. I'd like to be sitting peacefully at home but all day long I keep wandering around with my gun, just like a dog, because I can't stand it there. I hate my own home!'

Aware that his tongue was muttering the complete opposite of what he intended the bailiff waved his arm and continued bitterly, 'If the world's doomed to perish, the sooner the better! No point in dragging things out and letting people suffer for nothing!'

The old shepherd took the pipe from his lips, screwed up one eye and peered down the small mouthpiece. His face was sad and covered with large, tear-like splashes. He smiled and said, 'It's a pity, my friend. God, a real pity! The earth, forests, sky, animals – all these have been fashioned and fitted for some purpose, there's a reason behind everything. But it'll all come to nothing. It's folk I feel most sorry for.'

Suddenly a heavy squall rustled through the wood as it approached the edge. Meliton looked towards where the noise was coming from and buttoned his coat right up.

'I must get back to the village,' he said. 'Goodbye, old friend . . . what's your name?'

'Poor Luke.'

'Well, goodbye Luke. It's been nice talking to you. Lady, *ici*!'

When he had taken leave of the shepherd, Meliton trudged along the edge of the wood and then down to a meadow which gradually turned into a marsh. Water squelched underfoot and the reddish heads of sedge (its stems were still green and lush) bowed towards the earth as if afraid of being trampled. Beyond the marsh, on the banks of the Peschanka, about which the old shepherd had just been talking, stood willows, and beyond them, showing blue in the mist, could be seen the squire's threshing-barn. One sensed the proximity of that bleak time which nothing can avert, when the fields darken, when the earth grows muddy and cold, when the weeping willow seems sadder than ever and tears trickle down her trunk, when the cranes alone are able to flee universal disaster. And even they, as if afraid of offending despondent nature by voicing their joy, fill the skies with their mournful, plaintive song.

Meliton wandered towards the river and heard the sounds of the pipe gradually dying away behind him. He still felt the urge to complain. Sadly he looked on both sides and he felt unbearably sorry for the sky, the earth, the sun, the moon, the woods, his Lady; and when the pipe's highest note suddenly shrilled and hung in the air, trembling like the voice of someone weeping, he felt extraordinarily bitter and resentful at the disorder that was apparent in nature.

The top note quivered, broke off – and the panpipes were silent.

The Kiss

On 20 May, at eight o'clock in the evening, all six batteries of a reserve artillery brigade, on their way back to headquarters, stopped for the night at the village of Mestechki. At the height of all the confusion – some officers were busy with the guns, while others had assembled in the main square by the churchyard fence to receive their billetings – someone in civilian dress rode up from behind the church on a strange horse: it was small and dun-coloured with a fine neck and short tail, and seemed to move sideways instead of straight ahead, making small dancing movements with its legs as if they were being whipped. When the rider came up to the officers he doffed his hat and said, 'Our squire, His Excellency, Lieutenant-General von Rabbeck, invites you for tea and would like you to come now . . .'

The horse performed a bow and a little dance, and retreated with the same sideways motion. The rider raised his hat again and quickly disappeared behind the church on his peculiar horse.

'To hell with it!' some of the officers grumbled as they rode off to their quarters. 'We want to sleep and up pops this von Rabbeck with his tea! We know what *that* means all right!'

Every officer in the six batteries vividly remembered the previous year when they were on manoeuvres with officers from a Cossack regiment and had received a similar invitation from a landowning count, who was a retired officer. This hospitable and genial count had plied them with food and drink, would not hear of them returning to their billets and made them stay the night. That was all very well, of course, and they could not have hoped for better. But the trouble was that this retired officer was overjoyed beyond measure at having young men as his guests and he regaled them with stories from his glorious past until dawn, led them on a tour of the house, showed them his valuable paintings, old engravings and rare guns, and read out signed letters from eminent personages; and all this time the tired and weary officers listened, looked, pined for bed, and continuously yawned in their sleeves. When their host finally let them go, it was too late for bed.

Now, was this von Rabbeck one of the same breed? Whether he was or not, there was nothing they could do about it. The officers put clean uniforms on, smartened themselves up and went off en masse to look for the squire's house. On the square by the church they were told that they could either take the lower path leading down to the river behind the church, and then go along the bank to the garden, or they could ride direct from the church along the higher road which would bring them to the count's barns about a quarter of a mile from the village. The officers decided on the higher route.

'Who is this von Rabbeck?' they argued as they rode along. 'Is he the one who commanded a cavalry division at Plevna?'[1]

'No, that wasn't von Rabbeck, just Rabbe, and without the "von".'

'It's marvellous weather, anyway!'

The road divided when they reached the first barn: one fork led straight on and disappeared in the darkness of the evening, while the other turned towards the squire's house on the right. The officers took the right fork and began to lower their voices . . . Stone barns with red tiled roofs stood on both sides of the road and they had the heavy, forbidding look of some provincial barracks. Ahead of them were the lighted windows of the manor-house.

'That's a good sign, gentlemen!' one of the officers said. 'Our setter's going on in front. That means he scents game!'

Lieutenant Lobytko, a tall, strongly built officer, who was riding ahead of the others, who had no moustache (although he was over twenty-five there wasn't a trace of hair on his face), and who was renowned in the brigade for his keen senses and ability to sniff a woman out from miles away, turned round and said, 'Yes, there must be women here, my instinct tells me.'

The officers were met at the front door by von Rabbeck himself

– a fine-looking man of about sixty, wearing civilian clothes. He said how very pleased and happy he was to see the officers as he shook hands, but begged them most sincerely, in the name of God, to excuse him for not inviting them to stay the night, as two sisters with their children, his brothers and some neighbours had turned up, and he didn't have one spare room.

The general shook everyone's hand, apologized and smiled, but they could tell from his face that he wasn't nearly as pleased to have guests as last year's count and he had only asked them as it was the done thing. And, as they climbed the softly carpeted stairs and listened, the officers sensed that they had been invited only because it would have caused embarrassment if they had *not* been invited. At the sight of footmen dashing around lighting the lamps in the hall and upstairs, they felt they had introduced a note of uneasiness and anxiety into the house. And how could any host be pleased at having nineteen strange officers descend on a house where two sisters, children, brothers and neighbours had already arrived, most probably to celebrate some family anniversary. They were met in the ballroom upstairs by a tall, stately old lady with black eyebrows and a long face – the living image of Empress Eugénie. She gave them a majestic, welcoming smile and said how glad and happy she was to have them as guests and apologized for the fact that she and her husband weren't able to invite the officers to stay overnight on this occasion. Her beautiful, majestic smile, which momentarily disappeared every time she turned away from her guests, revealed that in her day she had seen many officers, that she had no time for them now, and that she had invited them and was apologizing only because her upbringing and social position demanded it.

The officers entered the large dining-room where about ten gentlemen and ladies, old and young, were sitting along one side of the table having tea. Behind their chairs, enveloped in a thin haze of cigar smoke, was a group of men with a rather lean, young, red-whiskered man in the middle, rolling his 'r's as he spoke out loud in English. Behind them, through a door, was a bright room with light blue furniture.

'Gentlemen, there's so many of you, it's impossible to introduce *everyone*!' the general was saying in a loud voice, trying to sound cheerful. 'So don't stand on ceremony, introduce yourselves!'

Some officers wore very serious, even solemn expressions; others forced a smile, and all of them felt awkward as they bowed rather indifferently and sat down to tea.

Staff-Captain Ryabovich, a short, stooping officer, with spectacles and lynx-like side whiskers, was more embarrassed than anyone else. While his fellow-officers were trying to look serious or force a smile, his face, lynx-like whiskers and spectacles seemed to be saying, 'I'm the shyest, most modest and most insignificant officer in the whole brigade!' When he first entered the dining-room and sat down to tea, he found it impossible to concentrate on any one face or object. All those faces, dresses, cut-glass decanters, steaming glasses, moulded cornices, merged into one composite sensation, making Ryabovich feel ill at ease, and he longed to bury his head somewhere. Like a lecturer at his first appearance in public, he could see everything in front of him well enough, but at the same time he could make little sense of it (physicians call this condition, when someone sees without understanding, 'psychic blindness'). But after a little while Ryabovich began to feel more at home, recovered his normal vision and began to take stock of his surroundings. Since he was a timid and unsociable person, he was struck above all by what he himself had never possessed – the extraordinary boldness of these unfamiliar people. Von Rabbeck, two elderly ladies, a young girl in a lilac dress, and the young man with red whiskers – Rabbeck's youngest son – had sat themselves very cunningly among the officers, as though it had all been rehearsed. Straight away they had launched into a heated argument, which the guests could not help joining. The girl in lilac very excitedly insisted that the artillery had a much easier time than either the cavalry or the infantry, while Rabbeck and the elderly ladies argued the contrary. A rapid conversational crossfire ensued. Ryabovich glanced at the lilac girl who was arguing so passionately about something that was so foreign to her, so utterly boring, and he could see artificial smiles flickering over her face.

Von Rabbeck and family skilfully drew the officers into the argument, at the same time watching their wine glasses with eagle eyes to check whether they were filled, that they had enough sugar, and one officer who wasn't eating biscuits or drinking any brandy worried them. The more Ryabovich looked and listened, the more he began to like this insincere but wonderfully disciplined family.

After tea the officers went into the ballroom. Lieutenant Lobytko's instinct had not failed him: the room was full of girls and young married women. Already this 'setter' lieutenant had positioned himself next to a young blonde in a black dress, bending over dashingly as though leaning on some invisible sabre, smiling and flirting with his shoulders. Most probably he was telling her some intriguing nonsense as the blonde glanced superciliously at his well-fed face and said, 'Really?'

If that 'setter' had had any brains, that cool 'Really?' should have told him that he would never be called 'to heel'.

The grand piano suddenly thundered out. The sounds of a sad waltz drifted through the wide-open windows and everyone remembered that outside it was spring, an evening in May, and they smelt the fragrance of the young leaves of the poplars, of roses and lilac. Ryabovich, feeling the effects of the brandy and the music, squinted at a window, smiled and watched the movements of the women. Now it seemed that the fragrance of the roses, the poplars and lilac wasn't coming from the garden but from the ladies' faces and dresses.

Rabbeck's son had invited a skinny girl to dance and waltzed twice round the room with her. Lobytko glided over the parquet floor as he flew up to the girl in lilac and whirled her round the room. They all began to dance . . . Ryabovich stood by the door with guests who were not dancing and watched. Not once in his life had he danced, not once had he put his arm round an attractive young woman's waist. He would usually be absolutely delighted when, with everyone looking on, a man took a young girl he hadn't met before by the waist and offered his shoulders for her to rest her hands on, but he could never imagine himself in that situation. There had been times when he envied his fellow-officers' daring and dashing ways and it made him very depressed. The realization that he was shy, round-shouldered, quite undistinguished, that he had a long waist, lynx-like side whiskers, hurt him deeply. But over the years this realization had become something of a habit and as he watched his friends dance or talk out loud he no longer envied them but was filled with sadness.

When the quadrille began, young von Rabbeck went over to the officers who were not dancing and invited two of them to a game of billiards. They accepted and left the great hall with him. As he had nothing else to do, and feeling he would like to take at least some part in what was going on, Ryabovich trudged off after them. First they went into the drawing-room, then down a narrow corridor with a glass ceiling, then into a room where three sleepy footmen leapt up from a sofa the moment they entered. Finally, after passing through a whole series of rooms, young Rabbeck and company reached a small billiard-room and the game began.

Ryabovich, who never played any games except cards, stood by the table and indifferently watched the players, cue in hand, walking up and down in their unbuttoned tunics, making puns and shouting things he could not understand. The players ignored him, only turning round to say, 'I beg your pardon', when one of them happened accidentally to nudge him with an elbow or prod him with a cue. Even before the first game was over, he was bored and began to feel he was not wanted, that he was in the way . . . He felt drawn back to the ballroom and walked away.

As he walked back he had a little adventure. Halfway, he realized he was lost – he knew very well he had to go by those three sleepy footmen, but already he had passed through five or six rooms and those footmen seemed to have vanished into thin air. He realized his mistake, retraced his steps a little and turned to the right, only to find himself in a small, dimly lit room he had not seen on the way to the billiard-room. He stood still for a minute or so, opened the first door he came to with determination and entered a completely dark room. Ahead of him he could see light coming through a crack in the door and beyond was the muffled sound of a sad mazurka. The windows here had been left open as they had in the ballroom and he could smell poplars, lilac and roses . . .

Ryabovich stopped, undecided what to do . . . Just then he was astonished to hear hurried footsteps, the rustle of a dress and a female voice whispering breathlessly, 'At last!' Two soft, sweet-smelling arms (undoubtedly a woman's) encircled his neck, a burning cheek pressed against his and at the same time there was the sound of a kiss. But immediately after the kiss the woman gave a faint cry and shrank backwards in disgust – that was how it seemed to Ryabovich.

He was on the point of crying out too and he rushed towards the bright chink in the door.

His heart pounded away when he was back in the hall and his hands trembled so obviously that he hastily hid them behind his back. At first he was tormented by shame and he feared everyone there knew he had just been embraced and kissed, and this made him hesitate and look around anxiously. But when he had convinced himself that everyone was dancing and gossiping just as peacefully as before, he gave himself up to a totally new kind of sensation, one he had never experienced before in all his life. Something strange was happening to him . . . his neck, which just a few moments ago had been embraced by sweet-smelling hands, seemed anointed with oil. And on his left cheek, just by his moustache, there was a faint, pleasant, cold, tingling sensation, the kind you get from peppermint drops and the more he rubbed the spot the stronger the tingling became. From head to heels he was overcome by a strange, new feeling which grew stronger every minute. He wanted to dance, speak to everyone, run out into the garden, laugh out loud. He completely forgot his stoop, his insignificant appearance, his lynx-like whiskers and 'vague appearance' (once he happened to hear some ladies saying this about him). When Rabbeck's wife went by he gave her such a broad, warm smile that she stopped and gave him a very searching look.

'I love this house so much!' he said, adjusting his spectacles.

The general's wife smiled and told him that the house still belonged to her father. Then she asked if his parents were still alive, how long he had been in the army, why he was so thin, and so on . . . When Ryabovich had replied, she moved on, leaving him smiling even more warmly and he began to think he was surrounded by the most wonderful people . . .

Mechanically, Ryabovich ate and drank everything he was offered at the dinner table, deaf to everything as he tried to find an explanation for what had just happened. It was a mysterious, romantic incident, but it wasn't difficult to explain. No doubt some girl or young married woman had a rendezvous with someone in that dark room, had waited for a long time, and then mistook Ryabovich for her hero in her nervous excitement. This was the most likely explanation, all the more so as Ryabovich had hesitated in the middle of the room, which made it look as though he were expecting someone . . .

'But who *is* she?' he thought as he surveyed the ladies' faces. 'She must be young, as old ladies don't have rendezvous. And intelligent – I could tell from the rustle of her dress, her smell, her voice.'

He stared at the girl in lilac and found her very attractive. She had beautiful shoulders and arms, a clever face and a fine voice. As he gazed at her, Ryabovich wanted *her*, no one else, to be that mysterious stranger . . . But she gave a rather artificial laugh and wrinkled her long nose, which made her look old. Then he turned to the blonde in black. She was younger, simpler and less affected, with charming temples and she sipped daintily from her wine glass. Now Ryabovich wanted her to be the stranger. But he soon discovered that she had a featureless face and he turned to her neighbour . . . 'It's hard to say,' he wondered dreamily. 'If I could just take the lilac girl's shoulders and arms away, add the blonde's temples, then take those eyes away from the girl on Lobytko's left, *then*.' He merged them all into one, so that he had an image of the girl who had kissed him, the image he desired so much, but which he just could not find among the guests around the table.

After dinner the officers, well-fed and slightly tipsy by now, began to make their farewells and expressed their thanks. Once again the hosts apologized for not having them stay the night.

'Delighted, gentlemen, absolutely delighted,' the general was saying and this time he meant it – probably because people are usually more sincere and better-humoured saying goodbye to guests than welcoming them.

'Delighted! Glad to see you back any time, so don't stand on ceremony. Which way are you going? The higher road? No, go through the garden, it's quicker.'

The officers went into the garden, where it seemed very dark and quiet after the bright lights and the noise. They did not say a word all the way to the gate. They were half-drunk, cheerful and contented, but the darkness and the silence made them pause for thought. Probably they were thinking the same as Ryabovich: would they ever see the day when they would own a large house, have a family, a garden, when *they* too would be able to entertain people (however much of a pretence this might be), feed them well, make them drunk and happy?

As they went through the garden gate they all started talking at once and, for no apparent reason, laughed out loud. Now they were descending the path that led down to the river and then ran along the water's edge, weaving its way around the bushes, the little pools of water and the willows which overhung the river. The bank and the path were barely visible, and the far side was plunged in darkness. Here and there were reflections of the stars in the water, quivering and breaking up into little patches – the only sign that the river was flowing fast. All was quiet. Sleepy sandpipers called plaintively from the far bank and on the near side a nightingale in a bush poured out its song, ignoring the passing officers.

The men paused by the bush, touched it, but still the nightingale sang.

'That's a bird for you!' approving voices murmured. 'Here we are, right next to him and he doesn't take a blind bit of notice! What a rascal!'

The path finally turned upwards and came out on to the high road by the church fence. The officers were exhausted from walking up the hill and sat down for a smoke. On the far bank they could make out a dim red light and they tried to pass the time by guessing whether it was a camp fire, a light in a window, or something else . . . Ryabovich looked at it and imagined that the light was winking at him and smiling, as though it knew all about that kiss.

When he reached his quarters Ryabovich quickly undressed and lay on his bed. In the same hut were Lobytko and Lieutenant

Merzlyakov, a gentle, rather quiet young man, who was considered well-educated in his own little circle. He was always reading the *European Herald*[2] when he had the chance and took it with him everywhere. Lobytko undressed, paced up and down for a long time, with the expression of a dissatisfied man, and sent the batman for some beer.

Merzlyakov lay down, placed a candle near his pillow and immersed himself in the *European Herald*.

'Who *is* she?' Ryabovich wondered as he glanced at the grimy ceiling. His neck still felt as if it had been anointed with oil and he had that tingling sensation around his mouth – just like peppermint drops. He had fleeting visions of the lilac girl's shoulders and arms, the temples and truthful eyes of the blonde in black, waists, dresses, brooches. He tried to fix these visions firmly in his mind, but they kept dancing about, dissolving, flickering. When these visions vanished completely against that darkened background everyone has when he closes his eyes, he began to hear hurried steps, rustling dresses, the sound of a kiss and he was gripped by an inexplicable, overwhelming feeling of joy. Just as he was abandoning himself to it, he heard the batman come back and report that there wasn't any beer. Lobytko became terribly agitated and started pacing up and down again.

'Didn't I tell you he's an idiot?' he said, stopping first in front of Ryabovich, then Merzlyakov. 'A man must really be a blockhead and idiot to come back without any beer! The man's a rogue, eh?'

'Of course, you won't find any beer in this place,' Merzlyakov said without taking his eyes off the *European Herald*.

'Oh, do you really think so?' Lobytko persisted. 'Good God, put me on the moon and I'll find you beer and women right away! Yes, I'll go now and find some . . . Call me a scoundrel if I don't succeed!'

He slowly dressed and pulled on his high boots. Then he finished his cigarette in silence and left.

'Rabbeck, Grabbeck, Labbeck,' he muttered, pausing in the hall. 'I don't feel like going on my own, dammit! Fancy a little walk, Ryabovich?'

There was no reply, so he came back, slowly undressed and got into bed. Merzlyakov sighed, put the *European Herald* away and snuffed the candle.

'Hm,' Lobytko murmured as he puffed his cigarette in the dark.

Ryabovich pulled the blankets over his head, curled himself into a ball and tried to merge the visions fleeting through his mind into one fixed image. But he failed completely. Soon he fell asleep and his last waking thought was of someone caressing him and making him happy, of something absurd and unusual, but nonetheless exceptionally fine and joyful, that had entered his life. And his dreams centred around this one thought.

When he woke up, the sensation of oil on his cheek and the minty tingling near his lips had vanished, but the joy of yesterday still filled his heart. Delighted, he watched the window frames, gilded now by the rising sun, and listened intently to the street noises. Outside, just by the window, he could hear loud voices – Lebedetsky, Ryabovich's battery commander, who had just caught up with the brigade, was shouting at his sergeant – simply because he had lost the habit of talking softly.

'Is there anything else?' he roared.

'When they were shoeing yesterday, sir, someone drove a nail into Pigeon's hoof. The medical orderly put clay and vinegar on it and they're keeping the horse reined, away from the others. And artificer Artemyev got drunk yesterday and the lieutenant had him tied to the fore-carriage of an auxiliary field-gun.'

And the sergeant had more to report. Karpov had forgotten the new cords for the trumpets and the stakes for the tents, and the officers had spent the previous evening as guests of General von Rabbeck. During the conversation, Lebedetsky's head and red beard appeared at the window. He blinked his short-sighted eyes at the sleepy officers and bade them good morning.

'Everything all right?' he asked.

'One of the shaft-horses damaged its withers – it was the new collar,' Lobytko answered, yawning.

The commander sighed, pondered for a moment and said in a loud voice, 'I'm still wondering whether to pay Aleksandra a visit, I really ought to go and see how she is. Well, goodbye for now, I'll catch you up by evening.'

A quarter of an hour later the brigade moved off. As it passed the general's barns, Ryabovich looked to the right where the house was. The blinds were drawn in all the windows. Clearly, everyone was still asleep. And the girl who had kissed Ryabovich the day before was sleeping too. He tried to imagine her as she slept and he had a clear and distinct picture of the wide-open windows, the little green branches peeping into her bedroom, the morning freshness, the smell of poplars, lilac and roses, her bed and the chair with that dress which had rustled the day before lying over it, tiny slippers, a watch on the table. But the actual features of that face, that sweet, dreamy smile, exactly what was most characteristic of her, slipped through his imagination like mercury through the fingers. When he had ridden about a quarter of a mile, he looked back. The yellow church, the house, the river and garden were flooded in sunlight and the river, with its bright green banks and its waters reflecting the light blue sky and glinting silver here and there, looked very beautiful. Ryabovich took a last look at Mestechki and he felt so sad, as if he were saying farewell to what was very near and dear to him.

But there were only long-familiar, boring scenes ahead of him. On both sides of the road there were fields of young rye and buckwheat, where crows were hopping about. Ahead, all he could see was dust and the backs of soldiers' heads; and behind, the same dust, the same faces. The brigade was led by a vanguard of four soldiers bearing sabres and behind them rode the military choristers, followed by trumpeters. Every now and then, like torchbearers in a funeral cortège, the vanguard and singers ignored the regulation distance and pushed on far ahead. Ryabovich rode alongside the first field-gun of the fifth battery and he could see the other four in front. These long, ponderous processions formed by brigades on the move can strike civilians as very peculiar, an unintelligible muddle, and non-military people just cannot fathom why a single field-gun has to be escorted by so many soldiers, why it has to be drawn by so many horses all tangled up in such strange harness, as if it really was such a terrible, heavy object. But Ryabovich understood everything perfectly well and for that reason he found it all extremely boring. He had long known why a hefty bombardier always rides with the officer at the head of every battery and why he is called an outrider. Immediately behind this bombardier came the riders on the first, then the middle-section trace-horses. Ryabovich knew that the horses to the left were saddle-horses, while those on the right were auxiliary – all this was very boring. The horsemen were followed by two shaft-horses, one ridden by a horseman with yesterday's dust still on his back and who had a clumsy-looking, very comical piece of wood fixed to his right leg. Ryabovich knew what it was for and did not find it funny. All the riders waved their whips mechanically and shouted now and again. As for the field-gun, it was an ugly thing. Sacks of oats covered with tarpaulin lay on the fore-carriage and the gun itself was hung with kettles, kitbags and little sacks: it resembled a small harmless animal which had been surrounded, for some reason, by men and horses. On the side sheltered from the wind a team of six strode along, swinging their arms. This gun was followed by more bombardiers, riders, shaft-horses and another field-gun – just as ugly and uninspiring as the first – lumbering along in the rear. After the second gun came a third, then a fourth with an officer riding alongside (there are six batteries to a brigade and four guns to a battery). The whole procession stretched about a quarter of a mile and ended with the baggage wagons, where a most likeable creature plodded thoughtfully along, his long-eared head drooping: this was Magar the donkey, brought from Turkey by a certain battery commander.

Ryabovich looked apathetically at all those necks and faces in front and behind. At any other time he would have dozed off, but now he was immersed in new, pleasant thoughts. When the brigade had first set off, he had tried to convince himself that the incident of the kiss was only some unimportant, mysterious adventure and that essentially it was trivial and too ridiculous for serious thought. But very quickly he waved logic aside and gave himself up to his dreams. First he pictured himself in von Rabbeck's drawing-room, sitting next to a girl who resembled both the girl in lilac and the blonde in black. Then he closed his eyes and imagined himself with another, completely strange girl, with very indeterminate features: in his thoughts he spoke to her, caressed her and leaned his head on her shoulder. Then he thought of war and separation, reunion, dinner with his wife and children . . .

'Brakes on!' rang out the command every time they went downhill. He shouted the command too, and feared that his own shouts would shatter his daydreams and bring him back to reality.

As they passed some estate, Ryabovich peeped over the fence into the garden. There he saw a long avenue, straight as a ruler, strewn with yellow sand and lined with young birches. With the eagerness of a man who has surrendered himself to daydreaming, he imagined tiny female feet walking over the yellow sand. And, quite unexpectedly, he had a clear mental picture of the girl who had kissed him, the girl he had visualized the previous evening during dinner. This image had planted itself in his mind and would not leave him.

At midday someone shouted from a wagon in the rear, 'Attention, eyes left! Officers!'

The brigadier drove up in an open carriage drawn by two white horses. He ordered it to stop near the second battery and shouted something no one understood. Several officers galloped over to him, Ryabovich among them.

'Well, what's the news?' asked the brigadier, blinking his red eyes. 'Anyone ill?'

When they had replied, the brigadier, a small skinny man, chewed for a moment, pondered and then turned to one of the officers: 'One of your drivers, on the third gun, has taken his knee-guard off and the devil's hung it on the fore-carriage. Reprimand him!'

He looked up at Ryabovich and continued: 'It strikes me your harness breeches are too long.'

After a few more tiresome comments, the brigadier glanced at Lobytko and grinned. 'You look down in the dumps today, Lieutenant Lobytko. Pining for Madame Lopukhov, eh? Gentlemen, he's pining for Madame Lopukhov!'

Madame Lopukhov was a very plump, tall lady, well past forty. The brigadier, who had a passion for large women, no matter what age, suspected his officers nurtured similar passions. They smiled politely. Then the brigadier, delighted with himself for having made a very amusing, cutting remark, roared with laughter, tapped his driver on the back and saluted. The carriage drove off.

'All the things I'm dreaming about now and which seem impossible, out of this world, are in fact very ordinary,' Ryabovich thought as he watched the clouds of dust rising in the wake of the brigadier's carriage. 'It's all so very ordinary, everyone experiences it . . . The brigadier, for example. He was in love once, now he's married, with children. Captain Vachter is married and loved, despite having an extremely ugly red neck and no waistline. Salmanov is coarse and too much of a Tartar, but *he* had an affair that finished in marriage. I'm the same as everyone else . . . sooner or later I'll have to go through what they did . . .'

And he was delighted and encouraged by the thought that he was just an ordinary man, leading an ordinary life. Now he was bold enough to picture *her* and his happiness as much as he liked and he gave full rein to his imagination.

In the evening, when the brigade had reached its destination and the officers were resting in their tents, Ryabovich, Merzlyakov and Lobytko gathered round a trunk and had supper. Merzlyakov took his time, holding his *European Herald* on his knees and reading it as he slowly munched his food.

Lobytko could not stop talking and kept filling his glass with beer, while Ryabovich, whose head was rather hazy from dreaming all day long, said nothing as he drank. Three glasses made him tipsy and weak and he felt an irrepressible longing to share his new feelings with his friends.

'A strange thing happened to me at the Rabbecks,' he said, trying to sound cool and sarcastic. 'I went to the billiard-room, you know . . .'

He began to tell them, in great detail, all about the kiss, but after a minute fell silent. In that one minute he had told them everything and he was astonished when he considered how little time was needed to tell his story: he had imagined it would take until morning. After he heard the story, Lobytko – who was a great liar and therefore a great sceptic – looked at him in disbelief and grinned. Merzlyakov twitched his eyebrows and kept his eyes glued to the *European Herald* as he calmly remarked, 'Damned if I know what to make of it! Throwing herself round a stranger's neck without saying a word first . . . She must have been a mental case . . .'

'Yes, some kind of neurotic,' Ryabovich agreed.

'Something similar happened to me once,' Lobytko said, assuming a frightened look. 'Last year I was travelling to Kovno . . . second class. The compartment was chock-full and it was impossible to sleep. So I tipped the guard fifty copeks . . . he took my luggage and got me a berth in a sleeper. I lay down and covered myself with a blanket. It was dark, you understand. Suddenly someone was touching my shoulder and breathing into my face. So I moved my arm and felt an elbow. I opened my eyes and – can you imagine! – it was a woman. Black eyes, lips as red as the best salmon, nostrils breathing passion, breasts like buffers! . . .'

'Just a minute,' Merzlyakov calmly interrupted. 'I don't dispute what you said about her breasts, but how could you see her lips if it was dark?'

Lobytko tried to wriggle out by poking fun at Merzlyakov's obtuseness and this jarred on Ryabovich. He went away from the trunk, lay down and vowed never again to tell his secrets.

Camp life fell back into its normal routine. The days flashed by, each exactly the same as the other. All this time Ryabovich felt, thought and behaved like someone in love. When his batman brought him cold water in the mornings, he poured it over his head and each time he remembered that there was something beautiful and loving in his life.

In the evenings, when his fellow-officers talked about love and women, he would listen very attentively, sitting very close to them and assuming the habitual expression of a soldier hearing stories about battles he himself fought in. On those evenings when senior officers, led by 'setter' Lobytko, carried out 'sorties' on the local village, in true Don Juan style, Ryabovich went along with them and invariably returned feeling sad, deeply guilty and imploring *her* forgiveness. In his spare time, or on nights when he couldn't sleep, when he wanted to recall his childhood days, his parents, everything that was near and dear to him, he would always find himself thinking of Mestechki instead, of that strange horse, of von Rabbeck and his wife, who looked like the Empress Eugénie, of that dark room with the bright chink in the door.

On 31 August he left camp – not with his own brigade, however, but with two batteries. All the way he daydreamed and became very excited, as though he were going home. He wanted passionately to see that strange horse again, the church, those artificial Rabbecks, the dark room. Some inner voice, which so often deceives those in love, whispered that he was *bound* to see her again. And he was tormented by such questions as: how could he arrange a meeting, what would she say, had she forgotten the kiss? If the worst came to the worst, he would at least have the pleasure of walking through that dark room and remembering . . .

Towards evening, that familiar church and the white barns appeared on the horizon. His heart began to pound. He did not listen to what the officer riding next to him was saying, he was oblivious of everything and looked eagerly at the river gleaming in the distance, at the loft above which pigeons were circling in the light of the setting sun.

As he rode up to the church and heard the quartermaster speaking, he expected a messenger on horseback to appear from behind the fence any minute and invite the officers to tea . . . but the quartermaster read the billeting list out, the officers dismounted and strolled off into the village – and no messenger came.

'The people in the village will tell Rabbeck we're here and he'll send for us,' Ryabovich thought as he went into his hut. He just could not understand why a fellow-officer was lighting a candle, why the batmen were hurriedly heating the samovars.

He was gripped by an acute feeling of anxiety. He lay down, then got up and looked out of the window to see if the messenger was coming. But there was no one. He lay down again but got up again after half an hour, unable to control his anxiety, went out into the street and strode off towards the church.

The square near the fence was dark and deserted. Some soldiers were standing in a row at the top of the slope, saying nothing. They jumped when they saw Ryabovich and saluted. He acknowledged the salute and went down the familiar path.

The entire sky over the far bank was flooded with crimson; the moon was rising. Two peasant women were talking loudly and picking cabbage leaves as they walked along the edge of a kitchen garden. Beyond the gardens were some dark huts. On the near bank everything was much the same as in May: the path, the bushes, the willows overhanging the river . . . only there was no bold nightingale singing, no fragrant poplars or young grass. Ryabovich reached the garden and peered over the gate. It was dark and quiet and all he could see were the white trunks of the nearest birches and here and there little patches of avenue – everything else had merged into one black mass. Ryabovich looked hard, listened eagerly, and after standing and waiting for about a quarter of an hour, without hearing a sound or seeing a single light, he trudged wearily away . . .

He went down to the river, where he could see the general's bathing-hut and towels hanging over the rail on the little bridge. He went on to the bridge, stood for a moment and aimlessly fingered the towels. They felt cold and rough. He looked down at the water . . . the current was swift and purled, barely audibly, against the piles of the hut. The red moon was reflected in the water near the left bank; tiny waves rippled through the reflection, pulling it apart and breaking it up into little patches, as if trying to bear it away.

'How stupid, how very stupid!' Ryabovich thought as he looked at the fast-flowing water. Now, when he hoped for nothing, that adventure of the kiss, his impatience, his vague longings and disillusionment appeared in a new light. He didn't think it at all strange that he hadn't waited for the general's messenger or that he would never see the girl who had kissed him by mistake. On the contrary, he would have thought it strange if he *had* seen her . . .

The water raced past and he did not know where or why; it had flowed just as swiftly in May, when it grew from a little stream into a large river, flowed into the sea, evaporated and turned into rain. Perhaps this was the same water flowing past. To what purpose?

And the whole world, the whole of life, struck Ryabovich as a meaningless, futile joke. As he turned his eyes from the water to the sky, he remembered how fate had accidentally caressed him – in the guise of an unknown woman. He recalled the dreams and visions of that summer and his life seemed terribly empty, miserable, colourless . . . When he returned to his hut, none of the officers was there.

The batman reported that they had all gone to 'General Fontryabkin's' – he'd sent a messenger on horseback with the invitation. There was a brief flicker of joy in his heart, but he snuffed it out at once, lay on his bed and in defiance of fate – as though he wanted to bring its wrath down on his own head – he did not go to the general's.

Verochka

Ivan Alekseyevich Ognyov remembers how the French windows rattled as he opened them that August evening and went out onto the verandah. Then he was wearing a light cape[1] and the broad-brimmed straw hat that now lay under his bed gathering dust with his topboots. In one hand he held a large bundle of books and notebooks, in the other a stout, knotty walking-stick.

In the doorway, lighting the way with a lamp, stood Kuznetsov his host, a bald old man with a long grey beard and wearing a snow-white piqué jacket. The old man was smiling and nodding benevolently.

'Goodbye, old chap!' Ognyov shouted to him.

Kuznetsov put the lamp on a small table and came out onto the verandah. Two long narrow shadows swept down the steps towards the flowerbeds, swayed for a moment and bumped their heads against the trunks of the lime trees.

'Goodbye – and thanks again, my dear fellow!' Ivan Alekseyevich said. 'Thanks for your generosity, your kindness, your affection . . . I shan't forget your hospitality as long as I live. You're such a good person, your daughter's so nice, everyone here's so kind, cheerful, generous . . . Really, such wonderful people that I'm lost for words!'

Carried away by his feelings and the effects of the home-made liqueurs he had just drunk, Ognyov spoke in a singing voice, like a theology student, and he was so touched that he expressed his emotions not so much in words as by blinking his eyes and twitching his shoulders. Kuznetsov, who was also slightly tipsy and overcome with emotion, leaned towards the young man and kissed him.

'I've become so used to you – it's as if I were your gun-dog!'

Ognyov continued. 'I've been coming here nearly every day and stayed overnight a dozen times. I've drunk so much of your liqueurs it doesn't bear thinking about! But what I have to thank you for most of all, Gavriil Petrovich, is for your help and cooperation. Without you I would have been busy with my statistics here until October. And that's just what I'm going to put in my preface: "It is my duty to express my gratitude to Kuznetsov, President of N— District Council for his kind assistance." Statistics has a brill-i-ant future![2] My profound respects to Vera Gavrilovna and please tell the doctors, the two magistrates and your secretary that I shall never forget their help. And now, old friend, let's embrace and kiss for the last time!'

Limp with emotion, Ognyov kissed the old man again and started going down the steps. On the bottom step he turned round.

'Shall we ever meet again?'

'God knows!' the old man replied. 'Probably not!'

'Yes, that's true. Nothing will induce you to go to St Petersburg and it's hardly likely I'll ever come back to this district. Well – goodbye!'

'Why don't you leave your books here?' Kuznetsov shouted after him. 'Why drag all that weight around? I could send them over tomorrow with one of the servants.'

But Ognyov was listening no longer and he quickly walked away from the house. Warmed by the liqueurs, at heart he felt glowing, cheerful – and sad. On the way he thought how often in life one chances to meet splendid people and what a pity it was that all that is left of these encounters is memories. It is the same when one glimpses some cranes on the horizon and a gentle gust of wind carries their mournfully exultant cries towards you. But a moment later, however eagerly you peer into the blue distance, you cannot see one speck or hear one sound – so people's faces and voices flash through our lives and are swallowed up by the past, leaving nothing but worthless scraps of memories. Having lived since early spring in N— district and visited the amiable Kuznetsovs almost every day, Ivan Ognyov had come to look upon the old man, his daughter, the servants as his own family; he had become familiar with every little detail of that house, the cosy verandah, the winding garden paths, the silhouettes of the trees over the kitchen and the bath-house. But the moment he passed through the garden gate all this would become but a memory, losing for him its meaning as part of reality for ever, and after one or two years all these cherished images would grow dim in his mind and fade together with the fruits and fancies of his imagination.

'Nothing in life is as precious as people!' thought Ognyov, deeply moved as he strode along the path towards the gate. 'Nothing!'

It was still and warm in the garden. A scent of still-blossoming mignonette, tobacco plant and heliotrope wafted from the flowerbeds. The spaces between the shrubs and tree trunks were filled with delicate, filmy mist saturated with moonlight; what Ognyov remembered for long afterwards were the spectral wisps of mist which were slowly but perceptibly following each other across the paths. The moon stood high above the garden and beneath it transparent patches of mist were hurrying eastwards. The whole world seemed to consist solely of black silhouettes and wandering white shadows. Seeing the mist on a moonlit August night almost for the first time in his life, Ognyov thought that it was not nature that he was witnessing but a stage set, where some clumsy pyrotechnists, intending to illumine the garden with Bengal lights, had concealed themselves in the shrubs and were discharging clouds of white smoke together with their flares.

As Ognyov approached the garden gate a dark shadow moved away from the low fence to meet him.

'Vera Gavrilovna!' he joyfully exclaimed. 'It's you! I've been looking for you everywhere . . . I wanted to say goodbye . . . Well, goodbye then, I'm leaving.'

'So early? It's only eleven o'clock.'

'Well, it's time I went. I've a three-mile walk and I haven't even packed yet. I have to be up early tomorrow.'

Before Ognyov stood Kuznetsov's daughter Vera, a girl of twenty-one, sad-faced as usual, carelessly dressed and most attractive. Young women who daydream a great deal and who spend days lying around lazily reading whatever comes to hand, who are bored and melancholy, generally tend to dress carelessly. To those of them whom nature has endowed with taste and a feeling for beauty this slight carelessness lends its own special charm. At least, when Ognyov later recalled pretty Verochka, he couldn't picture her without that loose-fitting blouse that hung creased in deep folds at the waist without touching her body, or that curl which had come loose from her piled-up hair onto her brow, or that red knitted shawl with the shaggy bobbles at the edges that was sadly draped over Verochka's shoulders in the evenings like a flag in calm weather, lying crumpled up during the day in the hall near the men's caps or on the chest in the dining-room and unceremoniously slept on by the old cat. That shawl and those creases in her blouse conveyed a feeling of idle ease, domesticity and placidity. Perhaps it was because he liked Vera that he saw in every button and frill something warm, cosy and innocent, something fine and poetic – just what was lacking in cold, insincere women with no feeling for beauty.

Verochka had a good figure, a regular profile and pretty, curly hair. Ognyov, who hadn't seen many women in his lifetime, thought she was beautiful.

'Well, I'm leaving,' he said, bidding her farewell at the gate. 'Think kindly of me! Thanks for everything!'

In that same singing, theology student's voice in which he had talked to the old man, blinking and twitching his shoulders again, he started to thank Verochka for her kindness, hospitality and cordiality.

'I mentioned you in every letter to my mother,' he said. 'If everyone were like you and your papa life would be a bed of roses. You're such wonderful people. So unpretentious, so friendly and sincere!'

'Where are you going now?' Verochka asked.

'First to my mother's at Oryol for a couple of weeks, then back to my work in St Petersburg.'

'And after that?'

'After that? I'll be working all winter and come spring it's back to somewhere in the provinces to collect material. Well, be happy, live a hundred years . . . Think kindly of me. We shan't meet again.'

Ognyov stooped and kissed Verochka's hand. And then, in mute emotion, he straightened his cape and rearranged his bundle of books.

'The mist's really come down tonight!' he said after a short pause.

'Yes. You haven't left anything at our place have you?'

'No, I don't think so . . .'

Ognyov stood for several seconds in silence, then he turned awkwardly towards the gate and walked out of the garden.

'Just a moment,' Verochka said, following him. 'I'll come with you as far as the wood.'

They set off along the path. Now there were no trees to obscure the view and one could see the sky and into the far distance. The whole of nature seemed to be hiding behind a gauzy, transparent haze, through which she gaily peered in all her beauty. Where the mist was thicker and whiter it lay unevenly near the ricks and bushes, or floated wispily across the path, clinging close to the earth as if trying not to spoil the view. Through the haze the whole path was visible as far as the wood, with dark ditches along its sides where thin bushes grew, trapping vagrant patches of mist. About a quarter of a mile from the gate they could see the dark strip of the Kuznetsovs' wood.

'Why has she come with me?' thought Ognyov. 'Now I'll have to see her back.' But after glancing at Verochka's profile he smiled warmly and said, 'I don't really feel like leaving in such wonderful weather. A truly romantic night – with the moon, silence – all the trimmings! Do you know what, Verochka? I'm twenty-nine, but I've never had a single love affair. Not one romantic episode in my whole life, so I know of lovers' trysts, paths of sighs and kisses only at second-hand. It's not normal! When you're cooped up in your room in town you don't realize what you're missing, but out here in the fresh country air you're very conscious of it. Somehow it's rather annoying.'

'Why are you like this?'

'I don't know. Probably because I've never had the time, but perhaps it's simply because I've never happened to meet the kind of women who . . . In fact, I don't have many friends and I never go out.'

For about three hundred paces the young pair walked in silence. Ognyov kept glancing at Verochka's bare head and her shawl and one after the other the memories of those spring and summer days came flooding back. That was when, far from his dreary Petersburg room, taking such delight in the kind attentions of fine people, in nature and in the work he loved that he failed to notice how dawn passed into sunset glow and how, presaging summer's end, first the nightingale, then the quail and soon afterwards the corncrake ceased their song ... Time had flown past unnoticed and that meant life had been so good, so easy. He began to recall aloud how reluctantly he, a young man of modest means, unaccustomed to society and travel, had come at the end of April to N— district, how he had been expecting to find boredom, solitude and an indifference to statistics[3] which he considered now queen of the sciences. Arriving one April morning at the little provincial town of N— he had put up at the inn kept by the Old Believer[4] Ryabukhin, where for twenty copecks a day they had provided a bright clean room, with the restriction that he should smoke out of doors. After a short rest and after discovering who was president of the rural council, he at once set off on foot to see Gavriil Petrovich Kuznetsov. The walk took him through two miles of lush meadows and young woodland. Beneath the clouds, filling the air with their silvery notes, skylarks hovered, whilst rooks circled over cornfields that were turning green, sedately and decorously flapping their wings.

'Heavens!' Ognyov had thought in surprise. 'Do they always breathe air like this here or does it smell like this just for today, in honour of my arrival?'

Expecting a cold, formal reception, he had entered the Kuznetsovs' house timidly, looking around distrustfully and shyly tugging his beard. At first the old man had frowned and failed to understand how the rural council could be of use to that young man with his statistics, but when Ognyov explained at length what statistical material was and where it was collected, Kuznetsov brightened up, smiled and began to examine his notebooks with childish curiosity. That same evening Ognyov was already dining with the Kuznetsovs, the potent liqueurs rapidly went to his head, and as he glanced at those placid faces and the lazy movements of his new friends, his body was filled with that delicious, drowsy indolence which makes one want to sleep, stretch oneself out and smile. And his new friends looked at him benignly, inquiring whether his father and mother were still alive, how much he earned a month and how often he went to the theatre.

Ognyov recalled his journeys through the neighbouring districts, the picnics, the fishing parties and the group excursion to the convent to see Mother Superior Martha, who gave each of the visitors a bead purse. He recalled those heated, endless, typically Russian arguments when the disputants, spluttering and banging their fists on the table, misunderstand and interrupt each other, contradict themselves with every sentence without even noticing, constantly change the subject and after arguing for two or three hours burst into loud laughter and exclaim: 'God alone knows what we've been arguing about! We began on a cheerful note and finished on a sad one!'

'Do you remember when you and I and the doctor rode over to Shestovo?' Ognyov asked Verochka as they approached the wood. 'That was when I met the holy fool.[5] I gave him five copecks and he crossed himself three times and flung it into the rye. Heavens, I'll be taking so many impressions away with me that if I could gather them into a solid mass they'd make a sizeable gold ingot! I don't understand why clever, sensitive people should herd together in St Petersburg and Moscow and not come out here. Is there really more breathing space on Nevsky Avenue and in those huge damp houses than here? Honestly, that existence in furnished rooms, packed from top to bottom with artists, academics and journalists, has always struck me as a complete sham!'

Twenty paces from the wood the path was crossed by a little narrow bridge with small pillars at the corners. This bridge always served as a brief stopping-place for the Kuznetsovs and their guests during their evening walks. From here, those who were so inclined could draw echoes from the wood and one could see the path disappearing into a dark cutting.

'Well, here's the bridge!' Ognyov said. 'You should turn back now.'

Verochka stopped and drew a deep breath.

'Let's sit down for a moment,' she said, sitting on one of the pillars. 'Everyone usually sits here to say goodbye before they leave.'

Ognyov settled himself beside her on his pile of books and carried on talking. Vera was breathing heavily from the walk and she wasn't looking at Ognyov, but to one side, so that he couldn't see her face.

'And suppose we suddenly meet in ten years' time?' he said. 'What shall we be like then? By then you'll be the respected mother of a family and I'll be the author of some respected, totally useless collection of statistical articles[6] as fat as forty thousand others. We shall meet and talk over the old days . . . Now we're more conscious of the present, it absorbs and excites us, but when we meet ten years from now we shan't remember the date or the month or even the year when we last met on this bridge. Most likely you will have changed by then. Do you think you'll have changed?'

Vera shuddered and turned her face to him.

'What?' she asked.

'I was just asking . . .'

'I'm sorry, I didn't hear what you were saying.'

Only then did Ognyov notice the change that had come over Vera. She was pale and breathing erratically, and her tremulous breathing communicated itself to her hands, lips and head; two curls instead of the customary one came loose and fell onto her forehead . . . She was evidently trying to avoid looking him in the eye and in an effort to conceal her agitation she kept adjusting her collar as if it were cutting into her neck and shifting her red shawl from one shoulder to the other.

'You must be cold,' Ognyov said. 'Sitting in the mist isn't very healthy. Let me see you *nach Hause*.'[7]

Vera said nothing.

'What's wrong?' Ognyov asked, smiling. 'You're so quiet, you don't answer my questions. Aren't you well – or are you cross?'

Vera pressed the palm of her hand firmly to the cheek that was turned towards him and immediately jerked it away.

'It's too awful,' she whispered with a look of intense pain. 'Too awful!'

'What's awful?' asked Ognyov, shrugging his shoulders and making no attempt to conceal his surprise. 'What's the matter?'

Still breathing heavily and twitching her shoulders Vera turned her back to him and gazed up at the sky for half a minute.

'I must speak to you, Ivan Alekseyevich,' she said.

'I'm listening.'

'It may seem strange to you . . . you'll be surprised, but I really don't care.'

Ognyov shrugged his shoulders again and prepared to listen.

'You see,' Verochka began, bowing her head and fingering a bobble on her shawl, 'this is what . . . I wanted to tell you . . . it will seem strange and . . . silly . . . but . . . I can't bear it any longer!'

Vera's words turned into an indistinct mumble and suddenly dissolved in sobs. The girl hid her face in her shawl, bowed her head even lower and wept bitterly. Ivan Alekseyevich cleared his throat in his confusion and, not knowing what to say or do, looked around in despair. Unaccustomed to sobbing and tears he felt that his own eyes were beginning to smart.

'Well really!' he stammered in dismay. 'Vera Gavrilovna! I'm asking you – whatever's the matter? Aren't you well, my dear? Or has someone upset you? If you tell me then perhaps I can . . . help.'

And when, in his efforts to console her, he allowed himself carefully to take her hands from her face, she smiled at him through her tears.

'I . . . I love you!' she said.

These words, so simple and ordinary, were spoken in simple, human language, but Ognyov turned away from Verochka in utter confusion and stood up – and his confusion was followed by panic.

That sad, glowing feeling and the sentimental mood induced by fond farewells and liqueurs suddenly evaporated and gave way to an acutely unpleasant sensation of awkwardness. As though his feelings had suffered an upheaval, he cast a sidelong glance at Verochka – and now that she had declared her love for him and shed that inaccessibility which is so attractive in a woman, she struck him as somehow shorter, plainer, darker.

'What's happening to me?' he asked himself in horror. 'Now . . . really . . . do I love her . . . or don't I? That's the problem!'

And now that the most important and difficult thing had finally been said, Vera breathed easily and freely again. She too stood up, looked Ognyov straight in the eye and started speaking quickly, passionately, irrepressibly.

Just as someone suddenly startled cannot recall afterwards the exact sequence of sounds that accompanied the catastrophe which stunned him, Ognyov cannot remember Verochka's words or phrases. All he remembers is the general drift of what she said, Verochka herself and the feelings that her words aroused. He remembers that voice, stifled and somewhat hoarse with emotion, and the rare music and passion of her intonation. Weeping and laughing, tears glistening on her eyelashes, she confessed that from the very first days of their friendship she had been struck by his originality, his intellect, his kind, clever eyes, by his aspirations and his aims in life; that she had fallen in love with him passionately, madly, deeply; that whenever she went from the garden into the house during the summer and saw his cape in the hall or heard his voice in the distance, her heart would thrill in anticipation of happiness. Even his weakest jokes made her laugh, in every figure in his notebooks she saw something exceptionally wise, majestic – and his knotty walking-stick seemed more beautiful than the trees themselves.

The wood, the wisps of mist and the dark ditches on the sides of the path seemed hushed as they listened to her. But in Ognyov's heart something strange and unpleasant was happening. When she declared her love Verochka had been enchantingly appealing, had spoken nobly and passionately; but now, instead of the pleasure and rejoicing in life that he would have liked to have felt, he experienced nothing but pity for her, pain, and regret that such a fine person should be suffering because of him. Heaven alone knew whether he was motivated by cold logic or if that incurable habit of remaining coolly detached which so often prevents people from living life to the full was manifesting itself, but Verochka's rapture and suffering struck him as cloying, trivial. And at the same time a feeling rebelled within him, whispering that all he was seeing and hearing now, as far as nature and personal happiness were concerned, was more serious than any statistics, books, eternal verities . . . And he was angry and reproached himself, although he did not understand where exactly he was to blame.

And to compound his embarrassment he had absolutely no idea what to say – yet speak he must. To tell her bluntly, 'I don't love you' was beyond him, nor could he bring himself to say 'Yes', since for all his soul-searching he could not find one spark of feeling within him . . .

He remained silent while she told him that for her there could be no greater happiness than to see him, to follow him wherever he wanted, there and then, to be his wife and helper, and that if he left her she would die of grief.

'I can't live here any more!' she said, wringing her hands. 'I'm sick of this house, these woods and the air. I cannot bear this perpetual peace, this aimless life. I cannot stand all these colourless, dull people – so alike you can't tell one from the other! They're all so well-meaning and good-natured only because they're well fed and because they don't have to suffer or struggle. But it's just to those great damp houses where people suffer, where drudgery and poverty make them bitter, that I *do* want to go!'

This too struck Ognyov as affected and frivolous. When Verochka had finished he still had no idea what to say, but silence was impossible, so he mumbled, "Vera Gavrilovna, I'm most grateful to you, although I do feel that I've done nothing to deserve such feelings on your part. Secondly, as a man of honour, I ought to tell you that happiness is based on . . . reciprocity . . . that is . . . when both parties love equally . . .'

But Ognyov immediately felt ashamed of his mumbling and stopped. He sensed at that moment that his expression was stupid, guilty, lifeless, that it was strained and false. Vera must have read the truth in his face because suddenly she became serious, turned pale and bowed her head.

'Please forgive me,' Ognyov muttered, unable to bear the silence. 'I have so much respect for you that this really hurts me!'

Vera turned sharply away and rapidly walked towards the house. Ognyov followed her.

'No, don't bother!' Vera said, waving him away. 'Don't come with me, I can go by myself . . .'

'But . . . I must see you home . . . after all . . .'

Everything he said, to the very last word, struck Ognyov as flat and loathsome. His feeling of guilt increased with every step he took. He fumed, clenched his fists and cursed his coldness and clumsiness with women. In an attempt to stir some measure of feeling he glanced at Verochka's pretty figure, at her hair and the traces left by her tiny feet on the dusty path; he recalled her words and tears, but all this merely moved him: it did not excite him.

'Ah well, you can't force yourself to fall in love!' he assured himself – and at the same time he thought, 'but when shall I ever fall in love without forcing myself? After all, I'm nearly thirty! I've never met anyone better than Verochka and I never shall . . . Oh, this wretched old age! Old age at thirty!'

Verochka walked ahead of him, quickening her steps and without looking back, her head bowed. It seemed that in her grief she had grown thinner and narrower in the shoulders . . .

'I can imagine what's going on inside her now,' he thought as he looked at her back. 'She must be feeling so ashamed and miserable that she wishes she were dead! Heavens, there's enough life, poetry and meaning in all this to melt a stone . . . But I'm . . . I'm stupid, ridiculous!'

At the gate Vera glanced back at him for an instant, wrapped her shawl more tightly around her hunched shoulders and hurried down the path.

Ognyov was left alone. As he went back to the wood he walked slowly, constantly stopping to look round at the gate and his whole bearing seemed to express utter disbelief in what he had done. He searched for Verochka's footprints along the path and could not believe that a young woman whom he liked so much had just declared her love and that he had so clumsily and boorishly 'spurned' her. For the first time in his life he had learnt from experience how little of what we do depends on our goodwill and he found himself in the position of a decent, sincere man who had brought cruel, undeserved suffering upon his neighbour despite himself.

His conscience troubled him and when Verochka disappeared from view it began to dawn on him that he had lost something very precious and close that he would never find again. He felt that with Verochka part of his youth had slipped away and that those moments he had lived through so fruitlessly would never be repeated.

When he reached the bridge he stopped and reflected. He wanted to find the reason for his strange coldness. It did not lie outside, but within him – that was clear. He frankly admitted to himself that it was not the cool detachment of which clever people boast so often, or that of a self-centred fool, but simply spiritual impotence, a lack of any deep appreciation of beauty, premature ageing brought on by his upbringing, his frantic struggle to earn a living, his bachelor existence in rented rooms.

From the bridge he walked slowly, reluctantly as it were, into the wood. Here, where in places sharply outlined patches of moonlight appeared against the impenetrable darkness and where he was aware of nothing but his own thoughts, he longed passionately to recapture what he had lost.

And Ognyov remembers going back to the house. Spurring himself on with memories, forcing himself to conjure up Verochka's image, he swiftly strode towards the garden. By now the mist had vanished from the path and the garden, and the bright moon looked down as if newly washed; only the sky in the east was hazy and overcast . . . Ognyov remembers his cautious steps, those dark windows, the heavy scent of heliotrope and mignonette. The familiar Karo, amicably wagging his tail, came up and sniffed his hand. This was the only living creature that saw Ognyov walk twice around the house, pause beneath Verochka's dark window and leave the garden with a deep sigh and gesture of despair.

An hour later he was in the town. Weary and despondent, he leaned his body and burning face against the inn gates and banged the knocker. Somewhere in the town a waking dog barked and as though in response to his knocking the watchman struck his iron plate near the church.

'Gadding about at night again . . . ?' grumbled the Old Believer innkeeper as he opened the gates in a long shirt resembling a woman's nightdress. 'Better be saying your prayers than gadding around like this . . .'

Ognyov went into his room, sank onto the bed and gazed at the lamp for a long, long time. Then he shook his head and started packing . . .

The Name-day Party

I

After the eight-course feast, with its interminable conversation, Olga Mikhaylovna went out into the garden. They were celebrating her husband's name-day, and she was completely exhausted by her duty to keep smiling and talking, by the clatter of dishes, by the servants' stupidity, by the long breaks during the meal and by the corset she had put on to conceal her pregnancy from the guests. She wanted to get right away from the house, to sit in the shade and to relax by thinking about the child that was due in about two months' time. She was always prone to thoughts like these whenever she turned left from the main avenue into the narrow path. Here, in the dense shade of plum and cherry trees, dry branches scratched her shoulders and neck, cobwebs brushed her face while she conjured up visions of a small creature of indeterminate sex, with vague features. And then she would feel that it was not the cobwebs but the tiny creature that was affectionately tickling her face and neck. When the thin wattle fence appeared at the bottom of the path, and beyond it the pot-bellied hives with earthenware roofs, when the motionless, stagnant air became filled with the scent of hay and honey and she could hear the gentle buzzing of bees, that tiny creature would take complete possession of her. She would sit pondering on a bench near the plaited osier hut.

This time too she walked as far as the bench, sat down and began to think. But instead of that tiny creature it was the big people she had only just left who filled her mind. She was deeply worried that she, the hostess, had abandoned her guests, and she remembered her husband Pyotr Dmitrich's and Uncle Nikolay Nikolaich's arguments over lunch about trial by jury, the press, and women's education. As usual, her husband had argued to flaunt his conservative views in front of the guests, but mainly so that he could disagree with her uncle, whom he disliked. But her uncle contradicted him, finding fault with every word to prove to the assembled guests that, despite his fifty-nine years, he, her uncle, still preserved the mental agility and liveliness of a young man. By the end of the dinner Olga herself could stand it no longer and began a clumsy defence of higher education for women – not because any defence was necessary, but simply to annoy her husband, whom she thought had been unfair. The guests found this argument very tiresome, but felt that they should intervene and make endless comments, although not one of them cared a scrap about trial by jury or women's education.

Olga was sitting on the near side of the wattle fence, just by the hut. The sun lay hidden behind clouds, the trees and air had a gloomy look, as though it was going to rain; but it was still hot and humid. The sad-looking hay that had been cut under the trees on St Peter's Eve remained ungathered. With its withered, many-coloured flowers, it gave off an oppressive, sickly scent. Everything was quiet. Beyond the fence bees buzzed monotonously.

Suddenly there was the unexpected sound of footsteps and voices. Someone was coming down the path towards the beehives.

'It's so close!' a woman's voice came. 'What do you think, is it or isn't it going to rain?'

'It is, my treasure, but not before tonight,' languidly answered a very familiar male voice. 'We're in for quite a shower.'

Olga reasoned that if she quickly hid in the hut they would move on without seeing her and she would not have to talk or force a smile. She gathered in her skirts, stooped and went inside. Her face, neck and arms were immediately immersed in air as hot and humid as steam. But for the humidity, the stifling smell of rye, dill and osiers that quite took her breath away, this thatched hut with its dim interior would have made the perfect hiding-place from her guests, where she could think about that little creature. It was cosy and quiet.

'What a lovely spot!' a female voice said. 'Let's sit down here, Pyotr.'

Olga peered through a chink between two osier plaits and saw her husband Pyotr with one of the guests, Lyubochka Sheller, a seventeen-year-old girl just out of boarding-school. With his hat pushed over the back of his head, and feeling heavy and lazy from too much wine, Pyotr sauntered along by the fence, kicking some hay into a little heap. Pink from the heat and pretty as ever, Lyubochka was standing with her hands behind her back watching the languid movements of his large, handsome body.

Olga knew that her husband was attractive to women and she did not like to see him with them. There was nothing really remarkable in Pyotr's lazily kicking hay into a pile on which he and Lyubochka could sit down and indulge in idle gossip; nor was there anything really noteworthy in the fact that pretty Lyubochka was looking at him so sweetly. Yet Olga felt annoyed with her husband and both frightened and pleased at the thought of being an eavesdropper.

'Sit down, my enchantress,' Pyotr said as he sank on to the hay and stretched himself. 'That's it. Now, tell me something interesting.'

'Well, really! You'll only fall asleep as soon as I start.'

'Fall asleep? Allah forbid. How could I fall asleep with such pretty little eyes looking at me?'

There was nothing remarkable, either, in her husband's words, in his sprawling over the hay in the presence of a lady, with his hat pushed over the back of his neck. Women had spoilt him – he knew that they were attracted to him and he had developed a special tone when talking to them, which, as everyone said, suited him. He was behaving towards Lyubochka as with any other woman. But Olga was jealous all the same.

'Please tell me,' Lyubochka said after a brief silence, 'if it's true what they say, that you're facing prosecution.'

'Me? Yes, it's true, I'm now looked upon as one of the criminal fraternity, my precious.'

'But why?'

'For nothing at all . . . it was mainly . . . it's mainly because of something to do with politics,' Pyotr said, yawning. 'It's the struggle between Left and Right. I'm a reactionary old stick-in-the-mud and I was bold enough to use – in official communications – expressions that such infallible Gladstones as our local Justice of the Peace Kuzma Grigoryevich Vostryakov (and Vladimir Pavlovich Vladimirov too) found offensive.'

Pyotr yawned again and went on, 'In this society of ours you may disapprove of the sun, the moon or anything you like, but God help you if you say anything about liberals! Liberals are like that toadstool over there – if you touch it accidentally it will shower you with clouds of dust.'

'What happened to you, then?'

'Nothing much; it was all a storm in a teacup. Some wretched schoolmaster – a loathsome type of clerical origin – filed a suit before our J.P., Vostryakov, against an innkeeper for slander and assault in a public place. According to the facts, both schoolmaster and innkeeper were blind drunk, both behaved equally nastily. Even if there had been a case to answer, both parties were at fault anyway. Vostryakov should have fined both of them for breach of the peace and thrown them out of court – and that would have been the end of the matter. But we don't do things that way! We always want to classify, to stick labels on people – the individual and facts take second place. However terrible a scoundrel your schoolmaster may be, he's bound to be right, for the simple fact that he's a schoolmaster. But innkeepers are always in the wrong just because they're innkeepers – they always grab what they can. Vostryakov sentenced the innkeeper to a term in prison, the innkeeper appealed to the Assizes who solemnly upheld Vostryakov's verdict. Well, I spoke my mind . . . got rather worked up about it . . . that's all.'

Pyotr spoke calmly, with a casual irony, but in fact he was terribly worried about the impending trial. Olga remembered how he had come back from those ill-fated proceedings and had tried desperately to conceal his despondency and feeling of dissatisfaction with himself from the servants. Being an intelligent man, he could not help thinking that he had gone too far in expressing disagreement – and how he had been forced to prevaricate to hide this feeling from himself and others! How many futile discussions had taken place, how much grumbling and forced laughter at things that were not at all funny! And when he learned that he had to stand trial, he had suddenly become weary and dejected, and begun to sleep badly and taken to standing by the window more often, drumming his fingers on the panes. He was too ashamed to admit to his wife that he was feeling depressed, and this had annoyed her.

'I hear you've been away, in Poltava,' Lyubochka said.

'Yes,' Pyotr replied. 'I got back two days ago.'

'I bet it was very nice there.'

'Yes, it was nice, very nice in fact. I must tell you, I happened to arrive just in time for the haymaking, which is the most idyllic time of year in the Ukraine. Here we have a large house, with a large garden, but what with all these servants, all the rushing around, it's quite impossible to see any haymaking. But on my farm down in the Ukraine forty acres of meadow open out before your eyes, you can see reapers from every window. There's mowing in the meadows and the garden, there's no visitors, none of this rushing around, so you just can't help seeing, hearing and feeling anything but haymaking. There's the smell of hay outdoors and in, scythes clatter away from dawn to dusk. The dear old Ukraine's a charming country, really. Believe me, when I drank water at those wells with their sweeps and filthy vodka at Jewish taverns, when the sound of Ukrainian fiddles and tambourines wafted over to me on calm evenings – then I was tempted by the enchanting thought of settling down on my farm and living a life miles away from these Assizes, smart conversations, philosophizing women and interminable dinners.'

Pyotr was not lying. He had been feeling depressed and he was really dying to get away from it all. He had gone to Poltava only to escape from his study, the servants, his friends and everything that would remind him of his wounded pride and his mistakes.

Lyubochka suddenly leapt up and waved her arms in horror.

'Oh, a bee, a bee!' she screamed. 'It's going to sting me!'

'Don't be silly, of course it's not!' Pyotr said. 'What a little coward you are!'

'No, no, it's going to!' Lyubochka cried, looking round at the bee as she quickly made her escape.

Pyotr followed her, his feeling of tenderness mingled with sadness as he watched her go. Looking at her he must have thought of his farm in the south, of solitude and – who knows? – perhaps he was even thinking how warm and snug life on his farm would be if that young, pure, fresh girl who was unspoilt by higher education, who was not pregnant, had been his wife . . .

When the voices and footsteps died away, Olga left the hut and set off towards the house. She wanted to cry and by now felt extremely jealous. She understood how tired Pyotr was, that he was dissatisfied with himself and ashamed; and people who are ashamed always avoid close friends more than anyone else and open their hearts only to strangers. She also understood that Lyubochka, like all those other women now drinking coffee in the house, posed no threat to her. But it was all so incomprehensible, so frightening, and Olga had now come to feel that Pyotr only half belonged to her.

'He has no right,' she muttered, trying to find the reason for her jealousy and her annoyance with her husband. 'No right at all. I'm going to let him know where he stands. This instant!'

She decided to find her husband right away and tell him the facts of the matter. The way he attracted women and sought their approval, as though it was a gift from heaven, was unspeakably degrading. He was behaving dishonourably when he gave perfect strangers what by right belonged to his wife, when he hid his heart and conscience from her and bared them to the first pretty face that came along. What had she done wrong? Finally, she was sick and tired of his lying. He was perpetually posing, flirting, saying what he did not mean and trying to appear other than he really was or should have been. What was the point of this prevarication? Was that sort of thing right for a respectable man? His lying was an insult to himself and to those to whom he dissimulated; and he did not care what kind of lies he told. If he could keep posing, showing off at the Bench, expatiating at dinner about the prerogatives of power just to spite her uncle, couldn't he see that it only went to show that he did not give a damn for the court, for himself or for anyone listening to him or watching?

As she came out on to the main avenue Olga tried to give the impression she was performing some domestic duty. The men were drinking liqueurs and eating soft fruit on the terrace. One of them, the examining magistrate, a stout, elderly gentleman, a clown and wit, must have been telling some rather risqué story since he suddenly pressed his hands to his fat lips when he saw the mistress of the house and sat back in his chair, eyes goggling. Olga did not care for their clumsy, overbearing wives, their gossip, their over-frequent visits, their adulation of her husband – whom they all hated. But now, when they were sitting there having drinks after a good meal, and showed no sign of leaving, she found their presence quite nauseating. But she smiled warmly at the examining magistrate and wagged a threatening finger at him so as not to appear ungracious. She crossed the ballroom and drawing-room smiling, making out that she was on her way to give orders to the servants and make some arrangements. 'I hope no one stops me, God forbid!' she thought, but she forced herself to stop for a moment in the drawing-room to listen – out of politeness' sake – to a young man playing the piano. After standing there for a minute she shouted 'Bravo, bravo, Monsieur Georges!', clapped twice and went on her way.

She found her husband in his study. He was sitting at his desk pondering something. His face had a stern, pensive, guilty look. This was not the Pyotr who had been arguing during the meal and whom the guests knew, but someone quite different – exhausted, guilty, dissatisfied with himself – whom only his wife knew. He must have gone into the study for some cigarettes. An open case lay before him, full of cigarettes, and one hand was resting in the desk drawer. He seemed to have frozen at the moment of taking them out.

Olga felt sorry for him. It was as clear as daylight that he was exhausted, worried and perhaps engaged in a battle against himself. Olga silently went over to the desk. Wanting to prove to him that she had forgotten the arguments over dinner and that she was no longer angry, she shut the cigarette case and put it in his side pocket.

'What shall I tell him?' she wondered. 'I'll say that deceitfulness is like a swamp, the further you go in, the harder it is to get out. Then I'll tell him: you've been carried away by that false role you've been acting out, you've gone too far. You've insulted people who were devoted to you and did you no harm. So please go and apologize to them, have a good laugh at yourself and you'll feel better. And if you want peace and solitude, let's go away from here together.'

When his eyes met his wife's, Pyotr suddenly assumed that indifferent, gently mocking expression he had worn at dinner and in the garden. He yawned and stood up.

'It's after five,' he said, glancing at his watch. 'Even if our guests take pity on us and depart at eleven, that still leaves another six hours. That's something cheerful to look forward to, need I say!'

Whistling some tune, he slowly left the study, walking in that familiar, dignified fashion. His unhurried footsteps could be heard as he crossed the hall and drawing-room, then his supercilious laugh as he called out 'Bravo, bravo!' to the young man at the piano. Soon the footsteps died away – he must have gone out into the garden. Now it was no longer jealousy or annoyance that took hold of Olga, but deep hatred for the way he walked, for that insidious laugh and tone of voice. She went over to the window, looked out into the garden and saw Pyotr walking down the avenue. One hand was in his pocket and he was snapping the fingers of the other. His head tossed slightly backwards, he solemnly ambled along, apparently very pleased with himself, the dinner, his digestion and nature all around.

Two small schoolboys – the sons of Mrs Chizhevsky, a landowner – who had just arrived with their tutor, a student in white tunic and very narrow trousers, appeared on the path. When they came up to Pyotr the boys and the student stopped, probably to congratulate him on his name-day. Exquisitely twitching his shoulders, he patted the children's cheeks and casually offered the student his hand without looking at him. The student must have praised the weather and compared it to St Petersburg's, since Pyotr replied in a loud voice, as if addressing a bailiff or court witness instead of a guest, 'Eh! Is it cold in St Petersburg then? Here, my dear young man, we have a salubrious climate and an abundance of fruits of the earth. Eh, what's that?'

Placing one hand in his pocket and snapping the fingers of the other, he strode off. Olga gazed at the back of his neck in amazement until he was lost to sight behind the hazel bushes. How had that thirty-four-year-old man acquired the solemn walk of a general? Where did that ponderous, impressive gait come from? Whence that authoritarian vibrancy of voice, all those 'What!'s, 'Well, sir!'s and 'My dear fellow!'s?

Olga remembered going to court sittings, where Pyotr sometimes deputized as president for her godfather, Count Aleksey Petrovich, to escape the boredom and loneliness at home during the first few months of her marriage. Seated in the president's chair in his uniform, with a chain over his chest, he underwent a complete transformation, what with those grandiose gestures, that thunderous voice, those 'What, sir?'s, those 'Hmm's, that casual tone. All normal human qualities, everything natural to him that she was used to seeing at home, had been swallowed up in grandeur. It was not Pyotr sitting in that chair, but some other man whom everyone called 'Your honour'. The consciousness of the power he wielded did not allow him to sit still for one minute, and he was always on the look-out for some opportunity to ring his bell, to scowl at the public, to shout . . . And where did he acquire that shortsightedness and deafness? He had suddenly become myopic and deaf, frowning imperiously as he told people to speak up and to come nearer the bench. From those lofty heights he could not distinguish faces and sounds at all well, and if Olga herself had approached him at these moments, he would most likely have shouted 'What's your name?' He talked down to peasant witnesses, yelled so loud at the public that they could hear him out in the street, and his treatment of barristers was quite outrageous. If a barrister approached him, Pyotr would sit sideways to him, squint at the ceiling to make it plain that the lawyer was not needed in court at all and that he had no wish either to listen to him or to acknowledge his existence. But if a shabby-suited solicitor happened to speak, Pyotr was all ears and sized him up with a devastatingly sarcastic look that seemed to say 'God, what lawyers we're afflicted with these days!' 'Just *what* are you trying to say?' he would interrupt. If some barrister with a florid turn of phrase ventured to use some word of foreign origin and said 'factitious' instead of 'fictitious', for example, Pyotr would suddenly come to life and ask 'What's that? What? Factitious? What does *that* mean?' Then he would issue the pompous admonition 'Don't use words you don't understand'. And when the barrister had finished his speech he would come away from the bench red-faced and bathed in perspiration, while Pyotr would settle back in his chair, celebrating his victory with a complacent smile. In the way he addressed barristers, he was imitating Count Aleksey Petrovich to a certain extent, but when the latter said 'Will counsel for the defence please be quiet?', for example, the remark sounded quite natural, as if a good-humoured old gentleman were speaking, but with Pyotr it was rather coarse and strained.

II

People were applauding – the young man had finished playing. Olga suddenly remembered her guests and hurried into the drawing-room.

'You play delightfully,' she said, going over to the piano. 'Delightfully. You have a wonderful gift! But isn't our piano out of tune?'

At that moment the two schoolboys and the student came in.

'Heavens, it's Mitya and Kolya!' Olga drawled joyfully as she went to meet them. 'How you've grown! I wouldn't have recognized you! But where's your mother?'

'Many happy returns to our host,' the student said breezily. 'I wish him all the best. Yekaterina Andreyevna Chizhevsky sends her congratulations and her apologies. She's not feeling very well.'

'How unkind of her! I've been looking forward all day to seeing her. When did you leave St Petersburg?' Olga asked the student. 'What's the weather like there?'

Without waiting for an answer she looked affectionately at the boys and repeated, 'How they've grown! Not so long ago they used to come here with their nanny, and now they're already at school! The old get older and the young grow up. Have you had dinner?'

'Oh, please don't worry,' the student said.

'Now you haven't eaten, have you?'

'Please don't worry.'

'Surely you must be hungry?' Olga asked impatiently and irritably, in a rough, harsh voice. She did not mean to speak like that and she immediately had a little coughing-fit, then smiled and blushed. 'How they've grown!' she said, softly.

'Please don't worry,' the student said yet again. He begged her not to go to any trouble; the children said nothing. It was obvious all three were hungry. Olga led them into the dining-room and told Vasily to lay the table.

'Your mother is so unkind,' she said, making them sit down. 'She's completely forgotten me. She's not very nice at all . . . you can tell her that. And what are *you* studying?' she asked, turning to the student.

'Medicine.'

'Oh, I have a weakness for doctors, you know! I'm very sorry my husband isn't one. What courage you must have, to do operations, for example, or to dissect corpses! It's terrifying! You're not afraid? I think I'd die of fright. Of course, you'll have some vodka?'

'It's all right, please don't bother.'

'After that journey you simply must have a drink. I like a drink sometimes, even though I'm a woman. Mitya and Kolya can have some Malaga.[1] It's not very strong, don't worry. What fine young men they are, really! Even ready for marriage.'

Olga talked non-stop. She knew from experience that with guests it suited her better and was in fact far easier to do the talking than to sit listening. When one is talking there's no need to be alert, to think of answers to questions and keep changing one's expression. But she accidentally raised some serious question and the student embarked on a long speech, so that she had to listen whether she liked it or not. The student knew that at some time she had been to a course of lectures, so he tried to look serious when speaking to her.

'What's your subject?' she asked, forgetting that she had already asked this.

'Medicine.'

'Oh, yes. So you're going to be a doctor?' she asked, getting up. 'That's good. I'm sorry I never went to lectures on medicine. Now, have your dinner, gentlemen, and then come out into the garden. I'll introduce you to some young ladies.'

Olga remembered that she had been neglecting the ladies for some time. She went out and looked at the clock: it was five to six. She was amazed that the time was passing so slowly and horrified that there were still six hours to midnight, when the guests would leave. How could she kill these six hours? What should she say? How should she behave towards her husband?

There wasn't a soul in the drawing-room or on the terrace – all the guests had wandered off to different parts of the garden.

'I really ought to suggest a walk to the birch grove, or boating before tea –' Olga thought, hurrying to the croquet lawn, where she could hear voices and laughter. 'And I must make the old men play cards.'

Grigory the footman came towards her from the croquet lawn carrying some empty bottles.

'Where are the ladies?' she asked.

'In the raspberry canes. The master's there as well.'

'Oh, good heavens!' came the furious cry from the croquet lawn. 'If I've told you once I've told you a thousand times! If you want to know your Bulgarians you must go and see them. You can't tell from the newspapers.'

Either because of this shout or something else, Olga suddenly felt dreadfully weak all over, especially in the legs and shoulders. She had no wish to speak, listen or move.

'Grigory,' she said listlessly, after a great effort, 'when you're serving tea or something please don't come bothering me, don't ask me questions and don't talk to me about anything. You can do it all yourself . . . and don't make a noise with your feet. I beg you to do this. I can't, because . . .'

She did not finish and walked on towards the croquet lawn. But on the way she remembered the ladies and went in the direction of the raspberry canes. The sky, the air and the trees were still just as gloomy, threatening rain. It was hot and close; huge flocks of crows, sensing bad weather, cawed as they wheeled over the garden. The nearer the paths were to the kitchen garden, the more neglected, dark and narrow they became. Over one of them that lay hidden in a dense thicket of wild pears, wood-sorrel, oak saplings and hops, great clouds of tiny black midges swarmed around her. Olga covered her face with her hands and tried hard to imagine that little creature . . . But all that came to mind were Grigory, Mitya, Kolya, the faces of the peasants who had come offering congratulations in the morning.

Hearing footsteps, she opened her eyes. Uncle Nikolay was fast approaching.

'Is that you, my dear? So glad to see you,' he said, panting. 'I'd like a couple of words with you.' He wiped his red, clean-shaven chin with his handkerchief, then suddenly stepped sharply backwards, clasped his hands and opened his eyes wide. 'My dear, how long is this going on for?' he said breathlessly. 'I'm asking you, isn't there a limit? I don't mean the demoralizing effect of his police sergeant's views on our little circle or the way he insults all that is finest and noblest in me and in all honest, thinking men. I'm not talking about that. But he could at least behave civilly. What's the matter with him? He shouts, growls, shows off, acts the little Bonaparte, doesn't let anyone get a word in edgeways. What the hell! Those grand gestures of his, that imperious laugh, that condescending tone! Who does he think he is, may I ask? Who *does* he think he is? He can't hold a candle to his wife, he's just a landowner lucky enough to have married money. Another of those *nouveau riche* upstarts. A cad and a rotter! I swear by God, either he's suffering from megalomania or that senile half-cracked Count Aleksey Petrovich is actually right when he says that children and young people take a long time to mature these days and carry on playing cabbies and generals until they're forty!'

'That's true, so true,' Olga agreed. 'Please let me pass now.'

'And where do you think it will all lead?' Uncle went on, barring her way. 'How will playing the bigot, acting the inquisitor finish? He's already facing prosecution, oh, yes! I'm delighted! Look where all his ranting and raving have landed him – in the dock! And not just the local Assizes, but the High Court of Justice! I can't think of anything worse than that! What's more, he's quarrelled with everyone. Today is his name-day party, but just look who's given it a miss – Vostryakov, Yakhontov, Vladimirov, Shevud, the Count – none of them have turned up. And who could be more of a die-hard reactionary than Count Aleksey Petrovich – even *he*'s not here. And he'll never come again, you mark my words!'

'Oh, heavens, what's all this got to do with me?' Olga asked.

'To do with *you*? You're his wife! You're clever, you've been to university, and it's in your power to make an honest worker out of him!'

'They don't teach you at lectures how to influence difficult people. I'll have to apologize to all of you, it seems, for having attended lectures!' Olga said sharply. 'Listen, Uncle, if your ears were bombarded all day long by someone practising the same scales, you wouldn't sit still and you'd run away. The whole year, day in, day out, I hear the same old thing, the same old thing. Heavens, it's high time you felt a little pity for me!'

Uncle pulled a very serious face, gave her an inquisitive look and curled his lips into a mocking smile.

'So that's how it is!' he chanted in his senile voice. 'I'm so sorry, madam!' he said with a stiff bow. 'If you yourself have fallen under his influence and changed your convictions, then you should have said so earlier. I'm sorry, madam!'

'Yes, I have changed my convictions!' she shouted. 'That should make you happy!'

'So sorry, madam!'

Uncle ceremoniously bowed for the last time – sideways on – drew himself in, clicked his heels and left.

'The fool,' Olga thought. 'I wish he'd clear off home.'

She found the ladies and young people among the raspberry canes in the kitchen garden. Some were eating the raspberries, while others who had had their fill were wandering among the strawberry beds or nosing around in the sugar-peas. Just to one side of the raspberry canes, near a spreading apple tree that was propped up on all sides by stakes pulled out of an old fence, Pyotr was scything the grass. His hair was hanging over his forehead, his tie had come undone, his watch-chain was dangling loose. Every step he took, every sweep of the scythe showed skill and enormous physical strength. Near him stood Lyubochka, with their neighbour Colonel Bukreyev's daughters Natalya and Valentina – or, as everyone called them, Nata and Vata, anaemic and unhealthy, plump blondes of about sixteen or seventeen in white dresses and strikingly alike. Pyotr was teaching them to scythe.

'It's very simple,' he was saying. 'All you have to know is how to hold the scythe and to take it calmly – I mean, not exerting yourself more than you need. Like this . . . Would you like to try now?' he asked, offering the scythe to Lyubochka. 'Come on!'

Lyubochka awkwardly took the scythe then suddenly blushed and burst out laughing.

'Don't be shy, Lyubochka,' Olga shouted, loud enough for all the ladies to hear and know that she had returned to them. 'Don't be shy. You have to learn. Marry a Tolstoyan, he'll make you wield the scythe.'

Lyubochka raised the scythe but burst out laughing again, which so weakened her she immediately put it down. She was both embarrassed and pleased that she was being spoken to like an adult. Nata, without smiling or showing any shyness, picked up the scythe with a serious, cold look, took a sweep and got it tangled up in the grass. Without smiling either, as serious and cold-looking as her sister, Vata silently picked up the scythe and plunged it into the earth. These operations completed, the sisters took each other by the arm and silently walked over to the raspberry canes.

Pyotr laughed and joked like a small boy, and this mischievous, childish mood, when he became excessively good-humoured, suited him far more than anything else. Olga loved him that way. But the boyish behaviour did not usually last long, which was the case this time. Having had his little joke he thought that he should introduce a note of seriousness into his playfulness.

'When I use a scythe I feel healthier, a more normal person, I can tell you,' he said. 'If you tried to force me to be satisfied solely with the life of the mind and nothing else I think I would go mad. I feel that I was not born for the cultural life! I should be reaping, ploughing, sowing, training horses.'

Pyotr started talking to the ladies about the advantages of physical labour, about culture, then turned to the harmfulness of money, to landed property. As she listened to her husband, for some reason Olga thought of her dowry.

'Surely the time will come,' Olga thought, 'when he won't be able to forgive me for being the richer. He's proud and touchy. Perhaps he'll come to hate me because of his great debt towards me.'

She stopped by Colonel Bukreyev, who was eating raspberries while participating in the conversation.

'Please join us,' he said, stepping to one side for Olga and Pyotr. 'The ripest ones are over here. And so, in Proudhon's[2] opinion,' he went on, raising his voice, 'property is theft. But I must confess that I don't accept Proudhon and don't rate him as a philosopher. As far as I'm concerned the French are not authorities on the matter, blast them!'

'Well, I'm a bit weak on my Proudhons and Buckles,'[3] Pyotr said. 'If you want to discuss philosophy, then my wife's the one. She's been to university lectures and knows all these Schopenhauers[4] and Proudhons backwards.'

Olga felt bored again. Once more she went down the garden along the narrow path, past the apple and pear trees, and again she appeared to be on some very important mission . . . Here was the gardener's cottage. Barbara, the gardener's wife, and her four small boys, with their big, close-cropped heads, were sitting in the doorway.

Barbara was pregnant too and the baby was due, according to her calculations, by Elijah's Day. After greeting her, Olga silently surveyed her and the children and asked, 'Well, how are you feeling?'

'Oh, all right.'

Silence followed. It seemed that both women understood each other without the need for words. Olga pondered for a moment and then said, 'It's terribly frightening having your first baby. I keep thinking that I won't get through it, that I'll die . . .'

'I thought that, but I'm still alive. You can worry about *anything* if you want to.'

Barbara, who was pregnant for the fifth time and a woman of experience, was rather condescending to her mistress and seemed to be lecturing her as she spoke, and Olga could not help sensing her authoritarian tone. She wanted to talk about her fears, the child, her sensations, but she was scared Barbara might think this trivial and naïve. And so she remained silent, waiting for Barbara to say something.

'Olga, let's go back to the house!' Pyotr shouted from the raspberry canes.

Olga liked waiting in silence and watching Barbara. She would have willingly stood there silently until night-time, although there was no need to. But she had to move on. The moment she left the cottage Lyubochka, Vata and Nata came running towards her. The two sisters stopped about two yards away, as if rooted to the spot, but Lyubochka ran and threw herself round Olga's neck.

'My dear, my darling, my precious!' she said, kissing her face and neck. 'Let's go and have tea on the island.'

'The island, the island!' echoed the identical, unsmiling Vata and Nata simultaneously.

'But it's going to rain, my dears.'

'It's not, it's not!' Lyubochka shouted, making a tearful face. 'Everyone wants to go, my dearest, my treasure!'

'Everyone's decided to have tea on the island,' Pyotr said, coming up to them. 'Now you make the arrangements . . . we'll all go in the rowing-boats, and the samovars and everything else can follow with the servants in the carriage.'

He took his wife by the arm and walked along with her. Olga wanted to tell her husband something nasty, hurtful – about the dowry even – and the more bluntly the better, she thought. But she pondered for a moment and said, 'Why hasn't Count Aleksey come? What a shame.'

'I'm only too pleased he hasn't,' Pyotr lied. 'I'm sick and tired of that old fool.'

'But before lunch you just couldn't wait for him to come!'

III

Half an hour later the guests were crowding along the bank near the posts where the boats were moored. There was much talk and laughter and so much unnecessary fuss that all the seating went wrong. Three boats were full to overflowing, while two others stood empty. The keys for these boats had been mislaid and people ran incessantly from river to house in search of them. Some said that Grigory had them, others said that they were with the estate manager, others thought it would be a good idea to send for the blacksmith to break the locks. And everyone spoke at once, interrupting and drowning each others' voices. Pyotr impatiently paced along the bank shouting, 'What the hell's going on here? The keys should always be kept on the windowsill in the hall. Who dared take them away? The manager can get his own boat if he likes.'

In the end the keys were found. Then they discovered that they were two oars short. Once again there was a loud commotion. Pyotr, tired of walking up and down, jumped into a kind of long, narrow canoe hollowed out from a poplar and pushed off so hard he nearly fell into the water. One after the other, the boats followed amid loud laughter and screams from the young ladies.

The white, cloudy sky, the trees along the bank, the reeds and the boats with people and oars were mirrored in the water; deep down under the boats, in that bottomless abyss, was a different sky, where birds flew. The bank where the estate was rose high and steep, and was densely wooded, while the other sloped gently, with green meadows and gleaming inlets. After the boats had travelled about a hundred yards, cottages and a herd of cows appeared from behind the willows which sadly leant over the gently sloping bank. Now they could hear songs, drunken shouts and the sound of an accordion. Here and there along the river darted the boats of fishermen who were setting up their nets for the night. In one boat some tipsy amateur musicians were playing home-made fiddles and a cello.

Olga sat at the rudder, smiling warmly and talking non-stop to entertain her guests, at the same time giving her husband sideways glances. His boat was ahead of all the others as he stood up working away with one oar. That light, sharp-nosed boat, which all the guests called 'an old dug-out' – for some reason Pyotr called it *Penderakliya* – moved swiftly. It had a lively cunning look and seemed to bear a grudge against that clumsy Pyotr – it was only waiting for the right moment to slip away from under him. Olga watched her husband, and she was revolted by his good looks that were universally admired, by the back of his neck, by his posing, by his familiar manner with women. She hated all the women who were sitting in the boat, envied them, and at the same time was in fear and trembling lest disaster struck and the shaky boat capsized.

'Don't row so fast!' she cried and her heart sank. 'Sit down in the boat, we all know how brave you are!'

And the others in the boat worried her too. They were all ordinary, decent people, but now the lot of them struck her as peculiar, evil. She could see nothing but falsehood in each one. 'Now,' she thought, 'that young man with the auburn hair and gold-rimmed spectacles and fine beard rowing away. He's a rich, smug, perpetually fortunate mother's little pet, everyone thinks he's honest, free-thinking and progressive. It's hardly a year since he took his degree and came to live in the country, but already he's proclaiming "*We* community workers". But before the year's out he'll be bored too, like so many others, he'll depart for St Petersburg, and to justify his flight he'll tell them everywhere that local councils are a waste of time, that he's terribly disenchanted. His young wife in that other boat simply has her eyes glued on him and she's convinced that he's a "servant of the community", but within one year she too will come to believe that local councils are useless. And that stout, immaculately shaven gentleman in the straw hat with the broad ribbon and with an expensive cigar between his teeth – he's fond of saying, "It's time we stopped daydreaming and got down to a real job of work!" He has Yorkshire pigs, Butlerov beehives,[5] rape seed, pineapples, a creamery and a cheese dairy, and Italian double-entry book-keeping. But every summer he sells some of his forests for timber, mortgages parts of his land so that he can spend the autumn with his mistress in the Crimea. And there's old Uncle Nikolay, who won't go home, despite being angry with Pyotr!'

Olga looked at the other boats, where she could discover only boring cranks, hypocrites or idiots. She thought of everyone she knew in the district, but could not call to mind one person about whom she could say or think anything that was good. All of them seemed undistinguished, colourless, stupid, narrow-minded, shifty and heartless. Either they did not say what they meant or they did not do what they wanted to. She was stifled by boredom and feelings of despair. She wanted suddenly to stop smiling, leap up and shout, 'I'm sick of the lot of you!', jump out of the boat and swim ashore.

'Come on, let's all give Pyotr a tow,' someone shouted.

'Give him a tow! Give him a tow!' the rest joined in. 'Olga, give your husband a tow!'

While she sat at the rudder, Olga had to seize the right moment and deftly catch hold of the chain at *Penderakliya*'s bows. As she leant over, trying to grasp it, Pyotr frowned and gave her a frightened look.

'Mind you don't catch cold!' he said.

'If you're scared on my account and the baby's then why do you torment me?' Olga thought.

Pyotr admitted defeat, but not wishing to be towed, he leapt from *Penderakliya* into a boat already bursting at the seams. He did this so clumsily that the boat listed sharply and everyone screamed with horror.

'He only jumped like that to please the ladies,' Olga thought. 'He knows how impressive it looks . . .'

Her arms and legs began to tremble, for which the feeling of jadedness, irritation, the forced smiles and the discomfort that she felt all over her body were to blame, she thought. To hide this trembling from her guests she tried to raise her voice, laugh, keep moving. 'If I suddenly burst into tears,' she thought, 'I'll tell them I have toothache.'

Now the boats at last put in at the 'Isle of Good Hope' – this was the name of the peninsula formed by a sharp bend in the river; it was covered with a copse of ancient birches, oaks, willows and poplars. Tables with steaming samovars were already in position under the trees, and Vasily and Grigory, in tailcoats and white knitted gloves, were busy near the crockery. On the far bank, opposite the 'Isle of Good Hope', stood the carriages that had brought the provisions, and baskets and parcels of food were being ferried from them to the island in a boat very similar to *Penderakliya*. The expressions of the footmen, coachmen – even of the peasant sitting in the boat – were solemn, festive, the kind one usually finds only among children and servants.

While Olga was making the tea and pouring out the first glasses, the guests busied themselves with fruit liqueurs and sweetmeats. Then followed the usual tea-time chaos, so trying and exhausting for the hostess. Grigory and Vasily had hardly served the tea than hands holding empty glasses were reaching towards Olga. One guest asked for tea without sugar, another wanted it strong, a third weak, a fourth said 'No more, thank you.' And Olga had to commit all this to memory and then shout, 'Ivan Petrovich, are you the one without sugar?' or 'Who asked for it weak?' But the guest who had asked for weak tea without sugar simply forgot what he had asked for, being carried away with the pleasant conversation, and took the first glass that was offered. Dejected figures wandered like shadows not far from the table, pretending that they were looking for mushrooms in the grass, or reading labels on boxes – these were the ones for whom there weren't enough glasses. 'Have you had some tea?' Olga would ask, and the guest in question would tell her not to worry and say, 'I don't mind waiting', although the hostess would have preferred her guests to hurry up instead of being prepared to wait.

Some of them were deep in conversation and drank their tea slowly, holding on to their glasses for half an hour, while others, especially those who had drunk a great deal over dinner, did not leave the table but drank glass after glass, so that Olga had a job refilling them. One young humorist sipped his tea through a lump of sugar and kept saying, 'Sinner that I am, I love to spoil myself with the Chinese Herb.' Now and then he sighed deeply as he asked, 'Please, just one more little dish-full.' He drank a lot, noisily crunched his sugar, thinking this was all very funny and original, and that he was giving a superb imitation of a merchant. No one appreciated that all these little things were sheer torture for the hostess: in fact it would have been difficult for anyone to guess, since Olga managed to keep smiling amiably and engage in idle tittle-tattle.

She was not feeling well, though. The crowd, the laughter, the questions, the young humorist, the flustered servants who were run off their feet, the children running round the table – all this irritated her. And she was irritated by the fact that Vata looked like Nata, Kolya like Mitya, so that it was impossible to tell which of them had had tea. She felt that her strained, warm smile was turning into a nasty scowl and that she would burst into tears at any moment.

'It's raining!' someone shouted.

Everyone looked up at the sky.

'Yes, it really is,' Pyotr confirmed, wiping his cheek. The sky let fall just a few drops – it wasn't really raining yet, but the guests abandoned their tea and began to hurry. At first they all wanted to go back in the carriages, but then they changed their minds and went towards the boats. On the pretext that she urgently had to see to supper, Olga asked if they minded if she travelled back on her own, by carriage.

The first thing she did when seated was to give her face a rest from smiling. She drove scowling through the village and gave bowing peasants angry looks. When she arrived home she went to the bedroom by the back entrance and lay down on her husband's bed.

'Good heavens!' she whispered, 'what's the use of all this hard labour? Why do these people hang around here pretending they're having a good time? Why all these false smiles? I don't understand, I just don't understand!'

She heard footsteps and voices. The guests had returned.

'They can do what they like,' Olga thought. 'I'm going to lie down a little longer.' But the maid came into the bedroom and said, 'Madam, Marya Grigoryevna's leaving.'

Olga leapt up, tidied her hair and rushed out of the room.

'Marya, what's wrong?' she asked in an offended voice, going up to Marya Grigoryevna. 'Why the rush?'

'I *must* go, my dear, I simply must! I've stayed too long already. The children are waiting for me at home.'

'You're so naughty! Why didn't you bring them with you?'

'My dear, I'll bring them over one day in the week if you like, but as for today . . .'

'Oh, yes!' Olga interrupted, 'I'd be delighted. Your children are so sweet. Give them all a kiss from me. But honestly, I'm quite offended. Why the hurry, I just don't understand!'

'I must be going, I really must . . . Goodbye, my dear, and look after yourself. In your condition . . .'

And they kissed. After seeing her guest to her carriage, Olga joined the ladies in the drawing-room. There the lamps had been lit and the men were just sitting down to cards.

IV

At a quarter past twelve, after supper, the guests began to leave. Olga stood at the porch to say goodbye.

'Really, you should have brought a shawl,' she said, 'it's getting rather chilly. I hope you won't catch cold!'

'Don't worry, Olga,' the guests replied as they climbed into their carriages. 'Well, goodbye. Remember, we're expecting you. Don't let us down!'

'Whoa!' said the coachman, holding back the horses.

'Let's be going, Denis! Goodbye, Olga.'

'Give the children a kiss from me!'

The carriage moved off and immediately vanished in the darkness. In the red circle cast by the lamp on the road, a new pair or team of three impatient horses would appear, their coachman silhouetted with hands stretched out in front of him. Once again there were kisses, reproaches and requests to come again or to take a shawl. Pyotr ran back and forwards from the hall, helping the ladies into carriages.

'Drive straight to Yefremovshchina,' he told the coachman. 'It's quicker if you go by way of Mankino, but that road isn't so good. You might overturn . . . Goodbye, my dear! *Mille compliments* to your artist friend!'

'Goodbye, darling Olga. Go inside now or you'll catch cold. It's damp.'

'Whoa! Up to your tricks again, eh!'

'Where did you get these horses from?' Pyotr asked.

'From Khaydarov, during Lent,' the coachman answered.

'They're superb!'

Pyotr slapped the trace-horse on the croup. 'Well, off with you! Safe journey!'

Finally the last guest departed. The red circle on the road flickered, drifted off to one side, dwindled and vanished – Vasily had taken the lamp away from the front door. Previously, when they saw their guests off, Pyotr and Olga usually performed a jig in front of each other in the ballroom, clapped their hands and sang 'They've gone, they've gone, they've gone!' But Olga did not feel up to that now. She went into the bedroom, undressed, and climbed into bed.

She thought that she would fall asleep immediately and that she would sleep soundly. Her legs and shoulders ached horribly, her head was reeling from all that talk and once again she felt strangely uncomfortable all over. Covering her head, she lay still for a little while, then stole a glance at the icon-lamp from under the blanket, listened to the silence and smiled.

'Good, good,' she whispered, tucking in her legs, which she felt had grown longer from all that walking. 'I must sleep, sleep.'

Her legs would not stay under the blankets, her whole body felt uncomfortable and she turned over on the other side. A large fly flew around the bedroom, buzzing and restlessly beating against the ceiling. She could also hear Grigory and Vasily treading carefully as they cleared the tables in the ballroom. Olga felt that only when those noises stopped would she feel comfortable and able to fall asleep. And once again she impatiently turned over.

She could hear her husband's voice in the drawing-room. One of the guests was probably staying the night, because Pyotr was telling someone in a loud voice, 'I wouldn't say that Count Aleksey Petrovich is a trickster. But he can't help giving that impression, since you all try to see him as other than he actually is. His eccentricity is misinterpreted as originality, his familiar manner as a sign of good-heartedness, and because of his complete lack of any views you take him for a conservative. Let's even go so far as to admit that he's a conservative of the purest stamp. But what is conservatism, all things considered?'

Furious with Count Aleksey Petrovich, with his guests and with himself, Pyotr unbosomed himself. He cursed the Count, his guests, and was so annoyed with himself he was prepared to hold forth or preach a sermon on any subject. After showing his guest to his room, he paced the drawing-room, walked around the dining-room, then up and down the corridor and around his study, then once more around the drawing-room, after which he went into the bedroom. Olga was lying on her back with the blanket only up to her waist (she was feeling hot now) and sullenly watching the fly banging against the ceiling.

'Do we have someone staying overnight, then?' she asked.

'Yegorov.'

Pyotr undressed and lay down on his bed. He silently lit a cigarette and he too started watching the fly. His face was gloomy and uneasy. Olga looked at his handsome profile for about five minutes without saying a word. For some reason she felt that if he were suddenly to turn his face towards her and say 'I feel so depressed, Olga', then she would have burst into tears or laughed, and she would have felt better for it. Her legs ached and her whole body felt uncomfortable – from nervous tension, she thought.

'Pyotr, what are you thinking about?' she asked.

'Oh, nothing,' her husband answered.

'You've started keeping secrets from me lately. That's not right.'

'Why isn't it?' Pyotr replied dryly, pausing briefly. 'We all have our own private lives, therefore we must have our secrets.'

'Private lives, secrets . . . that's only words! Do you realize that you're insulting me?' Olga said, sitting up. 'If you feel depressed, why do you hide it from me? And why do you find it more convenient to confide in strange women rather than talk to your wife? In fact I heard you pouring out your heart this afternoon to Lyubochka, near the beehives.'

'Well, congratulations. I'm delighted you heard.'

This remark meant 'Leave me in peace, don't disturb me when I'm trying to think.' Olga flared up. All the annoyance, hatred and anger which had been accumulating in her during the day suddenly seemed to boil over. She wanted to say exactly what she thought about it all to her husband there and then, without waiting until the morning; she wanted to insult him, have her revenge. Trying hard not to shout she said, 'Just try and see how terribly, terribly vile all this is! I've felt nothing but hatred for you all day long – it's all your fault!'

Pyotr sat up too.

'Terribly, terribly vile!' Olga went on, beginning to shake all over. 'You've no need to congratulate *me*! You'd better congratulate yourself! It's a downright disgrace! You've taken your lying so far, you're ashamed to be in the same room as your wife. You're such a phoney! I can see right through you and I understand every step you take!'

'Olga, when you're not feeling too well again, please warn me. I can go and sleep in the study then.'

With these words Pyotr took a pillow and walked out of the bedroom. Olga had not anticipated this. For several minutes – speechless, her mouth wide open, and trembling all over – she looked at the door through which her husband had disappeared, trying to understand the meaning of it all. Was it one of those tricks resorted to by dishonest people during an argument, when they are in the wrong, or was it a deliberate insult to her pride? How was she to take it? Olga remembered her officer-cousin, a nice cheerful young man who often laughingly told her that when 'my good lady wife starts nagging me at night', he usually took a pillow and went away whistling to his study, leaving his wife looking stupid and ridiculous. This officer was married to a rich, frivolous, silly woman whom he did not respect and could barely tolerate.

Olga leapt up from the bed. She thought that now there was only one course of action – to dress herself as quickly as she could and leave that house for ever. The house was her property, but that was hard luck for Pyotr. Without first asking herself whether it was necessary, she dashed into the study to tell her husband about her decision (the thought 'Woman's logic!' flashed through her mind) and say something offensive and sarcastic by way of farewell.

Pyotr lay on the couch and pretended he was reading the paper.

A lighted candle stood on a chair nearby and his face lay hidden behind the paper.

'Please explain the meaning of this, I'm asking you!'

'"Please explain . . ."' mimicked Pyotr, not showing his face. 'I'm fed up, Olga! Word of honour, I'm worn out, and I don't feel up to it right now . . . We can quarrel tomorrow.'

'No, I know you only too well!' Olga continued. 'You hate me! Yes, yes! You hate me for being richer than you! You'll never forgive me for that and you'll always tell me lies.' (The thought 'Woman's logic' flashed through her mind again.) 'I know you're having a good laugh at me now . . . I'm even convinced that you only married me for social status and those vile horses . . . Oh, I'm so unhappy!'

Pyotr dropped his paper and sat up. He was stunned by this unexpected insult. He smiled as helplessly as a child, looked at his wife in bewilderment and, as if warding off blows, held out his hands to her and said pleadingly, 'Olga!'

Expecting her to say more horrible things, he leant hard on the back of the couch, and his whole body looked just as helpless and childish as his smile.

'Olga, how could you say a thing like that?' he whispered.

Olga came to her senses. Suddenly she was aware of her mad love for that man, remembering that he was Pyotr, her husband, without whom she could not live one day, and who loved her madly too. She burst into loud sobs, in a voice that did not sound like hers at all, clasped her head and ran back into the bedroom.

She slumped on to the bed and the room echoed to the sound of broken, hysterical sobbing, which suffocated her and cramped her arms and legs. Remembering that a guest was staying about three or four rooms away, she buried her head under the pillow to smother the sobs, but the pillow slipped on to the floor and she almost fell herself as she bent down to pick it up. She tried to pull the blanket up to her face, but her hands would not obey her and convulsively tore at everything she tried to grasp.

She felt that all was lost now, that the lie she had told to insult her husband had smashed her life to smithereens. Her husband would never forgive her – the insult she had inflicted on him was not the kind to be smoothed away by caresses or vows. How could she convince her husband that she herself did not mean what she said?

'It's all over, it's finished!' she cried, not noticing that the pillow had once again slipped on to the floor. 'For God's sake!'

By this time her cries must have wakened the guest and the servants. Next day the whole district would know about her hysterics and everyone would blame Pyotr. She made an effort to control herself, but her sobs grew louder by the minute. 'For God's sake!' she shouted in a voice hard to recognize as hers and not understanding just why she was shouting. 'For God's sake!'

She felt that the bed had collapsed under her and that her legs had become tangled up in the blanket. Pyotr came into the bedroom in his dressing-gown, carrying a candle.

'Olga, that's enough!' he said.

She raised herself to her knees, screwed up her eyes in the candlelight and said between her sobs, 'Please understand, please understand!'

She wanted to tell him that the visitors, the lies that he and she had told, had exhausted her, that now she was inwardly boiling. But all she could say was 'Understand, *please* understand!'

'Come on, drink this,' he said, giving her some water.

Obediently, she took the glass and began to drink, but the water spilled over and trickled down her hands, breast and knees. Pyotr silently put her back in bed, covered her with the blanket, took the candle and left.

'For God's sake!' Olga shouted again. 'Pyotr, you *must* understand!'

Suddenly something gripped her so violently beneath the stomach and back that her tears were cut short and she bit the pillow in pain. But the pain immediately subsided and she burst out sobbing again.

The maid entered, inquiring anxiously as she straightened the blanket, 'Madam, my dear madam, what's wrong?'

'Clear out of here,' Pyotr snapped as he went over to the bed.

'Please understand, please understand,' Olga began.

'Olga, I beg you, calm yourself!' he said. 'I didn't mean to offend you. I wouldn't have left the bedroom if I'd known you would take it like this. I just felt depressed. I'm telling you this as an honest man.'

'Please try and understand . . . you lied, I lied . . .'

'I *do* understand . . . Well, that's all right now. I do understand,' Pyotr said tenderly, sitting on the bed. 'You spoke in the heat of the moment, it's understandable . . . I swear I love you more than anything in the world and when I married you the thought that you were rich never entered my mind. My love had no bounds . . . that's all, I assure you. I've never needed money and I've never known its value, so I can't appreciate the difference between your position and mine. I've always thought that we were both equally rich. And that remark about my acting deceitfully in small matters. Up to now my life has been run on such frivolous lines that somehow it's been impossible to manage without petty lies. Now *I* feel low too. Let's stop this conversation, for God's sake!'

Olga felt a sharp pain again and grasped her husband's sleeve.

'Oh, such a dreadful pain!' she said hurriedly. 'It's terrible!'

'To hell with all these visitors!' Pyotr muttered as he stood up. 'You shouldn't have gone to the island today!' he shouted. 'And I'm a fool for letting you! God in heaven!'

He scratched his head irritably, waved his arm as if to wash his hands of the whole matter and left the room.

Afterwards he came back several times, sitting on the bed and talking a great deal, gently and angrily in turn. But Olga hardly heard a thing. The sobs alternated with terrible pains, each new one sharper and more prolonged than the last. At first she held her breath and bit the pillow during the spasms, but then she began to produce ear-splitting, obscene shouts. Once, when she saw that her husband was near, she remembered that she had insulted him and without asking herself if she was being delirious or if it really was Pyotr, she seized his hand in both of hers and started kissing it.

'Both you and I lied . . .' she began, trying to excuse herself. 'Please understand, *please*. They've tormented the life out of me, I've no more patience . . .'

'Olga, we're not alone!' Pyotr said.

She raised her head and saw Barbara kneeling by the chest of drawers, taking the lower drawer out – the top ones had already been removed. When she had done this, Barbara stood up, flushed from her efforts, and started opening a small chest with a cold, solemn look on her face.

'Marya, I can't open it,' she whispered. 'Perhaps you can do it for me.'

The maid Marya, who was digging out some wax from a candlestick with some scissors to make room for a new candle, went over to Barbara and helped her open the chest.

'I don't want anything left shut,' Barbara whispered. 'Open that little box as well.' She turned to Pyotr and said, 'You should send for Father Mikhail, sir, to open the altar doors. You must!'

'Do what you like,' Pyotr said between short gasps, 'only get a doctor or midwife as soon as you can, for God's sake. Has Vasily gone? Send someone else as well. Send your husband!'

'I'm in labour,' Olga realized. 'Barbara,' she groaned, 'it will be stillborn.'

'It'll be all right, ma'am, it'll be all right,' Barbara whispered. 'With God's help it'll live.' (It seemed she was incapable of saying 'it will'.)

When Olga came to, after another stab of pain, she was no longer sobbing or tossing about, but moaning instead. She could not help moaning, even in the intervals between the pains. The candles were still burning, but daylight was already breaking through the shutters. Most likely it was about five o'clock. A strange, very meek-looking woman in a white apron was sitting at a round, bedroom table. From her posture it was obvious that she had been there a long time. Olga guessed that she was the midwife.

'Will it soon be over?' she asked and detected a special, unfamiliar note in her own voice which she had never heard before. 'I must be dying in labour,' she thought.

Pyotr came gingerly into the bedroom in his day-time clothes and stood at the window with his back to his wife. He raised the shutters and looked out.

'How it's raining!' he said.

'What's the time?' Olga asked, just to hear that unfamiliar tone in her voice again.

'A quarter to six,' the midwife answered.

'But what if I really am dying?' Olga wondered as she looked at her husband's head and at the windows with the rain beating against them. 'How will he live without me? Who will he drink tea with, dine with, talk to in the evenings, sleep with?'

And he struck her as a little orphan. She felt sorry for him and wanted to tell him something pleasant, affectionate, comforting. She remembered that he was intending buying some hounds in the spring but she had stopped him as she thought hunting was a cruel and dangerous sport.

'Pyotr, go and buy those hounds,' she groaned.

He lowered the blind and went over to the bed, meaning to say something, but at that moment Olga had a spasm and she produced an obscene, piercing shriek.

She was numb from all the pain and the repeated shouting and groaning. She could hear, see, speak at times, but she understood little and was aware only of feeling pain or that she was about to feel it. She had the impression that the party was long ago, not yesterday, but a whole year, that this new life of pain had lasted longer than her childhood, high school days, courses of lectures and marriage put together, and that it would carry on like that for ages and ages, without end. She saw them bring the midwife her tea, call her to lunch at noon and then to dinner. She saw how used Pyotr had become to entering, standing for a long time by the window and leaving, how some strange men, her maid and Barbara had taken to coming in and out. All Barbara could say was 'it'll be, it'll be', and she became very angry whenever anyone closed the drawers in the chest. Olga saw the light change in the room and at the windows – at times there was twilight, then it was dim, as in a mist; at others, there was bright daylight, as at dinner the day before, then twilight once again. And each of these changes appeared to last as long as her childhood, her high school days, the university courses . . .

In the evening two doctors – one bony, bald, with a wide reddish beard, the other swarthy and Jewish-looking, with cheap spectacles

– performed an operation on Olga. She was completely indifferent to those strange men touching her body: no longer did she feel any shame, she had lost her willpower, and anyone could do what he liked with her. If at that moment someone had attacked her with a knife or insulted Pyotr, or deprived her of her right to that little creature, she would not have said one word.

She was given chloroform for the operation. Afterwards, when she woke up, she still had the pains and they were unbearable. It was night. Olga remembered a similar night, with its peace, icon-lamp, midwife sitting motionless by the bed, the chest with its drawers pulled out, Pyotr standing at the window, but that was long, long ago . . .

V

'I haven't died,' Olga thought when she became aware of her surroundings again and the pains had gone.

A bright summer's day looked in through the two wide-open bedroom windows. Sparrows and magpies chattered incessantly in the garden outside.

The drawers in the chest were shut now; her husband's bed had been made. There was no midwife, no Barbara, no maid in the bedroom, only Pyotr standing motionless as before at the window, looking into the garden. There was no crying child, no congratulations or rejoicing, and clearly the small creature had been stillborn.

'Pyotr!' Olga called out to her husband.

Pyotr looked round. A long time must have passed since the last guest had left and Olga had insulted her husband, since Pyotr had become noticeably thinner and pinched-looking.

'What's the matter?' he asked, going over to the bed.

He looked away, twitched his lips and smiled like a helpless child.

'Is it all over?' Olga asked.

Pyotr wanted to reply, but his lips trembled and his mouth twisted like an old man's – like toothless Uncle Nikolay's.

'Olga,' he said, wringing his hands, and suddenly large tears gushed from his eyes. 'Olga! I don't need your money, courts . . .' (here he sobbed) 'differing opinions, those guests, your dowry . . . I don't need anything! Why did we lose our child? Oh, what's the use of talking!'

He waved his arm in defeat and left the bedroom.

But Olga did not care about anything now. Her head was muzzy from the chloroform, she felt spiritually drained. The dull indifference to life that had come over her when the two doctors were performing the operation still had not deserted her.

A Dreary Story

(FROM AN OLD MAN'S MEMOIRS)

I

There lives in Russia an eminent Professor Nikolay Stepanovich Such-and-Such, a Privy Councillor and a man of great distinction. He has so many decorations, both Russian and foreign, that whenever he wears them his students call him the 'icon-stand'. He moves in the very best circles: at least, over the past twenty-five–thirty years he has been on the most intimate terms with every single famous Russian scholar. Nowadays he has no one to make friends with. But if we turn to the past we'll find that the long list of his celebrated friends ends with such names as Pirogov,[1] Kavelin[2] and the poet Nekrasov[3] who bestowed on him their most sincere and warmest friendship. He's a member of all Russian and three foreign universities. And so on . . . All this – and a lot more might be added – makes up my so-called 'name'.

This name of mine is very popular. It's familiar to every literate Russian and is mentioned in foreign lecture-rooms with an additional 'honoured' or 'distinguished'. It's one of those few fortunate names it would be a sign of bad taste to abuse or take in vain in public or in print. And that is only right. You see, my name is closely associated with the concept of a celebrated, richly gifted and unquestionably useful man. I am hard-working, with the stamina of an ox, which is important, and I have talent, which is even more important. What's more, while I'm on the subject, I'm a well-bred, modest and decent fellow. Never have I poked my nose into literature or politics, never have I sought popularity by arguing with ignoramuses, never have I delivered speeches at dinners or at my colleagues' funerals . . .

Generally speaking, there's not a single blemish on my scholarly name – and it has no reason to complain. It is fortunate.

The bearer of this name – myself – I would describe as a man of sixty-two, bald, with false teeth and an incurable nervous tic. I'm as dull and ugly as my name is brilliant and impressive. My head and hands tremble with weakness. Like one of those heroines in Turgenev,[4] my neck resembles the skinny handle of a doublebass, my chest is hollow, my shoulders narrow. When I talk or lecture my mouth twists to one side. When I smile my face is a mass of ghastly, senile wrinkles. There is nothing inspiring about my pathetic figure. Perhaps only when I'm suffering from the tic do I have that special look which is bound to arouse in any observer the grimly inspiring thought: 'That man's obviously not long for this world.'

I still lecture fairly well, as I always have done; as before, I can still hold my audience's attention for two hours. My fervour, my elegant exposition and my humour almost completely conceal the defects of my voice, which is dry, harsh and sing-song, like a sanctimonious preacher's. But I write badly. The portion of my brain that controls the faculty of writing has refused to function. My memory is fading, my thoughts have little consistency and whenever I put them to paper I always feel that I have lost the knack of linking them organically, that my phrasing is monotonous and my language sketchy and feeble. Often I don't write what I mean. When I'm writing the conclusion I've already forgotten the beginning. Often I forget ordinary words and I always have to waste a great deal of energy to avoid superfluous phrases and unnecessary parentheses – both of which are unmistakable proof of my declining mental faculties. Amazingly, the simpler the subject the more painful the effort. I feel far more at ease and intelligent with scientific articles than with letters of congratulation or with memoranda. And another thing: I find it easier to write in German or English than in Russian.

As for my present mode of life I must give first place to the insomnia from which I've been suffering of late. If someone were to question me as to what constitutes the fundamental, basic feature of my life now I would reply: insomnia. From force of habit I still undress and go to bed exactly at midnight. I fall asleep quickly, but between one and two o'clock I wake up, feeling that I haven't slept a wink. I get out of bed and light a lamp. For an hour or two I pace up and down and look at those long-familiar pictures and photographs. When I am weary of walking I sit down at my table and stay there motionless, thinking of nothing, desiring nothing. If there's a book in front of me I draw it towards me and mechanically read it, without any interest. This was how I read in one night an entire novel with the odd title: *What Song the Swallow Sang.*[5] Or to occupy my mind I force myself to count to a thousand or imagine a colleague's face, trying to remember when and under what circumstances he joined the Faculty. I like to listen for sounds. Sometimes my daughter Liza will mutter something rapidly in her sleep two rooms away, or my wife will cross the drawing-room and invariably she'll drop the matchbox; or the warped cupboard will creak; or the lamp burner will suddenly start humming – for some reason all these sounds excite me.

To lie awake at night is to be conscious every minute that you are not normal, and that is why I so long for the morning and the day, when I have the right not to sleep. Many wearisome hours pass before the cock crows in the yard – he is my first herald of good tidings. The moment he crows I know that within an hour the house-porter will wake up and come upstairs for some reason, angrily coughing. And then the light will gradually grow pale at the windows, voices will ring out in the street.

My day begins when my wife arrives. She enters in her petticoat, her hair undone, but washed and smelling of flower-scented eau-de-Cologne and looking as if she has come in by accident. Every time she says the same thing, 'Sorry, I only dropped in for a moment . . . Had another bad night?'

Then she puts the lamp out, sits by the table and starts talking. I'm no prophet, but I know in advance what she's going to talk about – the same thing every morning. Usually, after anxious inquiries about my health, she'll suddenly mention our son, who is an army officer stationed in Warsaw. After the twentieth of every month we send him fifty roubles – and this is our main topic of conversation.

'Of course, it's hard for us,' my wife sighs, 'but it's our duty to help until he can finally fend for himself. The boy's in a strange country, his pay's not very much . . . But if you like we can send him forty roubles instead of fifty next month. What do you think?'

Everyday experience might have taught my wife that constant talk about expenses doesn't reduce them in any way, but my wife refuses to learn from experience and every morning she regularly discusses our officer son and tells me that bread, thank God, is cheaper, but sugar is two copecks dearer – and all this as if she were communicating some important news.

I listen, mechanically agree and probably because I've had a bad night, strange, inappropriate thoughts grip me. I look at my wife and I wonder like a child. In bewilderment I ask myself if this extremely stout, clumsy old woman with her dull look of petty anxiety and fear that we might starve, her eyes clouded by constant brooding over debts and privation, who can talk of nothing but expenses and who smiles only when prices come down – could this woman possibly be the same slim Varya with whom I once fell in love so passionately for her fine, lucid mind, her pure soul, her beauty, because she felt 'sympathy' for my studies as Desdemona did for Othello?[6] Could this really be the same Varya, my wife who once bore me a son?

I gaze intently into this flabby, clumsy old woman's face, trying to discover my Varya, but of her past self nothing remains except her concern for my health and her habit of calling my salary 'our salary', my cap 'our cap'. It pains me to look at her and to provide her with a few scraps of comfort I let her say what she likes – and I even keep quiet when she criticizes people unfairly or picks on me for not going into private practice or publishing textbooks.

Our conversations always end the same way. My wife suddenly remembers that I haven't had my tea and takes fright.

'What am I sitting here for?' she says, getting up. 'The samovar's been on the table for ages and here I am chattering away. Heavens, I've become so forgetful!'

She quickly goes out but she stops at the door to ask, 'Did you know we owe Yegor five months' wages? We mustn't let the servants' wages run up, I've told you that so many times! It's far easier paying them ten roubles a month than fifty every five months!'

In the doorway she stops again to say, 'The one I feel most sorry for is our Liza. She's a student at the Conservatoire, she's always mixing in good society, yet just look how she's dressed! That fur coat would make anyone ashamed to be seen in the street with it. It wouldn't matter so much if she were *anyone's* daughter, but everyone knows that her father is a famous professor, a Privy Councillor!'

And after reproaching me with my name and position she finally leaves. So begins my day. Nor does it get any better.

While I'm drinking my tea in comes my daughter Liza in her fur coat and little hat, carrying some music books – all ready to go to the Conservatoire. She is twenty-two, but she looks younger. She's pretty and a bit like my wife when she was young. She kisses me affectionately on the temple and hand.

'Good morning, Papa. How are you?' she asks.

As a child she was very fond of ice cream and I often took her to a café. Ice cream was her criterion of excellence. If she wanted to praise me she would say, 'Papa, you're all ice creamy!' One of her fingers would be called 'pistachio', another 'cream', another 'raspberry' – and so on. Usually when she came in to say good morning I would sit her on my knee and kiss her fingers.

'Vanilla . . . pistachio . . . lemon . . .' I would say.

And even now, for old time's sake, I still kiss Liza's fingers and mutter, 'Pistachio, cream, lemon . . .', but it somehow doesn't sound right. I'm as cold as ice cream myself, I feel embarrassed. When my daughter comes in and touches my temple with her lips I give a sudden start, as if stung by a bee, produce a forced smile and turn my face away. Ever since I first began to suffer from insomnia one question has constantly been nagging me: my daughter often sees me, an elderly, distinguished man, blush painfully because I haven't paid our footman his wages. She sees how often my worrying over petty debts makes me stop work and thoughtfully pace the room for hours on end. So why has she never once come to see me without her mother's knowledge to whisper, 'Papa, here's my watch, my bracelets, earrings, dresses . . . pawn the lot, you need the money'? When she sees her mother and myself trying to keep up appearances why doesn't she give up the expensive pleasure of studying music? I could never accept her watch, or bracelets or any other sacrifices – God forbid! I don't need them.

And this leads me to think of my son, the army officer in Warsaw. He is an intelligent, honest and sober person. But that's not enough for me. I fancy that if I had an old father and knew that there were times when he was ashamed of being so poor, I would give up my commission to someone else and take a job as a labourer. Such thoughts about my children poison me. But what good are these thoughts? Only a narrow-minded or embittered man can harbour malicious thoughts about ordinary mortals for not being heroes. But enough of that.

At a quarter to ten I have to go and deliver a lecture to my dear boys. I get dressed and walk down the road I have known for thirty years and which has a history of its own for me. Here is the large grey building with the chemist's shop. Here there used to be a small house with an ale bar – there I planned my thesis and wrote my first love letter to Varya, in pencil, on a page with the heading *Historia Morbi*.[7] Next comes the grocer's, once kept by a little Jew who sold me cigarettes on credit and later by a fat woman who was fond of the students because 'every one of them had a mother'. Now it's occupied by a red-haired shopkeeper – a very phlegmatic man who drinks his tea from a copper teapot. And here are the grim university gates that have long needed repairing, a bored janitor in a sheepskin jacket, a broom, heaps of snow . . . Such gates cannot make a healthy impression on a bright young boy from the provinces who imagines that the Temple of Learning really is a temple. All in all, the dilapidated university buildings, the gloomy corridors and grimy walls, the lack of light, the dismal aspect of the steps, coat-hooks and benches play a leading role as a conditioning factor in the history of Russian pessimism. And here is our garden. I fancy it has grown neither better nor worse since I was a student. I do not like it. It would have been much more sensible to have grown some lofty pines and fine oaks there instead of shrivelled-up limes, yellow acacias and skimpy, clipped lilacs. Most students' moods are influenced by their environment, therefore they should be able to see only what is noble, impressive and elegant at all times at their place of study. God preserve them from spindly trees, broken windows, grey walls and doors upholstered with torn oil-cloth.

When I approach my own entrance the door is flung open and I'm met by my old colleague, contemporary and namesake, Nikolay the porter. He lets me in, clears his throat and says, 'It's very frosty, Professor!' Or if my fur coat is damp: 'It's raining, Professor!'

Then he runs on ahead and opens all the doors on the way. In my study he solicitously takes off my coat, at the same time managing to communicate some item of university news. Thanks to the close camaraderie that exists between all university porters and caretakers, he knows simply everything that is going on in all four faculties, in the registry, the Vice-Chancellor's study and the library. There's absolutely nothing he doesn't know about. When the latest news is a Dean's or Vice-Chancellor's resignation, for example, I can hear him talking to the young janitors, naming candidates for the vacancy, explaining that So-and-So wouldn't be approved by the Minister, or that So-and-So would turn it down himself. Then he goes into fantastic detail about some mysterious papers that were received in the registry about a secret conversation alleged to have taken place between the Minister and a trustee – and so on. If you spare all the details, in general he's almost always right. His descriptions of each candidate's character, although highly original, turn out to be correct as well. If you need to know in what year someone defended a thesis, took up his post, retired or died, then call on this old soldier's prodigious memory and he will not only tell you the year month and day, but will also furnish all the details that accompanied this or that event. Only someone who loves his work can have such a memory.

He is a custodian of university traditions. From the porters who were his predecessors he has inherited many legends of university life and to this repository of wealth he has added many riches of his own, acquired during years of service. Many are the stories he will tell you – long or short – if you so desire. He can tell of extraordinary sages who knew everything, of remarkable scholars who would go without sleep for weeks on end, of science's innumerable martyrs and victims. In his stories good always triumphs over evil, the weak over the strong, the wise over fools, the humble over the proud, the young over the old . . . There's no need to take all his cock-and-bull stories and fables at their face value, but if you sift them you will be left with what is truly important: our fine traditions and the names of real, universally recognized heroes.

In our society all information about the academic world is confined to a few anecdotes about the phenomenal absent-mindedness of elderly professors and two or three witticisms variously ascribed to Gruber,[8] myself or Babukhin.[9] For an educated public this is rather feeble. If people loved learning, scholars, students as Nikolay does, its literature would long ago have included entire epics, legends and chronicles which it unfortunately lacks these days.

Whenever he tells me the news Nikolay assumes a grave expression and we get down to business. If an outsider could observe the ease with which Nikolay uses scientific terminology at these times he might easily conclude that here was an academic masquerading as an old campaigner. Incidentally, those rumours about the erudition of university porters are greatly exaggerated. True, Nikolay knows more than a hundred Latin terms, can put a skeleton together, can occasionally prepare specimens or amuse the students with some long, learned quotation. But a simple theory such as the circulation of the blood, let's say, is as great a mystery to him now as it was twenty years ago.

At a table in my study, bent low over a book or some preparation, sits Pyotr Ignatyevich my demonstrator, a hard-working, modest but untalented man of about thirty-five, already bald and with a fat belly. He slaves away from dawn to dusk, reads a great deal and can remember everything he has read – in this respect he's a perfect treasure. But in all other respects he's a mere drudge – in other words a learned blockhead. The drudge-like features that distinguish him from someone of genuine talent are as follows: his horizon is narrow and severely restricted to his speciality; outside his special subject he is like a child. I can remember going into his office one morning and saying, 'What terrible news! I've heard that Skobelev's[10] died.'

Nikolay crosses himself, but Pyotr Ignatyevich turns to me and asks, 'Who is this Skobelev?'

Another time – this was somewhat earlier – I tell him that Professor

Perov[11] has died and my dear old Pyotr Ignatyevich asks 'What did he lecture on?'

I fancy that if Patti[12] sang into his ear, if hordes of Chinese invaded Russia, if there was an earthquake, he wouldn't turn a hair and would calmly keep squinting down his microscope. In short, 'What's Hecuba to him?'[13] I would give anything to see this dry old stick in bed with his wife.

Another feature is his fanatical faith in the infallibility of science and above all in everything written by Germans. He has great confidence in himself and in his preparations, he knows the purpose of life and is a total stranger to those doubts and disappointments which make more talented people go grey. There's his cringing deference to authority and complete absence of any desire for independent thought. It's impossible to make him change his mind about anything and it's impossible to argue with him. Just try and argue with a man who is firmly convinced that medicine is queen of the sciences, that doctors are a superior breed and that medical traditions are the finest. The sole surviving tradition from medicine's tarnished past is the white tie, still worn by doctors. For scholars and any educated person there can only be traditions that apply to the university as a whole, without distinction between medicine, law, etc. But it's hard for Pyotr Ignatyevich to agree with this and he is prepared to argue with you until doomsday.

I have a clear picture of his future. In the course of his life he'll make a few hundred preparations of unparalleled purity, write many dreary but very decent articles, turn out a dozen or so conscientious translations. But he'll never set the world alight. For that you need imagination, inventiveness, vision, but Pyotr Ignatyevich is blessed with none of these things. In brief, he's not a master in science, but a journeyman.

Pyotr Ignatyevich, Nikolay and I speak in an undertone. We feel a little uneasy. You always have this special kind of feeling when you can hear your audience booming away like the sea on the other side of the lecture-room door. Thirty years haven't inured me to this feeling and I have it every morning. Nervously I button up my frock-coat, ask Nikolay unnecessary questions, get cross. I may seem to be behaving like a coward, but this is something quite different from cowardice, something which I can neither put a name to nor describe.

'Well then, it's time to go in,' I say.

And we proceed into the hall, in the following order: first is Nikolay with the preparations or charts, then myself – and after me lumbers the old drudge, head humbly bowed. Or, when it's necessary, a corpse is carried in first on a stretcher, followed by Nikolay, and so on. On my appearance the students stand up, then they sit down and the roar of the sea suddenly subsides: the ocean is becalmed.

I know what I'm about to lecture on, but have no idea *how* I'm going to lecture, what I shall begin with and how I shall conclude. I haven't a single sentence ready in my mind. But I only have to cast my eyes over the lecture-hall (it is built like an amphitheatre) and utter the obligatory: 'At last week's lecture we stopped at . . .' for the sentences to spring from my inner self in long procession – and then I'm off! I speak with irrepressible speed and passion and feel that no earthly power could stem the flow of words. To lecture well – so that your audience will profit from your lecture and not be bored – you need not only talent but a certain knack, experience, the clearest possible awareness of your own strengths, of your audience and the subject of your lecture. Besides that, you need to be on your toes, to be ever-vigilant and never lose sight of your objective for one moment.

A good conductor does twenty things at once when interpreting a composer: he reads the score, waves his baton, watches the singer, motions sideways towards the drums or French horns, and so on. That is just what I do when lecturing. Before me are one hundred and fifty faces, all different, with three hundred eyes staring straight at me. My aim is to vanquish this many-headed hydra. If I can keep their level of concentration and comprehension clearly in mind every minute of my lecture, then they are in my power. My other enemy dwells within me. This is the infinite variety of forms, phenomena and laws, and the mass of ideas – my own and other people's – conditioned by them. Every minute I must be skilful enough to snatch from this vast body of material what is most important and vital and at the same time keep pace with the speed of my thoughts and present them in a form that will be intelligible to the hydra and arouse its attention; at the same time I must be ever-vigilant, so that I convey my ideas not simply as they happen to accumulate, but in the specific order which is essential for the correct composition of the picture I'm trying to paint. Further, I endeavour to use polished language, to ensure that my definitions are brief and precise, my phraseology as simple and elegant as possible. Every minute I have to hold myself in check and remember that I have only an hour and forty minutes at my disposal. In brief, I have my work cut out. At one and the same time I have to play the scholar, the pedagogue and the orator – and woe betide me if the orator gets the better of the pedagogue and scholar, or vice versa.

After lecturing for about a quarter or half an hour, you suddenly notice that the students are beginning to stare at the ceiling or at Pyotr Ignatyevich. One of them feels for his handkerchief, another fidgets in his seat, another smiles at his own thoughts . . . This means their attention is flagging and action is necessary. I seize the first opportunity and crack a joke. The one hundred and fifty faces grin broadly, eyes gaily sparkle, the sea briefly roars. I laugh as well. Their concentration has been revived and I can continue.

No debate, diversion or game has ever given me such enjoyment as lecturing. Only when lecturing have I been able to let myself go completely and come to understand that inspiration is not an invention of poets, but really does exist. And I don't think that even after his most piquant labour Hercules ever felt such voluptuous exhaustion as I do after lecturing.

All that is in the past – now lecturing is nothing but sheer torture for me. Barely half an hour goes by before I start to feel an overwhelming weakness in my legs and shoulders. I sit in an armchair, but I am not used to lecturing sitting down. A minute later I get up and continue standing – then I sit down again. My mouth goes dry, my voice grows hoarse, my head spins . . . To hide my condition from the audience I keep drinking water, cough, frequently blow my nose as if I have a cold, casually make irrelevant jokes and finish by announcing the break before I should. But above all I feel ashamed.

My conscience and reason tell me that the best thing I could do now would be to deliver a valedictory lecture to my boys, to say one last word to them, to give them my blessing and surrender my post to a younger and stronger man than myself. But as God is my judge I lack the courage to act according to my conscience.

Unfortunately I am neither philosopher nor theologian. I know perfectly well that I have no more than six months to live. I think I should really be concerned most of all with the gloom beyond the grave and the ghosts that will haunt my sepulchral slumbers. But for some reason my heart rejects these questions, although my mind fully recognizes their full import. Now that I am on the brink of death only science has any interest for me – it is the same as twenty to thirty years ago. When I draw my last breath I shall still believe that science is the most important, beautiful and vital thing in man's life, that it always has been and always will be the highest manifestation of love and that only through science will man conquer nature and himself. Although this belief may appear naïve and based on false assumptions, it's not my fault if this is what I believe and not otherwise. This is my creed and I am powerless to destroy it.

But this is beside the point. All I ask is for people to indulge my weakness and to understand that to tear from his professorial chair and his students a man for whom the fate of the bone medulla is of more interest than the ultimate purpose of the universe would be equivalent to seizing him and nailing him in his coffin without waiting for him to die.

Because of my insomnia and the strain of fighting my increasing weakness strange things are happening to me. In the middle of my lecture tears suddenly choke me, my eyes begin to smart and I feel a passionate, hysterical urge to stretch my hands out and complain out loud. I want to shout out loud that fate has sentenced me, a famous man, to death and that within about six months another person will be holding sway in the lecture-hall. I want to cry out that I've been poisoned. New thoughts that I've never known before have poisoned the last few days of my life and they continue to sting my brain like mosquitoes. Just now my position seems so terrible that I want my entire audience to leap from their seats in horror and rush panic-stricken for the exit, shrieking in despair.

Such moments are not easy to endure.

II

After the lecture I stay at home and work. I read journals, theses, or prepare my next lecture; sometimes I do some writing. My work is constantly interrupted as I have to receive visitors.

The door bell rings. It's a colleague who has come to discuss some academic matter. He enters with his hat and walking-stick. Thrusting both at me he says, 'I've just dropped in for a minute . . . only a minute! Now, don't get up, my dear colleague! Just a couple of words . . .'

From the start we try to show each other how exceptionally polite we are and how terribly delighted we are to see each other. I sit him in an armchair and he makes me sit as well – as we do this we carefully stroke each other's waist, touch each other's buttons and it seems that we are feeling each other and are afraid of burning our fingers. We both laugh, although we don't say anything amusing. Seated in our chairs, we lean our heads towards each other and speak in subdued voices. However cordially disposed we might be to each other, we cannot help gilding our conversation with all kinds of pretentious piffle like: 'As you so justly deigned to observe', or 'As I already had the honour of informing you.' And we cannot help laughing out loud if one of us cracks a joke, however poor. His business completed, my colleague abruptly gets up, waves his hat at my work and begins to say goodbye. Again we paw each other, again we laugh. I see him into the hall. Here I help him on with his fur coat, but he makes every effort to decline so signal an honour. Then, when Yegor opens the front door, my colleague assures me that I will catch cold, but I pretend that I'm prepared to accompany him right out into the street even. Finally, when I'm back in my study, my face is still smiling – from inertia I suppose.

A little later the bell rings again. Someone enters the hall, spends a long time removing his coat and coughing. Yegor announces that a student has arrived. 'Ask him in,' I tell Yegor. A minute later in comes a young man of pleasant appearance. For the past year relations between us have been strained: he makes a dreadful hash of his exams and I give him the lowest mark. Every year I have about seven young hopefuls like him whom I fail – or 'plough' in student slang. Those who fail their exams, either through inability or sickness, usually bear their cross patiently and don't try to bargain with me. The only ones who come to my house to bargain are the sanguine, expansive types for whom hard cramming spoils their appetite and prevents them from going to the opera regularly. To the first I am merciful, the latter I keep 'ploughing' all year round.

'Please sit down,' I tell my visitor. 'What is it?'

'Sorry to trouble you, professor,' he begins, faltering and not looking me in the eye. 'I wouldn't have taken the liberty of disturbing you if . . . I . . . er . . . I've sat your exam five times and I've been . . . er . . . ploughed every time. I'm begging you, please be good enough to pass me, because . . .'

The argument all these idlers defend themselves with is invariably the same: they have passed all their other subjects with distinction, only in mine have they come to grief, which is all the more surprising, since they have always studied my subject so diligently and know it backwards. They have failed because of some mysterious *misunderstanding*.

'Forgive me, my friend,' I tell my visitor, 'but I cannot pass you. Go and study your lecture notes a bit more and come and see me again. Then we shall see.'

A pause. I have the urge to make my student suffer a little for preferring beer and the opera to learning and I say with a sigh, 'I think it would be best if you gave up medicine altogether. If someone of your ability can't pass his exams it's obvious you have neither the desire nor the vocation to become a doctor.'

The young hopeful's face lengthens. 'I'm sorry, professor, but it would be very odd if I did that, to say the least,' he laughs. 'Study for five years and then suddenly chuck it all in!'

'Well, why not? It's better to lose five years than spend the rest of your life doing something you don't like.'

But immediately I feel sorry for him and hasten to add, 'Well, do as you like. Study a bit more and then come and see me again.'

'When?' the idler asks in an empty voice.

'Whenever you like. How about tomorrow?'

And in his good-natured eyes I can read, 'All right, I'll come, but you'll only plough me again, you bastard!'

'Of course,' I say, 'you won't know any more medicine even if you sit my exam another fifteen times. But it's all good character training – for that you should be grateful.'

Silence follows. I get up and wait for my visitor to leave, but he stands there looking out of the window, fingering his beard and thinking. The whole thing's becoming a bore.

The young hopeful's voice is agreeably mellow, his eyes are intelligent and mocking, his complacent face is somewhat bloated from too much beer-drinking and lying around on his sofa for hours. No doubt he could tell me many interesting things about the opera, his love affairs, his fellow-students of whom he is very fond, but unfortunately it isn't the done thing to discuss such matters. Yet I would gladly listen.

'Professor! On my word of honour, if you pass me I'll . . . er . . .'

The moment we arrive at 'word of honour' I gesture in despair and sit at my desk. The student ponders for another minute.

'In that case, goodbye,' he says dejectedly. 'I'm sorry . . .'

'Goodbye, old chap. Look after yourself.'

Hesitantly he goes into the hall, slowly puts on his coat and probably spends a long time when he's out in the street mulling everything over again. And then, failing to think up anything except 'old devil' with regard to myself, he goes into a cheap restaurant for a glass of beer and something to eat, then back home to bed. May your ashes rest in peace, honest toiler!

The bell rings for the third time. In comes a young doctor wearing a new black suit, gold-rimmed spectacles and – naturally – a white tie. He introduces himself. I sit him down and ask what I can do for him. Rather nervously, this youthful devotee of learning tells me first that this year he has passed his qualifying exam for his doctorate: it only remains to write the thesis. He would like me to supervise him and he would be *awfully* obliged if I could suggest a subject.

'Delighted to be of assistance, my dear colleague,' I say, 'but let's first see if we agree about what a thesis is. The word is generally taken to mean an essay which is the product of original work. Isn't that so? But compositions written on someone else's subject and under someone else's guidance have a different name . . .'

The candidate says nothing. I fly into a rage and leap from my chair. 'Why do you all come to me!' I shout angrily. 'That's what I don't understand. Do you think I'm running a shop? I don't peddle research subjects! For the umpteenth time I'm asking you all to leave me in peace! Apologies for being so blunt, but I'm really sick to death of all this!'

The candidate makes no reply – only a slight flush appears around his cheekbones. His face expresses profound respect for my distinguished name and erudition, but I can see from his eyes that he despises my voice, my pathetic figure, my nervous gestures. In my wrath I strike him as some kind of freak.

'This isn't a shop!' I fume. 'Why don't you want to be independent – that's what amazes me! Why do you find freedom so repellent?'

I say a great deal, but still he remains silent. In the end I gradually calm down – and of course I give in. The candidate will get a subject not worth a brass farthing from me, he'll write a thesis of no use to anyone, under my supervision, he'll defend it with merit in a tedious oral and be awarded a higher degree that is of no use to him.

The doorbell could go on ringing for ever, but for the moment I shall confine myself to four visits. It rings a fourth time and I hear familiar footsteps, the rustle of a dress, a dear voice.

Eighteen years ago an oculist colleague of mine died, leaving a seven-year-old daughter Katya and sixty thousand roubles. In his will he appointed me guardian. Until she was ten, Katya lived with my family, then she was sent to boarding-school and spent only the summer holidays with us. I never had the time to take care of her education and supervised it only in fits and starts, which is why I can say very little about her childhood.

The first thing I remember about her and which remains a fond memory is the extraordinary trustfulness she showed when she came into my house and with which she let herself be treated by doctors, a trustfulness which always illumined her little face. She would sit somewhere out of the way with her cheek bandaged, invariably looking attentively at something – whether it was myself writing or leafing through a book, or my wife bustling about the house, or the cook peeling potatoes in the kitchen, or the dog playing, her eyes always expressed the same thing: 'Everything that happens in this world is wise and wonderful.' She was inquisitive and very fond of talking to me. Seated at the table opposite me she would sometimes follow my movements and ask questions. She was interested in what I was reading, what I did at the university, whether I was scared of corpses, what I did with my salary.

'Do students fight at the university?' she would ask.

'Yes they do, my dear.'

'Do you make them go down on their knees?'

'Yes I do.'

She found it funny that the students fought and that I made them go down on their knees and she would burst out laughing. She was a gentle, patient, good child. I often happened to see something taken away from her, saw her punished without reason, or her curiosity left unsatisfied. At such times a touch of sadness would colour her perpetually trusting expression – and that was all. I was incapable of standing up for her, but only when I saw her sadness did I long to draw her close to me and comfort her like some old nanny with the words: 'My poor darling orphan!'

I also remember how she loved dressing up and sprinkling herself with scent. In this respect she was like me: I too am fond of nice clothes and perfume.

I do regret that I had neither the time nor the inclination to observe the origin and growth of that passion which took possession of Katya when she was fourteen or fifteen. I mean her passionate love for the theatre. When she came home from school for the summer holidays she would talk of nothing with such delight and enthusiasm as plays and actors. She would exhaust us with her endless talk of the theatre.

My wife and children wouldn't listen and I alone lacked the courage to refuse her an audience. Whenever she felt like sharing her excitement she would come into my study and plead, 'Nikolay Stepanych, let me talk about the theatre with you!'

I would point at the clock and say, 'You've got half an hour. Begin!'

Later she started bringing home by the dozen portraits of actors and actresses whom she worshipped. Then she tried several times to get parts in amateur theatricals and finally, when she finished boarding-school, she announced that she was born to be an actress.

I never shared Katya's enthusiasm for the theatre. As I see it, if a play's any good there's no need to trouble actors in order to get the intended impression – reading should suffice. If a play's bad, no acting will make it good.

When I was young I often went to the theatre and now my family takes a box about twice a year, to give me 'an airing'. Of course, this does not entitle me to criticize the theatre and I won't say much about it. In my view the theatre hasn't improved over the past thirty to forty years. It's still impossible to get a glass of water in the corridors or the foyer, the attendants still fine me twenty copecks for my fur coat, although I can see nothing dishonourable in wearing warm clothes in winter. The orchestra still plays in the intervals without the slightest need for it, adding a new, unsolicited impression to that which has already been conveyed by the play. The gentlemen still go to the bar in the intervals to drink spirits. If there's no progress in small matters there's no point in seeking it in the really important ones. When an actor, cloaked from head to foot in theatrical traditions and prejudices, tries to declaim that simple, straightforward soliloquy 'To be or not to be' in a way that is far from simple – and for some reason invariably accompanied by hissing and general bodily convulsions – when he tries to convince me at all costs that Chatsky,[14] who talks so much with fools and is in love with a foolish girl, is a very clever man and that *Woe from Wit* isn't a dull play, the stage seems to exhale that same old routine which bored me so much forty years ago, when I was regaled with classical lamentations and breast-beating. And on each occasion I leave the theatre more conservative than when I went in. You can convince the sentimental, gullible herd that the theatre in its present state is a school, but anyone who knows what a school really is will not rise to this bait. I cannot predict what will happen in fifty or a hundred years, but as things are the theatre can serve only as a kind of diversion. But this kind of entertainment is too expensive to be enjoyed in the long term. It deprives the state of thousands of healthy, talented young men and women who might have become good doctors, farmers, schoolmistresses, officers had they not devoted themselves to the stage. It robs the public of the evening hours, the best time for intellectual work and friendly conversation – not to mention the wasted money and moral damage to the theatre-goer when he sees murder, fornication or slander badly handled on the stage.

Katya's views were completely different. She assured me that even in its present state the theatre was superior to lecture-rooms, books – superior to anything in this world. The stage was a force that united all the arts, the actors were missionaries. No art or science on its own could have such a strong, beneficial influence on the human soul as the stage and it was no surprise that third-rate actors enjoyed greater popularity in Russia than the finest scholar or artist. And no public activity could give so much pleasure and satisfaction as the stage.

So one fine day Katya joined a theatrical troupe and went off – to Ufa[15] I think – taking a great deal of money with her, a host of rainbow-hued hopes and grandiose notions about the venture.

Her first letters written on the journey were marvellous. I read them and was simply amazed that those small sheets of paper could contain so much youth, spiritual purity, heavenly innocence and at the same time such subtle and business-like judgements as would have done credit to a keen male intellect. The Volga, the countryside, the towns she visited, her colleagues, her successes and failures – these she did not so much describe as glorify in song. Every line breathed that trustfulness which I was used to seeing on her face – and with all this there were masses of grammatical mistakes and practically no punctuation.

Barely six months passed when I received a highly romantic,

rapturous letter beginning: 'I'm in love.' In it was enclosed a photograph of a young man with clean-shaven face, broad-brimmed hat and a plaid draped over one shoulder. The following letters were just as splendid, but now punctuation marks made an appearance, there were no more grammatical mistakes and there was a strong masculine flavour to them. What a wonderful idea it would be, wrote Katya, to build a large theatre somewhere on the Volga. It had to be a limited company and rich businessmen and shipowners must be brought in to invest in it. There would be lots of money, the takings would be tremendous and the actors would perform on a partnership basis. This was all very well in theory, but I feel such schemes can only originate in a male head.

Anyway, everything clearly went well for eighteen months or two years: Katya was in love, she had faith in her work and she was happy. But then I began to notice in her letters unmistakable signs of decline. It began with complaints about her colleagues – the first and most ominous symptom. If a young scholar or literary man embarks on his career bitterly complaining about other scholars or literary men it's a sure sign he is already worn out and unfit for the work. Katya wrote that her companions skipped rehearsals and never knew their parts. By the absurd plays they put on, by their behaviour on stage, every one of them showed utter contempt for the public. For the sake of box-office receipts – which was all they could talk about – serious actresses sank to singing music-hall songs, while tragic actors performed in sketches satirizing deceived husbands, the pregnancies of unfaithful wives and so on. The amazing thing is – generally speaking – that the provincial stage hasn't folded up to now and that it can still hang on by such a rotten, tenuous thread.

In reply I wrote Katya a long and admittedly very boring letter. Amongst other things I wrote: 'I've often chatted with elderly actors – the nicest of people and very well-disposed towards me. From my conversations with them I learned that in their work they were guided less by their own intelligence and freedom of choice than by fashion and society's mood. The best of them in their time had happened to act in tragedies, operettas, Parisian farces and in pantomimes, and in whatever they performed they felt they were on the right road and were doing something useful. So, as you can see, you mustn't look for the reason for this evil in the actors themselves but somewhere deeper, in the art itself and the whole of society's attitude to it.' My letter only irritated Katya. 'We're talking at cross purposes,' she replied. 'I didn't mean those exceedingly worthy people who are well-disposed towards you, but a gang of rogues who have absolutely no sense of decency. They are a pack of savages who went onto the stage only because no one else would employ them – these people call themselves artists only because they have the cheek to. Not one genuine talent among them, but plenty of mediocrities, drunkards, schemers and scandalmongers. I just cannot tell you how bitter it makes one feel that the art I love so dearly has fallen into the clutches of those who are loathsome to me. Bitter, because even the best of men only observe evil from the distance, don't wish to come any nearer and instead of taking a stand write platitudes and pointless sermons in the most ponderous style . . .' – and so on, in the same vein.

Shortly afterwards I received the following letter: 'I have been cruelly deceived. I cannot go on living. Dispose of my money as you think best. I loved you as a father and as my only friend. Farewell!'

He too belonged to the 'pack of savages', so it turned out. Later on I was able to guess from certain hints that she attempted suicide: apparently she tried to poison herself. I could only suppose she must have been seriously ill after that, since the next letter was from Yalta, where the doctors had most probably sent her. In her last letter she asked me to send her (in Yalta) one thousand roubles as soon as possible and it finished with these words: 'I'm sorry this letter's so depressing. Yesterday I buried my baby.' After living for about a year in Yalta she came home.

She travelled for about four years and I must confess that throughout those four years I played a pretty unenviable and strange part as far as she was concerned. Earlier, when she announced that she was going on the stage and then wrote about her love affair; when she was overcome by sporadic fits of extravagance; when time and again

I had to respond to her demands by sending one thousand, two thousand roubles; when she wrote that she intended taking her life and then about the death of her child – on each occasion I became flustered and all my concern for her fate amounted to was a great deal of reflection and the penning of long, boring letters which I needn't have written at all. And yet, all said and done, I was like a father to her and loved her as my own daughter!

Now Katya lives about a quarter of a mile from me. She has taken a five-roomed flat and installed herself quite comfortably and in her own distinctive taste. If someone were to make a sketch of her surroundings the predominant mood would be one of indolence. For indolent bodies there are soft couches and soft stools; for indolent legs soft carpets; for indolent eyes faded, dull or matt colours; for the indolent spirit an abundance of cheap fans and trifling pictures on the walls, where originality of execution prevails over content, an excessive number of small tables and shelves crammed with absolutely worthless, useless junk, amorphous rags instead of curtains . . . All this, together with a phobia of bright colours, proportion and space – not to mention spiritual sloth – shows a perversion of natural taste into the bargain. For days on end Katya lies on her couch reading – mostly novels and short stories. She leaves the house only once a day, in the afternoon, to come and see me.

I am at my work, while Katya sits silently on a nearby sofa, wrapped up in her shawl as if she's feeling the cold. Whether it's because I'm so fond of her or because I've grown used to her frequent visits since she was a little girl, her presence doesn't stop me concentrating. Now and then I mechanically ask her something and I get a sharp rejoinder; or when I want a moment's relaxation I turn towards her and watch her pensively browsing through some medical journal or the newspaper. It is then that I notice she has lost that earlier trusting look. Now her expression is cold, apathetic, vacant, the kind you find with passengers who have to wait a long time for their train. She still dresses beautifully and simply, but carelessly. Her dress and hair have taken a great deal of punishment from lying for days on end on sofas and rocking-chairs – that is plain to see. No longer is she inquisitive, which she was before. No longer does she ask me questions – it's as if she has sampled everything in life and does not expect to hear anything new.

Towards four o'clock there are sounds of movement in the hall and drawing-room: Liza is back from the Conservatoire, bringing some of her female friends home with her. I can hear them playing the piano, trying out their voices and laughing out loud. Yegor is laying the table, making the crockery rattle.

'Goodbye,' says Katya. 'I won't drop in on your family today – I hope they'll forgive me. I don't have the time. Come and see me.'

As I see her into the hall she looks me up and down sternly and says irritably, 'You're getting even thinner! Why don't you go and see a doctor? I'll drive over to Sergey Fyodorovich's and get him to come and have a look at you.'

'It's not necessary, Katya.'

'I don't understand why your family does nothing about it. A fine lot, I must say!'

Impulsively she puts on her fur coat and two or three hairpins invariably fall to the floor from her carelessly arranged hair. She is too lazy and in too much of a hurry to tidy it. She clumsily hides the straggling locks under her hat and leaves.

When I enter the dining-room my wife asks, 'Was that Katya just now? Why didn't she come and see me? It's really most odd!'

'Mama!' Liza says reproachfully. 'If she doesn't want to – then blow her! It's not for us to go down on our knees!'

'As you like, but it shows total disregard. Sitting in the study for three hours without a thought for us! Well, she can do as she likes.'

Varya and Liza both hate Katya. This hatred is beyond my comprehension and one must probably be a woman to understand it. I would stake my life that out of the hundred and fifty young men whom I see almost every day in my lecture-room, and out of the hundred elderly ones I happen to meet every week, you would be hard put to find even one capable of understanding this hatred and revulsion for Katya's past – I mean her extra-marital pregnancy and illegitimate child. On the other hand I can't remember a single woman or young girl of my acquaintance who would not have nurtured these feelings, whether consciously or instinctively. And that's not because women are more virtuous or any purer than men. After all, virtue and chastity aren't very different from vice if they are not free of malice. I explain this simply as women's backwardness. That dreary feeling of compassion and those pangs of conscience that modern men experience at the sight of misfortune tell me far more about culture and moral development than hatred and revulsion. Modern women are just as given to tears and are as insensitive as they were in the Middle Ages. And I think that those who advise them to be educated like men are completely in the right.

The other reasons why my wife doesn't like Katya are for having been an actress, for her ingratitude, pride, weird behaviour and for all those innumerable vices that one woman always manages to find in another.

Besides myself and my family two or three of my daughter's friends, together with Aleksandr Adolfovich Gnekker, Liza's admirer and suitor, are dining with us. Gnekker is a young, fair-haired man, no more than thirty, of medium height, very stout, broad-shouldered, with reddish sideburns around his ears and a dyed moustache, which makes his podgy, smooth face look like a toy. He is wearing a very short jacket, an embroidered waistcoat, trousers with a large check pattern – very wide at the top and narrow at the bottom – and yellow, flat-heeled shoes. His eyes protrude like a crab's, his tie resembles a crab's neck and I even think that young man's whole body smells of crab soup. He calls every day, but no one in my family knows anything about his background, where he was educated or what his income is. He neither plays nor sings, but he has some sort of connection with music and singing, sells pianos for someone somewhere, is frequently at the Conservatoire, knows all the celebrities and arranges concerts. He criticizes music with an air of great authority and I've noticed that everyone is keen to agree with him.

Rich people always have their parasites around them and it's the same with the arts and sciences. It seems that there is no art or science in this world which is free of 'foreign bodies' such as this Mr Gnekker. I am no musician and perhaps I may be wrong about Gnekker – whom I hardly know, as it happens. But the air of authority and dignity with which he stands by the piano and listens when someone sings or plays strikes me as all too suspicious.

You may be a fine gentleman or person of high distinction a hundred times over, but if you have a daughter you can never be secure from the petty bourgeois atmosphere that match-making, courtship and weddings often bring into your house and into your state of mind. I, for example, can never reconcile myself to that triumphant expression on my wife's face whenever Gnekker is dining with us, nor can I reconcile myself to those bottles of Lafite, port and sherry which are brought out especially for him, so that he can see with his own eyes how grandly and sumptuously we live. Nor can I stomach that erratic laughter of Liza's, a habit she picked up at the Conservatoire, and the way she screws up her eyes whenever we have male visitors. But above all I just cannot understand why a person who is so utterly alien to my habits, my academic interests, to the whole tenor of my life and who is so completely different from those I love, should come and dine with me every day. My wife and the servants whisper mysteriously that he is the 'fiancé', but I still cannot understand the reason for his presence: it fills me with as much bewilderment as if they'd seated a Zulu next to me at the table. Also, I find it strange that my daughter, whom I look upon as a child, should like that tie, those eyes, those soft cheeks . . .

Previously I either enjoyed my dinner or felt indifferent towards it, but now it only arouses boredom or irritation. Ever since I became a professor and started hob-nobbing with the Faculty deans, for some reason my family has considered it necessary to make drastic changes in our diet and dining habits. Instead of those simple dishes to which I was used in my student days and as an ordinary doctor they now feed me with a kind of thick soup with objects resembling white icicles floating around in it, and kidneys in madeira. My civil rank (equivalent to a general's) and my fame have robbed me forever of cabbage soup, savoury pies, goose with apple sauce and bream with buckwheat. And they have also deprived me of Agasha my maid, a chatty, amusing old woman in whose place Yegor, a dull-witted arrogant young fellow, now serves dinner with a white glove in his right hand. The intervals between courses are short, but they seem excruciatingly long because there is nothing to fill them. Gone are the former gaiety, spontaneous conversation, the jokes and the laughter; gone are those mutual endearments and the joy which used to infect the children, my wife and myself when we gathered at the dinner-table. For a busy man like myself dinner was a time of relaxation and happy reunion: for my wife and children it was like a holiday – admittedly very brief – but bright and joyful, since they knew that for half an hour I didn't belong to science, nor to my students, but to them alone and no one else. No more getting tipsy from one glass of wine, no more Agasha, no more bream with buckwheat, no more of those commotions which always accompanied every little dinner-time incident – for example, the cat and the dog fighting under the table or Katya's bandage falling from her cheek into her soup.

To describe the dinners we have now is just an unappetizing as eating them. My wife's face wears a look of solemnity, of affected seriousness and that habitual worried expression of hers as she anxiously inspects our plates and says, 'I see you don't like the roast . . . Tell me, you don't really like it, do you?' And I have to reply, 'You're worrying for nothing, dear, it's very tasty . . .' And to this she retorts, 'You always stand up for me, Nikolay, you never tell the truth. Why is Mr Gnekker eating so little?' - and so it goes on throughout the entire meal. Liza laughs her staccato laugh and screws up her eyes. I look at both women and only now over dinner do I clearly see that the inner lives of the two of them have long escaped my field of vision. I have the feeling that once I lived in a house with a real family, but that now I'm dining as a guest of someone who isn't really my wife and that what I'm seeing is not my real daughter Liza. Both have undergone a marked change and I've failed to notice the long process which brought about this change. So it's no wonder that I can't make anything of it. How did this change come about? I don't know. Perhaps the whole trouble is that God gave my wife and daughter less strength than he gave me. From childhood I've been used to withstanding external pressure and have steeled myself pretty well. Such disasters in life as fame, becoming a professor, moving from modest comfort to living beyond one's means, mixing with celebrities and so on have scarcely touched me and I have remained immune to them, unscathed. But all of this has fallen on my unsteeled wife and daughter like a great pile of snow and crushed them.

Gnekker and the young ladies talk of fugues, counterpoint, singers and pianists, Bach and Brahms, while my wife, afraid of being suspected of musical ignorance, gives them a responsive smile and murmurs, 'Charming! . . . Really? . . . Go on! . . .' Gnekker eats solidly, jokes solidly and lends a condescending ear to the young ladies' remarks. From time to time he has the urge to talk bad French and then – for some mysterious reason – he finds it necessary to address me as *votre excellence.*

But I feel glum. It's obvious I inhibit all of them as much as they inhibit me. I have never been closely acquainted with class antagonism before, but something exactly like that bedevils me now. I seek only bad qualities in Gnekker, in no time do I find them and I'm tormented by the thought that a man who is outside my circle should aspire to my daughter's hand. His presence affects me badly in yet another way. Usually when I'm on my own or with people I like, I never ponder my own merits – and if I do they strike me as footling, as though I had become a scholar only yesterday. But with people like Gnekker around my merits strike me as the loftiest mountain, whose summit is lost in the clouds and around whose foothills slither Gnekkers barely visible to the naked eye.

After dinner I go into my study and light my only pipe of the day – a relic of my filthy old habit of puffing smoke from dawn to dusk. While I am smoking my wife comes in and sits down for a chat. Just as in the morning I know in advance what we are going to talk about.

'You and I must have a serious talk, Nikolay,' she begins. 'It's about Liza. Why do you turn a blind eye?'

'To what?'

'You pretend not to notice a thing – and that's bad. You mustn't be so indifferent. Gnekker is serious about Liza. What do you say to that?'

'I really can't say if he's a bad person as I don't know him well enough. But I've told you a thousand times that I don't like him.'

'But this is impossible, impossible . . .'

She gets up and walks around excitedly.

'You can't possibly take such an attitude to a serious step like this!' she says. 'When our daughter's happiness is at stake you must put aside all personal considerations. I know you don't like him. Very well . . . But if we refuse him now and break it off, what guarantee is there that Liza won't bear a grudge against us for the rest of her life? Goodness knows, eligible bachelors are few and far between these days and it's quite likely someone else will never turn up. He's deeply in love with Liza and she's fond of him. Of course, he doesn't have a proper job, but that can't be helped. God willing, he'll find something in time. He's from a good family and he's well off.'

'Where did you hear that?'

'He told us himself. His father has a big house in Kharkov and an estate nearby. In short, Nikolay, you'll definitely have to go to Kharkov.'

'Why?'

'You can make inquiries there . . . You know some professors there and they'll help you. I'd go myself but I'm a woman, I can't . . .'

'I'm not going to Kharkov,' I say sullenly.

My wife takes fright and a look of intense pain appears on her face.

'For God's sake, Nikolay,' she begs, in between sobs. 'For God's sake, take this burden away! I'm going through hell!'

I find it painful to look at her.

'Very well, Varya,' I say tenderly. 'All right, I'll go to Kharkov if you want me to and I'll do everything you want.'

She presses her handkerchief to her eyes and goes to her room to cry. I am left on my own.

A little later a lamp is brought in. The armchair and lampshade cast those familiar shadows of which I have long grown tired on the walls and floor, and when I look at them I feel night has already come and with it my damned insomnia. I lie on my bed, then I get up again, walk up and down – and then I lie down again. Usually after dinner, as evening approaches, my nervous excitement reaches fever pitch. For no reason I start crying and bury my head under the pillow. At these moments I'm afraid that someone might come in, or that I might suddenly die. I'm ashamed of my tears and altogether I feel something insufferable is going on inside me. I feel that I can't bear to look at my lamp, my books, the shadows on the floor any more, I can't bear to hear those voices in the drawing-room. Some invisible, incomprehensible force is roughly driving me out of the house. I leap up, hurriedly dress and, taking every precaution not to be seen by anyone in the house, I slip out into the street. Where can I go?

The answer to this question has long been in my mind – to Katya.

III

As usual she is lying on the ottoman or on a couch reading. When she sees me she idly raises her head, sits up and stretches out her hand to me.

'You're always lying down,' I say after a short pause and a rest. 'It's not good for you. You should find something to do!'

'What?'

'I said you should find something to do.'

'What? A woman can only be a menial worker or an actress.'

'All right, if you don't want to do menial work then go on the stage.'

She says nothing.

'You ought to get married,' I say, half-joking.

'There's no one I want to marry. Besides, there's no point.'

'But you can't go on like this.'

'Without a husband? What does it matter! I could have as many men as I liked if I wanted to.'

'That's not nice, Katya!'

'What's not nice?'

'Well, what you just said.'

Noting that I am upset and eager to erase the bad impression Katya says, 'Let's go. This way – there!'

She leads me into a small, very cosy room and points at a writing desk.

'There . . . I've arranged it all for you,' she tells me. 'You can work here. You can come every day and bring your work with you. They only interrupt you at home. Will you do this? Yes?'

Not wishing to upset her with a refusal I reply that I will come and work at her place, that I like the room very much. Then we both sit down in the cosy little room and start talking.

Instead of giving me pleasure as they did before, warmth, comfort and agreeable company only arouse a strong desire to complain and grumble. Somehow I feel better after a little grousing and complaining.

'Things are bad, my dear!' I begin with a sigh. 'Very bad.'

'What's wrong?'

'I'll explain, my dear. The finest, most sacred right of kings is the right to pardon and I've always felt like a king, since I've made unlimited use of this right. I've never judged, I've made allowances, I've readily forgiven everyone right and left. Where others have protested or waxed indignant, I've merely advised and persuaded. All my life I've been concerned solely with making my company tolerable for my family, my students, my colleagues and my servants. And I know that this attitude to people has had a civilizing influence on all those around me. But no longer am I a king. Something is happening to me that is fit only for a slave. Day and night evil thoughts haunt me and feelings I had never known before – of hatred, contempt, indignation, exasperation and dread – have come to dwell in my heart. I've become excessively strict, demanding, irritable, rude, suspicious. What was once a pretext for an extra joke or hearty laughter utterly depresses me now. And my sense of logic has also altered. Once I despised only money, but now I feel malicious – not towards money, but towards the rich, as if they were to blame. Where I used to hate violence and tyranny I now hate the perpetrators of violence, as if they alone were to blame and not all of us who are incapable of educating each other. What does it all mean? If these new thoughts and feelings are the result of a change in my convictions how did the change come about? Has the world become worse? Have I become better? Or was I blind before and indifferent? But if this change originated from a general decline in physical and intellectual powers – after all, I'm a sick person and I'm losing weight every day – then my position is indeed pathetic: it can only mean that my new thoughts are morbid, abnormal, that I should be ashamed of them and make light of them . . .'

'Illness has nothing to do with it,' interrupts Katya. 'It's simply that your eyes have been opened, that's all. You've seen what for some reason you closed your eyes to before. In my opinion the most important thing is to make a clean break with your family and get away from them.'

'You're talking nonsense.'

'But you don't love them any more, so why act against your conscience. Call that a family! They're nobodies! If they were to drop dead today no one would miss them tomorrow.'

Katya despises my wife and daughter as much as they loathe her. These days it's practically impossible to speak of people's rights to despise each other. But if one were to accept Katya's point of view and admit this right exists, then obviously she's just as entitled to despise my wife and Liza as they are to detest her.

'Nobodies!' she repeats. 'Have you had any lunch today? How come they didn't forget to invite you to the table? How is it that they are still aware you exist?'

'Katya,' I say sternly, 'please be quiet, I beg you.'

'Do you honestly think I enjoy talking about them? I wish I'd never set eyes on them. Now, listen to me, my dear: give everything up and go away. Go abroad. And the sooner the better.'

'Rubbish! What about the university?'

'And leave the university too. What do you need it for? It just doesn't make sense. You've been lecturing for thirty years now and where are your pupils? Are there many famous scientists among them? Count them, go on! To breed doctors who exploit ignorance and earn their hundreds of thousands of roubles – you don't need to be a talented or good man for that! You're redundant!'

'Good God, how harsh you are!' I exclaim, horrified. 'How harsh! Now be quiet, or I'll go! I've no answer to these sharp words of yours!'

The maid enters to announce that tea is ready. Over the samovar we both change the subject, thank God. After my good old grumble I want to indulge another weakness of old age – reminiscing. I tell Katya about my past and to my own great surprise I go into details I never suspected I would remember so well. And she shows emotion and pride as she listens with bated breath. I'm particularly fond of telling her about my student days at a theological college when I dreamed of going on to university.

'I often used to stroll in the college gardens,' I tell her. 'From some distant tavern a song and an accordion's grating would be borne to me on the breeze, or a troika with bells ringing would tear past the college fence – all this would suffice to fill not only my heart, but my stomach, legs and arms with a sudden feeling of happiness. As I listened to the accordion or those bells dying away I would imagine myself a doctor and I'd paint pictures in my mind, each better than the last. And as you can see, now my dreams have come true. I've received more than I ever dared dream of. For thirty years I've been a much-loved professor, I've had excellent colleagues, enjoyed fame and distinction. I've loved – I married for passionate love – I've had children. In brief, as I look back on it, my whole life seems a beautiful, skilfully fashioned composition. All that remains is not to spoil the finale and for that I must die like a man. If death really is a threat, then I must meet it in a manner worthy of a teacher, scholar and citizen of a Christian country: courageously and with equanimity. I'm spoiling the finale, though. It's as if I'm drowning and I'm running to you begging for help, but all you say is: "Then go and drown – that's exactly what you should do."'

But then a bell rings in the hall. Katya and I recognize the sound. 'That must be Mikhail Fyodorovich,' we say.

And in fact a minute later my colleague, the literary historian Mikhail Fyodorovich, enters, a tall, well-built, clean-shaven man of fifty, with thick grey hair and black eyebrows. He is a good fellow and first-class colleague. He hails from a fairly fortunate, ancient, talented and noble family which has played a prominent part in the history of our country's literature and enlightenment. As for him, he's intelligent, gifted, highly educated, but not without certain oddities. To some extent we are all strange and a little weird, but in his idiosyncrasies there is something truly exceptional and fraught with danger for his friends. I know quite a few of the latter for whom his numerous virtues are completely obscured by these quirks of his.

On entering he slowly removes his gloves.

'Good evening!' he says in his velvety bass. 'Having tea? That's most welcome. It's hellishly cold.'

Then he sits down at the table, takes himself a glass and immediately starts talking. What is most distinctive about the way he talks is that constantly jocular tone, a kind of mixture of philosophizing and buffoonery – as with Shakespeare's gravediggers. He's always talking about serious matters, but he never talks seriously. His judgements are always sharp and provocative, but thanks to his soft, even, jocular tone, the sharp words don't jar on the ear and you soon get used to them. Every evening he brings with him half a dozen stories of university life and he usually begins with them when he sits down at the table.

'Oh Lord!' he sighs, twitching his black eyebrows mockingly. 'There's such clowns in this world!'

'What do you mean?' asks Katya.

'Well, when I came out of the lecture-room this morning whom should I meet on the stairs but that silly old fool NN—. There he comes with that horsey chin sticking out as usual and looking for someone to hear him complain about his migraine, his wife and the students who don't want to go to his lectures. Oh, I think to myself, he's spotted me, I'm finished, all is lost . . .'

And more in the same vein. Or he fires off like this: 'Yesterday I was at our dear So-and-So's public lecture. Perhaps I shouldn't say this, but I'm amazed that our alma mater has the nerve to put such imbeciles and certified nitwits as him on public display. Why, he's an international fool! You won't find a fool to equal him in the whole of Europe in a month of Sundays! Just imagine – when he lectures he lisps, just as if he's sucking boiled sweets . . . He gets in such a flap that he can hardly decipher his own handwriting, his piffling little thoughts hobble along with the speed of an abbot on a bicycle. But worst of all, you can't make head or tail of what he wants to say. The boredom's deathly – even the flies drop dead! The only other kind of boredom you can compare with it is what we get at the annual ceremony in the assembly hall, on degree day, when the traditional oration is read – damn and blast it!'

Immediately there is an abrupt transition.

'About ten years ago, as Nikolay Stepanovich will recall, it was my turn to deliver the oration. It was hot and stuffy, my uniform was pinching me under the arms – it was sheer hell! I read for half an hour, an hour, an hour and a half, two hours . . . "Well, I think, praise the Lord there's only ten pages left!" And there were four pages at the end that could easily be skipped and I was counting on leaving them out. "So," I think, "only six pages to go!" But then – just imagine! – I glance in front of me and lo and behold there's some beribboned general sitting with a bishop in the front row. The poor devils were bored out of their minds and kept goggling their eyes to stay awake. But for all that they were still trying to look as if they were listening, pretending that they understood and liked my oration. "Well," I think, "if you like it so much you can damned well have it! That'll teach you!" So I soldier on and read all four pages.'

As you usually find with sarcastic people, only his eyes and eyebrows smile when he speaks. At such moments there is neither hatred nor malice in them, but a great deal of wit and that peculiar foxy cunning which you only find with very observant people. To continue with his eyes, I noticed another peculiarity about them. Whenever he takes a glass from Katya or listens to what she says, or glances after her when she leaves the room for a short while to fetch something, I notice something gentle, beseeching, pure in their expression . . .

The maid takes the samovar away and puts on the table a large piece of cheese, some fruit and a bottle of Crimean champagne – a rather poor wine to which Katya had become partial when she lived in the Crimea. Mikhail Fyodorovich takes two packs of cards from the shelf and starts playing patience. But despite his claim that some varieties of patience call for nimbleness of thought and concentration, he still doesn't stop distracting himself with his talk as he plays. Katya closely follows the cards, helping him more by gesture than by words. She drinks no more than two glasses the whole evening. I drink a quarter of a glass and the rest of the bottle falls to the lot of Mikhail Fyodorovich who can knock back any amount without ever getting drunk.

Over patience we settle all kinds of questions, mainly on the highest level and our dearest love – science – catches it more than anything else.

'Science, thank God, has had its day,' solemnly proclaims Mikhail Fyodorovich. 'Its goose is cooked! Oh yes, sir! Mankind is already feeling the need to replace it with something else. Science arose out of superstition, was nourished by superstition and now constitutes the very essence of superstition, like those obsolete grandmamas – alchemy, metaphysics and philosophy. And in actual fact, what has science given mankind? After all, the difference between learned Europeans and Chinamen who have no science is trivial, purely superficial. Chinamen have never had any science – and what have they lost as a result?'

'Flies don't have science either,' I say, 'but what does that prove?'

'There's no need to get cross, Nikolay. I'm only saying this here, between ourselves. I'm more tactful than you think and I'd never talk like this in public. God forbid! The superstition that the arts and sciences are superior to agriculture, commerce and handicrafts is alive and kicking among the masses. Our part of society thrives on superstition and God forbid that you or I should destroy it!'

During patience the younger generation catches it as well.

'Nowadays our students have degenerated,' sighs Mikhail Fyodorovich. 'I don't mean ideals and all that stuff, but if only they would work and think intelligently! Oh yes it's all a question of "How sadly I behold our generation".'[16]

'Yes, they've degenerated terribly,' Katya agrees. 'Tell me, have you had a single outstanding student over the past five or ten years?'

'I can't speak for the other professors, but *I* don't remember having had any.'

'I've seen many students in my lifetime and those young scholars of yours, many actors . . . and what do you think? Not once have I had the honour of meeting a single interesting person, let alone geniuses and high flyers. They're all so dull, mediocre, so puffed up with pretension . . .'

All this talk of degeneracy invariably affects me as if I'd accidentally overheard an unpleasant conversation about my daughter. I find it offensive that these accusations are unfounded and based on such hackneyed clichés, such bugbears as degeneracy, lack of ideals, or harking back to the good old days. Every accusation, even if it is made in the company of ladies, should be formulated with the greatest possible precision, otherwise it is not an accusation at all, but vain backbiting, unworthy of decent men.

I'm an old man, I've been working at the university for thirty years, but I don't see any degeneracy or lack of ideals and I don't think things are any worse now than before. My porter Nikolay, whose experience in these matters is not to be underestimated, maintains that the students of today are neither worse nor better than before.

If I were asked what I dislike about my present students I wouldn't reply immediately or in much detail, but my answer would be precise enough. I'm aware of their shortcomings, so I don't need to resort to platitudes. I don't like their smoking, drinking strong alcohol, marrying late in life, being so devil-may-care and often so heartless that they allow some of their number to starve by not paying their subscription to the students' aid society. They don't know modern languages and can't express themselves correctly in Russian. Only yesterday a hygienist colleague of mine complained that he has had to double the number of lectures, as his students' physics is so poor and because they are utterly ignorant of meteorology. They gladly succumb to the influence of the most modern writers – and not even the best ones at that – but they are completely indifferent to such classics as Shakespeare, Marcus Aurelius, Epictetus or Pascal,[17] for example. Their lack of experience in worldly matters shows most of all in this inability to distinguish the great from the small. All difficult problems of a more or less social character (for instance, land settlement in unpopulated areas) they decide by organizing public subscriptions, not by scientific research and investigation, although the latter is fully at their disposal and is more in line with their vocation. Eagerly they become house surgeons, registrars, laboratory assistants, house physicians and are ready to carry on doing these jobs until they are forty, although an independent spirit, a feeling of freedom and personal initiative are needed in science for example, as much as in art or commerce. I have my students and my audience – but no assistants or successors. Therefore I like them and am touched by them, but I'm not proud of them. And so on . . .

However numerous these shortcomings may be they can generate pessimistic or quarrelsome moods only in the faint-hearted or weak. All of them are accidental and transient and depend entirely on living conditions. A few decades will suffice for them to vanish or give way to other, fresh defects that can't be avoided and which in turn will frighten the faint-hearted. Students' transgressions often annoy me, but the annoyance is nothing in comparison with the joy I've been having now for thirty years when I talk with my students, lecture to them, note their attitudes and compare them with people from different social circles.

Mikhail Fyodorovich continues with his muckraking, while Katya listens. Neither notices the deep abyss into which they are gradually being sucked by the apparently innocent diversion of condemning their neighbour. They don't realize how ordinary conversations can gradually turn into mockery and sneering, and how both of them are beginning to resort to the techniques of outright slander.

'You really do come across some killingly funny types,' says Mikhail Fyodorovich. 'Yesterday I dropped in on our dear Yegor Petrovich and whom do I find there but one of your medics – third-year, I think. His face was in Dobrolyubov style,[18] with that same stamp of profound thought on his brow. We get talking. "The things you hear about, young man," I say. "I've been reading about a certain German – I forget his name – who's extracted a new alkaloid from the human brain – *idiotin*." And what do you think?

He believed it and even assumed a respectful expression. "You have to hand it to us scientists!" he says. And the other day I went to the theatre. I take my seat. Right in front of me, in the very next row, one of our students is sitting – evidently a lawyer – and the other a shaggy medic. The medic's soused to the gills, not paying a blind bit of attention to what was happening on stage, just dozing away, his head nodding. But the moment an actor embarks on a loud soliloquy or simply raises his voice my medic gives a start, pokes his neighbour in the ribs and asks, "What's he on about? Are they noble sentiments?". "Yes, noble sentiments," replies the lawyer. "Bra-avo!" roars the medic. "Noble sentiments! Bra-avo!" You see, that drunken moron hadn't gone to the theatre for art's sake, but for noble sentiments! He wants to be uplifted!'

Katya listens and laughs. She has the most peculiar sort of guffaw, breathing in and out in a rapid, regular rhythm, just as if she were playing a concertina, so that the only part of her face that seems to be laughing is her nostrils. But I lose heart and don't know what to say. Then I flare up, lose my temper, leap from my chair.

'Will you please shut up!' I shout. 'Why are you sitting there like two toads, poisoning the air with your breath? It's enough!'

And without waiting for them to stop their spiteful gossip I prepare to go home. It's high time anyway – past ten o'clock.

'I think I'll stay a bit longer,' says Mikhail Fyodorovich. 'Do I have your permission, Yekaterina Vladimirovna?'

'You do,' replies Katya.

'*Bene*. In that case please ask for another bottle.'

Both of them see me into the hall with candles and while I'm putting on my fur coat Mikhail Fyodorovich says, 'You've grown terribly thin lately and you've aged, Nikolay Stepanovich. What's wrong? Are you ill?'

'Yes, a little.'

'And he won't go and see a doctor,' gloomily interposes Katya.

'Why ever not? You can't go on like this. God helps those who help themselves, my dear fellow. Remember me to your wife and daughter and my apologies for not calling on them. In a few days I'm going abroad. Before I go I'll come and say goodbye. I'm leaving next week.'

I leave Katya's place feeling irritated and alarmed by all that talk about my illness and dissatisfied with myself. I ask myself whether I shouldn't after all consult one of my colleagues. And immediately I picture my colleague silently going over to the window after examining me, reflecting for a while and then turning towards me, trying to stop me reading the truth on his face – and then casually saying, 'Although I can't see anything much at the moment I would still advise you, my dear colleague, to give up work . . .' And that will put paid to my last hope.

And who among us doesn't cherish hopes? Now when I make my own diagnosis and treat myself I sometimes hope that I'm the victim of my own ignorance, that I'm mistaken about the albumen and sugar in my urine, about my heart and those oedemas that I've already noticed twice in the mornings. When I read through the therapeutic textbooks with a hypochondriac's zeal and change the medicine every day, I always feel that I will stumble upon something that will be of comfort. It's all so petty!

Whether the sky is overcast or if it is filled with the light of the moon and the stars, every time I come home I look at it and reflect that death will soon come to take me. You might think that at these moments my thoughts would be as deep as the sky, bright and striking . . . But no! I think about myself, about my wife, Liza, Gnekker, the students, about people in general. My thoughts are ineffectual, trifling, I deceive myself– and then my outlook on life might be expressed in words used by the famous Arakcheyev[19] in one of his intimate letters: 'Everything that is good in this world cannot be free of evil – and there is always more bad than good.' In other words, everything is vile, there's no point in living and I must consider the sixty-two years of my life as wasted. I catch myself thinking these things and try and convince myself that they are accidental, ephemeral and aren't deeply ingrained in me. But then I immediately think: 'If this is so, then why do I have the urge to go and visit those toads every evening?'

And I solemnly promise myself not to go to Katya's any more, although I know very well that I'll go again tomorrow.

As I ring my front door bell and go upstairs I feel that I have no family any more and I have no desire to get it back. Clearly, those new, Arakcheyevan thoughts within me are neither accidental nor passing, but possess my whole being. With a sick conscience, feeling dejected and sluggish and barely able to move my limbs – as if a thousand pounds had been added to my weight – I get into bed and soon fall asleep.

And then – insomnia . . .

IV

Summer comes and life changes.

One fine morning Liza comes to see me and says jokingly, 'Let's go, Your Excellency! It's all ready.'

'My Excellency' is led into the street, put into a cab and driven away. To occupy my mind I read the shop signs backwards: *traktir* (tavern) becomes Ritkart. That would do very well for a baronial surname – Baroness Ritkart! Further on I drive through open country, past a cemetery which makes no impression on me at all, although I shall soon be lying there. Then I drive through a wood and through open country again. There's nothing of interest. After a two-hour drive 'His Excellency' is taken to the ground floor of a dacha and accommodated in a small, very cheerful little room with blue wallpaper.

I have insomnia at night again, but instead of waking up in the morning and listening to my wife I am lying in bed – not asleep, but in that drowsy, half-conscious state when you know you're not asleep, yet still have dreams of a sort. At midday I get up and from habit I sit down at the desk; I don't do any work, though, and I amuse myself with the yellow French paperbacks that Katya sends me. Of course, it would be more patriotic of me to read Russian authors, but I must confess that I don't really have much enthusiasm for them. Apart from two or three old-timers, the whole of contemporary literature seems less literature than a special kind of cottage industry which exists only to be patronized by those who are reluctant to avail themselves of its produce. The best of these home-produced artefacts cannot be called remarkable and cannot be praised without strong reservations. The same must be said of all those literary novelties which I've read over the past ten to fifteen years, none of which can be called remarkable or praised without a 'but'. The product may be intelligent, uplifting, but lacking in talent. It may be talented and uplifting, but it's unintelligent. Or – finally – it may be talented and intelligent, but it's not uplifting.

I wouldn't go so far as to say that French books are talented, intelligent and uplifting. Nor do they satisfy me. But they aren't so boring as Russian books and it's not uncommon to find in them what is essential for artistic creativity – a feeling of personal freedom which you don't find in Russian authors. I can't remember one new book where the author doesn't try from the first page to shackle himself with all kinds of conventions and contracts with his conscience. One is afraid to speak of the naked body, another has bound himself hand and foot with psychological analysis, another stands in need of a 'warm attitude to man', a fourth deliberately pads out whole pages with nature description so as not to be suspected of tendentiousness . . . One wants to appear lower class in his writings, whilst another simply *has* to be one of the gentry, and so on. They have a sense of purpose, are careful, shrewd, but they have neither the freedom nor the courage to write what they like and therefore there is no creativity.

All this applies to so-called belles-lettres.

As for serious Russian articles – on sociology, say, or art and so forth – I don't read them simply because I'm scared of them. In my childhood and youth I was terrified of porters and theatre ushers for some reason and this fear is with me to this day. I fear them even now. It's said that we fear only what we don't understand. And indeed it's very difficult to understand why porters and ushers should be so self-important, overbearing and imperiously ill-mannered. Reading serious articles I experience exactly the same vague fear. Their incredible pomposity, their bantering, magisterial style, the familiarity with which they treat foreign authors, their ability to retain their dignity whilst labouring in vain – all this I find incomprehensible, frightening and utterly unlike the humility and the calm, gentlemanly tone to which I've become accustomed when reading our medical and scientific authors. Not only articles, but even translations made or edited by serious-minded Russians I find difficult to read. The arrogant, condescending tone of the prefaces, the mass of translator's footnotes that ruin my concentration, the question marks and parenthetical 'sics' with which the generous translator has peppered the entire article or book are an invasion of the author's personality – and of my independence as a reader.

Once I was called to give expert evidence at a Court of Assizes. In the adjournment one of my fellow experts drew my attention to the prosecutor's rude treatment of the defendants, who numbered two cultured women. I don't believe I was exaggerating in the least when I replied to my friend that the prosecutor's treatment was no worse than that which prevails among authors of serious articles. In fact, their manners are so rude that it doesn't bear talking about. Either they treat each other and those writers they criticize with excessive obsequiousness, at the expense of their own dignity, or they go to the other extreme and deal with them far more ruthlessly than I have done in these memoirs and in my thoughts about my future son-in-law Gnekker. Charges of irresponsibility, impure motives and all kinds of criminal activity even, are the standard embellishment of these serious articles. But, as young doctors are fond of putting it in their articles, this is the *ultima ratio*! Such attitudes are bound to be reflected in the morals of the young generation of writers and therefore it doesn't surprise me in the least that, in the new books added to our stock of belles-lettres over the past ten to fifteen years, the heroes drink too much vodka, while the heroines are hardly what you'd call chaste.

I read French books and glance out of the open window. I can see the spikes of my garden fence, two or three spindly little trees and beyond the fence the road, the fields, then a broad strip of pine forest. I often enjoy looking at a boy and girl, both fair-haired and ragged, climbing the fence and laughing at my bald pate. In their sparkling little eyes I can read the words: 'Go up, thou bald head!'[20] They must be almost the only ones who don't care a rap about my fame or rank.

Now I don't have people coming to see me every day. I shall mention only the visits of Nikolay and Pyotr Ignatyevich. Nikolay usually comes on a Sunday or saint's day, ostensibly on business, but really just to see me. He turns up very tipsy, which he never is during the winter.

'How are things?' I ask as I go out into the hall to meet him.

'Professor!' he says, pressing hand to heart and looking at me with a lover's ardour. 'Your excellency! May God punish me! May lightning strike me dead on this very spot. *Gaudeamus igitur juvenestus!*'[21]

And he eagerly kisses me on my shoulders, sleeves, buttons.

'Is everything all right?'

'Professor! As God is my witness . . . !'

He never stops gratuitously invoking the deity and I soon get bored with him, so I dispatch him to the kitchen where they give him a meal. Pyotr Ignatyevich also comes on holidays, especially to see me and to share his thoughts. He usually sits next to me at table. Unassuming, spruce and sensible, he doesn't dare cross his legs or lean his elbows on the table and in his soft, even, smooth pedantic little voice relates what he considers very interesting and spicy novelties that he has gleaned from journals and books. All these items are identical and follow the same pattern: a Frenchman has made a discovery. Someone else, a German, has exposed him by proving the discovery was made as long ago as 1870 by some American. And a third (also a German) has outsmarted both of them by demonstrating that the two of them had committed a gaffe by mistaking air bubbles under a microscope for dark pigment. Even when he wants to amuse me Pyotr Ignatyevich talks at great length and diffusely, like someone defending his dissertation with an infinitely detailed itemization of bibliographical sources, endeavouring not to make one slip-up in the dates, issues of the journals, or in the names. He never calls anyone plain and simply Petit, but always Jean-Jacques Petit.[22] Sometimes he stays for dinner and throughout the meal tells the same spicy stories, which depress the whole company. If Gnekker and Liza mention fugues or counterpoint in his presence, Brahms or Bach, he humbly drops his eyes and shows embarrassment. He is ashamed that such trivial matters can be discussed in the presence of such serious-minded people as himself or me.

In my present mood five minutes are enough for him to bore me as if I'd been seeing and listening to him from time immemorial. I loathe the poor devil. His quiet, even voice and pedantic language make me droop, his stories stupefy me. He nourishes the kindest feelings towards me and only talks to give me pleasure. But I pay him back by staring straight at him, as if I want to hypnotize him. 'Go away, go away!' I think to myself. 'Go!' But he cannot read my mind and stays on and on and on . . .

When he's with me I just can't shake off the thought that when I die he'll very likely be appointed to succeed me and my poor lecture-room seems like an oasis where the spring has run dry. I'm rude to Pyotr Ignatyevich, taciturn and sullen – as if he were to blame for such thoughts, not I. When he starts rapturously praising German scholars I no longer good-humouredly chaff him as I used to.

'Your Germans are asses . . .' I mutter gloomily.

That reminds me of the late Professor Nikita Krylov,[23] when he was once bathing with Pirogov at Revel. He became furious with the freezing cold water and cursed those 'German scoundrels'. I behave badly towards Pyotr Ignatyevich and only when he's leaving and I look through the window and glimpse his grey hat beyond the fence do I feel like calling out to him: 'Please forgive me, my dear fellow!'

Lunch is even more boring than during the winter. That same Gnekker, whom I now hate and despise, dines with me almost every day. Once I tolerated his presence in silence, but now I make caustic remarks at his expense, which make my wife and Liza blush. Carried away by malicious feelings I often come out with complete inanities. For example, once after I'd given Gnekker a long, contemptuous look I suddenly blurted out, for no apparent reason:

> Eagles lower than hens can fly
> But hens will ne'er soar into the sky.[24]

What's most annoying is that 'hen-Gnekker' turns out to be far cleverer than 'eagle-professor'. Knowing that my wife and daughter are on his side he adopts the tactic of answering my caustic sallies with a condescending silence. 'The old boy's off his rocker,' he must be thinking, 'so why talk to him?' Or he good-humouredly pulls my leg. It's quite amazing how low a man can sink. I'm capable of spending the entire meal dreaming that one day Gnekker will turn out a confidence trickster, that Liza and my wife will see the error of their ways and that I'll tease them – and similar ridiculous fantasies when I already have one foot in the grave!

And now there are misunderstandings of which I previously became aware only by hearsay. However ashamed it makes me feel, I shall describe one of them that happened the other day after dinner.

I am sitting in my room smoking my pipe. In comes my wife. She sits down and starts talking about how nice it would be if I went to Kharkov – now that the weather's warm and I have the time to spare – to find out what kind of man this Gnekker is.

'All right, I'll go,' I agree.

Pleased with me, my wife gets up and goes to the door, but immediately she turns back.

'By the way, I have one more request. I know you'll be angry, but it's my duty to warn you . . . I'm sorry I have to say this, Nikolay, but all your friends and neighbours have started talking about your being at Katya's so much. She's clever and educated – that I don't dispute – and it must be pleasant spending time with her, but at your age and for someone in your social position it's a bit odd that you should find pleasure in her company . . . Besides, she has such a reputation that . . .'

The blood suddenly drains from my head, my eyes flash. I leap up, clutch my head and stamp my feet.

'Leave me alone!' I shout in a voice that isn't mine. 'Leave me alone! Leave me!'

I probably look terrible and my voice must sound strange in the extreme, since my wife suddenly goes pale and shrieks – also in a frantic voice which isn't hers. Hearing our cries in rushes Liza, then Gnekker, followed by Yegor . . .

'Leave me alone!' I shout. 'Get out! Leave me!'

There's no feeling in my legs, as if they aren't there at all, and I feel that I am falling into someone's arms. Then, briefly, I can hear someone weeping and I sink into a faint which lasts two or three hours.

And now about Katya. She arrives every day in the late afternoon and this of course cannot fail to go unnoticed by neighbours or friends. She comes in for a few minutes and then takes me for a drive. She keeps her own horses and a new chaise which she bought this summer. On the whole she lives quite lavishly: she has rented an expensive detached villa with a large garden in the country and moved all her furniture there from town. She keeps two maids and a coachman. I often ask her, 'Katya, what will you live on once you've squandered all your father's money?'

'We'll see . . . ,' she replies.

'That money deserves to be treated more seriously, my dear. It was earned by a good man, by honest labour.'

'I know – you've already told me.'

At first we drive through open country, then through the pine wood which is visible from my window. Nature looks as beautiful as ever, although the devil whispers that when I'm dead in three or four months those pines and firs, those birds and white clouds in the sky won't notice I've gone. Katya likes driving and finds it pleasant to have me sitting next to her – and in such fine weather. She's in a good mood and doesn't say any of those nasty things.

'You're a very good man, Nikolay Stepanovich,' she says. 'You are a rare specimen and no actor could portray you. As for myself or Mikhail Fyodorovich – even a bad actor could manage us, but no one could manage you. And I envy you – I envy you terribly! After all, what am I, all said and done? What?'

She reflects for a moment and then she asks, 'Nikolay Stepanovich, I'm a negative phenomenon, aren't I? Yes?'

'Yes,' I reply.

'Hm . . . what am I to do then?'

What can I tell her? It's easy enough to say, 'Work!', 'Give all you have to the poor', 'Know thyself' – and because it's so easy to say I'm lost for a reply.

When my colleagues from the therapy department are teaching the art of healing they advise their students to 'individualize each separate case'. You only need to follow this advice to see that the techniques recommended in textbooks as the very best and most applicable to routine cases turn out completely unsuitable in individual cases. It's the same with moral ailments.

But I have to give some reply.

'My dear, you have too much time on your hands,' I tell her. 'You must find something to do. In fact, why don't you go on the stage again, if that's your real vocation?'

'I can't.'

'Your tone and manner seem to imply you're a victim. I don't like that, my dear. It's your own fault. Remember how at first you got angry with people and the way things were, but you did nothing to improve one or the other. You didn't combat evil, but simply crumpled up and so you're a victim of your own feebleness – not of the struggle. Of course, you were young then and inexperienced, but now everything can be different. Yes, go ahead! You will toil, you will serve sacred art . . .'

'Don't try and pull the wool over my eyes, Nikolay Stepanovich,' Katya interrupts. 'Let's agree once and for all – we'll talk about actors, actresses and writers, but let's leave art in peace. You're a fine, rare person, but I don't think you understand enough about art to call it sacred, in all honesty. You have no instinct for art, no ear. All your life you've been too busy, so you never had time to acquire that feeling. In general I don't like all this talk about art,' she continues nervously. 'I don't like it! It's been vulgarized enough already, thank you very much!'

'Who's vulgarized it?'

'Some people by drunkenness, newspapers by their condescending attitude, clever people by their philosophy.'

'Philosophy's got nothing to do with it.'

'Yes it has. When someone philosophizes it shows he doesn't understand.'

To avoid a possible flare-up I hasten to change the subject and then say nothing for a long time. Only when we are driving out of the wood and approaching Katya's village do I return to the earlier topic.

'You still haven't answered my question: why don't you want to go back to the stage?'

'Really, Nikolay Stepanovich, that's cruel of you!' she cries and suddenly blushes furiously. 'Do you want me to spell the truth out loud? Very well, if that's what you want! I've no talent! No talent and a great deal of vanity. So there you are!'

Having made this confession she turns her face away and tugs violently on the reins to hide the trembling in her hands.

As we drive up to the villa we can see from the distance Mikhail Fyodorovich strolling by the gates and impatiently awaiting us.

'It's that Mikhail Fyodorovich again!' says Katya in exasperation. 'Take him away from me – please! I'm sick and tired of him . . . he's all washed up. Blow him!'

Mikhail Fyodorovich ought to have gone abroad long ago, but every week he keeps postponing his departure. A few changes have come over him lately: now he has a somewhat pinched look, wine goes to his head, which it never used to before, his black eyebrows are turning grey. When our chaise draws up at the gates he can't hide his delight and impatience. Fussily he helps Katya and myself down, fires questions at us, laughs and rubs his hands. The gentle, imploring expression I'd noticed only in his eyes before now suffuses his whole face. He is happy, yet he's ashamed of his joy, ashamed of his habit of visiting Katya every evening and he feels he must justify his appearance with some patent absurdity such as: 'I happened to be driving past on some business, so I thought I'd drop in for a moment.'

The three of us go inside. First we have tea, then those long-familiar two packs of cards, the large piece of cheese, the fruit, the bottle of Crimean champagne, make their appearance on the table. Our topics of conversation aren't new – they're exactly the same as during the winter. University students, literature and the theatre all come in for abuse. The air grows thicker, stuffier from all that spiteful gossip and no longer two toads as in winter but a trio of them poison it with their exhalations. Besides the velvety baritone laughter and loud guffaws that put me in mind of an accordion the maid who is serving us can also hear an unpleasant grating laugh, like a general's chuckle in a cheap stage farce.

V

There are terrifying nights, with thunder, lightning, rain and wind – they are called 'sparrow nights' by country folk. One such sparrow night took place in my personal life . . .

I wake up after midnight and suddenly jump out of bed. For some reason I feel I'm suddenly going to die. Why do I feel this? In my body there is not one sensation that would seem to indicate an early demise, but my heart is assailed with such horror it's as though I'd suddenly seen the sinister glow of some vast conflagration.

I quickly strike a light and drink some water straight from the carafe. Then I rush to the open window. The night is magnificent, with a scent of hay and some other delightful smell. I can see the spikes of my garden fence, the gaunt sleepy trees by the window, the road, the dark strip of the wood. There's a tranquil, very bright moon in the sky and not one cloud. All is quiet, not a leaf stirs. I feel that everything is looking at me and trying to hear how I'm going to die.

I'm terrified. I close the window and run back to bed. After feeling for my pulse and not finding it in my wrist, I start looking for it in my temples, my chin, then again in my wrist. Everything I touch is cold and clammy with sweat. I breathe faster and faster, my body trembles, all my inside is in turmoil and it feels as if my face and bald patch are covered with a cobweb.

What shall I do? Call my family? No, there's no point in that – I don't know what my wife and Liza would do if they came in.

I hide my head under the pillow, close my eyes and wait . . . and wait. My back is cold and it seems as if it's being drawn into me, and I have the feeling that death is bound to creep up on me from behind . . .

'Kee-vee, kee-vee!' something shrieks in the silence of the night and there's no telling where it's coming from – my chest or the street?

'Kee-vee, kee-vee!'

God, how frightening! I would have drunk some more water but I'm too scared to open my eyes and afraid to raise my head. This fear of mine is unaccountable, animal-like – why I'm feeling so frightened is quite beyond me. Is it because I want to live or because some new, as yet unknown pain is in store for me?

In the room above someone groans or laughs. I listen hard. Soon afterwards I can hear footsteps on the stairs. Someone hurries down and then up again. A minute later I can again hear footsteps downstairs: someone stops outside my door and listens.

'Who's there?' I shout.

The door opens and I boldly open my eyes and see my wife. Her face is pale and her eyes tear-stained.

'Can't you sleep, Nikolay?' she asks.

'What do you want?'

'For God's sake go and see Liza. There's something the matter with her.'

'All right . . . with pleasure,' I mutter, delighted that I'm no longer alone. 'All right . . . straight away.'

I follow my wife and listen to her, but I'm too agitated to take in anything. The patches of light from her candle dance on the stairs, our long shadows quiver, my feet become entangled in the skirts of my dressing-gown. I gasp for breath and I sense that something is chasing me and wants to grab my back. 'I'm going to die now, right here, on these stairs,' I think. 'Now . . .' But we've gone up the stairs, along the dark corridor with the Italian window and we enter Liza's room. She's sitting on the bed in her nightdress, her bare feet dangling; she's groaning.

'Oh God!' she mutters, screwing up her eyes at our candle. 'I can't bear it any more!'

'Liza, my child,' I say. "What's wrong?'

Seeing me, she shrieks and flings her arms around my neck.

'My kind Papa,' she sobs. 'Good kind Papa . . . my darling sweet pet . . . I don't know what's wrong with me. I feel awful!'

She hugs and kisses me and babbles those fond words that I used to hear from her when she was a little child.

'Calm yourself, my child - please!' I say. 'You mustn't cry. I feel awful too.'

I try to tuck her in, my wife gives her some water and the two of us jostle each other around the bed in confusion. I jog my wife's shoulder with mine and this reminds me of how once we used to bathe our children together.

'Help her, won't you!' begs my wife. 'Do something!'

But what can I do? Nothing. That girl is depressed about something but I understand nothing, know nothing and can only mutter, 'It's all right . . . it will pass . . . Now, go to sleep . . . sleep.'

To make matters worse a dog suddenly starts barking in the yard, quietly and hesitantly at first, then followed by a noisy duet. I've never attached much significance to omens such as dogs howling or owls hooting, but now my heart sinks and I hurry to find an explanation for that howling.

'It's all nonsense,' I think. 'It's just how one organism influences another. My extreme nervous tension has infected my wife, Liza, the dog – that's all . . . This transmission explains presentiments, forebodings.'

After returning to my room a little later to write Liza a prescription I no longer think about imminent death, but I feel so wretched and miserable that I actually regret not having died suddenly. For a long while I stand motionless in the middle of the room, wondering what to prescribe for Liza. But the groans above the ceiling die away and I decide not to prescribe anything. But still I stand there . . .

There's a deathly silence that rings even in the ears, as some writer put it. Time passes slowly, the streaks of moonlight on the windowsill stay quite still and seem frozen. Dawn is a long time away.

But then the garden gate creaks, someone creeps in, breaks a twig off one of the spindly trees and cautiously taps on the window.

'Nikolay Stepanovich!' I hear someone whisper. 'Nikolay Stepanovich!'

I open the window and fancy I'm dreaming. Beneath the window, huddled close to the wall, stands a woman in a black dress, brightly lit by the moon and looking at me with big eyes. Her face is pale, stern, weird in the moonlight, just like marble; her chin is trembling.

'It's me!' she says. 'It's me – Katya!'

In the moonlight all women's eyes look large and black, people seem taller and paler – this was probably why I didn't recognize her right away.

'What do you want?'

'Forgive me,' she says, 'but for some reason I suddenly felt so incredibly miserable that I could bear it no longer. So I came here. There was a light in your window . . . and . . . I decided to knock . . . Forgive me . . . Oh, if only you knew how depressed I was feeling! What are you doing now?'

'Nothing . . . can't sleep.'

'I had a kind of premonition. Still, that's all nonsense.'

She raises her eyebrows, tears shine in her eyes and her whole face is illumined with that familiar, trusting look I hadn't seen for so long.

'Nikolay Stepanovich!' she pleads, holding out both arms to me. 'My dear friend, I beg you . . . I implore you . . . If you don't despise my friendship and respect for you, please grant my request!'

'What is it?'

'Take my money!'

'Don't be ridiculous! What do I want with your money?'

'You could go away somewhere for your health. You need treatment. You will take it, won't you, dear? Yes?'

She eagerly looks into my face.

'You *will* take it? Yes?' she repeats.

'No, my dear, I won't . . .' I say. 'But thank you . . .'

She turns her back to me and lowers her head. Probably the tone of my refusal made any further discussion of financial matters impossible.

'Go home and sleep,' I say. 'We'll see each other tomorrow.'

'Does this mean you don't consider me your friend?' she asks dejectedly.

'I'm not saying that. But your money is useless to me now.'

'I'm sorry . . .' she says, lowering her voice a whole octave.

'I understand you . . . To be indebted to a person like me . . . a retired actress . . . Oh well, goodbye . . .'

And she leaves so quickly that I don't even manage to say goodbye.

VI

I'm in Kharkov.

Since it would be fruitless and beyond my powers to struggle against my present mood, I've decided that the last days of my life will be irreproachable – at least in a formal sense. If I'm being unfair to my family, as I fully realize, I'll try my very best to do what they want. If I really have to go to Kharkov – then to Kharkov I shall go. Besides, I've become so indifferent to everything lately that it's really all the same to me where I go – Kharkov, Paris or Berdichev.[25]

I arrived in Kharkov at about noon and put up at a hotel not far from the cathedral. The jolting of the train made me feel sick, the draughts went right through me and now here I am sitting on my bed, clutching my head and waiting for the nervous tic to start. Today I really ought to go and see some professor friends, but I've neither the inclination nor the strength.

The old hotel waiter comes in and asks if I have bed linen. I keep him for about five minutes and question him about Gnekker – the object of my journey. The waiter turns out to be a native of Kharkov, who knows the city like the back of his hand, but he doesn't know of any house owned by a Gnekker. I ask him about estates in the country – I get the same reply.

In the corridor the clock strikes one, two, three . . . The final months of my life, whilst I'm waiting for death, seem far longer than the whole of my life up to now. Never before could I resign myself to the slow passage of time as I can now. Before, when I waited for a train at a station, or invigilated at an examination, a quarter of an hour seemed a eternity. But now I can sit all night on my bed without moving, reflecting with complete indifference that tomorrow night will be just as long and dreary – and the night after that . . .

The corridor clock strikes five, six, seven. It's growing dark.

There's a dull pain in my cheek – the tic is starting. To occupy my mind I revert to my earlier outlook, when I wasn't so apathetic. Why, I ask myself, should a famous man, at the top of his profession, be sitting in this small hotel room on a bed with a strange grey quilt? Why am I looking at a cheap tin washstand and listening to the jarring sound of that wretched clock in the corridor? Is all this in keeping with my fame and elevated position in society? And I answer these questions with a sarcastic smile. I'm amused by the naïvety with which I once – when I was young – used to exaggerate the importance of fame and the exclusive status celebrities appear to enjoy. I am well-known, my name is uttered in awe, my portrait has been in *The Cornfield*[26] and *World Illustrated*.[27] I've even read my biography in a German journal – and what does it all add up to? Here I am sitting all alone, in a strange town, on a strange bed, rubbing my aching cheek with my hand. Family squabbles, ruthless creditors, the rudeness of railway guards, the bothersome passport system,[28] the expensive and unhealthy food at buffets, people's general boorishness and bad manners – all this and much more which would take too long to enumerate, affects me no less than any lowly tradesman, known only in his little back alley. What is so special about my position? Let's suppose I'm a celebrity a thousand times over, that I'm a hero, the pride of Russia. Bulletins about my illness appear in every paper, now I receive in the post letters of sympathy from my colleagues, students and the public, yet none of this will save me from dying miserably in a strange bed and in utter loneliness. No one's to blame for this of course but (sinner that I am) I don't like having such a popular name. It strikes me that it's cheated me.

Around ten o'clock I fall asleep and I sleep soundly, despite the tic. I would have slept for a long time had someone not woken me up. Soon after one o'clock there's a sudden knock at the door.

'Who's there?'

'A telegram for you.'

'You might have waited till the morning,' I say angrily as I take the telegram from the hotel boy. 'Now I shan't get to sleep again.'

'Sorry sir. I saw a light in your room, so I thought you were awake.'

I open the telegram and first I glance at the signature: it's my wife's. What does she want?

YESTERDAY GNEKKER SECRETLY MARRIED LIZA COME BACK

As I read the telegram my fear is short-lived. It's not Liza's or Gnekker's behaviour that alarms me, but my own indifference to the news of their marriage. Philosophers and true sages are said to be dispassionate, but that's false: indifference is spiritual paralysis, premature death.

I go back to bed again and wonder how to occupy my mind. What can I think about? I feel I've thought over everything already and that there's nothing left capable of stimulating my mind now.

When daylight comes I'm sitting on my bed, knees clasped, and for want of anything else to do I try to know myself. 'Know thyself' is fine, practical advice, only it's a pity the ancients didn't get round to showing us how to make use of their advice.

Before, whenever I had the urge to understand someone else or myself, it wasn't their actions – where everything follows convention – that I used to take into account, but their desires: tell me what you want and I'll tell you who you are.

And now I examine myself and ask: what *do* I want?

I want our wives, children, friends, students to love us not for our prestige, not for the way we're branded and labelled, but as ordinary human beings. What else? I would have liked to have had helpers and successors. What else? I'd like to wake up a hundred years from now and at least have a quick look at what's going on in science. I'd like to live another ten years . . . And then?

Nothing more. I keep thinking for a long, long time but can't hit upon anything. And however much I rack my brains and whenever I let my thoughts roam, obviously something of fundamental importance, something that is absolutely crucial is lacking in my desires.

In my passion for science, in my urge to live, in my sitting here on this strange bed, in all the thoughts and feelings and conceptions I form about everything and in my endeavour to know myself, there is no common link which might bind them into one whole. Every feeling, every idea I entertain lives a separate life. Not even the most skilful analyst could discover any 'general idea' or the God of living man in any of my judgements about science, the stage, literature, students, in any of the pictures painted by my imagination.

And if *that*'s not there, then nothing is there.

My present plight is so wretched that serious illness, fear of death, the impact of circumstances and people have sufficed to capsize and to completely shatter what once I considered my entire outlook, everything which once brought meaning and joy to my life. Therefore it's no wonder that I've darkened the last months of my life with thoughts and feelings worthy of a slave and barbarian, that I'm so apathetic now and don't even notice when dawn comes. When a man lacks something which is stronger and superior to all outside influences, then a cold will suffice for him to become unbalanced and to see an owl in every bird and to hear the howling of dogs in every noise. And all his pessimism or optimism, together with his thoughts – great or small – are in that case meaningful solely as symptoms, nothing else.

I am defeated. If that's so, there's no point in carrying on thinking or talking. I shall just sit and wait in silence for whatever comes.

In the morning the boy brings me tea and a local paper. Mechanically I read the advertisements on the front page, the editorial, extracts from papers and journals, the Chronicle of Events. Among other things I find the following announcement: 'Yesterday that famous scholar the distinguished Professor Nikolay Stepanovich Such-and-Such arrived by express in Kharkov and is staying at Such-and-Such hotel.'

Resounding reputations are apparently created to live their own separate lives, apart from those who bear them. Now my name is wandering serenely around Kharkov; in three months' time it will be engraved in gold letters gleaming bright as the sun on my tombstone – that's when I myself will be under the grass . . .

There's a light tap on the door. Someone wants me.

'Who's there? Come in!'

The door opens and I am so startled I step backwards, hurriedly wrapping the folds of my dressing-gown around me. Before me stands Katya.

'Hullo,' she says, out of breath after walking up the stairs. 'You weren't expecting me, were you? Well . . . I've come here too.'

She sits down and goes on talking, falteringly and without looking at me.

'Why don't you say hullo? I'm here too, I arrived this morning. I found out that you were staying in this hotel, so I came to see you.'

'But I'm amazed . . . just like a bolt from the blue! Why have you come here?'

'Me? Oh well . . . I had a sudden urge, so I came . . .'

Silence. Suddenly she impetuously gets up and comes over to me.

'Nikolay Stepanovich!' she says, turning pale and pressing her hands to her bosom. 'Nikolay Stepanovich! I can't go on living like this! I can't! For God's sake tell me quickly, right now – what am I to do? Tell me what to do.'

'What can I say?' I ask in bewilderment. 'There's nothing to say.'

'But *please* tell me, I beg you!' she continues, gasping and shaking all over. 'I swear it, I can't live like this any more. I'm at the end of my tether!'

She sinks onto a chair and starts sobbing. With her head tossed back she wrings her hands, stamps her feet. Her hat falls off and dangles on a piece of elastic, her hair is dishevelled.

'Help me, help me!' she pleads. 'I can't go on like this any more!'

She takes a handkerchief from her travelling bag and pulls out with it several letters which fall from her lap onto the floor. I pick them up and in one of them I recognize Mikhail Fyodorovich's handwriting and happen to read part of a word – 'passionat . .'

'There's nothing I can tell you, Katya,' I say.

'Help me!' she sobs, seizing my hand and kissing it. 'You're my father, my only friend! You're clever, educated, you've lived a long life! You were a teacher once! Tell me what to do!'

'In all honesty, Katya, I don't know.'

I am bewildered, embarrassed, moved by her sobbing and I can hardly stand.

'Let's have some lunch, Katya,' I say, forcing a smile. 'Now stop crying!'

And I immediately add in a sinking voice, 'Soon I shall be dead, Katya . . .'

'Just one word, one word!' she weeps, stretching out her arms. 'What can I do?'

'Really, you're so strange,' I mutter. 'I don't understand. Such a clever girl – then suddenly all these tears! Really!'

Silence follows. Katya tidies her hair, puts on her hat, crumples the letters together and stuffs them in the bag – all this without hurrying or speaking. Her face, her bosom, her gloves are wet with tears, but her expression is cold and stern now . . . I look at her and feel ashamed that I'm happier than her. Only on the brink of death, in my twilight days, have I discovered that I lack what my philosopher colleagues call a general idea, but that poor girl's spirit never knew and will never know sanctuary all its life. All its life!

'Come on Katya, let's have lunch,' I say.

'No thank you,' she replies coldly.

Another minute passes in silence.

'I don't like Kharkov,' I say. 'It's very grey – a grey kind of town!'

'Yes, perhaps it is . . . Yes, it's ugly . . . I'm not staying long . . . just passing through. I'm leaving today.'

'Where are you going?'

'To the Crimea . . . I mean, the Caucasus.'

'Oh. For long?'

'I don't know.'

Katya gets up and without looking at me she stretches out her hand with a cold smile.

I feel like asking: 'So, you won't be at my funeral?' But she doesn't look at me, her hand is as cold as a stranger's. Without saying a word I escort her to the door . . . And now she's left me and she's walking down the long corridor without looking back. She knows I'm watching her and she'll probably look back at the corner.

But no, she doesn't look back. I glimpse her black dress for the last time, her footsteps die away . . . Farewell, my treasure!

Gusev

I

It is dark now, soon it will be night.

Gusev, a discharged soldier, sits up in his bunk and says in an undertone, 'Can you hear me, Pavel Ivanych? A soldier in Suchan[1] told me that when they were at sea their ship collided with an enormous fish and stove a hole in its bottom.'

The nondescript person whom he is addressing and whom everyone in the ship's sickbay knows as Pavel Ivanych says nothing, as if he doesn't hear.

And again silence descends . . . The wind plays in the rigging, the screw throbs, waves lash, bunks creak, but the ear has long grown accustomed to all this and everything around seems to be silently slumbering. It is boring. The three patients – two soldiers and one sailor – who have been playing cards all day are already dozing and talking in their sleep.

The ship is beginning to pitch, it seems. The bunk beneath Gusev slowly rises and falls as if it is breathing – once, twice, a third time. Something hits the floor with a ringing noise – a mug must have fallen down.

'The wind's broken loose from its chains,' says Gusev, listening hard.

This time Pavel Ivanych coughs and answers irritably, 'First you say the ship's colliding with a fish, then the wind's broken loose from its chains. Is the wind a wild animal then, that can break loose from its chains?'

'That's what folk say.'

'Then folk are as ignorant as you are, they say all sorts of things. A man should have a head on his shoulders and use his brains, you foolish man.'

Pavel Ivanych is subject to seasickness. When the sea is rough he is usually bad-tempered and the least trifle irritates him. But in Gusev's opinion there is absolutely nothing to be angry about. What's so strange or surprising about that fish, for instance, or the wind breaking loose from its chains? Suppose that fish were as big as a mountain and its back as hard as a sturgeon's? Suppose too, that far away, where the world ends, there are thick stone walls and the fierce winds are chained to those walls . . . If they haven't broken loose then why do they charge all over the ocean like maniacs and struggle to break free, like dogs on a leash? Where then do they go in calm weather if they're not chained up?

Gusev ponders long over mountain-sized fish and thick rusty chains; then he grows bored and starts thinking of his homeland where he is now returning after five years' service in the Far East. He pictures the large snow-covered pond . . . on one side there's a red-brick pottery with a tall chimney and clouds of thick black smoke, on the other is the village. His brother Alexis is driving in his sledge out of the fifth yard from the end with his little son Vanka sitting behind him in large felt over-boots, and his little girl Akulka, who is wearing felt boots too. Alexis has been drinking, Vanka is laughing, but Akulka's face is hidden because she has wrapped herself up.

'You'll see, he'll get them kids frostbitten,' thinks Gusev. 'Oh Lord,' he whispers, 'grant them sense and understanding so they honours their parents and aren't cleverer than their mama and papa.'

'Them boots need resoling,' the sick sailor babbles in his deep voice. 'Oh yes they do!'

Gusev's thoughts break off and instead of the pond a large eyeless bull's head appears for no earthly reason, whilst the horse and sledge no longer drive along but whirl round in a cloud of black smoke. Still, he is glad that he has seen the folk at home. His joy takes his breath away, sends shivers all over his whole body and makes his fingers twitch.

'The Lord's arranged for us to meet again!' he rambles deliriously, but at once he opens his eyes and looks for some water in the darkness.

He drinks and lies back – and again that sledge drives past, again that eyeless bull's head, smoke, clouds . . . and so it goes on until daybreak.

II

A dark blue circle first emerges from the darkness – it is a porthole; then Gusev gradually begins to distinguish his neighbour Pavel Ivanych in the next bunk. Pavel is sleeping sitting up as he would choke lying down. His face is grey, his nose long and sharp and his eyes enormous because he has grown so terribly thin. His temples are sunken, his beard sparse, his hair long. By looking at his face it is impossible to tell what class he is – gentleman, merchant or peasant. From his expression and long hair he might be a hermit or a lay brother in a monastery, but if you listen to him speak he doesn't sound like a monk. The pitching, the humidity and his illness have exhausted him, he finds breathing difficult and he keeps moving his parched lips. Noticing that Gusev is looking at him he turns his face to him and says, 'Now I'm beginning to see . . . Yes, I understand everything perfectly now.'

'Understand what, Pavel Ivanych?'

'I'll tell you . . . What's always puzzled me is how serious cases like you, instead of being somewhere nice and peaceful, should end up in a ship, where there's pitching, humidity, heat – in short, where you're threatened with death on all sides. But now it's all clear to me . . . yes . . . Your doctors let them put you on the ship to get rid of you. They're sick of messing around with cattle like you. You don't pay them anything, you're a damned nuisance and you spoil their records by dying – so you're cattle! And getting rid of you isn't difficult. The first requirement is to lack all conscience and humanity and the second is to cheat the steamship line. You can ignore the first

– we're all artists in that respect and you can always manage the second with a little practice. Five sick men don't stand out in a crowd of four hundred fit soldiers and sailors. So, they bundle you on board, mix you up with the healthy ones, quickly tot you all up and in all the confusion they find nothing wrong. Only when the ship's under way do they notice the paralytics and consumptives in the last stages lying around the deck.'

Gusev doesn't understand Pavel Ivanych. Thinking that he is being told off he says in self-defence, 'I was lying on deck because all me strength had gone. I got frozen stiff when they was unloading us from the barge onto the ship.'

'It really gets your back up,' Pavel Ivanych continues. 'The worst of it is they know perfectly well you won't last the long journey, yet still they put you here! Supposing you make it to the Indian Ocean – then what? It doesn't bear thinking about . . . And that's all the thanks you get for loyal service and a clean record!'

Pavel Ivanych's eyes fill with anger and he frowns in disgust.

'I'd like to have a go at that lot in the papers!' he gasps. 'I'd make the feathers fly all right!'

The two sick soldiers and the sailor are awake and already playing cards. The sailor is half lying in his bunk while the soldiers are sitting near him on the floor in the most uncomfortable positions. One of the soldiers has his right arm in a sling and the hand is swathed in a great bundle, so that he holds his cards in his right armpit or the crook of his elbow while he plays with the left.

The ship is pitching heavily so that it is impossible to stand up, drink tea or take any medicine.

'Were you a batman?' Pavel Ivanych asks Gusev.

'Yes, a batman.'

'My God!' says Pavel Ivanych with a sad shake of the head. 'Uprooting a man from his home, dragging him ten thousand miles and then making a consumptive out of him – and all this for what, I wonder? To make a servant out of him for some Captain Kopeykin[2] or Midshipman Dyrka.[3] There's a lot of logic in that, I must say!'

'It's not hard work, Pavel Ivanych. You get up in the morning, clean the boots, put the samovar on, sweep the rooms – after that there's nothing more to do. The lieutenant spends the whole day drawing plans, so you can say your prayers, read a book, go into the street – whatever you fancy. God grant everyone such a life!'

'Very nice, I must say! The lieutenant draws his plans while you sit all day in the kitchen pining for home . . . Plans – I ask you! It's not plans that matter, but human life. You only live once, life must be respected.'

'Of course, Pavel Ivanych. A bad man will be shown no mercy anywhere, whether at home or in the army. But if you live proper and obey orders then who's going to harm you? The officers are all educated gents, they understand . . . Not once in five years was I in the guardhouse and if me memory don't play me false I wasn't beaten more than once.'

'For what?'

'For fighting. I'm always spoiling for a fight, Pavel Ivanych. Four Chinamen comes into our yard, carrying firewood or something, I can't remember what. Well, I was feeling a bit fed up . . . so I . . . well knocks 'em about a bit, one of the buggers' noses starts bleeding. The lieutenant sees it through the window, gets real mad he does and gives me a clout on the ear.'

'You stupid, pathetic man,' whispers Pavel Ivanych. 'You haven't got a clue about anything.'

He is utterly exhausted by the pitching of the ship and closes his eyes. His head first falls backwards, then drops onto his chest. Several times he tries to lie flat but doesn't succeed because of his difficulty with breathing.

'Why did you lay into those Chinamen?' he asks a little later.

'Can't really say. They comes into the yard so I bashes 'em.'

There is silence . . . The card players carry on playing for a couple of hours with enthusiasm and a good deal of foul language, but the pitching exhausts even them. They throw aside their cards and lie down. Once more Gusev visualizes the big pond, the pottery, the village . . . Once more the sledge drives past, again Vanka laughs while silly Akulka throws open her fur coat and sticks her legs out as if to say: 'Just look, all of you! My snow-boots aren't like Vanka's. They're new!'

'Five years old and still she's got no sense,' Gusev rambles. 'Instead of kicking your legs out you ought to be getting your soldier uncle a drink. I'll give you a nice present . . .'

Then Andron, a flintlock gun on his shoulder, comes along with a hare he has killed and after him comes that decrepit old Jew Isaiah who offers to barter the hare for a piece of soap. Just inside the hut there's a small black calf and there's Domna, sewing a shirt and crying about something – and once again that eyeless bull's head, black smoke . . .

Overhead someone gives a loud shout and several sailors run past: it seems that they are dragging something bulky over the deck or that something has fallen with a crash. Again they run past. Has there been an accident? Gusev raises his head, listens and sees the two soldiers and the sailor playing cards again. Pavel Ivanych is sitting up and moving his lips. He's choking, he hasn't the strength to breathe and he's thirsty, but the water is warm and foul. The pitching doesn't stop.

Suddenly something strange happens to one of the card-playing soldiers. He calls hearts diamonds, muddles the score and drops his cards; then with a frightened and stupid smile he looks around at everyone.

'Won't be a jiff, lads,' he says and lies down on the floor.

All of the men are bewildered. They call him, but he doesn't respond.

'Maybe you don't feel well, Stephan?' asks the soldier with the sling. 'Eh? Maybe we ought to get a priest. Eh?'

'Have some water, Stephan,' says the sailor. 'There mate, drink that.'

'What yer banging his teeth with that mug for?' says Gusev angrily. 'Can't you see, you nitwit?!'

'What?'

'What!' Gusev mimics him. 'There's no breath in him, he's dead. 'That's *what*! God help us, what a gormless lot!'

III

The pitching has stopped and Pavel Ivanych has cheered up. No longer is he angry and his expression is boastful, animated, mocking. It is as if he wants to say, 'Now I'm going to tell you a story that'll make you all split your sides with laughter!' The porthole is open and a gentle breeze is blowing on Pavel Ivanych. There is the sound of voices and the plash of oars in the water. Just beneath the porthole someone starts wailing in a shrill, unpleasant voice – most probably a Chinaman singing.

'Yes, now we're in the roadstead,' says Pavel Ivanych, smiling sarcastically. 'Only one more month and we'll be in Russia. Oh yes, my highly esteemed army brutes! As soon as I get to Odessa I'll go straight to Kharkov. I've a friend in Kharkov, a literary man. I'll call on him and say, "Well, old chap, leave your vile plots about female amours and the beauties of nature for the moment and expose this two-legged scum . . . Now, *there's* material for you!"

He reflects for a while and then asks, 'Gusev, do you know how I fooled them?'

'Fooled who, Pavel Ivanych?'

'Well, that lot I've just been talking about. You know, there's only first and third class on this ship and only peasants are allowed to go third – that is, the riff-raff. But if you're wearing a jacket and look anything like a gent or a bourgeois, then first you must travel – if you please! You must cough up five hundred roubles even if it kills you! "Why did you make these rules?" I ask. "Want to raise the prestige of the Russian intelligentsia that way, I suppose?". "Not a bit of it. We don't allow it simply because no respectable gentleman should travel third, it's foul and disgusting there." "Really? Much obliged for your concern for respectable people. But whatever it's like in third, disgusting or nice, I haven't got five hundred roubles. I haven't pilfered government money, I haven't exploited the natives, I haven't done any smuggling, I haven't flogged anyone to death. So it's for you to judge if I have any right to travel first class, let alone reckon myself one of the Russian intelligentsia." But logic will get you nowhere with that lot, so I pulled a fast one over them. I put on a workman's coat and high boots, made a face like a drunken lout and off I go to the agent. "Give us one of them tickets, your honner," I say.'

'From what background are you?' asks the sailor.

'Clerical. My father was an honest priest who always told the bigwigs of this world the truth to their faces and suffered dearly for it.'

Pavel Ivanych is exhausted from talking and gasps for breath, but still he goes on, 'Yes, I tell people the truth to their faces . . . I fear nothing and no one. In this respect there's a vast difference between you and me. You're a benighted, blind, downtrodden lot, you see nothing and what you do see you don't understand . . . If you're told the wind breaks loose from its chains, that you're cattle, savages, you believe it. If someone punches you on the neck you kiss his hand. If some brute in a raccoon coat robs you and tosses you a fifteen-copeck tip you say, "Allow me to kiss your hand, sir." You are pariahs, a pathetic lot. But I'm a different proposition. I'm alive to everything, I see everything, like an eagle or a hawk do when they fly over the earth and I understand everything. I'm protest incarnate. If I see tyranny – I protest. If I see a canting hypocrite – I protest. If I see a triumphant swine – I protest. I'm invincible, no Spanish Inquisition could ever force me to keep quiet. Oh no! Cut my tongue off – I'll mime my protest. Brick me up in a cellar – I'll shout so loud I'll be heard a mile off. Or I'll starve myself to death, so that'll be another load on their black consciences. Kill me – and my ghost will haunt you. "You really are insufferable, Pavel Ivanych," I'm told by all who know me. Well, I'm proud of my reputation. I've served three years in the Far East, but they'll remember me there for a hundred! I've had blazing rows with everyone. "Don't come back," my friends write from western Russia. Then I damned well *will* come back – just to spite them! Oh yes I will! That's life as I see it, that's what I call living.'

Gusev doesn't listen and looks through the porthole. On the translucent, delicate turquoise water, bathed in dazzling, hot sunshine, a boat is tossing. In it stand naked Chinamen holding up cages of canaries and calling out, 'It sing! It sing!'

Another boat knocks against the first, a steam cutter races past. And now another boat appears with a fat Chinaman sitting in it eating rice with chopsticks. The water heaves lazily, white seagulls lazily glide over it.

'I'd like to bash that greasy one on the neck,' thinks Gusev, looking at the fat Chinaman and yawning.

He is drowsy and feels that all nature is drowsing too. Time is flying. The day passes unnoticed, unnoticed the darkness descends . . . No longer is the ship at anchor, but moving somewhere further on.

IV

Two days pass. Pavel Ivanych is no longer sitting up, but lying down; his eyes are closed and his nose seems to have grown sharper.

'Pavel Ivanych!' Gusev calls out. 'Hey, Pavel Ivanych!'

Pavel Ivanych opens his eyes and moves his lips.

'Not feeling well?'

'It's nothing,' Pavel Ivanych replies breathlessly. 'Nothing at all . . . On the contrary, I even feel better. You see, I can lie down now . . . it's a bit easier . . .'

'Well, thank God for that, Pavel Ivanych!'

'When I compare myself to you poor devils I feel sorry for you . . . My lungs are in good shape and it's only a stomach cough. I can go through hell – let alone the Red Sea! Besides, I take a critical attitude to my illness and medicines. But you lot – why, you're so ignorant! It's very hard for you . . . very, very hard!'

The pitching has stopped and the sea is calm, but it is as hot and humid as a bath-house. It is hard to listen, let alone speak. Gusev hugs his knees, lowers his head on them and thinks of his homeland. God, how delightful to think of the snow and cold in this stifling heat! You're riding in a sledge. Suddenly the horses shy and bolt . . . Whether it's roads, ditches, gullies, they tear along like mad, right through the village, across the pond, past the pottery and then out across open country. 'Hold them back!' the pottery workers and passers-by shout at the top of their voices. 'Hold them!' But why hold them back? Let the keen cold wind lash your face and bite your hands, let the clods of snow kicked up by the horses' hooves fall on cap, collar, neck and chest. Let the runners screech, traces and swingletrees snap – to hell with them! But what delight when the sledge overturns and you fly full tilt into a snowdrift face first and you get up white all over, with icicles on your whiskers – no hat, no mittens and your belt undone! People laugh, dogs bark . . .

Pavel Ivanych half opens one eye, looks at Gusev and softly asks, 'Gusev, did your commanding officer steal?'

'How should I know, Pavel Ivanych? We don't know about such things – they never reach our ears.'

And then there is a long silence. Gusev muses, rambles deliriously and constantly drinks water. He finds speaking and listening difficult and he is afraid of being spoken to. One hour, then a second, then a third pass. Evening comes on, then night, but he does not notice and still sits dreaming of the frost.

It sounds as though someone has entered the sickbay, voices ring out, but after five minutes everything goes quiet again.

'May he rest in peace,' says the soldier with the sling. 'He was a restless sort of bloke!'

'What?' asks Gusev. 'Who?'

'He's dead. They've just carried him up.'

'Ah well,' Gusev mutters, yawning. 'May he rest in peace.'

'What do you think, Gusev?' asks the soldier with his arm in a sling, after a brief silence. 'Will he go to heaven or not?'

'Who do you mean?'

'Pavel Ivanych.'

'Of course he will. He suffered so long. What's more, he's from the clergy and priests have a lot of relatives. Their prayers will save him.'

The soldier with the sling sits on Gusev's bunk.

'As for you, Gusev, you're not long for this world,' he softly says. 'You'll never make it to Russia.'

'Did the doctor or his assistant tell you that?' asks Gusev.

'No, it didn't need anyone to tell me – I can see it . . . You can tell at once if someone's going to die, it's obvious. You don't eat, you don't drink and you're so thin it's a shocking sight. In a word, it's consumption. I'm not telling you this to frighten you, but you might want the sacrament and last rites. And if you have any cash you'd better give it to the senior officer.'

'I didn't write home,' sighs Gusev. 'I'll die and they won't know a thing about it.'

'They'll know all right,' the sick sailor says in a deep voice. 'When you die they enter your name in the ship's log and they'll hand a note to the Commandant at Odessa, who'll forward it to your parish, or wherever . . .'

This talk frightens Gusev and a vague longing starts to trouble him. He drinks some water – that's not what he wants; he stretches towards the porthole and breathes in the hot moist air – that's not it; he tries to think of his homeland and the frost – that's not it either. Finally he feels that just one more minute in that sickbay and he'll be bound to choke to death.

'I feel bad, mates,' he says. 'I'm going on deck. Help me up, for Christ's sake!'

'All right,' agrees the soldier with the sling. 'You won't make it on your own. I'll carry you – just hold on to my neck.'

Gusev puts his arms around the soldier's neck and the soldier puts his sound arm around him and carries him up. On the deck sailors and discharged soldiers are sleeping side by side – there are so many it's difficult to pick a way through.

'Get down,' the soldier with the sling says quietly. 'Follow me slowly and keep hold of my shirt . . .'

It is dark. There are no lights on deck or on the masts or in the surrounding sea. Still as a statue, right at the very tip of the bows, stands a sailor on watch, but he too seems to be sleeping. It appears that they have given free rein to the ship and that it's sailing where it likes.

'They're going to throw Pavel Ivanych into the sea now,' says the soldier with the sling. 'First in a sack – then into the water.'

'Yes, that's how they do it.'

'But it's better to lie in the ground at home. At least your mother'll come and weep at your grave.'

'That's true.'

There's a smell of dung and hay. Bulls stand with lowered heads at the rail – one, two, three – eight of them. And there's a small pony. Gusev stretches his hand out to stroke it, but it shakes its head, bares its teeth and tries to bite his sleeve.

'Damn you!' says Gusev angrily.

Both he and the soldier slowly pick their way to the bows, stand by the rail and look up and down in silence. Overhead are the deep sky, bright stars, peace and tranquillity – it's exactly like being at home in one's village. But down below all is darkness and chaos. The tall waves roar – why, no one can tell. Whichever way you look each wave tries to rise above the others, chases and crushes its neighbour – until a third, just as savage and hideous, with a gleaming white mane, piles into it with a great crash.

The sea is without meaning, without compassion. Had the ship been smaller, had it not been made of thick iron, the waves would have smashed it without any compunction and devoured all the people, with no distinction between saints and sinners. Like the sea, the ship has a mindless, cruel look too. This beaked monster forges ahead and slices millions of waves in her path. She fears neither the dark nor the wind, nor the vast wastes, nor the solitude. It cares for nothing and had people been living in the ocean this monster would have crushed them too, sinners and saints alike.

'Where are we now?' asks Gusev.

'Don't know. In mid-ocean, I think.'

'I can't see land.'

'How could we! They say we won't see land for a week.'

Both soldiers watch the white foam with its phosphorescent gleam and silently reflect. Gusev is first to break the silence.

'There's nothing to be frightened of,' he says. 'Only it's a bit scary, like sitting in a dark forest. But suppose they was to lower a boat in the water now and an officer ordered me to go sixty miles over the sea to catch fish – well, I'd go. Or if some Christian, let's say, were to fall overboard this very minute I'd go in after him. A German or Chinaman I wouldn't save, but I'd go in after a Christian.'

'Are you afraid of dying?'

'Oh yes. I'm worried how they'll get by at home. My brother ain't the steady type. He drinks, beats his old woman for nothing, has no respect for his parents. Without me it'll all go to pot. And mark my words – my father and my old mother'll have to go out begging . . . But I can't stand proper, mate, and I can't breathe here. Let's get some sleep.'

V

Gusev returns to the sickbay and lies down in his bunk. That same vague longing still torments him, but he just cannot work out what he really needs. There is a tightness in his chest, his head is throbbing, his mouth is so parched that he can barely move his tongue. He dozes and mumbles deliriously. Exhausted by nightmares, coughing and the stifling heat, he falls into a sound sleep by morning. He dreams that they have just taken the bread out of the oven in the barracks, that he has climbed into the stove, is having a steam-bath and is beating himself with birch twigs. He sleeps for two days and at noon on the third two sailors come down and carry him out of the sickbay.

They sew him up in sailcloth, putting in two iron bars to weigh him down. Stitched up in sailcloth he resembles a carrot or a radish: wide at the head, narrow at the feet. They take him on deck before sunset and lay him on a plank; one end of the plank rests on the ship's rail, the other on a box placed on a stool. The discharged soldiers and crew stand around, their heads bared.

'Blessed be the Lord,' chants the priest. 'As it was in the beginning, is now and ever shall be!'

'Amen!' three sailors sing.

The soldiers and the crew cross themselves and look sideways at the waves. It is strange that a man has been sewn up in sailcloth and that in a moment he will fly into those waves. Could such a thing really happen to *them*?

The priest scatters earth over Gusev and makes an obeisance. They sing 'Eternal Memory'.

The officer of the watch tilts one end of the plank. Gusev slides down, flies off head first, turns a somersault and – splash into the water! The foam covers him and for a moment he seems wrapped in lace; but the moment passes and he vanishes beneath the waves.

Quickly he sinks towards the bottom. Will he reach it? They say it's three miles deep. After sinking eight or ten fathoms he begins to move more and more slowly, swaying rhythmically as if he is deliberating. Then, caught by a current, he is borne quicker sideways than downwards.

And now he meets on his descent a shoal of tiny pilot-fish. Seeing the dark body the fish stop dead in their tracks, then all of them suddenly turn tail and vanish. Less than a minute later they again swoop on Gusev as swift as arrows and trace zigzags in the water around him . . .

Then another dark shape looms. It is a shark. With dignity and indifferently, apparently not even noticing Gusev, it glides beneath him and Gusev sinks onto its back. Then it turns belly upwards, basks in the warm, limpid water and lazily opens its jaws with their two rows of teeth. The pilot-fish are delighted: they stop and wait to see what will happen next. After toying with the body the shark nonchalantly puts its jaws under it, cautiously touches it with its teeth and the sailcloth tears along its full length, from head to foot. One of the weights falls out, scares the pilot-fish, strikes the shark on the side and rapidly goes to the bottom.

But meanwhile, up above where the sun is setting, clouds are massing, one like a triumphal arch, another like a lion, a third like a pair of scissors. A broad green shaft of light comes out from the clouds, reaching to the very centre of the sky. A moment later a violet ray settles next to it, then a golden ray, then one of pink. The sky turns a delicate lilac. Surveying this magnificent, magical sky, the ocean frowns at first, but before long it too takes on gentle, joyous, ardent hues which are difficult to name in the language of man.

The Duel

I

It was eight in the morning, a time when officers, civil servants and visitors usually took a dip in the sea after the hot, stuffy night, proceeding to the Pavilion afterwards for tea or coffee. When Ivan Layevsky, a thin, fair-haired young man of about twenty-eight, came down for his bathe in slippers and with his Ministry of Finance peaked cap, he met many of his friends on the beach, including Samoylenko, an army doctor.

The stout, red-faced, flabby Samoylenko with his large, close-cropped head, big nose, black bushy eyebrows, grey side-whiskers and no neck to speak of, with a hoarse soldier's voice as well, struck all newcomers as an unpleasant army upstart. But about two or three days after the first meeting his face began to strike them as exceptionally kind, amiable, handsome even. Although a rude-mannered, clumsy person, he was docile, infinitely kind, good-humoured and obliging. He called everyone in town by their Christian names, lent money to everyone, gave medical treatment to all, arranged marriages, patched up quarrels and organized picnics, where he grilled kebabs and made a very tasty grey mullet soup. He was always helping people and interceding for them, and there was always something that made him happy. He was generally regarded as a saint, with just two weaknesses: firstly, he was ashamed of his own kindness and tried to conceal it behind a forbidding expression and an affected rudeness; secondly, he liked to be called 'General' by the medical orderlies and soldiers, although he was only a colonel.

'Just answer one question for me, Alexander,' Layevsky began when he and Samoylenko were right up to their shoulders in the water. 'Suppose you fell in love and had an affair with the woman. Suppose you lived with her for more than two years and then, as happens so often, you stopped loving her and felt she was no more than a stranger. What would you have done in that event?'

'Very simple. I would say "Get out, my dear" – and that would be that.'

'That's easy enough to say! But supposing she had nowhere to go? Supposing she was all on her own, with no family, not a penny to her name, no job . . .'

'What of it? Five hundred roubles down, to keep her quiet, or twenty-five a month and no arguments. Very simple.'

'Let's assume you could pay her the five hundred or twenty-five a month, but the woman I'm talking about is educated and has her pride. Could you really offer someone like that *money*? How would you pay her?'

Samoylenko wanted to give him an answer, but at that moment a large wave broke over them both, crashed onto the beach and roared back over the shingle. The two friends came out of the water and started dressing.

'Of course it's difficult living with a woman if you don't love her,' Samoylenko said, shaking the sand out of his boot. 'But you must consider, Ivan, would it be humane? If it were me, I wouldn't let her see I didn't love her any more and I'd stay with her until my dying day.' Suddenly he felt ashamed of these words and thought again. 'In my opinion we'd be better off if there weren't any women at all, damn them!'

The friends dressed and went into the Pavilion where Samoylenko was one of the regulars, and even had his own cups, saucers and glasses reserved for him. Every morning he was served a cup of coffee, a tall, cut-glass tumbler of iced water and a glass of brandy on a tray. First he would drink the brandy, then the hot coffee, then the iced water, all of which obviously gave him great enjoyment, as afterwards his eyes would gleam and he would gaze at the sea, stroking his side-whiskers with both hands, and say: 'A remarkably beautiful view!'

Layevsky was feeling jaded and lifeless after a long night of gloomy, empty thoughts which had disturbed his sleep and only intensified the humidity and darkness, it seemed. Nor did the swim and the coffee make him feel any better. 'Alexander, may we carry on this conversation?' he said. 'I shan't hide anything and I'm telling you quite candidly, as a friend: things with Nadezhda are bad . . . very bad! Forgive me for letting you into my secrets, but I must tell *someone*.'

Samoylenko had anticipated that he was going to tell him this; he lowered his eyes and drummed his fingers on the table.

'I've lived with her for two years and now I don't love her any more . . .' Layevsky said. 'To be more precise, I've come to realize I never *did* love her. These two years have been sheer delusion.'

Layevsky had the habit of closely studying his pink palms, biting his nails or crumpling his shirt cuffs during a conversation. And this is what he did now. 'I know only too well you can't help,' he said, 'but I'm telling you, talking things over is the only salvation for failures, or Superfluous Men[1] like yours truly. I always feel I have to start generalizing after anything I do, I have to find an explanation and justification for my absurd existence in some sort of theory or other, in literary types – for example in the fact that we gentlefolk are becoming degenerate, and so on . . . All last night, for example, I consoled myself by thinking how right Tolstoy is, how ruthlessly right! And it made me feel better. A really great writer, my friend, say what you like!'

Samoylenko, who had never read Tolstoy and had been meaning to read him every day, was taken aback and said: 'Yes, all writers draw on their imagination, but he writes directly from nature . . .'

'Good Lord!' Layevsky sighed, 'how civilization has crippled us! I fell in love with a married woman, and she with me. At first there was kissing, and quiet evenings, and promises, and Spencer,[2] and ideals, and mutual interests . . . What a sham! Essentially, we were just running away from her husband, but we deluded ourselves into thinking we were running away from the emptiness of our lives. We imagined our future like this: first, until we got to know the Caucasus and the people here, I would wear my civil service uniform and work in a government office; then, out in the wide open spaces, we would buy a little plot of land, work by the sweat of our brows, cultivate a vineyard, fields, and so on. If you yourself or that zoologist friend of yours, von Koren, had been in my place, perhaps you would have lived with Nadezhda for thirty years and left your heirs a thriving vineyard and three thousand acres or so of maize. But I felt a complete failure, from the very first day. It's insufferably hot and boring in this town, no one you can make friends with, and out in the country, under every bush and stone you think you're seeing poisonous spiders, scorpions and snakes. Beyond the fields there's nothing but mountains and the wilderness. Foreign people, foreign landscape, pathetic cultural standards – all this, my friend, is a different proposition from strolling along the Nevsky in your fur coat, arm-in-arm with Nadezhda and dreaming of sunny climes. Here you have to go at it hammer and tongs – and I'm no fighter. Just a wretched bag of nerves, an old softy . . . I realized from the very first day that my ideas about the life of labour and vineyards aren't worth a tinker's cuss. And as for love, I must inform you that life with a woman who's read Spencer and gone to the ends of the earth for you is just about as boring as living with any village girl. There's that same old smell of ironing, face powder and medicine, the same curling-papers every morning, the same self-deception . . .'

'You can't run a household without ironing,' Samoylenko said, blushing because Layevsky was speaking so frankly about a woman he knew. 'Ivan, I can see you're feeling a bit low this morning, aren't you? Nadezhda is a beautiful, cultured woman and you're a highly intelligent man . . . Of course, you're not married,' Samoylenko continued, looking round at the neighbouring tables, 'but after all, that's not your fault . . . What's more, one has to cast aside one's prejudices and keep up with modern ideas on the subject. I'm all for civil marriage myself, yes . . . But I do think that once you've started living with someone you must stay that way till your dying day.'

'But without loving her?'

'I'll tell you why, here and now,' Samoylenko said. 'About eight years ago there was an old shipping-agent living here, a very intelligent man. This is what he used to say: the most important thing in family life is patience. Are you listening, Ivan? Not love, but patience. Love can't last very long. You've been in love for two years but now your domestic life has entered that stage when you have to bring all your patience into play to maintain your equilibrium, so to speak . . .'

'You can believe that old agent of yours if you like, but his advice makes no sense at all to me. Your old gentleman could have been fooling his partner, testing his stamina, at the same time using the unloved woman as something essential for his exercises. But *I* haven't fallen that low yet. If I wanted to put my powers of endurance to the test, I'd buy dumb-bells or a lively horse, but I'd leave human beings alone.'

Samoylenko ordered some chilled wine. After they had drunk a glass each Layevsky suddenly asked, 'Can you please explain what softening of the brain is?'

'It's . . . how can I best explain it to you? It's an illness where the brain gets softer, as if it were decomposing . . .'

'Is it curable?'

'Yes, if it hasn't gone too far. Cold showers, plasters . . . and some sort of medicine you have to drink.'

'Oh. Well, so you see the state I'm in. I can't live with her, it's more than I can cope with. While I'm sitting here with you I can philosophize and smile all right, but the moment I'm home I really get very down in the dumps. I feel so bad, so absolutely awful, that if someone told me I must live with her, let's say just one more month, I think I'd put a bullet through my brains. And at the same time I just can't leave her. She's got no one else, she can't work, neither of us has any money . . . Where could she go? And to whom? I just can't think . . . Well now, tell me what to do.'

'Hm . . . yes . . .' Samoylenko mumbled, at a loss for a reply. 'Does she love you?'

'Yes, as much as anyone of her age and temperament needs a man. She'd find it as difficult to part with me as with her powder and curling-papers . . . I'm an indispensable component of her boudoir.'

Samoylenko was taken aback by this. 'You're really in a foul mood today, Ivan,' he said. 'Probably it's lack of sleep.'

'Yes, I had a bad night . . . And I feel generally pretty rough, old chap. It all seems so futile, I feel so nervy, so weak . . . I must get away from here!'

'But where to?'

'Up north. To pines, mushrooms, people, ideas . . . I'd give half my life to be somewhere near Moscow or Tula now, to have a swim in a river, then cool down, then wander around for about three hours, with the most wretched student even, and talk, talk, talk . . . You remember the scent of that hay! And those evening walks in the garden when you can hear the piano in the house, the sound of a passing train . . .'

Layevsky smiled with pleasure, his eyes filled with tears and in an effort to hide them he leant over to the next table for a box of matches without getting up.

'It's eighteen years since I was up north,' Samoylenko said. 'I've forgotten what it's like there. If you ask me, nowhere's as magnificent as the Caucasus.'

'There's a painting by Vereshchagin[3] in which some prisoners condemned to death are languishing at the bottom of a terribly deep well. Your magnificent Caucasus strikes me as exactly the same kind of bottomless pit. If you offered me two choices – being a chimney-sweep in St Petersburg or a prince in this place – I'd opt for the chimney-sweep.'

Layevsky thought for a moment. As he looked at that stooping figure, those staring eyes, that pale sweaty face with its sunken temples, the gnawed finger nails and the slipper hanging down from Layevsky's heel, revealing a badly darned sock, Samoylenko felt a surge of pity. Then, probably because Layevsky reminded him of a helpless child, he asked:

'Is your mother still alive?'

'Yes, but we never see each other. She never forgave me for this affair.'

Samoylenko was very fond of his friend. In his eyes Layevsky was a thoroughly decent 'hail-fellow-well-met' type, a genuine student, the kind of person with whom one could have a good laugh over a drink and a real heart-to-heart chat. What he understood about him he disliked intensely. Layevsky drank a great deal, and at the wrong time, played cards, despised his work, lived beyond his means, often used bad language, wore slippers in the street and quarrelled with Nadezhda in public. Samoylenko liked none of this. But the fact that Layevsky was once a university student, in the arts faculty, that he now subscribed to two literary reviews and often spoke so cleverly that only few could understand him, that he was living with a woman of culture – all this was beyond Samoylenko's understanding and it pleased him; he considered Layevsky his superior and respected him.

'Just one more thing,' Layevsky said, shaking his head. 'Just between ourselves. I'm not telling Nadezhda for the moment, so don't let the cat out of the bag when you see her. The day before yesterday I received a letter saying her husband had died of softening of the brain.'

'May he rest in peace!' Samoylenko sighed. 'But why are you hiding it from her?'

'Showing her that letter would mean "Off to the altar, please!" Things between us have to be cleared up first. When she's convinced that we can't go on living together I'll show her the letter. There'll be no danger then.'

'Do you know what, Ivan?' Samoylenko said and his face took on a sad, pleading expression, as if he was about to beg for something very nice and was afraid of being refused. 'Get married, my dear chap!'

'Why?'

'Do your duty by this beautiful woman! Her husband has died – this is the way Providence has of showing you what to do!'

'But please try and understand, you silly man! That's impossible. Marrying someone you don't love is just as vile and dishonourable as celebrating Mass and not believing in God.'

'But it's your duty!'

'Why is it my duty?' Layevsky asked irritably.

'Because you took her away from her husband and therefore you assumed responsibility.'

'Well, I'm telling you in plain language, I don't love her!'

'Then if you don't love her, show her some respect, spoil her a little.'

'Respect, spoil?' Layevsky said, mimicking him. 'Do you think she's a Mother Superior? . . . You're not much of a psychologist or physiologist if you think that respect and honour on their own will do you much good when you live with a woman. What women need most is bed.'

'Ivan, Ivan!' Samoylenko said, embarrassed.

'You're a big baby, all theories. As for me, I'm old before my time and a pragmatist, so we shall never see eye to eye. Let's change the subject.' Layevsky called out to one of the waiters, 'Mustafa, how much do we owe you?'

'No, no,' the doctor said, grasping Layevsky's arm anxiously. 'I'll do the honours. I ordered.' And he called out to Mustafa, 'Charge it to me.'

The friends got up and walked in silence along the front. They stopped at the main boulevard to say goodbye and shook hands.

'You gentlemen are too spoilt!' Samoylenko sighed. 'Fate has sent you a young, beautiful, educated woman and you don't want her. If only God would send me some hunch-backed old crone, how happy I should be – as long as she was affectionate and kind. I'd live in my vineyard with her and . . .' Samoylenko suddenly pulled himself up. 'As long as the old witch could keep my samovar on the boil!'

After bidding Layevsky farewell he went off down the boulevard. Whenever that ponderous, majestic, stern-faced man strolled along the boulevard in his snow-white tunic and impeccably polished boots, thrusting his chest out and flaunting his splendid Order of Vladimir (with ribbon) he was very pleased with himself and thought the whole world was looking at him in delight. Without turning his head, he looked from side to side and concluded that the boulevard had been beautifully planned, that the young cypresses, the eucalyptus and those unsightly, anaemic-looking palm trees were very beautiful in fact and, given time, would cast a broad shade, and that the Circassians were a decent, hospitable people. 'Strange that Layevsky doesn't like the Caucasus,' he thought. 'Most strange.' Five soldiers with rifles saluted as they passed him. On the pavement, on the other side of the boulevard, a civil servant's wife was walking along with her schoolboy son.

'Good morning, Marya Konstantinova!' Samoylenko called out,

smiling pleasantly. 'Have you been for a bathe? Ha, ha, ha . . . My regards to Nikodim Aleksandrych.'

He walked on further, still smiling pleasantly, but when he spotted a medical orderly coming towards him he suddenly frowned, stopped him and asked, 'Is there anyone at the hospital?'

'No one, General.'

'What?'

'No one, General.'

'Very good . . . Carry on.'

Swaying majestically, he went over to a soft drinks kiosk, where an old, full-bosomed Jewess who pretended to be a Georgian was sitting behind the counter.

'Please give me a glass of soda water!' he said, so loud, he might have been giving orders to a regiment.

II

The main reason for Layevsky's dislike of Nadezhda was the falsity – or the apparent falsity – of everything she did. All he had read attacking women and love, it seemed, couldn't have been more applicable to himself, Nadezhda and her husband. When he arrived home she was already dressed and had done her hair, and she was sitting at the window drinking coffee, looking through a literary review with an anxious look on her face. He reflected that simply drinking coffee hardly warranted such a worried look and that her fashionable hair-do had been a sheer waste of time, since there was no one around worth pleasing in this kind of place and no point in the exercise anyway. And reading that review was only another pretence. He thought that she had only dressed up and had done her hair to look pretty, and in the same way the reading was just to make herself look clever.

'Do you mind if I go for a bathe today?' she asked.

'Why not? I don't suppose the mountains will cave in if you do or if you don't.'

'I only asked because the doctor might be annoyed.'

'Well, go and ask him. I'm not qualified to speak on the subject.'

What Layevsky disliked most about Nadezhda on this occasion was her bare white neck and the little curls around the back, and he remembered that when Anna Karenina stopped loving her husband, she had conceived a particular loathing for his ears. 'How true, how true!' he thought. Feeling weak and despondent, he went to his study, lay down on the couch and covered his face with a handkerchief to keep the flies away. Dull, lazy, monotonous thoughts lumbered through his mind like a long train of peasant carts on a foul autumn evening and he lapsed into a drowsy, depressed state of mind. He thought he was guilty as far as Nadezhda and her husband were concerned and that her husband's death was his fault. He felt he was to blame for ruining his own life, for betraying the wonderful world of noble ideas, learning, work, which did not seem to exist or be capable of realization in this seaside resort with its hungry, prowling Turks and lazy Abkhazians,[4] but only in the north with its opera, theatres, newspapers and great diversity of intellectual life. Only there could one be honourable, clever, noble-minded and pure – not in this sort of place. He accused himself of being without ideals or guiding principles in life, although he only had a vague idea what that meant. Two years before, when he had fallen in love with Nadezhda, he thought all he had to do to escape the nastiness and futility of life was to become her lover and go away with her to the Caucasus. Similarly, he was convinced that he only had to abandon Nadezhda and go to St Petersburg to achieve his every desire.

'Escape!' he muttered as he sat biting his nails. 'Escape!'

He imagined himself going on board ship, having lunch, drinking cold beer, chatting with the ladies on deck, then catching a train at Sevastopol – and away! Hail, Freedom! Stations flash past one after the other, the air grows cooler and sharper. Now he can see birches and firs, that's Kursk, now Moscow . . . Cabbage soup, mutton with buckwheat, sturgeon, beer at station buffets – in brief, no more of this barbarity, but *Russia*, the real Russia. The passengers discuss trade, new singers, Franco-Prussian accord. Everywhere life is vigorous, cultured, intelligent, brimming with energy. Faster, faster! Here at last is the Nevsky Avenue, Great Morskoy Street, then Kovensky Lane, where once he had lived with students. Here is that dear grey sky, drizzle, those drenched cab-drivers . . .

'Ivan Andreich!' someone called from the next room. 'Are you in?'

'I'm here!' Layevsky answered. 'What is it?'

'I've got some papers.'

As Layevsky lazily got to his feet, his head was reeling and he went into the next room yawning and shuffling his slippers. One of his young colleagues was standing by the window that overlooked the street and laying out government papers along the sill.

'Won't be a second, old man,' Layevsky said softly and went off to find an ink-pot. He returned to the window, signed the papers without reading them and remarked, 'It's hot!'

'Yes, sir. Are you coming to the office today?'

'I don't think so . . . I'm not feeling too good. My dear chap, please tell Sheshkovsky I'll look in after dinner.'

The clerk left. Layevsky lay down on his couch again and thought, 'So, I must carefully weigh up the pros and cons and come to a decision. Before I leave this place I must settle my debts. I owe about two thousand roubles. I've no money . . . Of course, that's not important. I could pay part of it now, somehow or other and I'll send some later from St Petersburg. The main problem's Nadezhda . . . I must get things straight between us, before I do anything else . . . Yes.'

A little later he was wondering if it might be best to go to Samoylenko for advice. 'I *could* go and see him,' he thought, 'but what's the use? I'd only say the wrong thing again, about boudoirs, women, what's honourable or not. And how the hell can I discuss what's honourable or not when the most urgent thing is to save my own skin, when I'm suffocating in this damned slavery and killing myself . . . It's time I realized that carrying on living as I am is shameful and an act of cruelty before which all else pales into insignificance!'

'Escape!' he murmured, sitting down. 'Escape!'

The deserted beach, the merciless heat and the monotony of the eternally silent, hazy, pinkish-violet mountains saddened him and seemed to be lulling him to sleep and robbing him of something. Perhaps he *was* very clever in fact, talented and remarkably honest; perhaps he might have made an excellent district official, public servant, orator, commentator on current affairs, champion of causes, had he not been shut in on all sides by sea and mountains. Who knows? And if this were true, wasn't it stupid to argue whether it was the right thing or not if a talented and useful man – a musician or artist, for example – tore walls down and fooled his jailers to escape from prison? For any man in that situation, everything was honourable.

After two o'clock Layevsky and Nadezhda sat down to lunch. When the cook served rice soup with tomatoes Layevsky said, 'The same old thing every day. Can't she make cabbage soup?'

'We haven't any cabbage.'

'That's strange, Samoylenko has cabbage soup, Marya Konstantinova has cabbage soup, only *I* am obliged to eat these sickly slops. It's no good, my dear.'

Like most married couples, at one time Layevsky and Nadezhda could not finish lunch without some scene or tantrums. But since Layevsky decided he did not love her any more, he tried to let Nadezhda have everything her own way, spoke gently and politely to her, smiled and called her darling.

'This soup's like liquorice,' he said, smiling. He was making a great effort to be friendly, but it was too much for him and he told her, 'No one looks after things in this house. If you're really so ill, or if you're too busy reading, I could see to the cooking, if you like.'

Earlier she would have replied, 'See to it, then', or 'It's obvious you want to turn me into a cook', but all she did now was give him a timid look and blush.

'Well, how do you feel today?' he asked affectionately.

'I'm all right today, just a little weak.'

'You must look after yourself, my dear. I'm terribly worried about you.'

In fact there *was* something wrong with Nadezhda. Samoylenko said she was suffering from intermittent fever and was giving her quinine. But another doctor, Ustimovich – a tall, skinny, unsociable person who stayed in during the day and strolled slowly along the front in the evenings, coughing away, his walking-stick pressed to his back with his hands – found she had some woman's complaint and prescribed hot compresses. Before, when Layevsky was in love with Nadezhda, her illness had made him feel sorry for her and worried, but now he could see it was mere pretence. That sallow, sleepy face and sluggish look, those yawning fits she had after attacks of fever and the way she lay under a rug during them, making herself look more like a little child than a grown woman, the stuffiness and unpleasant smell in her room – to his mind all this served to destroy any romantic illusions and was enough to throw cold water on any ideas of love and marriage.

For a second course he was served spinach and hard-boiled eggs, while Nadezhda had jelly and milk, as she wasn't well. At first, when she anxiously touched the jelly with her spoon and then lazily started eating it, washing it down with milk, the gulping noise aroused such violent hatred that it made his head itch. The way he felt, he knew very well, would have insulted a dog even, but he was not angry with himself, but with Nadezhda for stirring such feelings in him and he understood why lovers sometimes murder their mistresses. Of course, he could never have committed murder himself, but if he had happened to be on a jury at that moment he would have found for the accused.

'*Merci*, my dear,' he said after dinner, and kissed Nadezhda on the forehead.

Back in his study he paced up and down for five minutes, squinting at his boots, after which he sat on the couch and muttered, 'Escape! Escape! Just get things straight and then escape!'

As he lay on the couch he remembered that he was possibly to blame for the death of Nadezhda's husband. 'It's stupid blaming someone for falling in or out of love,' he said, trying to convince himself as he lay there lifting his legs up to put his boots on. 'Love and hatred are beyond our control. As for her husband, I was possibly one of the causes of his death, indirectly. But there again, is it my fault that I fell in love with his wife, and his wife with me?'

As he walked along Layevsky thought, 'I'm just like Hamlet in my indecision! How truly Shakespeare observed it! Oh, how truly!'

III

To ward off boredom and to cater for the desperate needs of new arrivals and bachelors who had nowhere to eat, owing to the complete absence of hotels in the town, Dr Samoylenko maintained a kind of *table d'hôte*. At the time in question only two of these gentlemen were taking meals with him, von Koren, a young zoologist who had arrived in the summer to study the embryology of the jellyfish in the Black Sea; and Deacon Pobedov, who had left theological college not long before and had been dispatched to this small town to stand in for the old deacon, who was away taking the cure. Each paid twelve roubles a month for lunch and dinner, and Samoylenko had made them promise faithfully to be there for lunch at two o'clock on the dot.

Von Koren was usually first to arrive. He would silently sit down in the drawing-room, pick up an album from the table and examine faded photographs of certain strange gentlemen in wide trousers and toppers, and ladies in crinolines and lace caps. Samoylenko could remember the names of only just a few and would comment with a sigh on those he had forgotten, 'A very fine person, of the highest intellect!'

When he had finished with the album, von Koren would take a pistol from the shelf, screw up his left eye and keep it pointed for a long time at Prince Vorontsov's[5] portrait; or he would stand in front of the mirror surveying his swarthy face, large forehead and hair that was as black and curly as a Negro's, then his faded cotton print shirt with its large floral pattern resembling a Persian carpet, then the broad leather belt he wore as a waistcoat. This self-contemplation gave him almost greater enjoyment than inspecting those photographs or that expensively mounted pistol. He was satisfied with his face and with his beautifully trimmed beard and broad shoulders that were clear proof of his good health and strong build. He was satisfied too with his terribly smart outfit – from the tie, which matched his shirt, right down to his yellow shoes.

While he was standing before the mirror looking through the album, Samoylenko was rushing bare-chested around the kitchen and pantry, without jacket or waistcoat. He sweated profusely as he excitedly fussed around the tables, preparing the salad, or some sort of sauce, or the meat, or cucumbers and onions for the soup, glaring furiously and alternately brandishing a knife and a spoon at the batman who was helping him.

'Vinegar!' he commanded. 'No, not the vinegar, I meant salad-oil!' he shouted, stamping his foot. 'And where are *you* going, you swine?'

'To get the oil, General,' replied the stunned batman in a high-pitched voice.

'Hurry up! It's in the cupboard. And tell Darya to put some more dill into the cucumber jar. Dill! Cover up that sour cream, you moron, or the flies will get to it!'

The whole house seemed to echo with his shouts. At about ten or fifteen minutes to two the deacon arrived – a thin young man of about twenty-two, long-haired, beardless and with a barely visible moustache. After he entered the drawing-room he crossed himself before the icon, smiled and held out his hand to von Koren.

'Hullo,' the zoologist said coldly. 'Where have you been?'

'Fishing for gobies in the harbour.'

'Why of course. It's quite evident, deacon, you'll never put your mind to doing some work.'

'Why ever not?' the deacon said smiling, shoving his hands into the cavernous pockets of his white cassock. 'Time enough for work tomorrow!'

'You always win,' the zoologist sighed.

Another fifteen or twenty minutes passed and still they weren't summoned to the table; and they could still hear the clatter of boots as the batman scurried from pantry to kitchen and back again, while

Samoylenko shouted, 'Put it on the table! What *are* you doing? Wash it first!'

The deacon and von Koren, who were starving by now, showed their impatience by tapping their heels on the floor, like a theatre audience. At last the door opened and the harassed batman announced, 'Lunch is ready!'

In the dining-room they were confronted by an angry, crimson-faced Samoylenko, who looked as if he had been boiled in that hot kitchen. He glanced at them malignantly and there was a horrified look on his face as he lifted the lid of the soup tureen and filled their plates. Only when he was convinced that they were enjoying the food, that it was to their taste, did he heave a gentle sigh and sink into his deep armchair. His face took on a languid, unctuous expression. Leisurely, he poured himself a glass of vodka and said, 'To the younger generation!'

After his talk with Layevsky, Samoylenko had passed the entire morning until lunch feeling rather heavy at heart, despite his generally excellent mood. He felt sorry for Layevsky and wanted to help him. Drinking his vodka before starting the soup he sighed and said, 'I saw Ivan Layevsky today. The poor devil's having a rough time of it. Materially, he's in a bad way, but the main problems are psychological. I do feel sorry for the young man.'

'Of all people I'm not sorry for *him*!' von Koren said. 'If that nice young gentleman were drowning I'd help him down with a stick and tell him, "Drown, my dear chap, please drown." '

'That's not true, you wouldn't do it.'

'And why not?' the zoologist said with a shrug of the shoulders. 'I'm just as capable of a good deed as you are.'

'Is making someone drown a good deed?' the deacon asked, laughing.

'If it's Layevsky – yes.'

'There's something missing in the soup,' Samoylenko said, trying to change the subject.

'There's no question about it, Layevsky's as harmful and dangerous to society as a cholera microbe,' von Koren went on. 'Drowning him would be rendering it a service.'

'It does you no credit speaking like that about your fellow human being. Tell me, why do you hate him?'

'Don't talk such nonsense, doctor. It's stupid hating and despising a microbe. But to think that any passing stranger just has to be thought of as your fellow human being, without discrimination – that's not rational at all, but a refusal to take any reasonable attitude towards people, if you don't mind my saying so. In short, it's the same as washing your hands of the matter. That Layevsky is a swine – I won't conceal the fact – and I regard him as such with the clearest conscience. But if *you* consider him your fellow, then go and drool over him as much as you like. If you consider *him* your neighbour that means you have the same attitude towards him as to the deacon and myself, and that means any old attitude. You're equally indifferent to everyone.'

'Calling the man a *swine*!' Samoylenko muttered, frowning with disgust. 'That's so awful, words just fail me!'

'People are judged by their actions,' von Koren went on. 'So now you can judge for yourself, deacon. There's something I'd like to tell you. Mr Layevsky's activities lie wide open before you, like a Chinese scroll, and you can read about them from beginning to end. What has he achieved in the two years he's been here? Let's count it on our fingers. Firstly, he's taught the people in this town to play whist. This game was unknown here two years ago, but now everyone's playing it from morning to night, even women and teenagers. Secondly, he's taught the people to drink beer, which was also unknown in this place. And the people are indebted to him for information regarding different brands of vodka, with the result that now they can tell Koshelyov from Smirnov No. 21 blindfold. Thirdly, when men used to sleep with other men's wives in this place before, they kept it a secret, for the same reasons that motivate burglars, who go about their business in secret and don't tell the whole world about it. Adultery used to be looked on as too shameful for the public eye. But Layevsky has shown himself to be a pioneer in this field, he's living quite openly with another man's wife. Fourthly . . .'

Von Koren quickly finished his soup and handed the batman his bowl. 'I saw through Layevsky the very first month we met,' he went on, turning to the deacon. 'We both came here at the same time. People of his sort love friendship, togetherness, unity and so on, because they always need partners for whist, for drinking and eating. What's more, they're great talkers and need an audience. We became friends – by that I mean he came over to my place every day and loafed around, interrupted my work and told me all about his mistress. At first he startled me by his extraordinary mendacity, which simply made me feel sick. As one friend to another, I told him off, asked him why he drank so much, why he lived beyond his means and ran up so many debts, why he neglected his work, why he read nothing, why he was so uncultured, why he was so ignorant – and his sole reply to all my questions was to smile bitterly and say, "I'm a failure, a Superfluous Man", or "What do you want from us, old man, we're just left-overs from the serf system?" or "We're *all* going to pot". Or he'd spin me a whole yarn about Onegin, Pechorin, Byron's *Cain*, Bazarov,[6] calling them "our fathers in the spirit and in the flesh". You must understand that *he*'s not to blame if official parcels lie around unopened for weeks, or if he drinks and sees that others get drunk with him. Onegin, Pechorin, and Turgenev, who invented failures and the Superfluous Man – they're to blame. The reason for his outrageous depravity and disgraceful carryings-on can't be found in him at all, but somewhere outside, in space. What's more – and this is a cunning stroke – he's not alone in being dissipated, lying, and vile, but *we* too – we "men of the eighties", we, "the lifeless, neurotic offspring of serfdom", we "cripples of civilization". The long and short of it is, we must realize that a man of Layevsky's calibre is great, even in decline; that his debauchery, ignorance and filthy ways are a quite normal evolutionary phenomenon, sanctified by the laws of necessity, that the reasons for all this are elemental, of world-shattering importance, and that we must cringe before Layevsky, since he's a doomed victim of the epoch, of trends of opinion, of heredity and all the rest of it. Whenever civil servants and their wives listened to him there would be sighs and gasps and for a long time I did not realize the kind of person I was dealing with – a cynic or a cunning rogue? People like him with a modicum of education, who appear to be intellectuals and with a lot to say about their own noble qualities, are dab hands at passing themselves off as highly complex characters.'

'Be quiet!' Samoylenko said, flaring up. 'I won't have you maligning the noblest of men in my presence!'

'Don't interrupt, Alexander,' von Koren said icily. 'I've nearly finished now. Layevsky is a fairly uncomplicated organism. This is his moral framework: slippers, bathing and coffee early in the morning, then slippers, exercise and conversation; at two – slippers, lunch and booze; bathing, tea and drinks at five, followed by whist and telling lies; supper and booze at ten; after midnight – sleep and *la femme*. His existence is bounded by this strict routine, like an egg by its shell. Whether he's walking, losing his temper, writing or having a good time, in the end everything boils down to drink, cards, slippers and women. Women play a fateful, overwhelming role in his life. He'll tell you he was already in love at the age of thirteen. When he was a first-year student, he lived with a woman who had a good influence on him and to whom he owes his musical education. In his second year he redeemed a prostitute from a brothel and raised her to his level – that's to say, made her his mistress. She stayed with him for six months and then fled back to Madame, an escape that caused him no end of spiritual distress. Alas, he suffered so much he was compelled to leave university and live at home for two years without doing a thing. But it was for the best. At home he started an affair with a widow who advised him to drop law and take up modern languages. And that's precisely what he did. The moment he finished the course he fell madly in love with this married woman he's with now – what's her name? – and had to run away with her to the Caucasus, presumably for the sake of his ideals . . . Any day now he'll tire of her and fly back to St Petersburg – and that will be because of his ideals too.'

'How do you know?' growled Samoylenko, looking daggers at the zoologist. 'Come on, better have something to eat.'

Boiled grey mullet *à la polonaise* was served. Samoylenko laid a whole fish on each of his guests' plates, pouring the sauce himself. Two minutes passed in silence.

'Women play an essential part in every man's life,' the deacon observed. 'There's no getting away from it.'

'Yes, but how great? For each one of us a woman is mother, sister, wife, friend. But to Layevsky she's everything – and at the same time she's only someone to go to bed with. Women – I mean living with one – are his whole purpose in life, his whole happiness. If he's cheerful, sad, bored, disenchanted it's always because of a woman. If his life has turned sour, then a woman's to blame. If a new life has brightly dawned, if new ideals have been unearthed, you only have to look for the woman. Only books or paintings featuring women satisfy him. According to him, the age we live in is rotten, worse than the forties and sixties, just because we cannot completely surrender ourselves to love's ecstasy and passion. These sensualists must have some sort of tumour-like growth which, by exerting pressure on the brain, has taken complete control of their minds. Just watch Layevsky when he's with people. You'll see, if you raise some general topic – cells, or the instincts, for example – he'll sit on one side, not listening or saying a word, lifeless and bored: none of it interests him, everything is trivial and second-rate. But just mention male and female, talk about female spiders devouring the male after mating, say, his face will light up, his eyes will burn with curiosity – in brief, he will come to life. However noble, elevated or unbiased his ideas may seem, they invariably centre around the same point of departure. You might be walking down the street with him and meet a she-ass, for example. He'll ask, "Tell me what you get, please, if you mate a she-ass with a camel?" And as for his dreams! Has he told you about his dreams? They are superb! First he'll dream he's getting married to the moon, then that he's been summoned to a police station and ordered to live with a guitar . . .'

The deacon broke into loud peals of laughter. Samoylenko frowned and angrily wrinkled his face to stop laughing, but he couldn't control himself and burst out laughing.

'And he never stops talking nonsense. Good Lord, the rubbish he talks!'

IV

The deacon was very easily amused – any little trifle was enough to send him into stitches and make him laugh until he dropped. It seemed he only liked company because people had their funny side and he could give them all comical nicknames. He called Samoylenko 'Tarantula', his orderly 'the Drake', and went into raptures when von Koren once called Layevsky and Nadezhda 'macaques'. He would hungrily peer into faces, listen without blinking and one could see his eyes fill with laughter and his face grow tense as he waited for a chance to let himself go and roar with laughter.

'He's a dissipated, perverted type,' the zoologist continued, while the deacon, expecting something funny, stared at him. 'You'll have to go a long way to find such a nobody. Physically, he's flabby, feeble and senile, while intellectually he's no different from any old merchant's fat wife who does nothing but guzzle, drink, sleep on a feather bed and have sex with her coachman.' Again the deacon burst out laughing. 'Now don't laugh, deacon,' von Koren said; 'that's stupid, after all.' Waiting until the deacon stopped, he went on, 'If this nonentity weren't so harmful and dangerous I wouldn't give him another moment's thought. His capacity for doing harm stems from his success with women, which means there's the danger he might have offspring and in this way he could present the world with a dozen Layevskys, all as sickly and perverted as himself. Secondly, he's highly contagious – I've already told you about the whist and the beer. Give him another year or two and he'll have the whole Caucasian coastline at his feet. You know how much the masses, especially the middle strata, believe in things of the mind, in university education, refinement of manners and polished self-expression. Whatever abomination he may perpetrate, everyone believes there's nothing at all wrong, that this is how it should be, since he's a cultured, liberally minded man with a university education. And the fact that he's a failure, a Superfluous Man, a neurotic, a victim of the times means that he's allowed to do whatever he likes. He's a nice young fellow, a good sort, so genuinely tolerant of human frailty.

He's obliging, easygoing, undemanding, not in the least high and mighty. One can have a nice little drink with him and swap dirty jokes, or have a chat about the latest gossip. The masses, who have always tended towards anthropomorphism in religion and morals, prefer those idols who have the same weaknesses as themselves. Judge for yourselves the wide field he has for spreading infection! What's more, he's not a bad actor, a clever impostor, there are no flies on *him*. Just take his little tricks and dodges, for example his attitude to civilization. He hasn't a clue about it, yet you can hear him say, "Oh, how civilization has crippled us! Oh, how I envy savages, those children of nature, ignorant of civilization!" You must understand that, at one time, in the old days, he was devoted to civilization heart and soul. He was its servant, he knew its innermost secrets, but it exhausted, disillusioned and cheated him. Can't you see that he's a Faust, a second Tolstoy? And he shrugs off Schopenhauer[7] and Spencer as schoolboys, gives them a paternal pat on the shoulder as if to say, "Well, Spencer, what have you got to say, old pal?" Of course, he's never read Spencer, but how charming he seems when he tells us – with mild, casual irony – that his lady friend "has read her Spencer". And people listen to him and no one wants to know that not only does this charlatan have no right to talk about Spencer in that tone, but that he isn't even fit to kiss his feet! Only a highly selfish, vile, disgusting animal would ever go about undermining civilization, authority and other people's gods, slinging mud at them with a playful wink, merely to justify and conceal its own impotence and moral bankruptcy.'

'I don't know what you expect of him, Kolya,' Samoylenko said, eyeing the zoologist more guiltily than hatefully. 'He's like everyone else. Of course, he has his weaknesses, but he keeps abreast of current ideas, does his work and is useful to his country. Ten years ago there was an old shipping-agent here, a man of the greatest intellect. What he used to say was . . .'

'Enough of that, enough!' the zoologist interrupted. 'You tell me he's working for the government. But what has he done? Have things improved here, are the clerks any more conscientious, honest, courteous, since *he* arrived on the scene? On the contrary, with the authority of a cultured, university man he's only sanctioned slackness. He's punctual only on the twentieth of the month, when he gets paid, the rest of the time he shuffles around at home in his slippers and tries to give the impression he's doing the Russian government a great favour by living in the Caucasus. No, Alexander, you shouldn't stand up for him. You're completely lacking in sincerity. If you were really so very fond of him and considered him your neighbour, then, before anything else, you wouldn't be so blind to his weaknesses, you wouldn't be so tolerant. Instead, you'd try to render him harmless, for his own good.'

'Which means?'

'Neutralizing him. Since he's incorrigible, there's only one way to do it . . .' Von Koren ran his fingers along his neck. 'Either by drowning him or . . .' he added, 'in the interests of humanity, in his *own* interest, such people should be exterminated. No doubt about it.'

'What are you saying?' Samoylenko muttered as he stood up and looked in amazement at the zoologist's calm, cool face. 'Deacon, what is he saying? Have you gone out of your mind?'

'I wouldn't insist on the death penalty,' von Koren said. 'If that's been proven harmful, then think of something else. If Layevsky can't be exterminated, then isolate him, strip him of his individuality, make him do community work.'

'What are you saying?' Samoylenko said, aghast. 'With pepper, with pepper!' he cried out in despair when he saw the deacon eating stuffed marrows without any. 'You're an extremely intelligent man, but what are you saying? Forcing our friend, such a proud, intelligent man, to do community work!'

'But if he's proud and tries to resist, then clap him in irons!'

Samoylenko was speechless and could only twiddle his fingers. The deacon peered into his stunned face, which really did look funny, and burst out laughing.

'Let's change the subject,' the zoologist said. 'Remember one thing, Alexander, primitive man was protected from men like Layevsky by the struggle for survival and natural selection. But nowadays, since civilization has significantly weakened this struggle and the process of natural selection too, the extermination of the weak and worthless has become our worry. Otherwise, if people like Layevsky were to multiply, civilization would perish and humanity would degenerate completely. *We*'d be the guilty ones.'

'If we're going to drown and hang people,' Samoylenko said, 'then to hell with your civilization, to hell with humanity! To hell with them! Now, let me tell you. You're a deeply learned man, highly intelligent, the pride of your country. But the Germans have ruined you. Yes, the Germans, the Germans!'

Since leaving Dorpat,[8] where he studied medicine, Samoylenko rarely saw any Germans and had not read one German book. But in his opinion the Germans were to blame for all the evil in politics and science. Even he could not say how he had arrived at this opinion, but he stuck firmly to it.

'Yes, the Germans!' he repeated. 'Now come and have some tea.'

All three stood up, put their hats on and went out into the small garden, where they sat in the shade of pale maple, pear and chestnut trees. The zoologist and the deacon sat on a bench near a small table, while Samoylenko sank into a wicker armchair with a broad, sloping back. The orderly brought them tea, preserves and a bottle of syrup.

It was very hot, about ninety in the shade. The burning air had become listless, inert; a long cobweb stretching down to the ground from the chestnut hung limp and motionless.

The deacon took his guitar – it was always lying on the ground near the table – tuned it and began to sing in a soft, thin voice, 'Oh, the young college boys were standing by the tavern . . .', but immediately stopped, as it was so hot, wiped the sweat from his brow and looked up at the deep blue, blazing sky. Samoylenko dozed off; he felt weak, intoxicated by the heat, the silence and that sweet afternoon drowsiness which swiftly took control of his limbs. His arms drooped, his eyes grew small, his head nodded on his chest. He gave von Koren and the deacon a sickly, sentimental look and murmured, 'The young generation . . . A great man of science and luminary of the church . . . You'll see, that long-skirted propounder of sacred mysteries will probably end up as a Metropolitan . . . and we'll all have to kiss his hand . . . Well, good luck to them.'

The sound of snoring soon followed. Von Koren and the deacon finished their tea and went out into the street.

'Going to catch gobies in the harbour again?' the zoologist asked.

'No, it's a bit too hot.'

'Let's go to my place. You can do up a parcel for me and copy something out. At the same time we can discuss what you are going to do. You must do some work, deacon, you can't go on like this.'

'What you say is fair and logical,' the deacon said, 'but my present circumstances do provide some excuse for my idleness. You know yourself that uncertainty as to one's position significantly increases apathy. The Lord alone knows if I'm here temporarily or for the duration. Here I am living in uncertainty, while the deaconess is vegetating at her father's and feeling lonely. I must confess this heat has fuddled my brains.'

'Nonsense,' the zoologist said. 'You should be able to get used to this heat and being without the deaconess. You shouldn't pamper yourself, take a firm grip.'

V

In the morning Nadezhda went for a bathe, followed by Olga her cook with jug, copper basin, towels and a sponge. Out in the roads two strange ships (obviously foreign freighters) with dirty white funnels lay at anchor. Some men in white, with white shoes, were strolling up and down the quayside shouting out loud in French, and they were answered by people on the ships. A lively peal of bells came from the little town church.

'It's Sunday!' Nadezhda remembered with great pleasure.

She was feeling quite well and her mood was gay and festive. She thought she looked very sweet in her new, loose dress of coarse tussore,[9] in her large straw hat with its broad brim pressed down so tightly over her ears that her face seemed to be looking out of a box. She thought that there was only one young, pretty, cultured woman in the town – herself. Only she knew how to dress inexpensively, elegantly and tastefully. Her dress, for example, had cost only twenty-two roubles, yet it was so charming! She was the only woman who could please the men in a town that was full of them and so they just could not help envying Layevsky, whether they liked it or not.

She was glad Layevsky had been cool and grudgingly polite towards her lately – at times he had been impertinent and even downright rude. Once she would have answered his outbursts and his contemptuous and cold, or strange and inscrutable, glances with reproaches, would have threatened to leave him or starve herself to death; but now she only replied with blushes, looked guilty, and rejoiced in the fact that he did not show any affection. It would have been even better and more pleasant if he had told her off or threatened her, since she felt entirely to blame. She thought she was the guilty one – firstly, for not showing any sympathy for his dreams of a life of toil, on account of which he had given up St Petersburg and come out here to the Caucasus. She was convinced that this was the true reason for his recent anger with her. When she was on her way to the Caucasus she thought that on the very first day she would find herself a quiet little place near the sea, with a cosy, shady little garden with birds and streams where she could plant flowers and vegetables, keep ducks and hens, entertain the neighbours, dole out medicine to the poor peasants and give them books. However, as it turned out, the Caucasus offered nothing but bare mountains, forests, enormous valleys – it was a place where one always had to be choosing, making a fuss, building. There just weren't any neighbours around, it was terribly hot, and one could easily be burgled. Layevsky was in no hurry to acquire a building-plot. Of that she was glad and it seemed they had both tacitly agreed never to mention that 'life of toil' again. His silence on the subject meant he was angry with *her* for not saying anything about it, so she thought.

Secondly, without his knowledge, she had spent about three hundred roubles over these two years on various trifles at Achmianov's shop. Buying cloth, silk, a parasol, little by little, she had run up a sizeable bill without even noticing it.

'I'll tell him today,' she decided, but immediately realized that it was hardly the best time to talk to Layevsky about bills in his present frame of mind.

In the third place she had already entertained Kirilin, an inspector in the local police, twice in Layevsky's absence – one morning when Layevsky had gone for a swim, and then at midnight, when he was playing cards. Nadezhda flushed as she recalled this and she looked at her cook as though she was frightened she might read her thoughts. These long, insufferably hot, tedious days; these beautiful, languorous evenings; these stifling nights; her whole life here, when from morning to night time hung heavily; the obsessive thought that she was the youngest and most beautiful woman in the town and that she was squandering her youth; and Layevsky himself, so honest, idealistic, but so set in his ways, perpetually shuffling about in his slippers, biting his nails and plaguing her with his moods – all these things gradually made her a victim of desire, so that, like a woman insane, she could think only of one thing, day and night. In her breathing, her glances, her tone of voice, the way she walked, she was ruled by desire. The roar of the waves told her how she must love, so did the darkness of evening, and the mountains too . . . And when Kirilin had begun courting her, she was neither able nor willing to resist, and she had given herself to him.

Now those foreign ships and men in white somehow put her in mind of a huge ballroom: the sounds of a waltz rang in her ears, mingling with French, and her breast trembled with inexplicable joy. She wanted to dance and to speak French.

Joyfully she thought that there was nothing so terrible in being unfaithful to him and her heart had played no part in that betrayal: she still loved Layevsky and this was plain from her jealousy of him, from feeling sorry for him and bored when he was out. As for Kirilin, he was just ordinary and a little on the coarse side, despite his good looks. She had already broken off with him and there would never be anything between them again. It was all over, finished, and it was no one's business – if Layevsky chanced to find out he would never believe it.

There was only one bathing-house on the beach – for ladies; the men swam out in the open. As she entered the bathing-house, Nadezhda met Marya Konstantinova Bityugov, the middle-aged wife of a civil servant, together with her fifteen-year-old schoolgirl daughter Katya. Both of them were sitting on a bench undressing. Marya Konstantinova was a kindly, emotional, refined lady who spoke with a drawl and over-dramatically. Up to the age of thirty-two she had been a governess, then she married Bityugov, a short, bald, extremely docile man who combed his hair over his temples. She was still in love with him, jealous of other women, blushed every time the word 'love' was mentioned, and assured everyone she was very happy.

'My dear!' she said, enraptured at seeing Nadezhda and assuming that expression all her friends called 'sugary'. 'My dear, I'm so pleased you've come! We shall bathe together – how delightful!'

Olga quickly threw off her dress and blouse and began undressing her mistress.

'Not quite so hot today, is it?' Nadezhda said, shrinking at her naked cook's rough hands. 'Yesterday I nearly died from the heat!'

'Oh yes, my dear! I almost suffocated. Can you believe it, I bathed three times yesterday, just imagine my dear, three times! Even my Nikodim was worried.'

'Well, how can people be so ugly?' Nadezhda thought as she looked at Olga and the civil servant's wife. She glanced at Katya and thought, 'Quite a good figure for a young girl!'

'Your Nikodim is very, very nice!' she said. 'I'm just mad about him.'

Marya Konstantinova replied, forcing a laugh, 'Ha, ha, ha! How delightful!'

Free of her clothes, Nadezhda had a sudden urge to fly and she felt that she had only to flap her arms to soar up into the sky. As she sat there undressed she saw Olga was looking at her white body rather disgustedly. The wife of a young soldier, Olga was living with her lawful husband and for this reason considered herself superior. Nadezhda also felt that Marya Konstantinova and Katya despised and feared her. This was unpleasant, so she tried to raise herself in their opinion and said, 'At home in St Petersburg the holiday season is in full swing right now. My husband and I have so many friends! We should go and see them.'

'Your husband's an engineer, I believe?' Marya Konstantinova asked timidly.

'I'm talking about Layevsky. He knows a lot of people. Unfortunately his mother's a terrible snob, and she's a little soft in the head . . .'

Nadezhda did not finish and plunged into the water; Marya Konstantinova and Katya followed her in.

'Society is so riddled with prejudices,' Nadezhda said. 'It's harder to get on with people than you think.'

Marya Konstantinova, who had worked as a governess with aristocratic families and who knew about high society, said, 'Oh, yes! Would you believe it, my dear, you had to dress for lunch *and* dinner at the Garatynskys', no question, so they gave me a dress allowance, apart from my salary, just as if I were an actress.'

She stood between Nadezhda and Katya as though shielding her daughter from the water that was washing over Nadezhda. Through the open doorway which led out to the sea they could see someone swimming about a hundred yards from the bathing enclosure.

'Mama, it's Kostya!' Katya said.

'Oh, oh!' Marya Konstantinova clucked in horror. 'Kostya, come back!' she shouted. 'Kostya, come back!'

Kostya, a boy of fourteen, dived and swam further away to show off to his mother and sister, but he tired and hurried back. It was plain from his serious, tense expression that he did not trust his own strength.

'Boys are so much trouble, my dear!' Marya Konstantinova said, feeling relieved now. 'It always seems that he's about to break his neck. Oh, my dear, how lovely to be a mother – but at the same time, it's a real worry! Everything scares you.'

Nadezhda put on her straw hat and struck out to sea. She swam ten yards or so and then floated on her back. She could see as far as the horizon, ships, people on the beach, the town, and all these sights, together with the heat and the translucent, caressing waves, excited her and whispered that she needed to live . . . live . . . A sailing-boat rushed swiftly past, vigorously cutting through the waves and air. The man at the rudder was looking at her and she felt how pleasant it was to be looked at.

After their bathe the ladies dressed and went off together. 'I'm usually running a temperature every other day, but I don't lose any weight, despite this,' Nadezhda said, licking her lips that were salty after the bathe, and smiling at bowing acquaintances. 'I've always been plump and now I seem to have put on even more weight.'

'My dear, it all depends on one's disposition. If you're not inclined to put on weight, like myself for example, then it makes no difference how much food you eat. But my dear, your hat's dripping wet.'

'It doesn't matter, it will soon dry.'

Nadezhda caught another glimpse of those French-speaking men in white strolling along the front. And once again, for some strange reason, she felt the joy rise up within her and she dimly remembered some great ballroom where she had once danced – or was it only a dream? And from deep down inside her came muffled, hollow whispers, telling her she was a petty-minded, vulgar, worthless, insignificant woman.

Marya Konstantinova stopped by her front gate and invited her to come in and sit down. 'Please do come in, my dear,' she said imploringly, and at the same time she looked anxiously at Nadezhda, half hoping she would refuse.

'Delighted,' Nadezhda agreed. 'You know how I love visiting you.' And she went into the house. Marya Konstantinova asked her to sit down, gave her coffee and rolls. Then she showed her photographs of her former charges – the Garatynsky girls, who were married now; and she showed her Katya and Kostya's examination marks. They were very good, but to make them appear even better she sighed and complained how difficult schoolwork was these days. She looked after her guest, but at the same time felt sorry for her and was worried in case her presence might have a bad effect on Kostya and Katya's morals. She was pleased Nikodim was out. Convinced that all men fell for *her sort*, she felt Nadezhda might have a bad influence on Nikodim Aleksandrych as well.

As she chatted with her guest, Marya could not forget that there was going to be a picnic later that afternoon and that von Koren had particularly requested her not to tell the 'macaques' about it – that is, Layevsky and Nadezhda. But she accidentally let it slip, blushed deeply and told her in an embarrassed voice, 'I do hope you'll join us!'

VI

The arrangements were to drive about five miles out of town along the southbound road, to stop near the inn at the junction of the Black and Yellow Rivers, where they would make some fish soup. Samoylenko and Layevsky led the way in a cabriolet, followed by Marya Konstantinova, Nadezhda, Katya and Kostya in a carriage drawn by three horses; in this carriage were the hamper and the crockery. In the next carriage sat Inspector Kirilin and young Achmianov – the son of the merchant whom Nadezhda owed three hundred roubles. Huddled up on a bench opposite them, legs crossed, was Nikodim Aleksandrych, a smart little man with his hair brushed over his temples. Last of all came von Koren, and the deacon, who had a basket of fish at his feet.

'Keep to the r-r-ight!' Samoylenko shouted at the top of his voice whenever they met a bullock cart or an Abkhazian on his donkey.

'Two years from now,' von Koren was telling the deacon, 'when I have the funds and staff, I'll be off on my expedition. I'm going up the coast from Vladivostok to the Bering Straits, then to the mouth of the Yenisey. We're going to make a map, study the fauna and flora and carry out detailed geological, anthropological and ethnographic surveys. It's up to you whether you come or not.'

'That's impossible,' said the deacon.

'Why?'

'I'm a family man, I'm tied down.'

'The deaconess will let you go. We'll see she has nothing to worry about. Even better, you might try to persuade her, for the good of society, to become a nun. That would enable you to become a monk yourself and come on the expedition as a regular priest. I can fix it.' The deacon remained silent. 'Is your theology up to scratch?'

'Pretty weak.'

'Hm . . . can't advise you there, because I don't know much about it myself. Give me a list of the books you need and I'll send them to you this winter from St Petersburg. You'll also have to read the memoirs of missionaries. There you'll find excellent ethnologists and experts in oriental languages. When you're familiar with their approach you'll find you can tackle the work more easily. Well, don't waste your time while you're waiting for books, come and see me and we'll study the compass and do some meteorology. All that's essential.'

'Well now . . .' muttered the deacon and he burst out laughing. 'I've applied for a post in Middle Russia and my archpriest uncle promised to help. If I join you I'll have troubled him for nothing.'

'I don't understand why you can't make your mind up. If you go on as you are, just an ordinary deacon, your only duty conducting services on Sundays and high holidays, and taking it easy the rest of the time, in ten years you'll be just the same – although you might have acquired whiskers and a beard. Whereas if you come on the expedition you'll be a different man in ten years' time, you'll be rich in the knowledge that you've achieved something.'

Cries of horror and delight came from the ladies' carriage. They were travelling along a road carved out of a sheer cliff and everyone felt they were racing along a shelf attached to a high wall and that at any moment they would all go hurtling over into the abyss. On the right stretched the sea, while on the left was a rugged brown wall covered in black patches, red veins and creeping roots, while up above bushy conifers seemed to be leaning down towards them and gazing in fear and curiosity. A minute later there was laughter and more shrieks – they had to pass under an enormous, overhanging rock.

'I don't know why the hell I've come with you,' Layevsky said. 'It's so stupid and trivial! I should be on my way north, running away, escaping, but for some reason here I am on this ridiculous picnic.'

'But look at that view!' Samoylenko told him when the horses had turned to the left and the Yellow River valley opened out before them, with the glinting river itself flowing yellow, turbid, insane . . .

'I can't see anything nice about it,' Layevsky answered. 'Always going into raptures over nature is to betray poverty of imagination. Compared with what my imagination can offer me all those streams and cliffs are absolute rubbish, nothing else.'

The carriages were travelling along the river bank now. The lofty, precipitous banks gradually closed in, the valley narrowed, confronting them now in the form of a gorge. The great crag which they were passing had been constructed by nature from huge rocks that were exerting such pressure on each other that Samoylenko had to grunt every time he looked at it. Here and there that gloomy, magnificent mountain was intersected by narrow defiles and clefts, from which dampness and a sense of mystery came wafting towards the travellers. Through the defiles they caught sight of other mountains – brown, pink, lilac, smoky, or suffused with light. Every now and then, as they passed the defiles, they could hear water pouring down from above, splashing over the rocks.

'Blasted mountains,' Layevsky sighed; 'they bore me stiff!'

At the point where the Black River flowed into the Yellow, where its ink-black waters stained the yellow as they did battle with them, stood Kerbalay the Tatar's inn, just off the road. The Russian flag flew over it and the name *Pleasant Inn* was chalked on the signboard. Nearby was a small garden, enclosed by a wattle fence, with tables and benches, and from a miserable looking thorny bush rose a solitary cypress, beautiful and dark. Kerbalay, a small sprightly Tatar in dark blue shirt and white apron, was standing in the road. Clasping his stomach he bowed low to the approaching carriages and smiled to reveal his brilliant white teeth.

'Hallo, my dear old Kerbalay!' Samoylenko shouted. 'We're just going on a little bit further, so bring us a samovar and chairs. Look lively now!'

Kerbalay nodded his close-cropped head and muttered something which only the occupants of the last carriage could make out, 'We've got trout today, General.'

'Bring it then, bring it!' von Koren told him.

About five hundred yards past the inn the carriages stopped. Samoylenko chose a small meadow strewn with rocks that made good seats. Here there was a tree felled in a storm, lying with bared, shaggy roots and dried-up yellow needles. A rickety plank bridge spanned the river and right opposite, on the far bank, was a little shed used as a drying-room for maize; with its four low piles it reminded one of the fairy-tale hut that stood on chicken's legs. A short ladder led down from the door.

Their first impression was that they would never get out of the place. Wherever they looked, the mountains loomed on all sides and seemed to be bearing down on them; the evening shadows swiftly closed in from the direction of the inn and the dark cypress, making the narrow, sinuous Yellow River valley look even narrower and the mountains higher. The river gurgled and cicadas chirped incessantly.

'Enchanting!' Marya Konstantinova said with deep sighs of delight. 'My dears, look how beautiful it is! So very quiet!'

'Yes, it really is nice,' agreed Layevsky, who liked this view. For some reason he felt suddenly sad when he gazed at the sky and then at the blue wisp of smoke curling out of the inn's chimney. 'Yes, very nice!' he repeated.

'Ivan Andreich, please describe the view for us!' Marya Konstantinova said.

'What for?' Layevsky asked. 'First-hand impressions are better than any description. The wealth of colour and sound that we all receive from nature through our senses is turned into an ugly, unrecognizable mishmash by writers.'

'Is that so?' von Koren asked coldly, selecting the largest rock near the water and trying to climb up it and sit down. 'Is that so?' he repeated and stared at Layevsky. 'What about *Romeo and Juliet*? Or Pushkin's Ukrainian Night?[10] Nature should prostrate herself before them.'

'That may be so,' Layevsky agreed, too lazy to offer any considered reply. 'However,' he said a little later, 'what exactly is *Romeo and Juliet*? Beautiful, poetic, divine love is only roses covering up the rottenness beneath. Romeo's an animal, like anyone else.'

'No matter what anyone tells you, you always turn it into . . .'

Von Koren glanced at Katya and did not finish.

'And *what* do I turn it into?' Layevsky asked.

'Well, for instance, if someone says, "What a lovely bunch of grapes," you reply, "Yes, but how ugly when they've been chewed and then digested into the stomach." Why say things like that? It's nothing very original and it's really a strange way of expressing yourself.'

Layevsky knew that von Koren did not like him and therefore was scared of him. When von Koren was around, he thought, people felt very awkward, as if someone were standing guard behind their backs. Ignoring this last remark he walked away and regretted having come.

'Ladies and gentlemen, quick march! Get some wood for the fire!' Samoylenko commanded.

Everyone wandered off at random, leaving only Kirilin, Achmianov and Bityugov behind. Kerbalay brought some chairs, spread a carpet and stood several bottles of wine on the ground. Inspector Kirilin, a tall, distinguished-looking man who wore a raincoat over his tunic in all weathers, put one in mind of those young provincial police chiefs with his proud bearing, solemn walk and deep, rather hoarse voice. He had a sad, sleepy look, as if he had just been woken against his will.

'What's *that* you've brought, you scum?' Kirilin asked Kerbalay, slowly enunciating every word. 'I asked you to serve Kvarel, but what have you brought, you Tatar pig? Eh? What?'

'We have plenty of our own wine, Inspector Kirilin,' Bityugov observed timidly and politely.

'So what? But I want you to have some of my wine as well. I'm on this picnic and I assume I've a perfect right to contribute my share. That's what I ass-ume! Bring ten bottles of Kvarel.'

'Why so many?' Bityugov asked in surprise, knowing full well that Kirilin had no money.

'Twenty bottles! Thirty!' shouted Kirilin.

'Don't worry,' Achmianov whispered to Bityugov, 'I'll pay.'

Nadezhda was in a gay, playful mood. She felt like skipping, laughing, shouting, teasing, flirting. In her cheap cotton dress with its pattern of blue dots, her little red shoes and that same straw hat, she felt as tiny, natural, light and ethereal as a butterfly. She ran across the rickety bridge and looked down at the water for a minute to make her head go round; then she cried out and ran laughing towards the shed, conscious that all the men – even Kerbalay – were feasting their eyes on her. In the swiftly approaching dusk, when the trees, mountains, horses and carriages had all merged together and a light gleamed in the windows of the inn, she climbed a mountain path that threaded its way up the hillside between boulders and prickly bushes, and sat on a rock. Down below, the bonfire was already burning. With sleeves rolled up, the deacon was walking about and his long black shadow moved in a radius around the fire. He was piling on wood and stirring the pot with a spoon tied to a long stick. Samoylenko, his handsome face coppery-red, was fussing around the fire as though at home in his own kitchen.

'But where's the salt, gentlemen?' he shouted fiercely. 'I bet you've forgotten it. And why are you all lounging about like country squires while I'm left to do all the work?'

Layevsky and Bityugov were sitting side by side on the uprooted tree, gazing pensively at the fire. Marya, Katya and Kostya were taking teacups, saucers and plates out of the baskets. Von Koren stood wondering at the water's edge, his arms folded and with one foot on a rock. Red patches of light cast by the bonfire wandered with the shadows over the ground near dark human shapes, trembled on the mountains, trees, bridge and drying-room. The steep, hollowed-out far bank was lit up all over and its reflection flickered in the river, to be torn to shreds by the fast-flowing, turbulent water.

The deacon went to fetch the trout which Kerbalay was cleaning and washing on the bank, but he stopped half-way to look around. 'Heavens, how beautiful!' he thought. 'Just people, rocks, a bonfire, twilight, a twisted tree – nothing more than that, but how beautiful!'

Near the drying-room on the far bank some strangers came into view. It was impossible to make them all out straight away in the flickering light and bonfire smoke drifting over the river, but one could make out some details – first a shaggy fur cap and a grey beard, then a dark blue shirt, rags hanging from shoulder to knee and a dagger across a stomach, then a swarthy young face with black eyebrows, thick and sharp as if drawn in charcoal. About five of these people were squatting in a circle, while another five or so went into the shed. One of them stood in the doorway, hands thrust behind him, with his back to the fire, and started telling what was undoubtedly a most interesting story because, after Samoylenko had put some more wood on the fire, making it flare up, scattering sparks and brightly illuminating the shed, two calm, deeply attentive faces could be seen looking through the doorway, while others in the circle had turned round to listen as well. Shortly afterwards the men in the circle struck up a slow-moving song, rather like those sung in church during Lent. As he listened the deacon pictured himself ten years from then, after he had returned from the expedition: he is a young monk and missionary, a celebrated writer with a glittering past; he is ordained Archimandrite, then Bishop. He celebrates Mass in the cathedral. With his golden mitre and image hanging round his neck, he steps up into the pulpit and proclaims as he makes the sign of the cross over the congregation with his three- and two-branched candelabrum, 'Look down from heaven, oh Lord. Behold and visit this vineyard, which Thy right hand hath planted!' And the children would respond, singing 'Holy God' in angelic voices.

'Deacon, where's that fish?' he heard Samoylenko say.

Returning to the bonfire, the deacon imagined a religious procession moving along a dusty road on a hot day in July. Leading the way are men with banners and women and girls carry the icons. They are followed by choirboys and a lay reader with a bandaged cheek and straw in his hair. Then (in the correct order) follow the deacon, then the parish priest with calotte and cross, and after them a crowd of peasant men, women and boys raising clouds of dust. And there in the crowd are the priest's wife and the deaconess in kerchiefs. Choirboys sing, children howl, quails call and a lark bursts into song. Now they stop to sprinkle the cattle with holy water. They move on and kneel to pray for rain. Then food, conversation . . .

'All that would be very nice too,' thought the deacon.

VII

Kirilin and Achmianov clambered up the mountain path. Achmianov lagged behind and stopped, while Kirilin went over to Nadezhda.

'Good evening!' he said, saluting.

'Good evening.'

'Oh, yes!' Kirilin said, gazing pensively at the sky.

'What does *that* mean?' Nadezhda asked after a short silence, noticing that they were both being watched by Achmianov.

'Well now, it means,' the police officer said, articulating every syllable, 'our love has withered without having time to blossom, in a manner of speaking. How else can I take it? Is this some special kind of flirtatiousness on your part or do you take me for some ruffian whom you can treat as you like?'

'It was a mistake! Leave me!' snapped Nadezhda looking at him in terror on that wonderful evening and asking herself in bewilderment if there actually had been a time when this man had attracted her and was close to her.

'Well then!' Kirilin said. He stood silently pondering for a moment, then he asked, 'What now? Let's wait until you're in a better mood. In the meantime, may I make so bold as to assure you I'm a respectable man and I forbid anyone to doubt it. No one plays games with me! *Adieu!*'

He saluted and made off through the bushes. A little later Achmianov hesitantly approached. 'A fine evening!' he said with a slight Armenian accent.

He was quite good-looking, dressed smartly and had the easy-going manner of a well-bred young man. But Nadezhda did not like him, as she owed his father three hundred roubles. What was more, she did not like the fact that a shopkeeper had been invited to the picnic, and she did not like being approached by him on an evening just when she felt so pure at heart.

'On the whole, the picnic's been a success,' he said after a pause.

'Yes,' she agreed, casually adding as though she had just remembered that debt, 'yes, tell them in your shop that Ivan Andreich will call soon to pay the three hundred . . . I don't remember exactly how much.'

'I'd lend you another three hundred just to stop you reminding me of that debt every single day. Why do you have to be so prosaic?'

Nadezhda burst out laughing. The funny thought occurred to her, that if she were sufficiently immoral and were so inclined, she could have settled that debt in one minute. What if she were to turn that handsome young idiot's head? How comical, absurd, how insane that would be! And suddenly she had the urge to make him fall in love with her, to take what she could, drop him and then sit back to see what happened.

'Allow me to give you a piece of advice,' Achmianov said timidly. 'I beg you to steer clear of Kirilin. He's been saying terrible things about you everywhere.'

'I'm not interested in hearing what any fool has to say about me,' Nadezhda said coldly and she became dreadfully worried; that amusing idea of having a game with young, handsome Achmianov suddenly lost its charm.

'I must go down now,' she said; 'they're calling.'

Down below the soup was ready. They poured it into the bowls and drank it with that air of ritual solemnity exclusive to picnics. They all found the soup delicious and declared they had never tasted anything so appetizing at home.

As usually happens on picnics, in all that jumble of napkins, packets, useless scraps of greasy paper floating around in the wind, no one knew where anyone else's glass or bread was, they spilt wine on carpet and knees, they scattered salt all over the place. All round it was dark now and the bonfire was dying out. Everyone felt too lazy to get up and put more wood on; everyone drank wine and Kostya and Katya were allowed half a glass each. Nadezhda drank one glass after another, became drunk and forgot Kirilin.

'A splendid picnic and an enchanting evening,' Layevsky said, exhilarated by the wine, 'but I prefer a good winter to all of this. "His beaver collar sparkles silver with frosty dust."'[11]

'Each to his taste,' von Koren observed.

Layevsky felt awkward: his back was hot from the fire, while von Koren's loathing was directed at his chest and face. This decent, clever man's hatred of him, which most probably was founded on some sound, underlying reason, humiliated him and made him feel weak. Lacking the strength to combat it he said in a cringing voice, 'I'm passionately fond of nature and I'm sorry I'm not a scientist. I envy you.'

'Well, I don't feel envious or sorry,' Nadezhda said. 'I don't understand how anyone can seriously study small beetles and bugs when the common people are suffering.'

Layevsky shared this opinion. He knew nothing whatsoever about the natural sciences and therefore he could not stand that authoritarian tone of voice and show of erudition and profound wisdom affected by students of ants' antennae and cockroaches' legs. It always annoyed him to think that these people presumed to solve questions embracing the origin and life of man on the evidence of these antennae, legs and something called protoplasm – for some reason he always imagined this as an oyster. But he saw that what Nadezhda had said was false and retorted (merely for the sake of contradicting her), 'It's not the bugs that are important, but the deductions you make from them!'

VIII

It was late – past ten – when they climbed back into the carriages. Everyone was seated, with the exception of Nadezhda and Achmianov, who were chasing each other along the opposite bank and laughing.

'Ladies and gentlemen, hurry up!' Samoylenko shouted at them.

'We shouldn't have served wine to the ladies,' von Koren said softly.

Exhausted by the picnic, by von Koren's hatred of him and by his own thoughts, Layevsky went to meet Nadezhda. She was in high spirits, radiant and she felt as light as a feather; when she seized him by both hands and laid her head on his chest, breathlessly laughing out loud, he took a step backwards and said sternly, 'You're behaving like a . . . tart.'

This was so very nasty that he even felt sorry for her. On his tired, angry face she read hatred, pity, self-annoyance, and suddenly she lost heart. She realized she had gone too far, had behaved far too irresponsibly, and sadly she climbed into the first empty carriage with Achmianov, feeling ponderous, fat, coarse and drunk. Layevsky got in with Kirilin, the zoologist with Samoylenko, the deacon with the ladies and the convoy moved off.

'That's typical of macaques,' von Koren began, wrapping himself in his cape and closing his eyes. 'You heard her say it, how she wouldn't want to study bugs and beetles, because the common people are suffering. That's how all macaques judge people like me. They're a servile, crafty breed, intimidated by ten generations of the knout and fist; they tremble, show feeling and cringe only when they're forced to. But just let your macaque loose where he can be free, where there's no one to grasp him by the scruff of the neck, and he will display himself and make his presence felt. Just look how brazenly he behaves at painting exhibitions, museums, theatres, or when he passes judgement, puffs himself up, gets on his hind legs, lashes out, criticizes . . . And he never fails to criticize – this shows how much of a slave he is! Just listen: professional people come in for more abuse than crooks and this is because three quarters of society consists of slaves, of these same macaques. You'll never find one of these slaves holding his hand out and offering you his sincere thanks for working.'

'I don't know what you expect!' Samoylenko said, yawning. 'That poor woman, in her simplicity of mind, wanted to have a serious talk with you and here you are jumping to conclusions. You're annoyed with him over something or other, so you have to drag *her* into it as well. But she's a fine woman!'

'Hey, that's enough! She's just an ordinary kept woman, dissolute and vulgar. Listen to me, Alexander, if you met a simple peasant woman who wasn't living with her husband, who did no work and could only giggle all the time, then you would tell her to go and do some work. So why are you so timid, so frightened of speaking the truth? Just because Nadezhda's living with a civil servant, not a sailor?'

'So what should I do with her then?' Samoylenko said angrily. 'Beat her?'

'Don't flatter vice. We only condemn vice behind its back, but that's the same as poking your tongue out when no one's there. I'm a zoologist or sociologist, which comes to the same thing. You're a doctor. Society trusts us and it's our duty to point out the dreadful damage that the existence of women like Nadezhda Ivanovna might inflict on it and generations to come.'

'Fyodorovna,' corrected Samoylenko. 'But what must society do?'

'Do? That's its own affair. In my opinion the most straightforward and the safest way is by force; she should be returned to her husband *manu militari*[12] and if he won't take her back then she should be sentenced to hard labour or some house of correction.'

'Ugh!' Samoylenko sighed. He was silent for a moment, then he quietly asked, 'Only a short time ago you were saying people like Layevsky should be exterminated . . . Tell me, if the state or society gave *you* the job, could you do it?'

'I wouldn't hesitate.'

IX

When they arrived home Layevsky and Nadezhda went into their dark, stuffy, dreary rooms. Neither said a word. Layevsky lit a candle while Nadezhda sat down and, without taking off her cloak or hat, looked at him with sad, guilty eyes.

He realized she was waiting for an explanation. But that would have been so boring and futile, so exhausting, and he felt depressed at having lost his temper and spoken rudely to her. He happened to touch the letter in his pocket that he had intended reading to her for days now and thought that by showing it to her this would help to distract her attention.

'It's high time things were sorted out,' he thought. 'I'll give her the letter and what will be, will be.'

He took the letter out and gave it to her. 'Read this. It concerns you.'

Then he went into his study and lay down in the dark on his couch without a cushion. Nadezhda read the letter and felt the ceiling had fallen down, that the walls had closed in on her. Suddenly everything seemed cramped, dark and frightening. Quickly she crossed herself three times and murmured, 'May he rest in peace . . . May he rest in peace.' And she burst into tears.

'Ivan!' she called. 'Ivan!'

There was no reply. Thinking Layevsky had come into the room and was standing behind her chair she sobbed like a child and asked, 'Why didn't you tell me before that he'd died? I wouldn't have gone on the picnic and I wouldn't have laughed in that dreadful way . . . The men said such vulgar things to me . . . What a disgrace, what a disgrace! Save me, Ivan, save me . . . I'm out of my mind . . . I'm ruined!'

Layevsky heard her sobs. He felt he was nearly suffocating and his heart was pounding. In his despair he got up, stood in the middle of the room, groped for the armchair near the table and sat down.

'This is a prison,' he thought. 'I must get away . . . I can't go on like this.'

It was too late now for cards and there were no restaurants in the town. He lay down again, stuffed his fingers in his ears to shut out the sobs and suddenly he remembered that he could call on Samoylenko. To avoid Nadezhda, he climbed into the garden through a window, over a fence and went down the street.

It was dark. A ship had just docked – a large liner judging by her lights. The anchor-chain rattled away. A small red light swiftly moved from shore to ship – this was the Customs boat.

'The passengers are snugly asleep in their cabins,' Layevsky thought and envied others their rest.

The windows in Samoylenko's house were open. Layevsky peered through one of them, then another. Inside it was dark and quiet.

'Are you asleep, Alexander?' he called. 'Alexander!'

He heard some coughing and then a cry of alarm. 'Who in the devil's name is that?'

'It's me, Alexander. Please forgive me.'

A few moments later the door opened, a lamp cast its soft light and the massive figure of Samoylenko appeared, all in white and with a white nightcap.

'What do you want?' he asked, breathing heavily and scratching himself as he stood there half asleep. 'Just a moment, I'll open up.'

'Don't bother, I can get through the window.'

Layevsky climbed through a small window, went up to Samoylenko and gripped his arm.

'Alexander,' he said in a trembling voice, 'save me! I beg you, I implore you! Try and understand! I'm in absolute agony. Another couple of days of this and I'll hang myself like . . . like a dog!'

'Wait a minute . . . What exactly are you on about?'

'Light a candle.'

'Oh, oh,' Samoylenko sighed, lighting a candle. 'Good heavens, it's already past one, my dear chap.'

'Forgive me, but I can't stay at home,' Layevsky said, greatly relieved at the candlelight and Samoylenko's presence. 'You, Alexander, are my best, my only friend. You are my only hope. Whether you want to or not, please save me, for God's sake! I must escape from here at all costs. Lend me some money!'

'Oh, good Lord, good Lord!' Samoylenko sighed, scratching himself. 'I was just falling asleep when I heard the ship's siren . . . and now you . . . Do you need much?'

'At least three hundred roubles. I must leave her a hundred and I need two hundred for the journey . . . I already owe you about four hundred, but I'll send you everything in the post . . . everything . . .'

Samoylenko grasped both side-whiskers in one hand, stood with legs apart and pondered. 'Well now,' he murmured pensively. 'Three hundred . . . All right. But I don't have that much. I'll have to borrow it from someone.'

'Please borrow it then, for God's sake!' Layevsky said and he could tell from Samoylenko's face that he wanted to lend him the money and that he would not let him down. 'Borrow it, I'll pay you back without fail. I'll send it from St Petersburg the moment I arrive, don't worry about that.' Brightening up he added, 'I'll tell you what, Sasha, let's have some wine.'

'All right, let's drink some wine.'

They both went into the dining-room.

'But what about Nadezhda?' Samoylenko asked, putting three bottles and a bowl of peaches on the table. 'She's not staying on, surely?'

'I'll arrange everything, everything,' Layevsky said, with a sudden surge of joy in his heart. 'Later on I'll send her money and then she'll come and join me. We'll sort things out all right once we're there. Your health, my friend.'

'Wait a moment!' Samoylenko said. 'Try this first . . . it's from my own vineyard. That one's from Navaridze's and this is an Akhatulov . . . Try them all and tell me quite frankly what you think . . . Mine's a little sharp, eh? Do you think so?'

'Yes. You've really cheered me up, Alexander. Thanks. I'm a new man.'

'Rather sharp?'

'Damn it, I don't know. But you're a wonderful, marvellous person.'

As he looked at his pale, excited, kind face Samoylenko remembered von Koren's opinion, that such people should be exterminated, and Layevsky struck him as a weak, defenceless child whom anyone could harm or exterminate.

'Be sure you make your peace with your mother when you go,' he said. 'This sort of thing's not very nice.'

'Yes, yes. Without fail.'

For a moment neither said a word. When the first bottle was finished Samoylenko said, 'You ought to make it up with von Koren too. You're always quarrelling.'

'Yes, he's a very fine, very clever man,' Layevsky agreed, now ready to praise and forgive everyone. 'He's a remarkable man, but I find him impossible to get on with. No! Our temperaments are too far apart. I'm a sluggish, feeble, servile sort of person. I might offer to shake hands with him when the time's right, but he'd turn away in contempt . . .' Layevsky sipped his wine, paced up and down and then continued, from the middle of the room, 'I understand von Koren perfectly. He's the firm, strong type, a despot. You've heard him always going on about expeditions and these are no idle words. He needs a desert, a moonlit night. All around, sleeping in tents and under the open sky, are his hungry, sick Cossacks, guides, bearers, doctor, priest, worn out by killing treks. He's alone, doesn't sleep and he sits like Stanley[13] on his camp-stool, feeling lord of the desert and master of these people. He's always going somewhere and his men groan and die, one after the other, but on and on he goes, until he himself perishes in the end. None the less he's still tyrant, still lord and master, since the cross over his grave can be seen by caravans thirty or forty miles off and it rules the desert. I'm only sorry this man isn't in the army. He would have made an excellent, brilliant commander. He would have known how to drown his cavalry in a river and build bridges from the corpses, and such daring is more necessary in war than any fortifications or tactics. Oh, I understand him perfectly! But tell me why is he hanging about here? What's he after?'

'He's studying marine animals.'

'No, my friend. No, no!' Layevsky sighed. 'A scientist on board ship told me the Black Sea is poor in fauna and that the excess of sulphuretted hydrogen in its depths makes organic life impossible. All serious zoologists work at the marine biological stations in Naples or Villefranche. But von Koren is stubborn and independent. He's working on the Black Sea because no one else is. He's severed all links with the university, he won't have anything to do with scientists or colleagues, as he's first and foremost a tyrant, and then a zoologist. He'll go far, you see. And now he's dreaming that when he gets back from his expedition he'll root out intrigues and mediocrity from our universities and make the professors crawl like worms. Despotism is just as powerful in the academic world as in war. But he's spending a second summer in this stinking little dump, as it's better to be boss in a village than underdog in town. Here he's lord and master. He rules everyone here with a rod of iron, crushes them with his authority. He's taken everyone in hand, pokes his nose into other people's business, gets involved in everything and everyone is scared of him. He senses I'm slipping through his fingers and he hates me for it. Didn't he tell you I should be exterminated and made to do community work?'

'Yes,' Samoylenko laughed.

Layevsky laughed too and drank some wine. 'He's even despotic in his ideals,' he said, laughing and nibbling a peach. 'Ordinary mortals working for the common good think of their fellow men – me, you, human beings in brief. But for von Koren people are amateurs and nonentities, too insignificant to serve any purpose in life. He does his work and he'll go on his expedition where he'll break his neck, not out of love for his fellow men, but in the name of some abstraction such as humanity, future generations, the ideal race. He's striving to improve the human race and in this respect we're nothing but slaves for him, just cannon fodder or beasts of burden. Some he would exterminate or pack off to labour camps, while others he would subject to strict discipline, making them get up and go to bed to the sound of the drum, like Arakcheyev.[14] Or he'd bring in eunuchs to mount guard over our chastity and morals, he'd order anyone stepping outside the bounds of our narrow, conservative morality to be shot. And all this to improve the human race. But what *is* the human race? An illusion, a mirage . . . Despots have always been illusionists. I understand him perfectly, my dear chap. I appreciate him and don't deny his importance: men like him provide a firm foundation for the world and if it were left to us alone we'd make as big a mess of it as those flies are making of that picture, for all our kindness and good intentions.'

Layevsky sat down by Samoylenko and said with genuine conviction, 'I'm a superficial, insignificant wreck of a man! The air I breathe, this wine, love – all in all, I've paid for everything in my life up to now with lies, idleness and cowardice. Up to now I've been deceiving others and myself and have suffered as a result. And even my sufferings have been cheap and vulgar. I bow humbly before von Koren's hatred, since I loathe and despise myself at times.' Highly excited, Layevsky once again paced the room. 'I'm glad I can see my own shortcomings so clearly and I admit them,' he said. 'That will help me to rise from the dead, become a new man. My dear fellow, if you only knew how passionately, with what yearning I long for this regeneration! I will be a real person, I promise you! I will be a man! I don't know whether it's the wine or if it's really happening, but it seems ages since I knew such bright, pure moments as I'm experiencing right now with you.'

'Time for bed, my dear chap,' Samoylenko said.

'Yes, yes . . . Forgive me. I'm going right now.'

Layevsky fussed around the furniture and windows in search of his cap.

'Thank you,' he muttered, sighing. 'Thank you . . . Kindness and a friendly word are better than any charity. You've given me a new lease of life.'

He found his cap, stopped for a moment and gave Samoylenko a guilty look.

'Alexander!' he begged.

'What?'

'My dear friend, please let me stay the night.'

'Be my guest . . . Why not?'

Layevsky lay down on the couch and went on talking to the doctor for a long time.

X

Three days after the picnic Marya Konstantinova unexpectedly called on Nadezhda. Without a word of greeting or taking her hat off she seized both her hands, pressed them to her breast and said in extreme agitation, 'My dear, I'm so upset, absolutely stunned. Yesterday, it seems, our dear, charming doctor told my Nikodim that your husband has died. Tell me, my dear, is it true?'

'Yes, it's true. He's dead,' Nadezhda replied.

'That's terrible, just terrible, my dear! But every cloud has a silver lining. Your husband was probably a wonderful, extraordinary, saintly person, but men like him are needed more in heaven than in this world.'

Every little feature and spot on Marya Konstantinova's face trembled, as though tiny needles were jumping about under her skin; she produced that sugary smile and said breathlessly, ecstatically, 'So, my dear, you're free! You can hold your head high now and not be afraid to look people in the face. From now on God, and everyone here, will bless your union with Layevsky. It's so enchanting it makes me tremble for joy! I'm lost for words. I'll see to the wedding arrangements, my dear. Nikodim and I have always been so fond of you, you must allow us to give our blessing to your lawful, unsullied union. When, when is the day?'

'I haven't given it any thought,' Nadezhda said, freeing her hands.

'But that's not possible, my dear. You *must* have thought about it!'

'Really, I haven't!' Nadezhda said laughing. 'What's the point of our marrying? I don't see the need for it. We'll carry on as before.'

'What are you saying!' Marya Konstantinova said, horrified. 'For God's sake, what are you saying?'

'Marrying won't improve anything. On the contrary, it would even make things worse. We would lose our freedom.'

'My dear! My dear, what are you saying!' Marya Konstantinova cried, stepping back and wringing her hands. 'You're quite outrageous! Come to your senses! Calm down!'

'What do you mean, *calm down*? I haven't lived yet and you tell me to calm down!'

Nadezhda recalled that she actually hadn't had much of a life up to now. After boarding-school she married someone she did not love. Then she went away with Layevsky and stayed the whole time with him on this boring, deserted coast, hoping for better things. Was that any kind of life?

'We ought to get married,' she thought, but then she remembered Kirilin and Achmianov, and she blushed.

'No, it's impossible,' she said. 'Even if Ivan Andreich went down on his knees and begged me, I'd still refuse.'

Marya Konstantinova sat silently for a minute on the couch, sad and serious, and staring at one point. Then she stood up and said coldly, 'Goodbye, my dear! Forgive me for disturbing you. Although it's not easy for me to say this, I must tell you that from now on it's all over between us and despite my deep regard for Ivan Andreich the doors of my house are closed to you.'

She pronounced this with great solemnity and seemed overcome by her own seriousness. Her face trembled again and assumed that mild, sugary expression. Holding out both her hands to a frightened, bewildered Nadezhda she pleaded, 'My dear, please allow me to be your mother or elder sister – for one minute! I'll speak to you frankly, just like a mother.'

Nadezhda felt such warmth, joy and self-pity deep down inside, it was as if her mother had in fact risen from the dead and was standing before her. Impulsively she embraced Marya Konstantinova and buried her face in her shoulder. Both burst into tears and sat sobbing on the couch for several minutes, without looking at each other, unable to speak one word.

'My dear, my little child!' Marya Konstantinova began. 'I'm going to tell you a few home truths and I shan't spare you!'

'Please do, for goodness' sake! Please do!'

'Trust me, my dear. You will remember that I was the only lady here who invited you home. You horrified me from the very first day, but unlike the rest, I just couldn't give you the cold shoulder. I suffered for that dear, kind Ivan Andreich as though he were my own son. He was a young man in a foreign country, inexperienced, weak, without his mother – and how I suffered! My husband was against making friends with him but I managed to win him over . . . We began inviting him home and of course that meant you as well, otherwise he would have taken offence. I have a daughter, a son . . . You understand. A child's tender mind and pure heart – you know the passage, "But whoso shall offend one of these little ones".[15] When I had you home I trembled for my children. Oh, when you're a mother you'll understand my fears. Everyone was amazed that I received you – please forgive me – like a respectable person and they kept dropping hints. And of course there was gossip and speculation. In my heart of hearts I condemned you, but you were so unhappy, pathetic, so outrageous in your behaviour that I wept for pity!'

'But why, why?' Nadezhda asked, shaking all over. 'What harm have I ever done anyone?'

'You've committed a terrible sin. You've broken the vow you made to your husband at the altar. You've seduced a young man who, if he had never met you, might have taken a lawful wife from a good family, someone of his own class, and might have been leading a proper life now, like everyone else. You've ruined his youth. Don't say anything, my dear, don't say anything! I just can't believe that men are to blame for our sins, the woman's always the guilty party. When it comes to family life men are so thoughtless, they live by their minds and not their hearts, they understand very little, but a woman understands everything. Everything depends on her. Much has been given to women, but much will be required of them. Oh, my dear, if women were sillier or weaker than men in this respect, God would never have entrusted them with bringing up boys and girls. And then, my dear, you trod the path of vice and left all sense of shame behind you. In your position another woman would have hidden herself, locked the doors and stayed at home, and you would only have appeared in God's temple, pale, all dressed in black, weeping. And everyone would have really been saddened and said "Oh Lord, this fallen angel returns to Thee . . ." But you cast all modesty aside, my dear, you lived quite brazenly, outrageously, as if you prided yourself on your sins. You behaved wantonly and laughed as I watched you. I shuddered in horror, afraid that heaven's thunder might strike our house when you were there.

'My dear, don't speak, don't speak!' Marya Konstantinova shrieked, seeing that Nadezhda wanted to say something. 'Trust me, I won't deceive you, I won't hide a single truth from your inner eye. Listen to me, my dear. God puts his mark on great sinners and this is what you bear. Remember, your dresses always were shocking!'

Nadezhda, who had always greatly admired her own dresses, stopped crying and looked at her in amazement.

'Yes, shocking!' Marya Konstantinova continued. 'Anyone can tell what your behaviour's like from the pretentious, gaudy dresses you wear. Whenever people looked at you they all had a good laugh to themselves, but I suffered terribly. And if you'll forgive me for saying so, my dear, you're not very clean! You gave me a fright when we met in the bathing-house. Your top dress isn't too bad, but what you wear *underneath*, your petticoat and slip . . . well my dear, it makes me blush! And poor Ivan Andreich's no one to knot his tie properly for him and one look at his linen and boots shows no one looks after the poor man at home. And he never has enough to eat, my dear. In fact, if there's no one at home to see to the tea and coffee you'll have to spend half your salary in the Pavilion. And your house is awful, just awful! No one in the whole town has flies, but your place is swarming with them, all the saucers and plates are black with them. And as for the windowsills and tables, there's dust, dead flies, glasses . . . Why keep glasses there? And you never clear the table, my dear. It makes one ashamed going into your bedroom, underwear just thrown anywhere, all those rubber things of yours hanging on the wall and that china *object*, whatever that may be, standing there . . . My dear! A husband should know nothing of these things and his wife should keep herself as pure as an angel for him. Every morning, as soon as it's light, I wake up and wash my face with cold water so that my Nikodim won't see me looking sleepy.'

'But those are trivial little things,' Nadezhda sobbed. 'If only I were happy, but I'm so miserable!'

'Yes, you're dreadfully unhappy!' Marya Konstantinova sighed, barely able to stop crying herself. 'And great sorrow awaits you in the future. A lonely old age, illnesses, then you will have to answer at the Day of Judgement. It's terrible, terrible! And now that fate is lending you a helping hand you stupidly turn your back on it. You must get married, there's not a moment to lose!'

'Yes, I should, I should,' Nadezhda said, 'but it's impossible!'

'But why?'

'It's impossible! Oh, if only you knew!'

Nadezhda wanted to tell her about Kirilin, about yesterday evening's meeting with young, handsome Achmianov on the quayside, and about her crazy, ridiculous idea of getting rid of that debt of three hundred roubles, about how amusing it had all been, about how she had returned home very late that evening feeling irrevocably ruined – like a prostitute. She herself did not know how it had all come about. And now she wanted to make an oath, with Marya Konstantinova as witness, that she would settle the debt, without fail. But she could not speak for sobbing and shame.

'I shall go away from here,' she said, 'Ivan can stay if he likes, but I'm going.'

'But where?'

'Back to central Russia.'

'And what will you live on there? You haven't a penny, surely?'

'I'll do some translating . . . or open a little lending library.'

'Stop daydreaming, my dear. You need money to start a library. Well, I'll leave you now, so please calm yourself, think it over and tomorrow you'll come and see me, all nice and cheerful. That will be delightful! Well, goodbye, my little angel. Let me give you a kiss.'

Marya Konstantinova kissed Nadezhda on the forehead, made the sign of the cross over her and quietly left. It was already growing dark and Olga had lit the lamp in the kitchen. Nadezhda went into the bedroom and lay down on the bed. She began to run a high fever. She undressed as she lay there, crumpling her dress down to her feet, then she rolled herself into a ball under the blanket. She felt thirsty, but no one was there to bring her a drink. 'I'll settle that debt!' she told herself and in her delirium she imagined she was sitting beside some sick woman whom she recognized as herself. 'I'll settle it! How stupid to think that just for some money I'd . . . I'll leave and send him the money from St Petersburg. First a hundred roubles . . . then another hundred . . . then another . . .'

Late that night Layevsky returned.

'A hundred to begin with, then another . . .' Nadezhda told him.

'You should take some quinine,' he said and thought to himself, 'It's Wednesday tomorrow, that ship will sail and I won't be on it. That means I'm stuck here till Saturday.'

Nadezhda knelt up in bed.

'I didn't say anything just now, did I?' she asked, smiling and screwing up her eyes in the candlelight.

'No. We'll have to send for the doctor tomorrow morning. Get some sleep now.'

He took a pillow and went towards the door. Ever since he finally made up his mind to go away and abandon Nadezhda she began to arouse pity and guilt in him. He felt rather shamefaced when he was with her, as though she were an old or sick horse that was going to be put down. He stopped in the doorway and looked back at her. 'I was feeling irritable at the picnic and I said something very rude to you. Please forgive me, for God's sake.'

With these words he went to his study and lay down, but it was a long time before he fell asleep.

The next morning, Samoylenko, in full ceremonial uniform (today was an official holiday), parading his epaulettes and medals, took Nadezhda's pulse and examined her tongue. As he came out of the bedroom, Layevsky, who was standing in the doorway, worriedly asked, 'Well, is it all right? Is everything all right then?' Fear, extreme anxiety and hope were written all over his face.

'Relax, it's nothing dangerous,' Samoylenko said. 'Just an ordinary fever.'

'That's not what I meant,' Layevsky said, impatiently frowning. 'Did you get the money?'

'My dear chap, do forgive me,' Samoylenko whispered, glancing back at the door in embarrassment. 'Please forgive me, for heaven's sake! No one has any spare cash and up to now I've managed to collect only five or ten roubles here and there – all in all, a hundred and ten. I'll be speaking to some other people today. Please be patient.'

'But Saturday's the last day!' Layevsky whispered, trembling with impatience. 'In the name of all that's holy, by Saturday! If I can't get away on Saturday, then I won't need anything . . . anything! I don't understand how a doctor can be short of money!'

'Good God, all right then. As you like,' Samoylenko whispered so rapidly and impatiently his throat squeaked. 'I've been stripped bare. I'm owed seven thousand and I'm up to my eyes in debt. Is that *my* fault?'

'Do you mean you'll have it by Saturday? Yes?'

'I'll try.'

'I *beg* you, my dear chap! You *must* see I have the money by Friday morning.'

Samoylenko sat down and wrote out a prescription for quinine solution with *kalium bromatum*,[16] rhubarb infusion, tincture of gentian and *aqua foeniculi*[17] – all in the same mixture, with rose syrup to take the bitterness away – and then he left.

XI

'You look as if you've come to arrest me,' von Koren said when he saw Samoylenko entering in full regalia.

'I was passing by and thought, why don't I drop in and have a taste of zoology?' Samoylenko said as he sat at the large table that the zoologist had knocked together himself from some simple boards. 'Good day, Your Grace!' he said, nodding to the deacon who was sitting by the window copying something out. 'I'll just stay for a few minutes, then I must rush home to see to lunch. It's time already . . . I'm not disturbing you, I hope?'

'Not at all,' the zoologist answered, laying out some papers covered with fine handwriting over the table. 'We're busy copying up some notes.'

'Oh . . . my God, my God . . .' Samoylenko sighed. From the table he gingerly picked up a dusty book, on top of which was a dry, dead insect, like a spider, and said, 'Really! Just imagine some little green beetle going about its business when along comes this frightful object. I can imagine how horrified it would be!'

'Yes, I suppose so.'

'Is it equipped with poison to defend itself from its enemies?'

'Yes, for protection and for attacking as well.'

'Well, well, well . . . And everything in nature, my dear gentlemen, has its function and reason,' Samoylenko sighed. 'But there's one thing I don't understand. You're a terribly clever man, so please explain this. You know, there are some small animals, no larger than rats, quite pretty to look at but extremely vicious and immoral. Let's suppose one of these tiny creatures is making its way through a forest. It sees a bird, catches it and eats it. It moves on and sees a small nest in the grass with eggs in it. It's not hungry any more as it's eaten its fill, but it bites into one of the eggs and pushes the others out of the nest with its paw. Then it meets a frog, has a little game with it. After tormenting it, off it goes licking its lips and then along comes a beetle. It crushes it with its paw. And so it harms and destroys everything in its path. And it clambers into other animals' lairs, ruins ant-hills just for the fun of it, cracks snails open with its teeth . . . If it comes across a rat, it starts a fight. If it sees a small snake or a baby mouse it just has to throttle them. And so it goes on, all day long. Tell me then, what's the use of such an animal? Why was it created?'

'I don't know what animal you're talking about,' von Koren said, 'most likely an insectivore. Well now, the bird was caught because it was careless. It destroyed the nest of eggs because the bird was stupid, built its nest badly and did not succeed in camouflaging it. And there was most likely some defect in the frog's colouring, otherwise your animal wouldn't have spotted it, and so on. Your animal destroys only weak, stupid, careless creatures – briefly, creatures with defects that nature doesn't consider necessary to hand down to posterity. Only the most artful, cautious, strong and developed animals survive. Therefore, quite unaware of the fact, your little animal serves a magnificent end – progress towards perfection.'

'Yes, yes . . . By the way, old boy,' Samoylenko said casually, 'lend me a hundred roubles, will you?'

'All right. Among the insectivores there's some very interesting examples. Take the mole. It's said to be useful because it destroys harmful insects. There's a story about some German who sent Kaiser Wilhelm I a moleskin coat, but it seems the Kaiser ordered him to be reprimanded for destroying so many useful animals. However, the mole can be just as cruel as your little beast and it's also a very great nuisance, as it wreaks havoc in the fields.'

Von Koren opened a money-box and took out a hundred-rouble note.

'Moles have a powerful thorax, like bats,' he went on, shutting the box, 'tremendously developed bones and muscles and unusually well-armed mouths. If they were as big as elephants they would be invincible, capable of annihilating everything. It's interesting – when two moles meet underground they both start digging a little platform for themselves, as if they'd agreed on it beforehand. They need this platform to make it easier to fight. When it's finished they battle away furiously and fight until the weaker drops.' Von Koren lowered his voice as he added, 'Now, take your hundred roubles, but on condition it's not for Layevsky.'

'And supposing it is for Layevsky!' Samoylenko said, flaring up. 'Is that any of your business?'

'I can't let you have money if it's to help Layevsky. I know your fondness for lending people money. You'd lend any old bandit money if he asked you. I'm sorry, I can't help you in that direction.'

'Yes, it *is* for Layevsky!' Samoylenko said, standing up and brandishing his right arm. 'Yes, for Layevsky! What the hell, no one has the right to damned well try and teach *me* what to do with my money! You don't want to lend me it, eh?'

The deacon burst out laughing.

'Don't get so excited, just think a minute,' the zoologist said. 'Doing Mr Layevsky a good turn is just as silly in my opinion as watering weeds or feeding locusts.'

'I think it's our duty to help our neighbours,' Samoylenko shouted.

'In that case, help that starving Turk lying beneath the fence! He's a labourer and he's more valuable, more useful than your Layevsky. Let *him* have the hundred roubles. Or contribute a hundred towards my expedition!'

'I'm asking you, are you going to let me have it or not?'

'Tell me frankly, what does he need the money for?'

'It's no secret. He has to travel to St Petersburg on Saturday.'

'Oh, so that's it!' von Koren drawled. 'Aha . . . we understand. And is she going with him, or what?'

'She's staying on for the time being. He's going to straighten his affairs out in St Petersburg and send her money, and then she'll go as well.'

'Very neat!' the zoologist said with a short, high-pitched laugh. 'Very neat. A brilliant idea.'

He rushed over to Samoylenko, faced up to him and stared him right in the eye. 'Tell me honestly, now,' he asked: 'he doesn't love her any more, does he? No?'

'No,' Samoylenko said, breaking into a sweat.

'How revolting!' von Koren said and his face clearly showed his disgust. 'There are two alternatives, Alexander: either you've both hatched this plot together or – pardon me for saying so – you're a stupid ass. Can't you see he's making a fool of you, in the most shameless fashion, as though you were a little boy? Surely it's clear as daylight that he wants to get rid of her and abandon her here. She'll be hanging round your neck and it's also clear as anything that you'll have to send her to St Petersburg at your own expense. Surely that fine friend of yours can't have dazzled you so much with his virtues that you're blind to what's patently obvious?'

'These are mere conjectures,' Samoylenko said, sitting down.

'Conjectures? But why is he travelling alone and not with her? And ask him why *she* shouldn't go on ahead, with him following afterwards? The crafty devil!'

Overcome by sudden doubts and misgivings about his friend, Samoylenko's spirits fell, and he lowered his voice.

'But that's impossible!' he said, recalling the night when Layevsky had stayed with him. 'He's going through so much!'

'What of it? Thieves and arsonists also suffer!'

'Let's suppose you're right,' Samoylenko said reflectively. 'Granted . . . On the other hand, he's a young man in a strange country . . . a student . . . we're students as well and he had no one to turn to here for help besides us.'

'Help him perpetrate his filthy tricks just because you were both at university at different times and neither of you did a stroke of work there! What nonsense!'

'Hold on, let's consider it calmly.' Shaking his fingers, Samoylenko worked it all out. 'Perhaps we could manage it like this . . . I'll give him the money, but I'll insist he gives me his word of honour to send Nadezhda the money for her fare within one week.'

'And he'll give you his word, he'll even shed a tear or two and convince himself it's all genuine. But what is his word worth? He won't keep it, and when you meet him a year or so from now, on Nevsky Prospekt, with his new lady-love on his arm, he'll start defending himself, saying civilization has crippled him and that he's a chip off the same block as Rudin.[18] Give him up, for God's sake! Steer clear of this muck, don't go raking around in it!'

Samoylenko pondered for a moment and then said in a determined voice, 'I'm going to lend him the money all the same. You do as you like, but I'm in no position to refuse someone on the basis of mere suppositions.'

'That's excellent. So go and embrace him if you like.'

'Well, give me the hundred roubles, then,' Samoylenko timidly asked.

'No, I won't.'

Silence followed. Samoylenko felt quite weak. His face took on a guilty, ashamed, ingratiating expression and somehow it was strange to see a huge man like him, with epaulettes and medals, looking so pathetic and bewildered, just like a child.

As he laid down his pen the deacon said, 'The local bishop doesn't do his parish rounds in a carriage, but on horseback. He makes a terribly moving sight, sitting on his little horse. His simplicity and humility are permeated with biblical grandeur.'

'Is he a good man?' von Koren asked, glad of a change of subject.

'Well what do you think? If he weren't how come that he's a bishop?'

'There are some very fine and talented bishops about,' von Koren said. 'The only pity is, though, many of them have this weakness – they imagine they're state dignitaries. One tries to Russianize everything, another criticizes science. It's not their business. They'd do better if they looked in at the consistory more often.'

'Laymen aren't qualified to judge bishops.'

'But why not, deacon? A bishop is a man, like myself.'

'He is and yet he isn't,' the deacon replied in an injured voice, picking up his pen. 'If you *were* the same, then divine grace would have descended on you, and you yourself would be a bishop. But as you're not a bishop that means you can't be such a man.'

'Don't talk rot, deacon!' Samoylenko said, becoming very upset. 'Listen, I have an idea,' he added, turning to von Koren. 'Don't lend me the hundred roubles. As you'll be eating here for another three months before winter's here, you can pay a quarter in advance.'

'I won't do it.'

Samoylenko blinked and turned crimson. Mechanically, he drew the book with the spider on it over towards him and inspected it. Then he stood up and reached for his hat.

Von Koren felt sorry for him. 'Living and working with a man like that!' the zoologist said, and indignantly kicked a piece of paper into the corner. 'Please try and understand that this is not goodness of heart or love, but cowardice, poison! Whatever reason achieves, it's wrecked by your ineffectual, half-baked emotions! When I had typhoid as a schoolboy, my aunt was so sorry she stuffed me with pickled mushrooms and I nearly died. Both my aunt and yourself should see that love for one's neighbour should not be in the heart or the pit of the stomach or the small of the back, but *here*!' von Koren tapped his forehead. 'Take it!' he said and flung a hundred-rouble note in front of him.

'Now don't upset yourself, Nicholas,' Samoylenko said meekly as he folded the banknote. 'I understand you very well, but . . . put yourself in my position.'

'You're an old woman, that's what!'

The deacon burst out laughing.

'Listen, Alexander, a last request!' von Koren said heatedly. 'You should make one condition when you give that swindler the money: either he takes his lady friend with him or he sends her on ahead. Otherwise don't let him have it. You can't stand on ceremony with him. Tell him that, but if you don't, then on my word of honour, I'll go to his office and throw him down the stairs. And I won't have anything more to do with you! So there!'

'All right. If he travels with her or sends her on ahead, that will suit him all the more,' Samoylenko said. 'He'll even be glad. Well, goodbye.'

He made a fond farewell and left, but before shutting the door behind him he looked round at von Koren, pulled a terrible face and said:

'It's the Germans who've corrupted you, my friend. Yes, the Germans!'

XII

Next day, a Thursday, Marya Konstantinova was celebrating her son Kostya's birthday. Everyone had been invited for pies at midday and for chocolate in the evening. When Layevsky and Nadezhda arrived in the evening, the zoologist was already sitting in the drawing-room drinking chocolate.

'Have you spoken to him?' he asked Samoylenko.

'Not yet.'

'Now be careful, don't stand on ceremony with him. The cheek of these people really defeats me! Surely they know very well what the Bityugovs think of their liaison, yet still they sneak their way in.'

'If you let yourself be ruled by every little prejudice, then you shouldn't go anywhere,' Samoylenko said.

'Is the mass's revulsion for extra-marital love and dissipation a prejudice then?'

'Of course. Prejudice and the readiness to hate. When soldiers spot a girl of easy virtue they guffaw and whistle. But just ask them how *they* carry on.'

'They don't whistle for nothing. Young girls strangle their illegitimate babies and go off to hard labour, Anna Karenina threw herself under a train, in villages gates are smeared with tar. Both of us – I don't know why – admire Katya's purity, everyone has a vague need for pure love, although he knows that such love doesn't exist. Surely all of *that* can't be prejudice? My dear fellow, all that's survived from natural selection. And if it weren't for that mysterious force that regulates sexual relationships, people like Layevsky would have shown you what's what and humanity would have gone to the dogs within two years.'

Layevsky came into the drawing-room. He greeted everyone and smiled an oily smile as he shook von Koren's hand. He waited for the right moment and told Samoylenko, 'Excuse me, Alexander, I have something to say to you.'

Samoylenko stood up, put his arm around his waist and they both went into Nikodim Aleksandrych's study.

'It's Friday tomorrow,' Layevsky said, biting his nails. 'Did you get me what you promised?'

'Only two hundred and ten. I'll have the rest today or tomorrow. Don't worry.'

'Thank God!' Layevsky sighed and his hands shook with joy. 'You're my salvation, Alexander, and I swear by God, by my own happiness and by anything else you care to name that I'll send you the money the moment I arrive. And I'll settle my old debt as well.'

'Look here, Ivan,' Samoylenko said, turning red in the face as he took hold of one of his buttons. 'Forgive me for meddling in your private affairs but . . . why don't you take Nadezhda with you?'

'You're so silly, how could I! One of us has to stay behind, or the creditors will start kicking up a fuss. After all, I owe the shops seven hundred roubles, perhaps more. You wait, I'll send them the money and keep them quiet, then she can leave as well.'

'Oh . . . But why can't you send her on ahead?'

'Good Lord, how could I do that?' Layevsky asked, horrified. 'After all, she's a woman, what could she do there on her own? What does she understand? It would only hold things up and be a waste of money.'

'That makes sense,' Samoylenko thought, but he remembered his conversation with von Koren, looked down and said gloomily, 'I can't agree with you. Either travel with her or send her on ahead . . . or . . . or . . . I shan't lend you the money. That's my last word on the subject.'

As he retreated he banged his back on the door and went into the drawing-room red-faced and dreadfully embarrassed.

'Friday . . . Friday,' Layevsky thought as he went back to the drawing-room. 'Friday . . .'

He was served a cup of chocolate; the hot liquid burnt his lips and tongue as he kept thinking, 'Friday . . . Friday . . .' For some reason he could not get the word Friday out of his mind; he could think of nothing else and all he knew (his heart, not his head, told him) was that he would not be leaving on Saturday.

Looking very neat and tidy, his hair brushed down over his temples, Nikodim Aleksandrych stood before him and asked, 'Please have something to eat . . . Please.'

Marya Konstantinova was showing her guests Katya's school marks, remarking in her drawling voice, 'They make things so terribly, terribly hard for students these days! They ask so much of them!'

'Mama!' groaned Katya, not knowing where to put herself for embarrassment.

Layevsky also looked at the marks and complimented her. Scripture, Russian Language, Conduct – 'excellents' and 'very goods' danced before his eyes: all this and the perpetually nagging thought of that Friday, Nikodim's hair brushed down over his temples and Katya's red cheeks, struck him as such an immense, crushing bore that he was ready to cry out loud in despair. 'Will it, will it really be impossible for me to escape from this place?' he asked himself.

Two card-tables were placed side by side and they sat down to play Post Office.

'Friday . . . Friday . . .' he thought, smiling as he took a pencil from his pocket. 'Friday . . .'

He wanted to weigh his position up carefully, but he was too frightened to think. The realization that the doctor had found him out in that deception he had so long and so carefully concealed from himself, terrified him. Whenever he contemplated the future he did not let his thoughts run away with him. He would just enter a railway carriage and leave – in that way he would solve the problem of his life, and he would not allow his thoughts to wander any further. Like a dim light in distant fields, now and then the thought flashed through his mind that somewhere (in a St Petersburg back street, in the remote future) he would have to resort to some little lie in order to get rid of Nadezhda and settle his debts. Only once would he have to lie and then he would experience a completely new lease of life.

That would be a good thing: at the price of some trivial little lie he would be able to purchase absolute respectability.

But now that the doctor had, in his refusal, crudely brought his duplicity to light, he realized that he would need to lie not only in the remote future, but today, in a month's time, and until the day he died perhaps. In fact, in order to make his escape, he would have to lie to Nadezhda, his creditors and his superiors at the office, and afterwards, to obtain money in St Petersburg, he would have to lie to his mother and tell her that he'd already broken with Nadezhda. His mother wouldn't let him have more than five hundred roubles, which meant he had already cheated the doctor, as he wouldn't be able to send him any money in the near future. And then, when Nadezhda arrived in St Petersburg, he would have to resort to a whole series of petty and major lies to get rid of her. Once again there would be more tears, boredom, that wretched existence again, remorse and consequently no new lease of life. It was all a great sham, nothing more. An enormous mountain of lies loomed up in Layevsky's mind, and he would have to take drastic measures to leap over it in one bound without lying in instalments. For example, he would have to get up from his seat, put his cap on and leave straight away without the money and without a word to anyone. But Layevsky felt he was not equal to that. 'Friday, Friday,' he thought. 'Friday.'

The guests wrote little notes, folded them in two and dropped them into Nikodim Aleksandrych's old top hat. When it was full Kostya pretended to be a postman and walked round the table handing them out. The deacon, Katya and Kostya were in raptures as they received comical messages and tried to reply with even funnier ones.

'We must have a talk,' Nadezhda read in her note. She exchanged glances with Marya Konstantinova, who produced one of her sugary smiles and nodded.

'What is there to talk about?' Nadezhda thought. 'If the whole thing can't be discussed then there's no point in saying anything.'

Before coming to the party she had knotted Layevsky's tie and this insignificant act had filled her heart with tenderness and sorrow. His anxious expression, his distraught glances, his pale face and the incomprehensible change that had recently come over him, the fact that she was harbouring a terrible, loathsome secret from him, the way her hands had trembled when she tried to tie the knot – all this told her that their days together were numbered. She looked at him fearfully and penitently, as if he were an icon. 'Forgive me, forgive me . . .' she thought. Achmianov could not keep his black, amorous eyes off her from across the table. Desires troubled her, she was ashamed of herself, afraid that one day even her anguish and sorrow would not prevent her from yielding to lust, afraid that, like a confirmed drunkard, she was powerless to control herself.

Unwilling to carry on an existence which was shameful for her and insulting to Layevsky, she decided that she would leave. Tearfully she would beg him to let her go, and if he offered opposition, she would leave secretly. She would not tell him what had happened: at least let him have pure memories of her to cherish.

'I'm in love, I'm in love, I'm in love,' she read. 'That's from Achmianov.'

She would go and live in some backwater, work, and send Layevsky money, embroidered shirts and tobacco anonymously, and only when he was old – or if he were dangerously ill and needed a nurse – would she return to him. In his old age he would find out the reason why she had refused to be his wife, why she had left him – then he would appreciate the sacrifice she had made and he would forgive her.

'You've got a long nose.' That must be the deacon or Kostya.

Nadezhda imagined firmly embracing Layevsky as she said goodbye, kissing his hand and vowing to love him forever. And later, among strangers in her backwater, she would think every single day that she had a friend somewhere, a man she loved, pure, noble, highly idealistic, who held unsullied memories of her.

'If you won't meet me today, then I shall take steps, I swear it. Please understand, one doesn't behave like this with respectable people.' That was from Kirilin.

XIII

Layevsky received two notes. He unfolded one of them and read, 'Don't leave, my dear chap.' 'Who could have written that?' he wondered. 'Not Samoylenko of course . . . And it's not the deacon, he doesn't know I want to go away. Von Koren perhaps?'

The zoologist bent over the table and drew a pyramid. Layevsky thought he could detect a smile in his eyes.

'Samoylenko's let the cat out of the bag, most likely,' Layevsky thought.

The next note was in the same rough handwriting, with long tails and flourishes: 'Someone won't be leaving on Saturday.'

'What stupid insults,' Layevsky thought. 'Friday, Friday . . .'

Something stuck in his throat. He touched his collar and tried to cough, but broke into loud laughter instead.

'Ha, ha, ha!' he guffawed. 'Ha, ha, ha!' 'What am I laughing at?' he asked himself. 'Ha, ha, ha!'

He tried to control himself by covering his face with one hand, but his chest and neck were choking with laughter and he did not succeed. 'How stupid, though!' he thought, roaring with laughter. 'Have I gone out of my mind?'

His guffaws became shriller and shriller until they sounded like a small spaniel yapping. He tried to get up from the table, but his legs would not obey him and strangely, as though it were pleasing itself, his right arm started jumping about on the table, convulsively trying to grab hold of the notes and crumple them up. The astonished glances, Samoylenko's serious, frightened face, the zoologist's coldly contemptuous sneers, told him he was having hysterics. 'How scandalous, how disgraceful,' he thought, feeling warm tears on his face. 'Oh, oh, what a disgrace! Nothing like this has ever happened to me.'

They supported him under the arms and led him off somewhere, holding his head from behind; a glass sparkled before his eyes and knocked against his teeth. Water spilled onto his chest; then he saw a small room with two beds standing in the middle, covered with clean, snow-white bedspreads. He slumped onto one of them and burst out sobbing.

'It's nothing, nothing . . .' Samoylenko was saying. 'It's quite common, quite common.'

At the bedside stood Nadezhda, frightened out of her wits, trembling all over and expecting something terrible.

'What's the matter?' she asked. 'What's wrong? For God's sake, tell me.' 'Did Kirilin write to him?' she wondered.

'It's nothing,' Layevsky said, laughing and crying. 'Leave me, dear . . .'

His face expressed neither hatred nor disgust – this meant he knew nothing. Nadezhda calmed down a little and went back to the drawing-room.

'Don't upset yourself, my dear!' Marya Konstantinova said, sitting down beside her and taking her hand. 'It will pass. Men are just as weak as we sinful women. You're both going through a crisis at the moment, it's so understandable! Well, my dear, I'm waiting for an answer. Let's have a talk.'

'No, let's not,' Nadezhda said, listening to Layevsky's sobs. 'I'm so depressed . . . Please let me leave now.'

'What are you saying my dear!' Marya said, taking fright. 'Surely you don't think I would let you go without any supper? Let's have something to eat, then you can go.'

'I feel so depressed,' Nadezhda whispered, clutching the back of her chair to stop herself falling.

'He's had a fit!' von Koren said gaily as he came into the drawing-room, but the sight of Nadezhda embarrassed him and he left.

When the fit was over Layevsky sat on the strange bed thinking: 'What a disgrace, howling like a silly schoolgirl! I must look so stupid and disgusting. I'll leave by the back door. No, that would mean I'm taking the fit seriously. I should try and make a joke of it.'

He had a look in the mirror, sat for a little while and then went into the drawing-room.

'Here I am!' he said, smiling. He suffered torments of shame and felt that his presence made the others feel ashamed too. 'Things like that happen,' he said, taking a seat. 'I was just sitting there when suddenly I had a terrible stabbing pain in my side . . . absolutely unbearable, my nerves couldn't take it and . . . what happened was so stupid! Ours is a neurotic age, can't be helped!'

He drank wine at supper, chatted and now and then – to the accompaniment of convulsive sighs – kept stroking his side as if to show he still had pain. And no one – except Nadezhda – believed him and he saw it. After nine o'clock everyone went walking along the boulevard. Fearing that Kirilin might attempt to talk to her, Nadezhda tried to stay close by Marya Konstantinova and her children. Fear and dejection weakened her and she felt a fever was coming on; she was very weary and could hardly move her legs. But she did not go home, since she was convinced she would be followed by Kirilin or Achmianov, or both of them. Kirilin was walking behind, with Nikodim Aleksandrych, softly chanting, 'I wo-on't allow myself to be tri-fled with! I wo-n't allow it!'

They turned off the boulevard towards the Pavilion and walked along the beach. For a long time they watched the phosphorescent glow of the sea. Von Koren started explaining the reason for the phosphorescence.

XIV

'But it's time I was off to whist . . . They're waiting,' Layevsky said. 'Goodbye, everyone.'

'Wait, I'm coming with you,' Nadezhda said, taking his arm. They said goodbye to the others and left. Kirilin also made his farewell, saying he was going the same way and walked along with them.

'Whatever will be, will be,' Nadezhda thought. 'Let it be . . .' She felt that all the nasty memories had left her mind and were walking by her side, breathing heavily in the dark, while she was like a fly that has fallen into an ink-pot, crawling along the road and staining Layevsky's side and arm black. If Kirilin does something horrible, she thought, then she would be to blame, not he. After all, there was a time when no man would talk to her like Kirilin and it was she who had severed this period like a thread, destroying it for ever. But who was to blame? Stupefied by her desires, she had begun to smile at a complete stranger, most probably because he was tall and well-built. After two meetings he bored her, and she dropped him – surely that entitled him to behave as he liked to her, she thought.

'I must say goodbye here, my dear,' Layevsky said, stopping. 'Ilya Mikhaylich will see you home.' He bowed to Kirilin, quickly crossed the boulevard, went across the street to Sheshkovsky's house, where the lights were burning in the windows. Then he could be heard banging the gate.

'I want to have a little talk with you,' Kirilin began. 'I'm not a street urchin, not a mere nobody . . . I demand serious attention!'

Nadezhda's heart pounded away. She did not answer.

'At first I ascribed the sharp change in your attitude to flirtatiousness,' Kirilin continued, 'but now I see that you simply don't know how to behave towards respectable people. You simply wanted a little game with me, like that Armenian boy, but I'm a respectable man and demand to be treated as such. And so, I'm at your service.'

'I feel so depressed,' Nadezhda said, and burst into tears. To hide them she turned away.

'I'm depressed as well, what of it?' Kirilin paused for a moment and then said distinctly and deliberately, 'I repeat, my dear lady. If you don't grant me a rendezvous today, I shall make a scene this evening.'

'Just let me off for today,' Nadezhda said in such a plaintive, thin voice, she did not recognize it.

'I must teach you a lesson. Excuse my bad manners, but I have to teach you a lesson. Yes, Madam, you must be taught a lesson. I demand two meetings – tonight and tomorrow. The day after you'll be quite free to go where the hell you like, with whoever you like. Tonight and tomorrow.'

Nadezhda went over to her gate and stopped. 'Let me go!' she whispered, trembling all over and unable to see anything in front of her in the dark except a white tunic. 'You're right, I'm a dreadful woman . . . I'm to blame, but let me go, I beg you.' She touched his cold hand and shuddered. 'I beg you.'

'Unfortunately, no!' Kirilin sighed. 'No! It's not my intention to let you go. I only want to teach you a lesson, to make you understand. Besides, Madam, I really don't trust women.'

'I feel *so* depressed.'

Nadezhda listened hard to the steady roar of the sea, glanced up at the star-strewn sky and felt she wanted to finish with everything there and then, to rid herself of the wretched sensation of a life of sea, stars, men, fevers.

'But not in my house,' she said coldly. 'Take me somewhere else.'

'Let's go to Myuridov's, that's the best place.'

'Where is it?'

'Near the old rampart.'

She walked rapidly down the street and then turned up a side-street leading to the mountains. It was dark. Pale patches of light from illuminated windows lay here and there on the road and she felt like a fly, perpetually falling into an ink-pot and then crawling out again into the light. Kirilin was following her. At one spot he stumbled, nearly fell and burst out laughing.

'He's drunk,' Nadezhda thought. 'So what . . . So what . . . So be it.'

Achmianov had also quickly taken leave of the company and had followed Nadezhda to invite her to go boating with him. He went up to her house and peered across the fence. The windows were wide open and there were no lights. 'Nadezhda!' he called. A minute passed. He called out again.

'Who's there?' – it was Olga.

'Is Nadezhda home?'

'No, hasn't come back yet.'

'Strange . . . very strange,' Achmianov thought, beginning to feel terribly anxious. 'She *was* on her way home . . .'

He went along the boulevard, down the street and then he looked into Sheshkovsky's windows. Layevsky was sitting at the table, without a frock-coat, staring at his cards.

'That's strange, most strange . . .' Achmianov muttered and he felt ashamed when he remembered Layevsky's fit. 'If she's not at home, then where is she?'

Again he went over to Nadezhda's house and looked at the dark windows. 'I've been tricked,' he thought, remembering that when they had met at midday at the Bityugovs she had promised to go boating with him in the evening.

The windows in Kirilin's house were dark and a policeman sat fast asleep on the bench by the gate. One glance at the windows and the policeman and everything became clear to Achmianov. He decided to go home and started off, but once again found he was near Nadezhda's flat. He sat down on a bench there and took his hat off; his head seemed to be burning with jealousy and injured pride.

The parish church clock struck only twice every twenty-four hours: at noon and midnight. Soon after it had struck midnight there came the sound of hurried footsteps.

'So it's at Myuridov's again, tomorrow evening,' Achmianov heard and he recognized Kirilin's voice. 'Eight o'clock. Until then, Madam.'

Nadezhda came into sight near the garden fence. Not noticing Achmianov on the bench, she flitted past like a ghost, opened the gate and entered the house, leaving the gate open. In her room she lit a candle and quickly undressed. But she did not lie on her bed, but fell on her knees in front of a chair, embraced it and pressed her forehead to it.

Layevsky came home after two in the morning.

XV

Layevsky had decided not to tell her the pack of lies all at once, but gradually, and the next day, after one o'clock, he went to Samoylenko's to ask for the money that would enable him to travel that Saturday, without fail. After yesterday's fit, which had added a further sharp feeling of shame to his already deeply depressed state of mind, staying any longer in that town was out of the question. If Samoylenko insisted on his conditions, he thought, then he might possibly agree to them and take the money. Tomorrow he could tell him at the very last moment, just when he was about to leave, that Nadezhda had refused to go with him. That evening he could try and persuade her that it was all in her best interests. But if Samoylenko, obviously under von Koren's influence, refused point-blank to give him the money or stipulated new conditions, then he could possibly leave for New Athos or Novorossiysk that same day on some cargo ship, or even a sailing-boat. From there he would have to swallow his pride and send his mother a telegram and stay there until she sent him his fare.

When he called at Samoylenko's he found von Koren in the drawing-room. The zoologist had just arrived for lunch and as usual he had opened the album and was studying pictures of men in top hats and ladies in lace caps.

'What a nuisance,' Layevsky thought on seeing him. 'He might get in my way.'

'Good morning,' he said.

'Good morning,' von Koren replied, without looking up.

'Is Samoylenko home?'

'Yes, he's in the kitchen.'

Layevsky went towards the kitchen, but as he looked through the doorway he saw Samoylenko was busy making a salad; he went back to the drawing-room and sat down. He had always felt ill at ease with the zoologist and now he was afraid of having to talk about the fit. More than a minute passed in silence. Suddenly von Koren looked up at Layevsky and asked, 'How do you feel after what happened yesterday?'

'Excellent,' Layevsky replied, turning red. 'It was really nothing very much.'

'Before yesterday I'd always thought that only ladies had hysterics, that's why I supposed at first you had St Vitus's dance.'

Layevsky smiled obsequiously and thought, 'How tactless of him. He knows only too well how bad I'm feeling.'

'Yes, strange thing to happen,' he said, smiling. 'I've been laughing about it all morning. The curious thing about hysterics is that you know they're ridiculous, you laugh deep down about them, yet they still make you cry. In this neurotic age we're slaves of our nerves.

They are our masters and do what they like with us. Civilization has doublecrossed us there!'

As Layevsky went on he was not pleased that von Koren was listening to him seriously and attentively, watching him intently, without blinking an eyelid, as if he were an object for study. And he was annoyed with himself for being totally unable to drive that obsequious smile from his face, despite his dislike for von Koren.

'However, I must confess,' he went on, 'there were some more immediate reasons for the hysterics, and fairly substantial ones at that. My health has recently had a severe shake-up. Add to that boredom, eternal poverty, lack of congenial company with mutual interests . . . My position is worse than a governor's.'

'Yes, your position is hopeless,' von Koren said.

These calm, cold words, partly mocking, partly prophetic, were insulting for Layevsky. As he recalled the contemptuous, disgusted way the zoologist had looked at him the day before, he paused for a moment and then asked, no longer smiling, 'And how did you find out about my position?'

'You mentioned it yourself only just now, and your friends take such a burning interest in you it's all one hears about all day long.'

'Which friends? Do you mean Samoylenko?'

'Yes, he's one.'

'I'd prefer it if Samoylenko and all the rest didn't worry about me so much.'

'Here's Samoylenko now; ask him to stop worrying about you so much.'

'I don't like your tone of voice,' Layevsky muttered, as if he realized only now that the zoologist hated and despised him, was taunting him and that he was his most deadly, most implacable enemy. 'Please reserve that tone of voice for someone else,' he said softly, without the strength to speak out loud for the hatred that was already choking his heart and chest – just like yesterday's urge to laugh.

In came Samoylenko, without his frock-coat, sweaty and crimson-faced from the hot kitchen. 'Oh, so you're here,' he said. 'Hullo, my dear chap. Had lunch? Now don't be shy, tell me if you've eaten.'

'Alexander,' Layevsky said, standing up, 'if I came to you with an intimate request, it doesn't mean I've freed you from your obligation to be discreet and respect other people's secrets.'

'What's wrong, then?' Samoylenko said in astonishment.

'If you don't have the money,' Layevsky went on, raising his voice and excitedly shifting from one foot to the other, 'then don't lend me any, refuse me. But why do you have to spread it all over town that my position's hopeless and so on? I cannot bear these acts of charity, good turns from people who talk big and in the end give you nothing! You can boast to your heart's content about your good deeds, but no one ever gave you the right to reveal my secrets!'

'What secrets?' Samoylenko asked in bewilderment, losing his temper. 'If you've come here for a slanging-match then you'd better leave now. Why don't you come back later?'

He remembered the rule, that when one is angry with a close friend, counting mentally up to a hundred has a calming effect. And he started counting, quickly.

'I beg you not to concern yourself about me!' Layevsky went on. 'Don't take any notice. And what business is it of anyone's who I am and what kind of life I lead? Yes, I want to get away! Yes, I run up debts, drink, live with another man's wife. I have fits, I'm a vulgar person, and I'm not as profound as some other people. But whose business is that? You should respect individuals!'

'Forgive me, my friend,' Samoylenko said when he had counted to thirty-five, 'but . . .'

'Respect individuals!' Layevsky interrupted. 'To hell with all this bitchiness, all these "oohs" and "ahs", this constant hounding, eavesdropping, this friendly sympathizing! They lend me money and then subject me to conditions as if I were a child! I'm treated like God knows what! I don't want *anything*!'

Layevsky started shouting and he staggered from agitation, afraid he might have another fit. The thought, 'So I shan't be leaving this Saturday', flashed through his mind. 'I don't want *anything*! All I ask, if it's all the same with you, is to be spared this supervision. I'm not a child, I'm not insane and I ask you to end this surveillance!'

The deacon entered and when he saw pale-faced Layevsky waving his arms and addressing these strange words to Prince Vorontsov's portrait, he stood by the door, as if rooted to the spot.

'This continual prying into my soul,' Layevsky went on, 'offends my dignity as a human being and I ask these volunteer sleuths to stop spying! It's enough!'

'What . . . what did you say?' Samoylenko asked – having counted to a hundred he grew crimson-faced as he walked over to Layevsky.

'It's enough!' Layevsky repeated, gasping for breath as he picked his cap up.

'I'm a Russian gentleman, doctor and colonel,' Samoylenko said slowly and deliberately. 'I have never spied on anyone and I won't allow myself to be *insulted*!' he shouted in a broken voice, laying particular stress on the last word. 'So will you shut up!'

The deacon, who had never seen the doctor look so magnificent, proud, crimson-faced and fearsome, put his hand over his mouth, ran out into the hall and stood roaring with laughter. As though he were peering through a mist, Layevsky saw von Koren stand up, put his hands in his trouser pockets and stay in that position, as if waiting to see what would happen next. The calmness of his posture struck Layevsky as provocative and insulting in the extreme.

'Please take back what you just said!' Samoylenko shouted.

Layevsky, who could no longer remember *what* he had said, replied, 'Leave me in peace! I want nothing! All I want is for you and these German–Jewish immigrants to leave me in peace! If not, I shall take steps! I will fight!'

'Now I understand,' von Koren said as he rose from the table. 'Before he departs, Mr Layevsky wishes to amuse himself with a little duelling. I can accord him that pleasure. Mr Layevsky, I accept your challenge.'

'Challenge?' Layevsky softly enunciated as he went over to the zoologist and looked hatefully at his dark forehead and curly hair. 'Challenge? If that's what you want. I hate you! I hate you!'

'Absolutely delighted. First thing tomorrow morning, near Kerbalay's, please yourself about the details. And now beat it!'

'I hate you!' Layevsky said softly, breathing heavily. 'I've hated you for a long time. A duel! Yes!'

'Get him out of here, Alexander, or I shall have to leave,' von Koren said. 'He might bite me.'

Von Koren's cool tone calmed the doctor. Suddenly he recovered his senses and he gripped Layevsky around the waist, muttering in an affectionate voice that shook with emotion as he led him away from the zoologist. 'My friends . . . my good, kind friends . . . You've just got a little excited, let's call it a day . . . it's enough. My friends . . .'

When he heard that soft, friendly voice Layevsky felt that something quite unprecedented and monstrous had happened to him, as if he'd nearly been run over by a train. He was close to tears, waved his arm in capitulation and ran out of the room.

'God, how dreadful to be the target of someone's hatred and to make the most pathetic, despicable, helpless spectacle of oneself in front of him!' he thought soon after as he sat in the Pavilion. And he felt as if the feeling of hatred that this man had just stirred in him had left a deposit of rust on his body. 'God, how idiotic!'

Some brandy with cold water cheered him up. He clearly pictured von Koren's calm, arrogant face, the expression he had worn the day before, his carpet-like shirt, his voice, his white hands, and an intense, passionate, all-consuming hatred welled up inside him and sought gratification. He imagined knocking von Koren to the ground and stamping on him. Down to the very last details, he recalled everything that had happened and was amazed how he could have smiled so obsequiously at that nonentity, how he could have valued the opinions of those obscure little nobodies living in a wretched dump that apparently was not even on the map and which no self-respecting Petersburger had ever heard of. If that nasty little town were suddenly to vanish or burn down, the telegram bearing this news would have been read in central Russia with the same boredom as any advert for second-hand furniture. Killing von Koren tomorrow, sparing his life, did not matter a damn, it was equally pointless and boring. He would wound him in the leg or arm, then have a good laugh at him; just as an insect with a torn-off leg loses its way in the grass, so he would be lost with his mute suffering in that sea of nonentities, all as insignificant as himself.

Layevsky went to Sheshkovsky's, told him everything and invited him to act as second. Then they both went off to the local postmaster's, invited him to be a second and stayed for lunch, over which they cracked a great deal of jokes and had a good laugh together. Layevsky poked fun at himself, saying he hardly knew how to fire a pistol and dubbing himself 'Royal Marksman' and 'William Tell'.

'That man must be taught a lesson,' he said.

After lunch they sat down to cards. Layevsky joined in, drank wine, and reflected how stupid and senseless duels were, all things considered, as they never solved any problem, but only aggravated them; all the same, at times there was no other course of action. For example, he couldn't report von Koren to the Justice of the Peace for that kind of thing! And the impending duel seemed all the more attractive, as after it he could not possibly stay any longer in that town. He grew slightly tipsy, amused himself at cards and felt everything was fine.

But when the sun set and it became dark, he was overcome by uneasiness. This was not fear of death, since while he was lunching and playing cards he felt confident somehow that the duel would come to nothing. It was fear of the unknown, of what was bound to happen the following morning for the first time in his life, and fear of the approaching night . . . He knew the night would be long and sleepless, and that not only would he have to think of von Koren and his hatred, but about that mountain of lies he would have to surmount and which he had neither the skill nor strength to avoid. It was as though he had suddenly been taken ill. All at once he lost interest in the cards and the other players, fidgeted and asked if he could go home. He wanted to be in bed as soon as possible, to lie quite still and to prepare his thoughts for the night that lay ahead. Sheshkovsky and the postmaster saw him home, then went to von Koren's to discuss the duel.

Layevsky met Achmianov near his flat. The young man was out of breath and excited.

'I've been looking for you, Ivan Andreich!' he said. 'Please come quickly.'

'Where?'

'A gentleman you don't know has some very urgent business with you. He begs you to drop in for just a minute, there's something he wants to discuss with you . . . It's a matter of life and death to him . . .'

In his excitement Achmianov pronounced these words with a strong Armenian accent, making two syllables out of 'life'.

'Who is he?' Layevsky asked.

'He told me not to reveal his name.'

'Say I'm too busy at the moment. I'll come tomorrow, if that suits him.'

'But that's impossible,' Achmianov said, horrified. 'He wants to tell you something that is so very important to you . . . *very* important! It will be disastrous if you don't go.'

'That's strange,' Layevsky muttered, unable to understand why Achmianov should be so worked up and what manner of secrets could be lurking in that dull, nasty little town that no one wanted. 'That's strange,' he repeated thoughtfully. 'All right, let's go. It's all the same to me.'

Achmianov quickly went on ahead and Layevsky followed. They went down the main street, then an alley.

'What a bore,' Layevsky said.

'Any moment now, we're nearly there.'

Near the old rampart they went along a narrow alley between two fenced patches of waste ground; then they entered a kind of large courtyard and went over to a small house.

'That's Myuridov's, isn't it?' Layevsky asked.

'Yes.'

'But why are we going in the back way? I don't understand. We could have come in from the street, it's quicker.'

'It doesn't matter.'

Layevsky found it odd too when Achmianov led him round to the back door and waved his hand at him, as if asking him to step softly and not make a sound.

'In here, in here,' Achmianov said, cautiously opening a door and tiptoeing into the hall. 'Quietly please, I beg you . . . they might hear.'

He listened hard, took a deep breath and whispered, 'Open this door and go in . . . Don't be scared.'

Bewildered, Layevsky opened the door and entered a room with a low ceiling and curtained windows. A candle stood on the table.

'Who do you want?' someone asked in the next room. 'Is that you, Myuridov?'

Layevsky went into the room and saw Kirilin, with Nadezhda beside him. He didn't hear what was said to him, moved backwards and didn't realize when he was back in the street again. His hatred for von Koren and his anxiety had completely disappeared. On his way home he clumsily waved his right arm and carefully inspected the ground under his feet, trying to walk where it was smooth. Back in his study he paced up and down, rubbing his hands together and awkwardly jerking his shoulders and neck, as if his waistcoat and shirt were too tight. Then he lit a candle and sat down at the table.

XVI

'The humane studies you're talking about will only satisfy men's thinking when they converge with the exact sciences as they advance and go along arm in arm with them. Whether they'll meet under the microscope or in the soliloquies of a new Hamlet, or in some new religion, I can't say. But I do think that another ice age will be upon us before that comes about. The most stable and vital part of all humane studies is the teaching of Christ, of course, but just look at the diversity of interpretations! Some scholars teach us to love our neighbours, but make an exception for soldiers, criminals and the insane. They make it legal for the first to be killed in war, the second to be locked up or executed, and the last to be prohibited from marrying. Other commentators teach us to love our neighbours without exception, irrespective of the pros and cons. According to them, if a consumptive or murderer or epileptic comes up to you and proposes to your daughter, you must give your consent. If cretins wage war on the sound in body and mind, the healthy must lay their heads on the block. If this advocacy of love for love's sake, like art for art's sake, were to grow strong, it would lead in the end to the total extinction of mankind and as a result one of the most enormous crimes ever to be seen on this earth would have been committed. There are countless different teachings and if this is so, then no serious mind can ever be satisfied with any one of them and would hasten to add its own commentary to the sum total. So, you should never base a question on philosophical or so-called Christian premises, as you call them, or you'll only stray further from the correct solution.'

The deacon listened attentively to the zoologist's words and inquired after a moment's thought, 'Is the moral law, that is inherent in everyone, an invention of the philosophers, or did God create it together with the body?'

'I don't know. But this law is so common to all nations and epochs it strikes me it has to be recognized as an organic part of man. It is not an invention, it exists and will continue to do so. I wouldn't go so far as to say that one day we'll be able to see it under the microscope, but there's already evidence that proves its organic links. Serious illness of the brain and all the so-called mental illnesses manifest themselves first and foremost in violations of the moral law, as far as I know.

'Very well. So, just as the stomach wants food, the moral sense requires us to love our neighbours. Right? But our natural self resists the voice of conscience and reason out of sheer selfishness and many ticklish questions arise as a result. And to whom should we turn for the solution of these problems if you don't want us to deal with them from a philosophical standpoint?

'Take note of the small store of precise knowledge that we in fact do possess. Trust what you can see, and the logic of facts. True, it's not much to go on, but on the other hand it's not as shaky and vague as philosophy. Let's suppose the moral law demands that you should love people. What then? Love should lie in the elimination of everything that in any way harms people and threatens them with present or future danger. Knowledge and what we can observe tell us that humanity is threatened by the morally and physically abnormal. If that is correct, then you must do battle with these freaks of nature. If you can't raise them to the norm, you'll at least have the strength and ability to render them harmless – by that I mean exterminate them.'

'That's to say, love is when the strong conquer the weak?'

'Without any doubt.'

'But it was the strong who crucified our Lord Jesus Christ!' the deacon retorted heatedly.

'That's just the point, it wasn't the strong who crucified him, but the weak. Civilization has weakened the struggle for existence and natural selection, which it is trying to annihilate. That gives rise to the rapid multiplication of the weak and their superiority over the strong. Just imagine if you succeeded in instilling bees with crude, raw human ideals. Where would it lead? The drones, who should be killed, would survive, eat all the honey, and corrupt and smother the others, and as a result we'd have the weak holding sway over the strong, so that the latter became extinct. Exactly the same is happening to humanity now, the weak oppress the strong. The savage who is strongest, wisest and who has the highest moral standards, who is as yet untouched by culture – he's the one who makes the most progress; he is the leader and master. But we civilized men crucified Christ and keep on crucifying him. That's to say, we are lacking in something . . . And this "something" must be restored or there'll be no end to this folly.'

'But what's your criterion for distinguishing between the strong and the weak?'

'Knowledge and the evidence of my senses. Consumptives and the scrofulous are known by their symptoms and the immoral and insane are judged by their actions.'

'But surely mistakes can happen!'

'Yes, but there's no point in worrying about getting your feet wet when a flood is threatening.'

'That's philosophy,' the deacon laughed.

'Not at all. You've been so spoiled by seminary philosophy that you see fog just everywhere. The abstract studies which your young head is stuffed with are only called this because they abstract your mind from reality. Look the devil straight in the eye and if it *is* the devil then say so and don't go running off to Kant or Hegel for an explanation.'

The zoologist stopped for a moment and then went on, 'Twice two are four and a stone's a stone. Tomorrow there's going to be a duel. It's all very well for us to say how stupid and ridiculous it is, that duels have outlived their time, that the nobleman's duel is essentially no different from a drunken tavern brawl. All the same, we won't wait, we'll go off and fight. That means there's a power which is stronger than all our discussions on the subject. We cry out that war is robbery, barbarity, horror, fratricide and we faint at the sight of blood. But the French or the Germans only have to insult us and immediately our spirits soar, we cheer passionately and throw ourselves on the enemy. You'll invoke God's blessing on our guns while our valour will arouse universal and genuine elation. Once again, that means there's a power, if not loftier, then at least stronger than us and our philosophy. We are as powerless to stop it as that cloud over there coming in from the sea. Don't be hypocritical, don't stick your tongue out at it behind its back and don't say, "Oh, it's stupid, it's out of date, it doesn't agree with the Scriptures!" Look it straight in the eye and acknowledge that it's reasonable and in the rightful order of things. And when for example it wishes to destroy some feeble, scrofulous, depraved tribe, don't hinder it with all your medical remedies and quotations from imperfectly understood Gospels. Leskov has a highly virtuous character called Danila,[19] who feeds a leper he found outside the town and keeps him warm in the name of love and Christ. If this Danila had really loved people, he would have hauled that leper as far away from the town as he could and thrown him into a ditch. Then he would have gone off to lend a hand to the healthy. Christ preached the love that is sensible, meaningful and useful, that's what I hope.'

'Get on with you!' the deacon laughed. 'You don't believe in Christ, so why do you mention him so much?'

'No, I do believe in him. But in my own special way, not yours. Oh, deacon, deacon,' the zoologist said, laughing, as he put his arm round the deacon and gaily added, 'Well, what now? Are you going to that duel tomorrow?'

'My cloth doesn't allow it, or I would come.'

'What do you mean *cloth*?'

'I'm in holy orders, by God's grace.'

'Oh, deacon, deacon!' von Koren repeated, laughing. 'I love talking to you.'

'You say you have faith,' the deacon said. 'But what is it? Now, I have an uncle, just an ordinary parish priest, whose faith is such that when he goes into the fields to pray for rain during a drought, he takes his umbrella and a leather coat to avoid a soaking on the way home. There's faith for you! When he speaks of Christ there's a halo over his head and all the peasant men and women sob their hearts out. He would have made that cloud stop and put any of your powers to flight. Yes . . . faith moves mountains.'

The deacon burst out laughing and slapped the zoologist on the shoulder. 'And so,' he went on, 'that's what you're teaching the whole time, plumbing the depths of the ocean, sorting out the weak from the strong, writing pamphlets and challenging people to duels. But everything stays where it was. You wait, though, one old man only has to whisper a word in the name of the Holy Spirit – or some new Muhammad to come galloping out of Arabia, scimitar in hand – and everything will be turned upside down, leaving not one stone standing on another in Europe.'

'But that's a load of rot, deacon!'

'Faith without actions is dead and actions without faith are even worse, a sheer waste of time, nothing more.'

The doctor appeared on the front. Seeing the deacon and the zoologist he went up to them.

'Everything's arranged, it seems,' he said, gasping for breath. 'Govorovsky and Boyko will be seconds. They'll be here at five tomorrow morning. What a lot of clouds!' he said, looking at the sky. 'Can't see a thing. We're in for a shower any minute now.'

'I hope you're coming with us,' von Koren asked.

'No, God forbid. I'm just plain exhausted. Ustimovich is going instead. I've already spoken to him.'

Far over the sea lightning flashed and there were hollow peals of thunder.

'It's so close before a storm!' von Koren said. 'I'll wager you've already been round to cry on Layevsky's shoulder.'

'Why should I go there?' the doctor replied, taken aback. 'Well, what next!'

Before sunset he had walked up and down the boulevard and street several times, hoping to meet Layevsky. He was ashamed of his outburst and of that sudden benevolent impulse that had followed. He wanted to apologize to Layevsky in jocular vein – to give him a little ticking-off, to calm him down and to tell him that duelling was a relic of medieval barbarism, but that Providence itself had shown them that duelling was a means of reconciliation. The next day the two of them, both fine, highly intelligent men, would – after exchanging shots - come to appreciate each other's integrity and become friends.

'But why should I go to see him?' Samoylenko repeated. 'I didn't insult him, he insulted me. Tell me, if you don't mind, why did he attack me? Have I ever done him any harm? I merely went into the drawing-room and suddenly, without rhyme or reason, he called me a spy! A fine thing! Tell me, what started it? What did you say to him?'

'I told him that his situation was hopeless. And I was right. Only honest people and crooks can escape from *any* situation, but anyone wanting to be crooked and honest at one and the same time will never find a way out. However, it's eleven already, gentlemen, and we have to be up early tomorrow.'

There was a sudden gust of wind. It raised clouds of dust on the sea front, whirled them round and drowned the sound of the sea with its howling.

'A squall!' the deacon said. 'Let's go, or I'll have my eyes full of dust.'

When they had gone, Samoylenko sighed and said, gripping his hat, 'I probably won't sleep now.'

'Don't worry,' the zoologist laughed. 'You can relax, the duel will come to nothing. Layevsky will magnanimously fire into the air – he can't do anything else – and most likely I shan't fire at all. To find myself in court because of that Layevsky, wasting my time because of him – the game's not worth the candle. By the way, what's the penalty for duelling?'

'Arrest, and should your opponent die, up to three years in prison.'

'The Peter and Paul?'

'No, a military prison, I think.'

'That young puppy should be taught a lesson!'

Lightning flashed on the sea behind them and for a brief moment lit up the roofs of the houses and the mountains. Near the boulevard the friends parted. When the doctor had disappeared in the darkness and his footsteps had already begun to die away, von Koren shouted after him, 'I'm scared the weather might spoil things tomorrow.'

'It might well do that. Let's hope it does!'

'Good night.'

'What? What did you say?'

It was difficult to hear anything against the roaring wind and sea, and the thunderclaps.

'Oh, nothing!' shouted the zoologist, and hurried home.

XVII

> . . . a crowd of oppressive thoughts[20]
> Throngs my anguished mind; silently
> Before me, Memory unfolds its long scroll;
> And with loathing, reading the chronicle of my life,
> I tremble and curse, and shed bitter tears,
> But I do not wash away these sad lines.
>
> PUSHKIN

Whether he was killed in the morning or made to look a fool – that is, allowed to go on living – it was all finished now. That dishonoured woman might kill herself in despair and shame, or she might drag out her wretched existence – either way she too was finished.

These were Layevsky's thoughts as he sat late that evening at his table, rubbing his hands together as always. The window suddenly banged open, the strong wind burst into the room and the papers flew off the table. Layevsky shut the window and bent down to pick them up. He experienced a new kind of sensation, a kind of awkwardness which he had never known before and his movements seemed foreign to him. He walked about gingerly, thrusting his elbows to each side, twitching his shoulders. When he sat down at the table he started rubbing his hands again. His body had lost its suppleness.

Letters should be written to close relatives the day before one is going to die and Layevsky remembered this. He took his pen and wrote 'Dear Mother!' with trembling hand.

He wanted to ask his mother, in the name of all-merciful God in whom she believed, to shelter and give the warmth of her affection to that unfortunate, lonely, impoverished and weak woman whom he had dishonoured, to forget and forgive everything, and at least partly expiate her son's terrible sin by her sacrifice. But then he remembered how his mother, a plump, heavily built old lady in a lace cap, used to go from house to garden in the morning, followed by her companion with a lapdog. He remembered how she would bully her gardener and servants in that imperious voice of hers and how proud and arrogant her face was. All this he remembered and he crossed out what he had written.

The lightning flashed vividly in all three windows, followed by a deafening roll of thunder – indistinct at first, but then crashing and crackling so violently that the window panes rattled. Layevsky stood up, went over to the window, and pressed his forehead to the glass. Outside, a mighty, beautiful storm was raging. On the distant horizon lightning constantly darted out of the clouds on to the sea in white ribbons, illuminating the towering black waves for miles around. To the left and right, and probably over the house as well, the lightning flashed.

'A thunderstorm!' Layevsky whispered, feeling an urge to pray to someone or something, even if only to the lightning or the clouds. 'What a lovely storm!'

He remembered how once when he was a child a storm had made him run bareheaded into the garden with two fair-headed blue-eyed girls chasing after him, how they were all soaked by the rain. They laughed with delight, but then came a violent thunderclap and the girls trustfully snuggled up close to him as he crossed himself and hurriedly started reciting, 'Holy, holy, holy.' Oh, where have you gone, in what ocean have you foundered, first glimmerings of beautiful, innocent life? No longer did he fear thunderstorms, he had no love for nature, he had no God, and all those trustful girls he had once known had long since been ruined by himself and his friends. Never had he planted one sapling, never had he grown one blade of grass in his garden at home and never in his life had he spared a single fly even, but had only wrecked, ruined, and told lies, lies, lies . . .

'Is there anything in my past life except vice?' he asked himself, trying to cling to some bright memory, as a man falling over a precipice clutches at bushes.

And the high school? The university? It was all a deception. He had been a bad student and had forgotten what he had been taught. And what of his service to the community? That was deception as well, since he had never done any work and received a salary for doing nothing, so his 'service' was nothing more than disgraceful embezzlement of government funds which goes unpunished in court. He had no need for the truth and had never sought it. Under the spell of vice and deception, his conscience had either slept or remained silent. Like a stranger or an alien from another planet, he had done nothing to help people in their everyday life, was indifferent to their sufferings, ideas, religion, knowledge, searchings, strivings; never had he spoken a kind word to anyone, never had he written one line that was not cheap or worthless, never had he done a thing for others. Instead, he had eaten their food, drunk their wine, seduced their wives, copied their ideas. And to justify his despicable, parasitical life in his own eyes and theirs, he had always tried to give the impression of being a nobler, superior kind of being. Lies, lies, lies . . . He clearly recalled what he had witnessed that evening at Myuridov's and he felt unbearably sick with loathing and anguish. Kirilin and Achmianov were repulsive, but they were after all carrying on what *he* had begun. They were his accomplices and pupils.

He had taken a young weak woman, who had trusted him more than her own brother, away from her husband, her circle of friends, her native land, and had brought her to this place, to endure stifling heat, fever, boredom. Day after day she had come to mirror his idleness, loose living and lying in herself – her feeble, dull, wretched life consisted of this, and only this. Later on, when he had had enough of her, he began to hate her, but was not man enough to drop her, and so he redoubled his efforts to entangle her in a web of lies . . . The people here added the finishing touches.

Layevsky first sat at the table, then went over to the window again. Then he would snuff the candle and light it again. He cursed himself out loud, wept, complained, asked for forgiveness. Several times he ran despairingly over to the table and wrote, 'Mother!'

Apart from his mother, he had no blood relatives or close friends at all. But how could his mother help him? And where was she? He felt like running to Nadezhda, falling at her feet, kissing her hands and feet and begging her to forgive him. But she was his victim and he feared her, just as though she were dead.

'My life is ruined!' he muttered, rubbing his hands. 'For God's sake, why am I still alive!'

He had cast down his dim star from the sky, it had faded and its trail merged with the darkness of night. Never would it return to the heavens again, as life is given only once and is never repeated. If he were able now to bring back all those days and years that had passed he would replace all the lies they held with the truth, all the idleness with work, all the boredom with joy; he would return innocence to those he had robbed of it, and he would have found God and justice. But this was as impossible as putting that fading star back in the sky and the hopelessness of ever achieving this reduced him to despair.

When the storm had passed he sat by the open window and calmly considered what was going to happen to him. Von Koren would kill him, most likely. That man's lucid, cold outlook admitted the extermination of the weak and the useless. And if this frame of mind deserted him at the critical moment, he could call on the hatred and revulsion Layevsky aroused in him. But if he missed, or merely wounded him, just to make a laughing-stock of his odious opponent, or if he fired into the air, what could he do then? Where could he go?

'Should I go to St Petersburg?' Layevsky asked himself. 'But that would mean starting that damnable old life all over again. Whoever seeks salvation by going somewhere else, like a bird of passage, will find nothing, since things will be the same wherever he goes. Should I seek salvation among people? But from whom and how? Samoylenko's kindness and goodness of heart will do as little to save me as that deacon's laughing at everything or von Koren's hatred. Salvation must be sought in oneself alone, and if I fail there's no point in wasting any more time. I will have to kill myself, that's all . . .'

He heard the sound of a carriage. It was already growing light. The carriage passed, turned and with wheels crunching over the damp sand came to a stop by the house. Two people were sitting in it.

'Wait a moment, I'm coming!' Layevsky told them through the window. 'I haven't slept. Surely it's not time already?'

'Yes, it's four o'clock. By the time we get there . . .'

Layevsky put on his coat and cap, stuffed some cigarettes into his pocket and stopped to think for a moment. There was still something he had to do, it seemed. In the street the seconds were quietly chatting, the horses snorted. These early morning sounds, on a damp day, when everyone was asleep and dawn was breaking, filled Layevsky with a feeling of despondency that was just like an evil omen. He stood thinking for a little while and then went into the bedroom.

Nadezhda was lying stretched full length on the bed with a rug up to her head. She lay so still that she looked like an Egyptian mummy – her head in particular. Silently watching her, Layevsky inwardly prayed for her to forgive him and he thought that if heaven was not an empty place, if God really did exist, then he would stay with her. But if God did not exist, then she might as well perish, as she would have nothing to live for.

Suddenly she started and sat up in bed. She raised her pale face, gave Layevsky a horrified look and asked, 'Is that you? Is the storm over?'

'Yes.'

She remembered what had happened, came to her senses, placed both hands on her head and trembled all over.

'I feel so miserable!' she said. 'If only you knew how miserable I feel!' She screwed her eyes up and continued, 'I was expecting you to kill me, or drive me out into the rain and the storm, but you seem to be hesitating, hesitating.'

Impulsively, he gave her a violent embrace, showered her knees and hands with kisses. After she had murmured something, shuddering as she recollected the past events, he smoothed her hair and as he gazed into her face he came to realize that this unhappy, depraved woman was the only person in his life who was near and dear to him and who could not be replaced.

When he left the house and sat in the carriage he felt he wanted to come back alive.

XVIII

The deacon got up, dressed, took his thick, knotty walking-stick, and quietly slipped out of the house. It was dark and at first he could not even see his white stick as he walked down the street. Not a star was in the sky and it looked like rain again. There was a smell of moist sand and sea.

'I hope I'm not attacked by Chechens,' the deacon thought as he listened to the lonely, ringing sound of his stick as it clattered on the road in the silence of the night.

When he was out of the town he began to make out both the road and his stick. Here and there in the black sky there were dim patches of light and before long a single star peeped out and timidly winked. The deacon was walking along a high rocky cliff-top, from which he could not see the sea down below; invisible waves lazily, heavily, broke on the beach and seemed to be sighing in pain. And how slowly they rolled in! One wave broke on the beach and the deacon counted eight paces before the next arrived; six paces later came a third wave. The world was probably like this when nothing was visible, with only the lazy, sleepy sound of the sea in the darkness; and he was conscious of that infinitely remote, unimaginable time when God hovered over the void.

The deacon felt nervous, thinking that God might punish him for associating with unbelievers and because he was even going to watch a duel, which would be trivial, bloodless and ludicrous. In any case, it was a pagan spectacle and it was quite unbecoming for a member of the clergy to be present at such an event. He stopped and wondered if he should go back. But a keen, restless curiosity overcame his doubts and he continued on his way.

He comforted himself by saying, 'Although they are unbelievers, they are still good people and will be saved.'

Then he lit a cigarette and said out loud, 'They're bound to be saved.'

What criterion was needed to assess people's virtues, so as to arrive at a fair judgement? The deacon remembered his enemy, an inspector at the school for sons of the clergy, who believed in God, never fought duels, lived a chaste life, but who once gave the deacon some bread with sand in it and who had once almost torn his ear off. If human life had turned out to be so inane that everyone respected that cruel, dishonest inspector who stole government flour and prayed in school for his health and salvation – how could *he* be justified in steering clear of people like Layevsky and von Koren just because they were unbelievers?

The deacon tried to solve this problem, but he remembered how comical Samoylenko had looked yesterday and this disrupted his train of thought. What a good laugh they would have later on! The deacon imagined himself sitting among the bushes watching them and when von Koren started boasting over lunch he could have a good laugh as he told him every single detail of the duel.

'How do you know all that?' the zoologist would ask. 'That's a good question,' he would reply. 'I was at home, but I *know*.'

It would be great fun to pen a comical description of the duel. His father-in-law would be amused when he read it – he was the type who would go hungry, as long as someone told him or sent him a story that was funny.

The Yellow River valley opened out before him. The rain had made the river wider and angrier, and it no longer grumbled but roared instead. Dawn began to break. The dull grey sky, those clouds scurrying towards the west to catch up with a bank of storm clouds, the mountains girdled with mist, the wet trees – all this struck the deacon as ugly and evil-looking. He washed himself in a stream, said his morning prayers and conceived a sudden longing for the tea and hot buns filled with sour cream served every morning at his father-in-law's table. He thought of the deaconess and that piece *Lost Hope* she played on the piano. What kind of person was she really? In just one week he had been introduced, engaged and married to her. He had lived with her less than a month, then he was sent here, so that up to now he hadn't had a chance to find out what sort of person she was. All the same, it was rather boring without her. 'I ought to drop her a few lines,' he thought.

The flag over the inn was soaked with rain and hung limply. And the inn's wet roof made it seem darker and lower than before. A bullock cart stood by the door. Kerbalay, two Abkhazians and a young Tatar girl in wide trousers (probably Kerbalay's wife or daughter) were carrying sacks filled with something from the inn and laying them on maize straw in the cart. Two asses were standing near the cart, heads bowed. When the sacks were loaded, the Abkhazians and the Tatar girl started covering them over with straw and Kerbalay hastily began to harness the asses. 'Contraband, most likely,' the deacon thought.

Here was the uprooted tree with its dry needles and over there a black patch where the bonfire had been. He recalled every detail of the picnic, the fire, the Abkhazians' songs, those sweet dreams of becoming a bishop and the church procession. The rain had turned the Black River even blacker and wider. The deacon cautiously crossed the rickety bridge which was now washed by the crests of the turbid waves and clambered up the short ladder into the drying-room.

'That man has a wonderful brain!' he thought as he stretched out on the straw and thought of von Koren. 'A wonderful brain, God bless him! Only he does have a cruel streak . . .'

Why did von Koren hate Layevsky, and why did Layevsky hate him? Why were they going to fight a duel? Had they known the poverty the deacon had suffered from early childhood; had they been brought up among ignorant, soulless, grasping people who begrudged them every scrap of food, who were rough and uncouth, who spat on the floor and belched during dinner and prayers; had they not been spoilt since childhood by living in comfort among a select circle of friends – how they would cling to each other, how eagerly they would overlook each other's faults and truly value what was best in every one of them! But there are so few even superficially decent people in the world! True, Layevsky was wild, dissolute, strange, but at least even he wouldn't steal, spit loudly on the floor or tell his wife, 'You like to guzzle all right, but you won't do any work.' *He* would never whip his child with horse reins or feed his servants with stinking salt beef. Surely all that was enough to earn him some sort of indulgence? What's more, wasn't *he* the first to suffer from his own shortcomings, like a sick person suffers from his own wounds? Instead of an absurd searching for degeneracy, decline, inherited failings and the rest of it in each other, just because they were bored, and for lack of understanding, wouldn't they do better to set their sights lower and direct their hatred and anger where entire streets reverberated with barbaric ignorance, greed, reproaches, filth, abuse, women's screams . . . ?

The sound of a carriage broke the deacon's train of thought. He peered through the doorway and saw a barouche with three men in it – Layevsky, Sheshkovsky and the local postmaster.

'Stop!' Sheshkovsky said.

All three climbed out of the carriage and surveyed one another.

'They haven't arrived yet,' Sheshkovsky said, wiping the mud off. 'All right, then. Until proceedings commence, let's find a suitable spot. It's impossible to move here.'

They went upstream and were soon out of sight. The Tatar coachman went inside the carriage, laid his head to one side and fell asleep. After waiting about ten minutes the deacon came out of the shed, took his black hat off so as not to be seen and made his way along the river bank, squatting in the bushes and maize and looking around. Heavy raindrops fell on him from the trees and bushes, and the grass and maize were wet.

'How degrading!' he muttered, lifting his wet, muddy skirts. 'I wouldn't have come if I'd known.'

Soon he heard voices and saw people. Layevsky, stooping, and with his hands in his sleeves, was swiftly pacing back and forth across the small clearing. His seconds stood right by the river bank rolling cigarettes.

'Most peculiar . . .' thought the deacon, not recognizing Layevsky's walk. 'Just like an old man.'

'How rude of them!' the postmaster said, looking at his watch. 'Perhaps those smart alecs think it's clever to be late, but if you ask me, they're behaving like pigs.'

Sheshkovsky, a fat man with a black beard, pricked his ears up and said, 'They're coming!'

XIX

'I've never seen anything like that before! How magnificent!' von Koren said as he appeared in the clearing and held out both hands to the east. 'Just look at those green rays!'

In the east two green rays stretched out from behind the mountains and they were truly beautiful. The sun was rising.

'Good morning!' the zoologist continued, nodding to Layevsky's seconds. 'I hope I'm not late.'

He was followed by his seconds, Boyko and Govorovsky, two very young officers of identical height, in white tunics, and the thin unsociable Dr Ustimovich, who was carrying a bundle of some sort in one hand, while he kept the other behind him. Putting the bundle on the ground, without a word of greeting to anyone, he placed his other arm behind his back and paced backwards and forwards across the clearing.

Layevsky experienced the weariness and awkwardness of a man who perhaps was soon going to die and therefore was the centre of attention. He wanted to have the killing over and done with, as soon as possible, or to be taken home. It was the first time in his life he had seen the sunrise. The early morning, the green rays, the damp and those men in wet jackboots were no part of his life at all, he had no need of them, and they had a cramping effect. None of this had the least connection with the night he had just lived through, with his trains of thought and feelings of guilt, and consequently he would gladly have left without waiting for the duel.

Von Koren was visibly excited and tried to hide this by pretending he was interested in those green rays. The seconds were embarrassed, exchanging glances as if to ask why they were there and what they had to do.

'I don't think there's any point in going on further, gentlemen,' Sheshkovsky said. 'It's fine here.'

'Yes, certainly,' von Koren agreed.

Silence followed. Ustimovich suddenly halted, turned sharply towards Layevsky and breathed into his face as he said in an undertone, 'Most likely they haven't managed to inform you of my terms. Each side pays me fifteen roubles and in the event of the death of one of the parties the survivor will pay the whole thirty.'

Layevsky knew this man from before, but only now did he have the first clear view of his lacklustre eyes, wiry moustache and his gaunt, wasted neck. This was a usurer, not a doctor! His breath smelt unpleasantly of beef.

'There are some peculiar people in this world,' Layevsky thought as he answered, 'All right.'

The doctor nodded and strode off again. It was obvious he did not need money at all, but had simply demanded it out of hatred. Everyone felt it was high time they began or finished what had been put in motion, but they did neither, merely walked around or stood smoking.

The young officers who were attending a duel for the first time and who now felt very sceptical about a contest between two civilians, which was quite unnecessary in their opinion, carefully inspected their tunics and smoothed down their sleeves. Sheshkovsky went over to them and said softly, 'Gentlemen, we must make every effort to stop this duel. We must reconcile them.' He blushed and went on, 'Yesterday Kirilin called on me to complain that Layevsky had caught him with Nadezhda, and *all that*.'

'Yes, we know,' Boyko said.

'Well, just have a look . . . Layevsky's hands are shaking, and all that. He can't even pick his pistol up. Fighting him would be as inhuman as fighting a drunk or someone with typhus. If they can't be reconciled, gentlemen, then perhaps we should postpone the duel . . . It's all damned stupid, I don't think I can even look.'

'You'd better have a word with von Koren.'

'I don't know the rules of duelling, blast it, and I don't want to know. Perhaps he'll think Layevsky's got cold feet and sent me over. He can think what he likes, however. I'll talk to him.'

Hesitantly and limping slowly, as though he had pins and needles in his foot, Sheshkovsky went towards von Koren and he looked the very embodiment of laziness as he sauntered over, clearing his throat. 'There is something I must tell you, sir,' he began, closely studying the floral pattern on the zoologist's shirt. 'It's confidential . . . I don't know the rules of duelling, damn it, and I don't want to know, so I'm not speaking as a second, and all that, but as a man, that's all.'

'Yes. Well what?'

'When seconds propose a reconciliation they are usually ignored as it's considered a formality. Pride, and all that. But I most humbly beg you to take a look at Ivan Layevsky. He's not normal today, he's not in his right mind, in a manner of speaking he's just pathetic. He's had a terrible misfortune. I cannot stand scandal' (here Sheshkovsky blushed and took a look round) 'but I have to tell you this because of the duel. Yesterday evening he found his lady friend at Myuridov's with a . . . certain gentleman.'

'How shocking!' the zoologist muttered. He went pale, frowned and spat noisily. 'Ugh!'

His lower lip quivered. He walked away from Sheshkovsky, not wishing to hear any more and once again, as if he had accidentally eaten something bitter, spat loudly. For the first time that morning he gave Layevsky a hateful look. His excitement and embarrassment passed and he shook his head and said in a loud voice, 'Gentlemen, I ask you, why are we waiting? Why don't we begin?'

Sheshkovsky exchanged glances with the officers and shrugged his shoulders. 'Gentlemen!' he said out loud, without addressing anyone in particular, 'Gentlemen! We suggest you settle your differences!'

'Let's get the formalities over with,' von Koren said. 'We've already discussed a reconciliation. What's next on the agenda? Now, let's get a move on, gentlemen, there's no time to waste.'

'All the same, we insist you make it up,' Sheshkovsky said, in the guilty tone of someone forced to get involved in other people's business. Blushing and placing his hand over his heart he continued, 'Gentlemen, we cannot find any causal connection between the insult and the duel. Insults which we sometimes inflict on each other out of human frailty have nothing to do with duels. You are educated, university men and naturally you see duels as an outmoded, empty formality, and all that. We see it like that too, otherwise we wouldn't have come, since we cannot allow people to shoot at each other in our presence, and all that.' Sheshkovsky wiped the sweat from his brow and went on, 'Please settle your differences, gentlemen, shake hands and let's all go home and have a drink on it. Honestly, gentlemen!'

Von Koren said nothing. When Layevsky saw them looking at him he said, 'I've nothing against Nikolay Vasilyevich. If he thinks I'm the guilty party, then I'm prepared to apologize.'

Von Koren took offence at this. 'Obviously, gentlemen,' he said, 'you would like to see Mr Layevsky return home as the chivalrous knight, but I cannot afford either him or you that pleasure. And there was no need to get up at the crack of dawn and ride six miles out of town just for a friendly drink and bite to eat, and to be told duels are outmoded formalities. Duels are duels and we should not make them out to be even more stupid and artificial than they actually are. I wish to fight!'

Silence followed. Officer Boyko took two pistols from a box, one was handed to von Koren and the other to Layevsky. Then followed a state of confusion which amused the zoologist and the seconds for a while. It turned out that not one of the whole assembled company had ever attended a duel before and no one knew precisely how they should stand, or what the seconds should say or do. But then Boyko remembered and he smiled as he began to explain.

'Gentlemen, who remembers Lermontov's description?' von Koren asked, laughing. 'And in Turgenev, Bazarov had a duel with someone or other . . .'[21]

'Why bring all that up now?' Ustimovich asked impatiently as he halted. 'Just measure out your distances, that's all.'

He took three steps as if to show how measuring should be done. Boyko counted out the paces, while his fellow officer bared his sword and scratched the ground at the extreme ends to mark the barrier.

Amid general silence the two opponents took up their positions.

'Moles!' the deacon recalled as he sat in the bushes.

Sheshkovsky said something, Boyko explained something further, but Layevsky did not hear; rather, he probably heard but did not understand. When the moment arrived he cocked the cold heavy pistol and pointed it upwards. He had forgotten to unbutton his coat and felt terribly cramped around the shoulders and armpits, and he raised his arm so awkwardly the sleeve seemed to be made of metal. He remembered the hatred he had felt yesterday for that swarthy forehead and curly hair and reflected that even then, when his hatred and anger were at boiling-point, he could never have fired at a man. Afraid the bullet might accidentally hit von Koren, he raised his pistol higher and higher, feeling that this terribly ostentatious show of magnanimity was tactless and not at all magnanimous; but he was incapable of acting in any other way. As he watched the pale, mocking face of von Koren, who was evidently convinced from the start that his opponent would fire into the air, Layevsky thought that it would be all over any moment, thank God, and that he only had to squeeze the trigger a little harder . . .

The pistol recoiled violently against his shoulder, a shot rang out and back came the echo from the mountains.

Von Koren cocked his pistol and looked towards Ustimovich, who was still striding back and forwards, hands behind his back, oblivious of everything.

'Doctor,' the zoologist said, 'please be so good as to stop going up and down like a pendulum. You're giving me spots before the eyes!'

The doctor stopped. Von Koren began taking aim at Layevsky.

'It's all over now!' Layevsky thought.

The barrel which was directed right at his face, the hatred and scorn in von Koren's whole bearing and posture, the murder that was about to be committed by a decent man in broad daylight in the presence of other decent men, the silence, that strange power that compelled Layevsky to stand firm and not run away – how mysterious, incomprehensible and terrifying all this was!

The time von Koren took to aim seemed longer to Layevsky than the whole night. He looked imploringly at the seconds; their faces were pale and they did not move.

'Hurry up and fire!' Layevsky thought, sensing that his pale, trembling, pathetic face must arouse even deeper loathing in von Koren.

'I'll kill him right now,' von Koren thought, aiming at the forehead and already feeling the trigger. 'Yes, of course I will . . .'

'He's going to kill him!' a desperate cry came from somewhere quite close.

At once the shot rang out. When they saw Layevsky still standing in the same place everyone looked where the cry had come from – and they saw the deacon.

Pale-faced, soaked, covered in mud, his wet hair clinging to his forehead and cheeks, the deacon was standing in the maize on the far bank, smiling peculiarly and waving his wet hat. Sheshkovsky laughed for joy, burst into tears and walked to one side.

XX

Shortly afterwards von Koren and the deacon met near the bridge. The deacon was disturbed, breathing heavily and avoiding people's eyes. He was ashamed of being so scared, and of his wet, muddy clothes.

'I thought you wanted to kill him,' he muttered. 'How alien to human nature! How extremely unnatural!'

'But where on earth did you come from?' the zoologist asked.

'Don't ask!' the deacon said, waving his arm. 'The devil's to blame, he tempted me here. So off I went and I nearly died of fright in the maize. But now, thank God, thank God . . . I'm very pleased with you,' the deacon muttered. 'And Grandpa Tarantula will be pleased too . . . What a laugh, eh, what a laugh! But I beg of you, most earnestly, not to breathe a word to a soul that I was here or I'll get it in the neck from the authorities. They'll say a deacon acted as second.'

'Gentlemen!' said von Koren. 'The deacon requests you not to tell anyone you saw him here. It could have unpleasant consequences for him.'

'How alien to human nature!' the deacon sighed. 'Please be generous and forgive me – but from the way you looked I thought you were definitely going to kill him.'

'I was strongly tempted to have finished with that scoundrel,' von Koren said, 'but your shout put me off, and I missed. I'm just not used to all this repulsive procedure, it's worn me out, deacon. I feel terribly weak. Let's drive back now.'

'No, please permit me to walk. I must dry myself out, I'm soaked and frozen stiff.'

'Well, please yourself,' the exhausted zoologist said wearily as he climbed into the carriage and closed his eyes. 'As you like.'

While they were walking round the carriages and taking their seats, Kerbalay stood by the roadside, clasped his stomach with both hands, made a low bow and showed his teeth. He thought that the gentlemen had come to enjoy the beauties of nature and to drink tea, and he could not fathom why they were getting back into their carriages. The procession moved off in complete silence; only the deacon stayed behind at the inn.

'Me come to inn, me drink tea,' he said to Kerbalay. 'Me want eat.'

Kerbalay knew Russian well, but the deacon thought that the Tatar would understand broken Russian better.

'You make fried egg, you serve cheese . . .'

'Come on, come on, Father,' Kerbalay said, bowing. 'I'll give you everything . . . There's cheese and wine . . . Eat what you like.'

'What's Tatar for "God"?' the deacon asked as he entered the inn.

'Your God, my God – just the same,' Kerbalay said, not understanding. 'God same for everyone, only people different. Some are Russians, some Turks, some English, there's all kinds of different people, but God is one.'

'All right then. If all nations worship the same God, then why do you Muslims treat Christians as your eternal enemies?'

'Why you angry?' Kerbalay asked, clutching his belly with both hands. 'You're priest, me Muslim, you say "I want to eat" and I give you food . . . Only the rich man make difference which your God, which my God. But it's all the same for the poor man. Please eat.'

While this theological discussion was in progress at the inn, Layevsky was driving home and he realized how terrifying it had been travelling at dawn, when the road, rocks and mountains were wet and dark, and an unknown future had held the terrors of a seemingly bottomless abyss. But now the raindrops hanging from the grass and stones sparkled like diamonds in the sun, nature smiled joyfully and that terrifying future was left behind. He looked at Sheshkovsky's gloomy, tear-stained face, at the two barouches in front with von Koren, his seconds and the doctor in them and it seemed they were all returning from a cemetery where they had buried some dreadful bore who had been a thorn in everyone's side.

'It's all over,' he thought, reflecting on his past and gingerly running his fingers over his neck.

On the right side of his neck, near the collar, a small swelling had come up as long and wide as his little finger and it was so painful it seemed someone had passed a hot iron over it. This was the bruise from the bullet.

And then, when he arrived home, a long, strange, sweet day stretched out in front of him, as vague as oblivion. As though released from prison or hospital, he scrutinized long-familiar objects and was astonished that tables, windows, chairs, light and sea brought him a keen, childlike joy that he had not known for such a long time. Nadezhda, pale and terribly thin, did not understand his gentle voice and strange walk. She hurried to tell him all that had happened to her. He probably couldn't hear her properly, she thought, and didn't understand her – if he knew everything he would curse and kill her. But he listened, stroked her face and hair, looked into her eyes and said, 'I've no one besides you.'

Afterwards they sat for a long time in the front garden, snuggling close to one another, saying nothing. Or they would give voice to their dreams of the happy life that lay ahead, speaking in brief, broken sentences, and he felt that never before had he spoken so long and so eloquently.

XXI

More than three months passed.

The day of von Koren's departure arrived. From early morning there had been a cold, heavy rain, a north-easterly had blown up and a strong sea was running. In that kind of weather, people said, a steamer would have difficulty in getting into the roadstead. According to the timetable, it should have arrived at ten in the morning, but when he went down to the quay at noon and after lunch, von Koren could make out nothing through his binoculars except grey waves and rain veiling the horizon.

By the end of the day the rain had stopped and the wind dropped appreciably. Von Koren had already reconciled himself to the fact that he would not be leaving that day and sat down to a game of chess with Samoylenko. But after dark the batman reported that lights had been sighted out at sea and that a flare had been seen.

Von Koren began to hurry. He slung a knapsack over his shoulders, kissed Samoylenko and the deacon, went round all the rooms for no reason at all, said goodbye to his batman and cook, and went out into the street feeling as if he had left something behind at the doctor's or at his flat. He walked at Samoylenko's side, the deacon following with a chest and the batman bringing up the rear with two suitcases. Only Samoylenko and the batman could make out the tiny, dim lights at sea, the others peered into the darkness without seeing a thing. The steamer anchored far from the shore.

'Come on now, quicker!' von Koren said, hurrying along. 'I don't want to miss it!'

Passing the little three-windowed house into which Layevsky had moved soon after the duel, von Koren could not resist taking a look through one of the windows. Layevsky was sitting writing, hunched up at a table, his back to the window.

'Well, I'm amazed!' the zoologist said quietly. 'Just look how he's pulled himself together!'

'Yes, you may well be amazed,' Samoylenko sighed. 'He sits like that from morn till night, just sits and works. He wants to pay off his debts. But he's living worse than a pauper, my dear chap!'

About half a minute passed in silence. The zoologist, the doctor and the deacon stood at the window, all watching Layevsky.

'So the poor devil didn't manage to get away,' Samoylenko said. 'Do you remember how hard he tried?'

'Yes, he's really pulled himself together,' von Koren repeated. 'His marriage, this daylong sweating and slaving for a crust of bread, that new look on his face, his walk even – it's all so extraordinary, words just fail me.' The zoologist grabbed Samoylenko's sleeve and went on in an emotional voice, 'Please tell him and his wife that I left this place full of admiration and that he has my very best wishes . . . and please ask him, if that's possible, not to bear any grudges. He knows me very well. He knows that had I foreseen the change in him at the time, I might have become his best friend.'

'Go in and say goodbye.'

'No, that would be embarrassing.'

'But why? God knows, you might never see him again.'

The zoologist pondered for a moment and said, 'That's true.'

Samoylenko softly tapped on the window. Layevsky shuddered and turned round.

'Ivan, Nikolay Vasilyevich wants to say goodbye,' Samoylenko said. 'He's just leaving.'

Layevsky got up from the table and went into the hall to open the door. Samoylenko, von Koren and the deacon went in.

'I've just dropped in for a moment,' the zoologist began as he took off his galoshes in the hall, already regretting that he had bowed to sentiment and called uninvited. 'I feel I'm intruding,' he thought; 'it's silly.'

'Forgive me for disturbing you,' he said, following Layevsky into his room, 'but I'm on my way now and I felt I had to come and see you. God knows if we'll ever meet again.'

'Delighted . . . Please come in . . .' Layevsky said, clumsily putting chairs in front of his guests as though wanting to bar their way. He stopped in the middle of the room, rubbing his hands.

'I should have left the others in the street,' von Koren thought.

'Don't think too badly of me, Layevsky,' he said firmly. 'Of course, one can't forget the past, it's too sad and I haven't come to apologize or to try and assure you I wasn't to blame. I acted in all sincerity and have since stuck to my convictions. It's true, and I'm delighted to see it, that I was mistaken about you, the best of us can take a tumble – that's only human destiny. If you don't trip on the main things, you'll stumble over the small. No one knows the real truth of the matter.'

'Yes, no one knows the truth . . .' Layevsky said.

'Well, goodbye . . . Good luck and God be with you.'

Von Koren offered Layevsky his hand; he shook it and bowed.

'Don't think too badly of me,' von Koren said. 'Remember me to the wife and tell her I was very sorry I didn't manage to say goodbye.'

'She's here.'

Layevsky went to the door and spoke into the next room.

'Nadezhda, Nikolay Vasilyevich wishes to say goodbye.'

Nadezhda came in. She stopped by the door and timidly surveyed the visitors. Her face was frightened and guilty and she held her hands to her sides, like a schoolgirl being told off.

'I'm leaving now, Nadezhda,' von Koren said, 'and I've come to say goodbye.'

Hesitantly she held her hand out to him, while Layevsky bowed.

'What a pathetic pair!' von Koren thought. 'They don't have an easy life.'

'I'll be in Moscow and St Petersburg,' he said. 'Is there anything I can send you?'

'But what?' Nadezhda said and exchanged anxious glances with her husband. 'I can't think of anything . . .'

'No, there's nothing,' Layevsky said, rubbing his hands. 'Give them our regards.'

Von Koren did not know what else he could or should say, but when he first came in he had contemplated saying a great deal of uplifting, kindly, significant things. Silently he shook Layevsky's and his wife's hands and went away feeling heavy at heart.

'What people!' the deacon whispered as he followed the others. 'Heavens, what people! "Verily the Lord's right hand hath sown this vine . . . Oh Lord, one hath conquered thousands, the other tens of thousands".' Solemnly he continued, 'Von Koren, you should know that today you overcame mankind's most powerful enemy – pride!'

'That's enough, deacon! What sort of conquerors do you think Layevsky and I are? Conquerors look down like eagles from their heights, but he's pathetic, timid, downtrodden and he bows like a Chinese dummy . . . I feel very sad.'

They heard footsteps behind them. Layevsky wanted to see von Koren off and was trying to catch them up. The batman stood on the quayside with the two suitcases and a little way off were four oarsmen.

'It's really blowing hard . . . brrrrr!' Samoylenko said. 'There must be a real gale out there. Oh dear! You've picked a fine time to leave, Nikolay!'

'I'm not scared of seasickness.'

'I don't mean that. I only hope those idiots don't have you in the water. You should have taken the agent's boat. Where is the agent's boat?' he shouted to the oarsmen.

'It's gone, General.'

'And the Customs boat?'

'She's gone too.'

'But why didn't you tell me?' Samoylenko said furiously. 'Blockheads!'

'It doesn't matter, don't let it upset you,' von Koren said. 'Well, goodbye, God protect you.'

Samoylenko embraced von Koren and made the sign of the cross over him three times.

'Now don't forget us, Nikolay . . . write . . . we'll expect you in the spring.'

'Goodbye, deacon,' von Koren said, shaking his hand. 'Thanks for your company and all the excellent conversations. Think about the expedition.'

'Yes, even to the very ends of the earth!' the deacon laughed. 'I didn't say no, did I?'

Von Koren recognized Layevsky in the dark and silently offered him his hand. The oarsmen were already down below holding the boat which banged against the wooden piles, although the pier offered protection from the main swell. Von Koren went down the ladder, leapt into the boat and sat by the rudder.

'Do write!' Samoylenko shouted. 'And look after yourself!'

'No one knows the real truth,' Layevsky thought, raising his collar and stuffing his hands into his sleeves.

The boat jauntily rounded the quay and went out into the open sea. It disappeared among the waves, then immediately rose up from a deep trough to the crest of a high wave, so that the men and even the oars were visible. For every eighteen feet the boat moved forward, she was thrown back twelve.

'Write!' Samoylenko shouted. 'What the hell possessed you to travel in this weather!'

'Yes, no one knows the real truth . . .' Layevsky thought, dejectedly surveying the restless, dark sea.

'The boat's tossed back,' he thought; 'it makes two movements forward and one back, but the oarsmen don't give up, they swing the oars tirelessly and have no fear of the high waves. The boat moves on and on, now it's disappeared from view. In half an hour the rowers will be able to see the ship's lights clearly and within an hour they'll be alongside the ladder. Life is like that . . . As they search for truth people take two paces forward and one back. Suffering, mistakes and life's tedium throw them back, but thirst for the truth and stubborn willpower drive them on and on. And who knows? Perhaps they'll arrive at the real truth in the end.'

'Goodbye!' shouted Samoylenko.

'No sight or sound of them now,' the deacon said. 'Safe journey!'

It began to drizzle.

PUBLISHING HISTORY AND NOTES

The Steppe

First published in the *Northern Herald* in 1888, 'The Steppe' marked a turning-point in Chekhov's career and his debut in the 'thick journals', to which he attached great importance. Grigorovich[27] had encouraged Chekhov to abandon 'trivial, rushed stories' (letter of 25 March 1886), and to do himself justice by writing longer, more substantial work. It was in this letter of encouragement that Grigorovich first expressed his very high hopes for Chekhov. At the time Chekhov wrote to Leontyev-Shcheglov,[28] 'The thought that I'm writing for a thick journal and that my trifle will be considered more seriously than is warranted prods my elbow like the devil a monk' (1 January 1888). And to Grigorovich, 'Whether it's a success or not, at all events I know it's my masterpiece. I can't manage anything better' (5 February 1888). And: 'I know that in the next world Gogol will be angry with me. He's Tsar of the Steppes in our literature. I've sneaked into his domain, with every good intention, but I've written a good deal of nonsense.'

Earlier, in 1887, Chekhov had written to Suvorin (10 February), 'In order not to dry up I'm going south at the end of March, to the Don regions, Voronezh and other places where I'll meet the spring and renew in my memory what has already begun to grow dim.' What had already begun to grow dim were the memories of childhood trips to the steppe to visit his grandfather. These memories are reflected and find lyrical expression in 'The Steppe'. After completing the story he writes, 'While I was writing I felt there was a smell of summer and steppe around me . . .' (letter to Pleshcheyev[29] of 3 February 1888) and he stresses that writing the story gave him great joy.

1. *Lady of Kazan*: In 1579 a young girl allegedly discovered the Kazan Icon of the Virgin in the ground. The event was annually celebrated after 1595 on 8 July.

2. *Lomonosov*: M. V. Lomonosov (1711–65), scientist, poet, grammarian. Son of a fisherman, he ran away to Moscow at the age of seventeen and subsequently became one of Russia's leading scientists and men of letters. Here he is being held up as a model for Yegorushka. Lomonosov is also mentioned as exemplar for the young Gorky in *My Universities* (1922; Harmondsworth: Penguin Books, 1979).

3. *'Puer bone, quam appellaris?' . . . 'Christophorus sum.'*: 'Good boy, what's your name?' 'Christophor'.

4. *'And the Cherubim'*: Ezekiel 10:19.

5. *Two-headed eagle*: Emblem of Imperial Russia.

6. *Molokans*: Dissenting sect, possibly so-called from their habit of drinking milk on fast-days. A hard-working people, highly successful in business and farming.

7. *Chernigov*: Ukrainian town about seventy-five miles from Kiev, situated on the River Desna, a tributary of the Dnieper.

8. *ancient barrows*: These barrows or tumuli were left by the Scythians, an Indo-European people who lived to the north of the Black Sea, in the Lower Don and Dnieper regions, from approximately 8th to 3rd century BC.

9. *Ilya Muromets or Solovey the Robber*: Russian folk heroes.

10. *bast shoes*: Peasant shoes or sandals made from inner bark of lime tree.

11. *Slavyanoserbsk*: Large town near North Donets River founded by the Serbs in 1753. Originally named Podgornoye, it was relocated because of floods in 1817 and renamed.

12. *Tim*: Small town in Kursk province on River Tim, in Don river basin.

13. *St Barbara*: Died c. 235. Patron saint of artillerymen, gunners and miners. Martyred under Maximinus Thrax.

14. *Lugansk*: Town in the Ukraine, north of Taganrog.

15. *Donets*: River of south-central Russia, rising in the Kursk steppes and flowing into the Don.

16. *tussore*: A strong coarse light-brown silk made in India.

17. *Vyazma*: Large town about 150 miles west of Moscow, famous for its gingerbread.

18. *Oryol*: Large town 200 miles south of Moscow, on the River Oka' founded as fortified town against the Crimean Tatars in 1564. Birthplace of Turgenev.

19. *Morshansk*: Small town 250 miles south-west of Moscow, on the River Tsna, on Volga uplands.

20. *Old Believer*: Also known as Dissenters, Old Believers rejected the reforms in the Russian Orthodox Church introduced by Nikon, Patriarch of Moscow, in the seventeenth century. Among these were: unification of the ritual, correction of books used in church services.
21. *St Peter's Day*: 29 June.
22. *Pyotr Mogila*: Bishop of Kiev in the first half of seventeenth century. Important theologian and champion of Enlightenment. Sent many young scholars to study in Western Europe.
23. *'Be not carried about . . .'*: Hebrews 13:9.
24. *summoning spirits like Saul . . .* : reference to biblical story that the ghost of Saul's father Samuel prophesied the end of his reign. Samuel 1:28.
25. *Basil [Vasily] the Great*: (329–79) Prominent church activist.
26. *St Nestor*: (*fl.* 1080) First notable Russian chronicler and hagiologist.
27. D. V. Grigorovich (1822–99). Short story writer, mainly of the misery of peasant life, with a strong humanitarian, sentimental attitude. He was one of the first to appreciate Chekhov's talent and to encourage him. (He had similarly offered encouragement to the young Dostoyevsky with his first work, *Poor Folk* (1846).) He corresponded regularly with Chekhov, who dedicated his collection *In the Twilight* (1887) to him and for which, through Grigorovich's good offices, he was awarded the Pushkin Prize. His *Literary Reminiscences* (1892–3) are a rich source of information about contemporary literary life. A friend of many of the most prominent figures in nineteenth-century Russian literature, as a writer he is only of secondary importance.
28. I. L. Leontyev-Shcheglov (1855–1911). Playwright and minor writer of fiction. After the sensational success of his comedy *In the Caucasian Mountains*, he started writing mainly for the theatre and his first works were praised by Chekhov, whom he first met in 1887 in St Petersburg. This was the beginning of a lasting friendship. Leontyev-Shcheglov left very interesting memoirs of Chekhov in the *Monthly Literary Supplement to the Cornfield*.
29. A. N. Pleshcheyev (1825–93). Journalist, critic, playwright, translator, minor poet. Together with Dostoyevsky he attended meetings of the Petrashevsky Circle, of which he was a prominent member. In 1849 (also with Dostoyevsky) he was arrested and exiled. First met Chekhov in 1885 and corresponded regularly with him. Was in charge of literary section of the *Northern Herald*.

Panpipes

First published in Suvorin's *New Times* (1887) and then, with minor changes, in the collection *In the Twilight* (1887).

1. *Elijah's Day*: 20 July.
2. . . . *since we got our freedom* . . . : Refers to the emancipation of the serfs, 1861.
3. *You had an eclipse* . . . : A total eclipse of the sun was recorded on 7 August 1887.

The Kiss

'The Kiss' was first published in *New Times* in 1887. According to Leontyev-Shcheglov the story was written incredibly quickly – within two days. Chekhov had sent Leontyev-Shcheglov the story for his opinion of the description of a brigade on the move. Leontyev-Shcheglov was astounded by the amazing accuracy of detail and acuteness of observation, remarking that he found it difficult to believe that the story had been written by a civilian and not by a 'hardened soldier'.

1. *Plevna*: Bulgarian town, forty miles south of the Danube, scene of fierce fighting between the Russians and Turks in 1877.
2. *European Herald*: A liberal monthly journal (1866–1918). Devoted to history, politics and literature. It published major works by Turgenev, Goncharov and Ostrovsky.

Verochka

First published in *New Times* (1887) and then in the collection *In the Twilight* (1887), with minor changes. It is possible that the moonlit garden with the floating wisps of mist was based on the garden at Babkino, a delightful estate owned by the highly cultured Kiselyov family. It was near Voskresensk (now Istra), about forty miles from Moscow. Chekhov rented a dacha on the estate for three successive summers.

1. *light cape*: In the mid 1880s this type of cape was fashionable among the educated classes of modest means.

2. *Statistics has a brill-i-ant future!* . . . : Statistical surveys flourished in the late 1870s–early 1880s. They were initiated and funded by local district councils.

3. *expecting to find boredom, solitude and an indifference to statistics*: In an article, 'The Misfortunes of Statistics' in the January 1887 issue of the *St Petersburg Gazette*, it was stated that statistics were banned in Saratov, Ryazan and Kursk, since disasters such as crop failure, hailstorms etc were blamed on them.

4. *Old Believer*: See 'The Steppe', note 20, p. 361.

5. *holy fool*: Idiot supposed to be blessed with gift of divine prophecy.

6. *totally useless collection of statistical articles*: In the same issue of *New Times* in which *Verochka* was printed there appeared the following wry announcement: 'Materials for the statistics of Kostroma Province were published recently. This is a finely printed volume, containing 250 pages, with 22 tables and 4 diagrams.'

7. *nach Hause*: home.

The Name-day Party

First published in the *Northern Herald* (1888), the story later underwent major stylistic changes and was significantly shortened. It was written in a great hurry, as Chekhov had thought that the story was needed for the September issue, not the October one, and admitted that he had 'muddled his arithmetic'. At the end of September he wrote to Pleshcheyev: 'Phew! I've just finished my story for the *Northern Herald*, my dear Aleksey Nikolayevich . . . It's turned out rather long, rather boring, but lively and with a "tendency"' (30 September 1888). In a letter to Suvorin of 2 October he states: 'I've finished my little story. It's written limply and carelessly.' A few days later he wrote to a female friend: 'The beginning and end can be read with interest but the middle is like a chewed mop' (letter of 9 October to E. M. Lintvareva). Chekhov was furious that he was not given sufficient time to correct the proofs and, in reply to Suvorin's complaint that the hero of the story had imperfections, Chekhov responded: 'I do realize that I cut my heroes to pieces and spoil them, that I waste good material. But in all honesty I would gladly have sat over 'The Name-day Party' for six months . . . but what can I do? . . . I start the story with the thought that I'm obliged to finish it by 5 October – a very short deadline.

If I exceed the deadline I'm letting you down and I won't get paid . . . I write the beginning calmly, not cramping myself, but by the middle I'm already growing timid and beginning to fear that the story will turn out too long: I must remember that the *Northern Herald* is short of cash and that I'm one of its expensive contributors. That's why my beginnings are always full of promise, as if I'd started a novel; but the middles are botched and timid, while the conclusions, as in a short tale, are pure fireworks' (letter of 27 October 1888).

Eventually, the story was published with a very large number of misprints, about which Chekhov complained bitterly to Pleshcheyev.

1. *Malaga*: A sweet fortified wine made in the region of Malaga, Spain.
2. *Proudhon's*: Pierre Joseph Proudhon (1809–65), French anarchist philosopher.
3. *Buckles*: Henry Thomas Buckle (1821–62), English historian and sociologist. Chekhov had read his *History of Civilisation* in translation in his younger days at Taganrog.
4. *Schopenhauers*: Arthur Schopenhauer (1788–1860), German pessimistic philosopher.
5. *Yorkshire pigs, Butlerov beehives*: Valued for their high-quality bacon, this breed of pig was raised in Europe and the USA, as well as England. The hives were named after Aleksander Mikhaylovich Butlerov (1828–86), famous Russian chemist who also published the best-selling *The Bee: Its Life and a Guide to Systematic Bee-Keeping* (1871).

A Dreary Story

First published in the *Northern Herald* (1889) and subsequently, after reworking, in the collection *Gloomy People* (1890). To some extent the prototype of the hero was A. I. Babukhin (1835–91), Professor at Moscow University, whose lectures Chekhov heard when a medical student. Chekhov worked on the story in Yalta, where he had gone in a depressed frame of mind after the death of his brother Nikolay. At the time Chekhov wrote to Pleshcheyev[29]: '. . . because of the heat and my vile, melancholy mood this story is turning out quite boring. But the subject is new. It's highly possible that it will be read with interest' (letter of 3 August 1889). And before sending it for publication Chekhov wrote to Pleshcheyev: 'I want to polish and varnish one or two things, but mainly to think about it. I've never written anything like it in my life, the themes are completely new for me' (letter of 3 September 1889). After returning to Moscow he wrote that he started: '. . . reworking my thing, mangled it right and left, threw out a large chunk of the middle and the whole of the ending, having decided to replace them with new ones' (letter of 7 September 1889 to A. M. Yevreinova).[30]

1. *Pirogov*: N. I. Pirogov (1810–81), famous military surgeon, Professor at the St Petersburg Medico-Surgical Academy.
2. *Kavelin*: K. D. Kavelin (1818–85), jurist, historian and liberal publicist. Active in the liberal movement of the 1860s.
3. *the poet Nekrasov*: N. I. Nekrasov (1821–77), famous for his civic poetry. Did much to focus attention of the educated classes on misery of the poor.
4. *Like one of those heroines in Turgenev, my neck . . .* : Reference to Turgenev's *Diary of a Superfluous Man* (1850). Chekhov was highly critical of Turgenev's portrayal of genteel young ladies, very unfavourably comparing them to other literary heroines, such as Anna Karenina.
5. *What Song the Swallow Sang*: Novel by F. Spielhagen (1829–1911), German writer, prominent in the 1860s for his anti-establishment attitude.
6. *Othello*: Cf. *Othello*, Act I, Scene 3:

> 'She lov'd me for the dangers I had pass'd,
> And I lov'd her that she did pity them'.

7. *Historia Morbi*: History of Disease.
8. *Gruber*: V. L. Gruber (1814–90), Professor of Anatomy at St Petersburg Medico-Surgical Academy.
9. *Babukhin*: A. Babukhin (1835–91), Professor of Medicine. It is possible that the hero of this story was based on Babukhin.
10. *Skobelev*: M. D. Skobelev (1843–82), general who distinguished himself in the Russo-Turkish War (1877–8).
11. *Professor Perov*: V. G. Perov (1833–82), genre and portrait painter. A leading exponent of social criticism in art, taught at Moscow College of Painting, Sculpture and Architecture.
12. *Patti*: Adeline Patti (1843–1919), famous opera singer. She made her debut in New York at the age of seven. Celebrated for her role as Lucia in Donizetti's *Lucia di Lammermoor* and as Amina in Bellini's *La Sonambula*, which she performed at Covent Garden in 1861. She enjoyed worldwide success and toured Russia several times.
13. *What's Hecuba to him?*: *Hamlet*, Act II, Scene 2: one of several references

to Shakespeare (especially *Hamlet*). The passage refers to an actor's skill in adapting to different roles. The full passage is:

> 'What's Hecuba to him or he to Hecuba
> That he should weep for her?'

14. *Chatsky*: Cynical hero of the famous verse comedy *Woe from Wit* (1822–4), by A. S. Griboyedov (1797–1829). Like Chatsky, Nikolay Stepanovich cannot abide Muscovite fools.
15. *Ufa*: Capital of Bashkir autonomous republic, south of the Urals, on River Belaya, founded as a Russian fortress in 1574.
16. *'How sadly I behold our generation'*: First line of Lermontov's lyric poem *Thought* (1838).
17. *Marcus Aurelius, Epictetus or Pascal*: Marcus Aurelius (AD 121–180), Roman emperor and Stoic philosopher; Epictetus (c. AD 50–139), Greek Stoic philosopher; Blaise Pascal (1623–62), French mathematician and philosopher.
18. *Dobrolyubov style*: N. A. Dobrolyubov (1836–61), radical literary and social critic, very popular among the young intelligentsia.
19. *Arakcheyev*: Count A. A. Arakcheyev (1769–1834), fanatical military disciplinarian, responsible for the notorious military colonies under Alexander I. Chekhov also refers to him in 'The Duel'.
20. *'Go up, thou bald head!'*: II Kings 2:23. Words with which the young Israelites teased the prophet Elisha.
21. *Gaudeamus igitur juvenestus!*: Correctly: *Gaudeamus igitur, juvenes dum sumus* (Let us rejoice while we are young). First line of the famous student song.
22. *Jean-Jacques Petit*: Almost certainly an error for Jacques-Louis Petit (1674–1750), famous French surgeon who served under the Marshal of Luxembourg. A member of the Royal Society of London, he died before completing his celebrated *A Treatise on Surgery* (begun in 1715).
23. *Krylov*: N. I. Krylov (1807–79), Professor of Roman Law at Moscow University.
24. *Eagles lower than hens can fly . . .*: From the fable *The Eagle and the Hens* by I. A. Krylov (1769–1844).
25. *Berdichev*: Ukrainian town about 110 miles south-west of Kiev.
26. *The Cornfield*: *Niva* (cornfield), a popular illustrated family magazine published in St Petersburg (1870–1918).
27. *World Illustrated*: St Petersburg weekly.
28. *passport system*: Passports were compulsory for travelling within Russia, as well as abroad.
29. *Plesheheyev*: See 'The Steppe', note 29, p. 361.

30. Anna Mikhaylovna Yevreinova (1844–1919), Doctor of Law. From 1885 editor of the *Northern Herald*.

Gusev

First published in *New Times* (1890), 'Gusev' was Chekhov's first story to be printed after his return by sea from Sakhalin. He wrote to Suvorin: 'Since my story was started on the island of Ceylon you can, if you like, to add a touch of chic, print underneath it: Colombo 12 November' (letter to Suvorin, 17 December 1890).

Some of Chekhov's experiences on his return from Sakhalin by sea are reflected in 'Gusev'. In another letter to Suvorin Chekhov writes: 'On the way from Singapore two corpses were thrown into the sea. When you see a dead man wrapped up in canvas, somersaulting into the water, and when you bear in mind that it's a few miles to the bottom it's terrifying, and you begin to think that you yourself will die and be thrown into the sea' (letter to Suvorin, 9 December 1890).

1. *Suchan*: A town in eastern Siberia, about sixty miles east of Vladivostok. An important coal-mining centre.
2. *Captain Kopeykin*: Character from Gogol's *Dead Souls*, part I (1842), whose story is told by the postmaster.
3. *Midshipman Dyrka*: A comic midshipman of this name is mentioned by Zhevakin in Gogol's two-act play *Marriage* (1842).

The Duel

First serialized in *New Times* (1890), then published in a complete edition, with corrections and new chapter divisions in 1892. When he first started the story Chekhov was not satisfied with it, telling Suvorin that there was 'no movement' and that it was 'rather complex'. At this time Chekhov was having frequent discussions with the zoologist V. A. Wagner (Vagner) on Darwinian and Nietzschean themes. Chekhov's brother Mikhail wrote that he would often debate with Wagner: '. . . the then fashionable subjects of degeneration, the rights of the strong, natural selection and so on, which were the basis of von Koren's philosophy . . . During these conversations Anton Pavlovich was always of the opinion that man's spiritual strength can always overcome any inherited shortcomings.'[22]

1. *Superfluous Men*: Characters in the tradition of Werther, Childe Harold, René who see themselves (and are seen) as disillusioned and at odds with society. A prime example is Lermontov's Pechorin (*A Hero of Our Time*, 1837–40). The term gained currency after the publication of Turgenev's *Diary of a Superfluous Man* (1850).
2. *Spencer*: Herbert Spencer (1820–1903), English radical thinker, founder of an evolutionist philosophy and a laissez-faire social policy.
3. *Vereshchagin*: V. V. Vereshchagin (1842–1904), Russian painter famous for his Central Asian themes.
4. *Abkhazians*: Natives of Abkhazia, an autonomous republic in Georgia.
5. *Prince Vorontsov*: Prince M. S. Vorontsov (1782–1856), appointed viceroy of the Caucasus in 1844.
6. *Onegin, Pechorin [Byron's Cain], Bazarov*: Eugene Onegin, eponymous hero of Pushkin's narrative poem *Eugene Onegin* (1831); Pechorin, hero of Lermontov's *A Hero of Our Time* (1840); Bazarov, hero of Turgenev's *Fathers and Sons* (1852). All these characters are types of 'Superfluous Men' (see note. 1).
7. *Schopenhauer*: See 'The Name-day Party', note 4, p. 364.
8. *Dorpat*: Modern Tartu. Chief cultural centre of Estonia, about 100 miles south-east of Tallin, famous for its university.
9. *tussore*: See 'The Steppe', note 16, p. 360.
10. *Pushkin's Ukrainian Night*: Reference to second canto of the narrative poem *Poltava* (1828).
11. *His beaver collar sparkles silver with frosty dust*: From the first chapter of *Eugene Onegin*.
12. *manu militari*: By military force.
13. *Stanley*: Henry Morton Stanley (1841–1904), explorer of equatorial Africa.
14. *Arakcheyev*: See 'A Dreary Story', note 19, p. 366.
15. *'But whoso shall offend one of these little ones'*: Matthew 18:6.
16. *kalium bromatum*: Potassium bromide.
17. *aqua foeniculi*: Fennel water.
18. *Rudin*: Eponymous hero of Turgenev's novel (1856) – another type of 'Superfluous Man'.
19. *Danila*: Character from N. S. Leskov's short story 'The Legend of Just Danila' (1888).
20. *. . . a crowd of oppressive thoughts . . .*: From Pushkin's *Remembrance* (1828).
21. *And in Turgenev, Bazarov had a duel with someone or other . . .*: Reference

to Bazarov's duel with Pavel Petrovich over Fenichka in *Fathers and Sons*. Significantly, Bazarov, Pechorin and Onegin all fight duels.

22. M. P. Chekhov, *Vokrug Chekhova* (*Around Chekhov*), published Moscow/Leningrad in 1933.

READ MORE IN PENGUIN

In every corner of the world, on every subject under the sun, Penguin represents quality and variety – the very best in publishing today.

For complete information about books available from Penguin – including Puffins, Penguin Classics and Arkana – and how to order them, write to us at the appropriate address below. Please note that for copyright reasons the selection of books varies from country to country.

In the United Kingdom: Please write to *Dept. EP, Penguin Books Ltd, Bath Road, Harmondsworth, West Drayton, Middlesex UB7 0DA*

In the United States: Please write to *Consumer Services, Penguin Putnam Inc., 405 Murray Hill Parkway, East Rutherford, New Jersey 07073-2136.* VISA and MasterCard holders call 1-800-631-8571 to order Penguin titles

In Canada: Please write to *Penguin Books Canada Ltd, 10 Alcorn Avenue, Suite 300, Toronto, Ontario M4V 3B2*

In Australia: Please write to *Penguin Books Australia Ltd, 487 Maroondah Highway, Ringwood, Victoria 3134*

In New Zealand: Please write to *Penguin Books (NZ) Ltd, Private Bag 102902, North Shore Mail Centre, Auckland 10*

In India: Please write to *Penguin Books India Pvt Ltd, 11 Community Centre, Panchsheel Park, New Delhi 110017*

In the Netherlands: Please write to *Penguin Books Netherlands bv, Postbus 3507, NL-1001 AH Amsterdam*

In Germany: Please write to *Penguin Books Deutschland GmbH, Metzlerstrasse 26, 60594 Frankfurt am Main*

In Spain: Please write to *Penguin Books S. A., Bravo Murillo 19, 1°B, 28015 Madrid*

In Italy: Please write to *Penguin Italia s.r.l., Via Vittorio Emanuele 45/a, 20094 Corsico, Milano*

In France: Please write to *Penguin France, 12, Rue Prosper Ferradou, 31700 Blagnac*

In Japan: Please write to *Penguin Books Japan Ltd, Iidabashi KM-Bldg, 2-23-9 Koraku, Bunkyo-Ku, Tokyo 112-0004*

In South Africa: Please write to *Penguin Books South Africa (Pty) Ltd, P.O. Box 751093, Gardenview, 2047 Johannesburg*

READ MORE IN PENGUIN